Forge Books by Elmer Kelton

STAND PROUD

— AND —

EYES OF THE HAWK

ELMER KELTON

FORGE®

A TOM DOHERTY ASSOCIATES BOOK | NEW YORK

This is a work of fiction. All of the characters, organizations, and events portrayed in these novels are either products of the author's imagination or are used fictitiously.

STAND PROUD AND EYES OF THE HAWK

Stand Proud copyright © 1984, 1990 by the Estate of Elmer Stephen Kelton

Eyes of the Hawk copyright © 1981 by the Estate of Elmer Stephen Kelton

A Forge Book
Published by Tom Doherty Associates
175 Fifth Avenue
New York, NY 10010

www.tor-forge.com

Forge® is a registered trademark of Macmillan Publishing Group, LLC.

ISBN 978-1-250-17779-7

Our books may be purchased in bulk for promotional, educational, or business use. Please contact your local bookseller or the Macmillan Corporate and Premium Sales Department at 1-800-221-7945, extension 5442, or by email at MacmillanSpecialMarkets@macmillan.com.

First Edition: September 2018

Printed in the United States of America

0 9 8 7 6 5 4 3 2 1

CONTENTS

STAND
PROUD

To Ann . . .

for all those good years . . .

INTRODUCTION

From the time I first began writing fiction more than fifty years ago, I was determined someday to write a novel about the development of the cattle industry in West Texas, the heyday of the open-range cattleman and cowboy. The concept ebbed and flowed during the years, changing shape and direction as my own concept of history broadened and changed.

Stand Proud is probably as near as I will ever come to fulfilling that longtime ambition. It was done on a broad canvas, spanning a period from the latter part of the Civil War until after the turn of the century, through the final years of the Indian as a free-roaming entity on the Texas plains and finally to the time when all the land was settled up, fenced up and a new regulatory mind-set was taking hold.

That period of more than forty years saw tremendous changes on the land, not all of them for the better. I tried to show them through the eyes of fictional cattleman Frank Claymore, who is something like the story I have heard all my life about the old-timer declaring that he had seen many changes during his long years, and he had been against every one of them.

Claymore is in some ways an amalgamation of many actual cattlemen I have known about or studied over the years. He borrows a great deal from the archetype of them all, Charles Goodnight, whose biography was so grandly written by J. Evetts Haley. Goodnight spent most of his early

life in Texas. When the Civil War began, he harbored reservations about the Confederacy, as many Texans did. To
avoid going east with Confederate regulars to fight against
Union troops, he chose to join a frontier company and scout
for Indians, thereby serving Texas without having to fire
upon the Union flag.

My Frank Claymore follows the same course. As the
story opens, he is forted up against the Indians with other
civilians in what was known as Fort Davis on the Clear
Fork, south of present-day Breckenridge. This is not to be
confused with a military post of the same name farther west
in the Davis Mountains. Much description of the fort and
its life is drawn from the classic *Interwoven,* by Sallie Reyn-
olds Matthews, who remembered it from her childhood,
and from the melancholy diaries of Sam and Susan New-
comb.

One of the needless tragedies of the Texas frontier was
the ill-considered, ill-fated battle of Dove Creek, fought
west of present-day San Angelo in the first days of 1865.
Against the advice of many experienced Indian fighters, a
set of Confederate irregulars attacked a migrating band of
Kickapoo Indians on the assumption that they might be hostile Comanches. The Kickapoos had been a friendly tribe,
but they proved to be fierce fighters in self-defense and
administered a grievous whipping to the attackers before
fleeing south to sanctuary in Mexico. No longer friendly,
they became a scourge along the Rio Grande.

Frank Claymore is hauled into that battle as a private soldier, much against his better judgment. It is a turning point
in his life.

Some years ago, while *Stand Proud* was in its planning
stages, an elderly ranchman named Ira Bird told me a story
about his father, a teenager late in the Civil War, too young
to join the regulars but old enough to scout the Indian frontier with a Ranger company. One day while on a scout into
what is now Coke County, he rode upon a tall hill and looked
down into a beautiful valley, its floor dotted by thousands

of grazing buffalo. Duty bade him ride away, but the scene haunted him for years. Later, married and starting a family, he went in search of that valley, found it and settled there. His descendants still live on Yellow Wolf Creek.

As I have often done with such stories that caught my imagination, I interpolated it into this narrative of Frank Claymore. Unable to forget the grand valley he has seen, Claymore returns to claim it and later in his life defends it against those he considers to be despoilers.

Often those who had the aggressive characteristics necessary to go into a raw land found those characteristics incompatible with the settled, ordered society which came later. Though they had cleared the path, civilization no longer had a place for them. It shoved them aside or plowed them under.

Claymore finds himself in that position in his later years. Early in life he is regarded as a hero, a trailblazer, a bringer of civilization to the wilderness. Late in life he is condemned as an exploiter, an impediment to progress. In truth, he has not changed. Society has changed, along with its concepts. A newspaper reporter tells Claymore, "In those days they wanted heroes. Today they are looking for villains. I am a writer. I write what they will read."

The irony is that the public often found villains in the same men it had once regarded as heroes.

In real life this happened to Goodnight and many others. Texas novelist Benjamin Capps explored the same phenomenon in his splendid *Sam Chance*.

Stand Proud brought me more adverse criticism than any of my other novels. Some readers and critics simply disliked Frank Claymore. They considered him irascible, unyielding, intolerant. I cannot argue with that; I intended him to be that way. Had he not been, he would not have accomplished as much as he did. His was not a time or place for the weak, the equivocal. Those could come later, after the taming. Then they would be safe to decry what their predecessors had done to make the land secure for them.

I saw Frank Claymore as a product of his time and the experiences of his formative years. The West Texas into which he came was raw and dangerous. He had to be tough-minded. Though he did not seek a leadership position, it was thrust upon him by others who considered his abilities superior to their own.

Early in the story, Claymore lacks full control over his life and suffers because of others' bad decisions. He is drawn into the frontier service against his will. While he is away serving the Confederacy, his one-time friend takes advantage of his absence to marry the woman Claymore loves. He is carried into the disastrous battle of Dove Creek and, through the folly of others, suffers a wound that will plague him the rest of his life.

The bitterness of these experiences hardens Claymore. It makes him vow that never again will he allow himself to fall under someone else's authority. Henceforth he will make his own decisions and ride his own road no matter what it costs him. There are times when it costs him dearly, for he is mortal, and his decisions are sometimes wrong.

He has difficulty communicating his feelings, even to his wife, so he is often misunderstood by those around him. This failure is at the root of many of his problems, as it often is with all of us. He has no patience with those he perceives to be idle or incompetent, for life has not allowed him the luxury of idleness, and the incompetence of others has almost killed him more than once.

Like most of his contemporaries, Claymore regards the Indian as an obstacle to be overcome and does not question the rightness of the white man's taking the land. That kind of introspection would come from later generations who would condemn Granddad for his heartlessness but nevertheless enjoy the results of his conquest and never seriously consider giving any of them away.

Late in life, as it happened with many old-time cattlemen and Indian fighters, Claymore would come to respect his former enemy, though he never returned what he had taken from him. Beset by a generation which took at the point of a pen instead of the point of a gun, he could appreciate what an honest and worthy adversary the Indian had been.

As a group, those early cattlemen who pushed their herds into new country were a tough, single-minded lot. They had to be if they were to survive. It is easy, after a century or more, to criticize them for not sharing the enlightened views which we have had the leisure and the security to develop over the last couple of generations. One must wonder, however, as we eat up the seed corn left to us by those pioneers, how we will be judged by future generations who may find no seed corn left.

Elmer Kelton
San Angelo, Texas

1

The jarring strike of the clock in the towering cupola drew Frank Claymore's unwilling eyes to the two-story courthouse. It was a Texas-plains impression of some forbidding Old World castle in which monstrous crimes had been wrought upon the innocent. Claymore had opposed the construction of this gray-stone insult, just one of many fights lost as the years stole his strength and diminished his influence. His taxes, reluctantly paid, had gone far toward building that courthouse. Now he was being tried in it, and the wolves were at his gate.

A deputy sheriff slouched at one corner of the hotel's front porch, trying to be inconspicuous as he watched Frank Claymore with nervous, weasel eyes.

There ain't no job too low for somebody who don't want to work, Claymore thought darkly.

Muttering, he moved toward a bench, attacking the floor with his cane at every step. It was hard to come to a tolerance for this kind of attention. For a time now, until just lately, it had seemed that hardly anyone except Homer Whitcomb and the hired hands paid attention to him. Older people didn't count for much anymore. He muttered a bit louder, taking crude comfort from mule-skinner language that had always been therapeutic.

Homer was at his elbow. "You say somethin', Frank?" He took Claymore's arm and tried to help him toward the bench. "You just set yourself down. Be a spell yet before court takes up again. Yonder comes the prosecutin' attorney to dinner, him and that whole pack."

Claymore jerked his arm free of Homer Whitcomb's solicitous hands. "I can set myself, thank you." Instantly he regretted his irritability, but he knew he would react no differently the next time. Long years of struggle had etched a belligerent independence into his grain, as time had conditioned the gentle Homer Whitcomb to overlook such provocations and permit them to leave no track. It had long galled Claymore that Homer showed no evidence of rheumatism, of stiffened joints that ached in protest over every quick move. Homer's hair remained indecently dark, though he was by two years the older. But, then, he had never been run over by a herd of cattle, had never carried a flint arrowhead amongst his vitals.

Homer had what Claymore regarded as a hound-dog face, loose skinned and wonderfully pliable, falling easier into smile than frown, seeming usually to harbor some private joke that he savored like old wine. To Claymore, a man who bore so little worry on his shoulders was shirking his responsibilities.

Claymore pushed aside a newspaper he found lying in the way, then settled himself upon the center of the bench so no one could share it with him. He glanced about with his eyes fierce in challenge of anyone who might have the temerity to try.

Homer asked, "Anything I can bring you, Frank?"

"I just had dinner. What the hell could I want?"

Homer seated himself in a nearby chair, showing no reaction. He was more than a working partner; he was a friend from far back down the long years. Like Frank Claymore, he had always done as he damn well pleased, and it had never pleased him to acknowledge the unpleasant.

Claymore studied the business-suited men passing through the gate of the white picket fence that surrounded the courthouse square, picking their way among the tied horses, the wagons and buggies. His vision was still sharp when he looked into the distance. He could see the special prosecuting attorney and his own lawyer walking side by side, conversing pleasantly, apparently the best of friends.

Claymore muttered again. When a man worked for you and accepted your pay, your enemies ought to be his enemies.

He did not understand lawyers. He did not understand *anybody* who spent his days sheltered beneath a roof, dealing in intangibles such as law or accounts receivable rather than something solid and real like cattle and horses. It was incomprehensible that two men could wrangle for hours in a courtroom and then shut off hostility at the moment of adjournment, like blowing out a lamp. He supposed his Anderson Avery was a good man, as lawyers went. At least he cost enough. But Claymore was not comfortable leaving his future in the hands of a man who had fought all his battles in the comfort of a courtroom, where the only blood he ever saw was in an opponent's eyes.

Anderson Avery mounted the hotel steps and asked politely if Claymore had enjoyed his dinner. Claymore only grunted. Special prosecuting attorney Elihu Mallard looked past the old rancher, fastening his attention upon the screen door and passing through as quickly as he could.

Afraid of me, Claymore thought with satisfaction. *Outside of the courtroom he ain't got the guts to look me in the eye.*

Inside the hotel lobby Mallard declared, loudly enough for Claymore to hear, "Sheriff, that man out there is on trial for his life. Why do you not have him in custody?"

The sheriff's voice was touchy. "I got Willis keepin' an eye on him. Anyway, he ain't fixin' to run off. I don't believe that old man ever ran from *anything*."

Homer Whitcomb nursed a secret smile that often irritated Claymore almost to violence. For the twentieth time he made reference to the prosecutor's name. "*Mallard.* Good handle for such a funny-lookin' duck."

To Homer, anyone outside the cattle-and-horse fraternity was peculiar.

Claymore grumped, "I've looked at better men over the sights of a rifle." The banked coals of courtroom anger stirred to a glow. "I wish it was still just the Indians. They faced you. These days you don't know who the enemy is half the time. They fight you with a pen instead of a gun."

He picked up the newspaper but could read only the Dallas masthead. He passed it to Homer. "You can still read without glasses. What does it say about me?"

"You don't want to hear all them lies."

Claymore demanded, "Read it!"

Reluctantly Homer folded the paper and held it almost at arm's length. He read slowly, stumbling now and again over an unfamiliar word as the article reviewed its version of Frank Claymore's spotted life. Claymore winced in pain when it touched upon the outlaw career of Billy Valentine. He interrupted Homer with an angry outburst. "Damn them, Homer! Damn them! Why can't they let Billy and all them other poor people just rest in peace?"

Homer shook his head and started to put the paper aside. Claymore motioned for him to continue reading. At length Homer came to a section that described Claymore as a greedy, evil old man, a despot of the range, a usurper of the children's grass. Homer looked up, reading the word again. "What's *usurper* mean?"

Claymore sighed. "I remember the stories they printed about me a long time ago. Said I was forgin' trails in the wilderness. Said I was turnin' them into highways and openin' the plains for civilization. I'm the same man. Old now, is all, instead of young. I was a hero then. Now I'm a greedy old despot. Where's the difference, Homer? I ain't changed."

Homer shook his head. "The *world* has changed."

Sheriff Ed Phelps walked out onto the porch, picking his teeth. He nodded civilly at Claymore but held his distance. Crowding forty, beginning to pack the first signs of tallow beneath his belt, he looked like a cattleman. Claymore felt more comfortable with him than the lawyers.

The deputy Willis motioned excitedly for the sheriff's attention. "Ed, I wisht you'd looky yonder. There's two Indians settin' under that big chinaberry tree."

Claymore said, "They're friends of mine."

The sheriff's eyebrow arched. "I thought you was an old Indian fighter."

Claymore frowned. "Used to be. Not anymore."

The deputy asked worriedly, "You want me to run them off, Ed?"

Testily Claymore repeated, "They're friends of mine."

The sheriff pondered the two figures squatted in the tree's generous shade. "They look harmless to me."

Claymore saw a smile in Homer's eyes. *Harmless,* he thought. *Hell of a lot these people know. They just ain't old enough to remember.*

Homer dropped the newspaper to the gray-painted gallery floor and stared wistfully off into the distance toward the open range, where the new spring grass was rising. Claymore hunched on the bench. He took out his watch, refusing to acknowledge the big clock in that hated cupola. He held the cane between his bony knees, tapping its tip against the toes of his foot-pinching black boots. Drowsiness came over him, for the trial had robbed him of his nap. He stared at the dreary courthouse, dreading his return to it. Gradually the dark stones seemed to dissolve before his half-closed eyes, and the town yielded to the open prairie. The years fell away from his weary shoulders, and in his mind he was again upon the Clear Fork of the Brazos River, where he had ridden so long ago with Homer and with others who were now but a fading memory . . .

Down from the rock-crested long hills into the broad valley of the Clear Fork the three horsemen had moved since dawn in a chill autumn mist, searching at first for their cattle, then watching in vain for a landmark to tell them where they were. The hills were brooding dark ghosts dimly seen through a blue-gray curtain drawn down by the season's first raw norther.

The sudden confrontation startled the Comanche hunting party as much as it surprised Frank Claymore and the two men who rode beside him. The riders reined up, stunned, facing each other across fifty yards of wet, brown-cured grass. Horses on both sides sensed the tension and danced nervously, wanting to run.

"My God!" declared George Valentine. "We're dead!"

Frank Claymore, barely the summer past twenty-two, felt as if the ground were opening up to engulf him. Shivering, he summoned the foresight to slip off the soft deerskin case that protected his long rifle from morning dampness. The Indians quickly spread out, widening their line. Frank had no idea whether this was a defensive move or preparation for a charge. He had never seen a hostile this near before. Ten—no, eleven. He looked expectantly at George Valentine for guidance. George, by a full three years his elder, captained the local flop-eared militia. But George trembled and offered no counsel.

Homer Whitcomb always had something to say whether it helped or not. "Them's Indians."

George asked plaintively, "What we goin' to do, Frank?"

Frank's first surge of fear made room for a little of annoyance. He was the youngest of the three. *Why do they always look to me?* He said, "You're the captain. You tell *us.*"

But George Valentine gaped in shuddering silence at the Indians waving their weapons in challenge. He was ready to break and run.

Frank said, "Let's stand our ground." He tried to put more steel into his voice than he felt. "If we run they'll overtake us and kill us one by one."

George tugged on his reins. "We've got to try." His voice was unnaturally high-pitched. "Maybe our horses are faster."

Frank knew George's panic was about to infect Homer. He felt it himself. It would probably be fatal to them all. He reached deep for nerve. "We can't outrun them, not all of us. Let's get down slow. Show them we'll fight."

Homer Whitcomb dismounted first. He sighted his rifle across the saddle, the reins wrapped around his wrist. If firing started, Homer might not have the horse; the horse might have Homer. *In the long run,* Frank thought gravely, *it probably would not matter.*

He remained in the saddle, rifle leveled toward the Comanches, until George was down. Then Frank eased slowly to the ground, though an inner voice shrilled at him to hurry. The Indians shouted. Frank watched them with a mixture of dread and morbid fascination. He fought down an insistent fear, wondering which warrior carried the leadership. The Indians flung away the blankets they had worn against the chill. Frank saw no paint on their faces. He was vaguely disappointed, for their plainness did not live up to his expectations. But he saw color enough in the buffalo-hide shields they raised in taunting gestures and in the feathers and animal tails ornamenting the edges. He saw no firearms. All the warriors brandished bows. That was no comfort, for they could loose arrows much faster than he could fire and reload cap and ball.

George's voice was still strained. "One shot, then they'll be on us before we can reload. We'll have to bluff them."

Frank flared but did not speak the thought. *If you know so damned much, why didn't you speak up before?*

Homer Whitcomb was never too frightened to talk. "The one on the black horse acts like the leader . . . the one with the red shield that looks like blood spilled all over it."

Shortly that warrior rode out alone toward the three white men. Frank tensed, expecting the rush.

Rachal! he thought in dismay. *Rachal may never know what happened to me.*

The Comanche gestured with the crimson shield on his

left arm and the bow in his right hand. His eyes fastened on Frank.

Homer said, "I believe he wants you to fight him."

The morning cold bit through Frank's soggy deerskin shirt. "I don't believe I want to do that." He looked at George, but George had nothing to offer.

Damn it, he thought, *why should they always assume I am smarter, or stronger, or braver?* But he recognized the dependency in the faces of George and Homer. Where he pointed, they would follow. If he panicked, so would they.

He studied the Indian and began as methodical a calculation as he could muster against a smothering fear. Frank was a good shot. Fatherless since ten, he had been sent into the woods by older brothers to fetch home meat while they tended crops. Far back east of here, on the Colorado River, Frank's rifle had often stood between the Claymores and hunger, for the land had been reluctant in its yield.

The Indian had only a bow, and arrows in a buckskin quiver on his shoulder.

It was not Frank's custom to call for help, not even from God. Prayer did not cross his mind. He said tightly, "Next time I may let you hunt cows by yourselves!"

Struggling against an instinct to cut and run, he left his brown horse and walked slowly into the middle ground where the challenging Indian waited. He had considered going mounted but reasoned that he could hold the long rifle steadier if he were on the ground. The Indian motioned for him to move closer. Twenty paces was as far as Frank would go. He held his breath while the Indian walked his horse toward him, shouting, gesturing with the feather-rimmed red shield. Frank could plainly see the dark round face. It struck him that the Comanche was no older than he. Perhaps his comrades had thrust this responsibility upon him as Frank's had done. Frank looked into the black eyes and thought he saw fear behind the bluster. Or perhaps he saw a mirroring of his own.

From a sheath at his waist the taunting warrior flourished

a long, crude knife. Frank guessed he was being challenged to a duel with the steel, but the prospect of a knife chilled him. He held the rifle steady, pointing at a tiny rawhide bag hanging from the Indian's neck. At this close range he could not miss. But he knew the other Indians would kill him.

The warrior sheathed the knife, then whooped and drummed his heels into the black horse's ribs. While Frank stared in surprise, the Indian swung the bow and rapped him smartly across the shoulder. Shouting his triumph, the young man whipped his horse around and raced back to his brothers. In startled reflex Frank came near shooting him. His legs threatened to crumple.

Death had brushed him like a raven's wing.

Frank backed toward the other cow hunters, his rifle still pointed at the warriors shouting approval for the young man's bravery. The pulse drummed at Frank's temples. He did not want to turn and let the others see his face washed colorless.

To his surprise, the Comanches pulled away, waving shields, yelping in victory. Frank held the rifle high as they dismounted to pick up their blankets. As quickly as they had appeared, they were enveloped in the chilling mist, leaving a deep silence.

His legs were wet from the tall grass, and his crudely pegged boots felt as if he had poured water into them. Homer Whitcomb gave up a long sigh and forced a nervous smile that endured but a moment. George Valentine stood immobile, his eyes downcast as fright gave way to shame.

Shivering, Frank looked from one to the other. His resentment ebbed. The two had done the best they could, considering their individual abilities. He had extended himself beyond what he had thought were his own limitations. He wished he could control his queasy stomach.

George blurted, "I wasn't goin' to run. If you say I was fixin' to run, I'll tell them you lie."

Frank felt warmth rising to his face. "I don't figure to tell anybody anything."

But he knew Homer would.

Frank swung into his saddle. "They may change their minds and have another try at us," he said as evenly as he could. "I think we've branded calves enough for one trip."

It was George's prerogative to make that judgment, but Frank assumed the lead and began to ride. Homer spurred quickly to catch up. George held back, nursing a wound that would not bleed. The camp people had elected him militia leader for reasons Frank had never understood. Perhaps it was because he looked more dashing than he was. Perhaps, and Frank thought this the most likely, it was because George owned more cattle than almost anybody. Frank had long thought they should have elected the strongest and smartest man in camp. They should have elected Sam Ballinger.

He was not certain of directions in the mist, but he hoped he was riding toward the Clear Fork. He thought George might have a better feeling for the way and correct him, but George did not speak. The distant trees, the long hills were but brooding phantoms. Frank's unspoken doubt did not leave him until he led the riders down the sloping bank of the Brazos tributary.

As they watered the horses Homer declared, "You've got the instinct, Frank. Me and George couldn't've found it."

Frank glanced at George, who kept his face turned away. Frank shrugged, glad he had trusted himself. He had no intention of letting the others know of his doubts. After a time he recognized a lightning-shuck tree, its ruptured black trunk resembling a bird with a broken wing dipped into the water. Up the bank a little way lay the dark pile of ashes and charred logs that remained of Sam Ballinger's cabin.

Through the mist he perceived a movement. Quickly he raised the rifle from the pommel of his saddle. His mouth was dry.

A familiar voice called through the gray curtain, "Who's that out yonder?"

Frank recovered enough to answer, "It's us, Sam."

The tall, gaunt frame of Sam Ballinger materialized cautiously out of the mist. Sam rode the biggest horse in Davis camp, a long-legged bay that could stand like a block of stone when a grown bull hit the end of a rope. Man and horse seemed carved one for the other.

Sam Ballinger had gray in his heavy sideburns and steel in his eyes. But he showed a kindly smile. "Been folks losin' sleep over you boys. You been gone three days."

The Indians were miles behind them. George was recovering some of his nerve. Though years younger than Sam, he asserted his authority. "What're you doin' out here by yourself? You know my orders against people leavin' camp alone."

Sam gave him a long silent stare without the smile. He turned to Frank. "See any of my cows?"

Homer, eager for Sam's approval, beat Frank to the answer. "We branded two calves for you. Heifer calves, they was."

Sam nodded his satisfaction. Heifer calves would build a herd. Bull calves were only to sell, and these days nobody was buying. "Thanks, Homer. I branded one for you and Frank this mornin'."

Like a son gingerly trying to advise his father, Frank said, "You oughtn't to ride out alone, Sam."

Sam did not yield an inch. "I can take care of myself." He had held out longer than any other farmer on the Clear Fork before finally taking his family to the settlement to fort up with the others at a place they had named Fort Davis. He had not gone until virtually forced at gunpoint by the Texas Confederate Rangers, who patrolled a long picket line north and south at frontier's edge. As soon as the Ballingers were gone, Indians had torched their cabin and the few possessions they had left behind. They had done the same to the small bachelor shack of pickets and sod that Frank had shared with Homer. Frank had accepted it as the fortunes of war, but Sam Ballinger had regarded it as a personal affront.

Sam looked up the slope at the ruins of his cabin and cursed, half under his breath. "I swear, Frank, I'll come back out here the soonest I'm able. I'll build me a house they'll never burn."

Frank nodded, wondering when that might ever be. Far to the east, war blistered Virginia and Georgia and sister states of the Old South. Here on the outermost fringe of Northwest Texas settlement, an older war continued. It had been fought in a hundred skirmishes across plains and hills that as yet had no names except those given by white cowmen or farmers, or by the Indians. They were Buzzard Peak and Walnut Creek and Blackjack Thicket. The Indian names were lost as white settlement stubbornly pushed the horse tribes northward and west, away from the deer and buffalo grounds won by right of conquest over other red men who had preceded them in these wide, grassy valleys, these raw-edged hills where the rough cedar and oak region known as the Cross Timbers yielded to the southeastern fringe of rolling plains.

Protected to some degree by military outposts such as Belknap and Cooper and Phantom Hill, audacious farmers and cattle owners had pushed into these game-rich grazing lands during the final years before the nation had come unraveled. Suddenly federal troops were gone. Many of the young Texas men volunteered or were conscripted for Confederate service, leaving a thinly guarded frontier more vulnerable than ever before. The western line of settlement had fallen under siege to Comanche and Kiowa, fracturing here and there and yonder as family after family abandoned the land to the constant probing, as men fell in sudden onslaught on field or road, as women and children died in isolated cabins taken by surprise. The settlers who did not choose to abandon the country fell back to redoubts such as Davis, which they called a fort though it was not. It had no military status, no soldiers except a rough-hewn and usually ineffective militia of its own residents, men who by and large had lost no Indians and did not wish to find any.

Few people on the Clear Fork knew or would have cared that a real fort of the same name existed two hundred miles farther west, in the dry mountains beyond the salty Pecos River. They simply banded together on a small plain above the river's east bank and named their rough settlement after the beleaguered president of the Confederacy. That the war back east was going badly they had only an inkling, for their isolation was severe, their own problems crushing enough.

When they needed to tend their drifted cattle or work their distant fields, men usually rode out in groups they hoped were large enough to discourage any Indians they might chance upon. Belatedly the Texas government had elected not to conscript additional young men from the frontier, for their guns were needed at home. The Confederacy had no troops to spare, so the settlers were left largely to defend themselves, augmented by a small and scattered force of state Rangers. Each man was considered a member of the militia and expected to give his share of time to its service. For some it was little more than a convenient alternative to the Confederate Army.

A fact seldom spoken aloud, for one could never be sure of another's conscience, was that many men were on the frontier because they had opposed secession and still held loyal to the Union. In the home guard, this far from that other war, a man was unlikely ever to fire upon the old flag. If he was lucky, he might not have to fire upon an Indian.

Frank Claymore never had.

As they neared the post the men who had followed began pressing ahead of Frank. His resentment gone, he could look upon Homer and George dispassionately. A man had to be taken as he was, not as another might wish him to be.

He had known Homer all his life. The Claymore and Whitcomb families had neighbored in Tennessee and had made the long wagon trek west together when Texas was yet an independent republic. They had settled on adjoining farms near Columbus when peg-legged Judge Willie Williamson was still conducting court there beneath a giant old live oak tree. Some of Frank's earliest recollections were of following Homer barefoot down to the Colorado River to watch him catch fish with a cane pole and homespun cotton string, of falling in and of Homer dragging him out upon the sandy bank to cough up muddy water. Homer had taught him about hunting, and they had often carried rifles longer than they were tall, seeking out squirrels in the river-bottom timber. Eventually student had become teacher, and Homer had become the follower.

Both had older brothers, so Frank and Homer had always known they stood no chance of inheriting the family farms; they would have to make their own way. In their teen years the boys cleared stumps and broke out new land for a farmer who, like most early Texans, had no more than a passing acquaintance with cash money. He paid them in old cows whose worn-down teeth had left them near worthless. Both Frank's parents had died by then. With kindly coaching from Homer's father, James, who had nothing to give the boys except counsel and affection, Frank and Homer pampered the cows and saved the calves, branding the C Bar W for Claymore & Whitcomb, trading bull calves for heifers, shaping a little herd. Inevitably the home country became overstocked and Frank's brothers declared his cattle a burden. Carrying little with them except the reluctant blessings of James and Nancy Whitcomb, the two young men drove their small fortune westward from water to water, subsisting upon other people's grass while they worked their slow way toward the frontier and free range. In the process they had happened upon George Valentine, whose older brother had hounded him off of the family farm after their father's death. In leaving, George had gathered what he considered his due, a sizable share of the cows carrying his father's brand, and drove hard to outdistance any angry pursuit. He had felt safer throwing his cattle in with the smaller bunch of Frank and Homer. The angry brother never came. Frank had since decided that most problems never materialize if a man holds himself always ready.

They had come at last to the Clear Fork, far up toward the headwaters of the Brazos. Frank had said this was far enough. He had liked the narrow, whispering river, the grass-blanketed valleys where buffalo might sometimes still be taken when fresh meat was needed. He had liked the ragged hills that seemed to stretch row upon row as far as he could see. Here, in the beginning, the land belonged to the first to squat upon it. There would be time enough later for legalities, for wrangling over titles, for the enrichment of lawyers and judges and the dispossession of those whose rifles and plows had opened the way. It was there for the taking, and Frank had chosen to take it.

That men of darker hue and Stone Age culture regarded it as their own by ancient birthright, confirmed in battle against fierce and persistent enemies, he had never considered. So far as he was concerned, he was the first man to set his feet upon the ground where he turned loose his cattle, where he had chosen to raise the picket cabin. That Homer shared it did not diminish his perception that it was his own.

George shared it only a little while. Because he was the older and owned more cattle, he had assumed an authority Frank had been unwilling to acknowledge. In due time George had put up his own cabin, salvaging what was left of a fragile friendship.

Frank chafed for that big war farther east to be over and done so he could get on with the business at hand. He wanted to reclaim permanently what belonged to him instead of riding out there like a thief in the company of an armed escort, then returning to the crowded and gloomy settlement miles from the place he wanted to be.

Thirty families lived in Davis on a flat patch of ground roughly a hundred yards square. One side was bucket-carrying distance from the river's flood-carved bank. An old stone house stood in one corner, a solid nucleus for the settlement. The other buildings were temporary, mostly of pickets. Cedar and post-oak trunks had been set upright in trenches and rawhide bound for the walls, the roofs made of poles covered by earth. The crude construction stood more for utility than for art, more for expediency than for permanence. Few people wished or expected to remain here for long.

Frank saw a homespun Confederate flag waving atop a pole raised in the middle of the fort. The flag aroused him to no patriotic emotion. He frowned at the partially finished picket wall supposed to surround and protect the place. Each man had been allotted a specified footage to build, but many had not found time or motivation. Frank and Homer and George had done theirs early. Sam Ballinger had done more than his share because he had a family who needed security. *Some bright morning,* Frank thought darkly, *a Comanche force may show up at the fringe of timber, and a bunch of laggard settlers will finish their fence right smartly.*

As the riders approached camp, Homer was telling Sam for the third time about their encounter with the Indians. He told about George wanting to run, as Frank had known he would. Face reddening, George spurred his horse and entered camp a couple of lengths ahead of the others.

Sam said, "Homer, there ain't no use you shamin' him so."

George was still in the lead as the horsemen circled a stockaded corner and rode into the square from the river side, where no fence had been built. Homer laughed. "Slow down, George. She's probably run off with some freighter."

Sam Ballinger turned on him sternly. "Never speak ill of a lady, Homer. Not even in jest."

Homer was taken aback. "She ain't no lady. She's just a girl."

Sam yielded nothing. "She'll be a lady. Respect her."

George moved his horse into a long trot across the traffic-packed quadrangle toward a small picket house where the Wakefield family lived. A stubborn will held Frank back. He would not have people thinking he was running after any woman, even Rachal. If George's unabashed eagerness won her favor, so be it. He held his brown horse to a walk, his dignity uncompromised.

It was just as well, for a flutter of movement drew his gaze to a picket corral beyond a far corner of the quadrangle. A girl stood in an open gate, a wooden milk bucket in her hand. She waved her bonnet. Even at the distance Frank knew the gesture was for him, not for George. She began running, heedlessly splashing milk from the bucket, depriving her younger brothers and sisters of their supper. Frank forced down an urge to spur his horse. He swung from the saddle and waited for her to come to him.

George Valentine veered across to meet her, but she gave him only a glance and a word. She might have thrown her arms around Frank had she not become aware of people watching. She stopped short. Her face flushed as she looked up at Sam Ballinger, watching her somberly. Sam was preacher-strict with his own daughters.

She controlled her smile. "I . . . we was commencin' to worry, Frank."

He wanted to reach out for her, but Sam Ballinger's towering presence inhibited him. Sam's son, about four, ran from the Ballinger family's picket house shouting, "Daddy!" Sam stepped down and grabbed him, moving so swiftly that he startled his big horse and had to grab the reins. Sam hugged the boy. His daughters waited by the ax-hewn door, their welcome restrained by hard-earned lessons in decorum.

George Valentine sat on his horse, face betraying his disappointment as he watched Frank and Rachal. Ill at ease, Frank was glad he had not reached for the girl. That would have made a spectacle for people to gossip about. Because so little news arrived from outside, everything done, said or imagined here was repeated and enlarged and changed

with every telling. Truth had no more chance than an unlucky buffalo that wandered too near this meat-hungry outpost. Frank would wait until darkness hid him and Rachal
from prying eyes. It would not, of course, hide them from
gossip.

"Tonight," he told her quietly, hoping the word would not
carry to George or Homer. But of course they would know.
A cow could not cough in this place without everybody
knowing.

"Tonight." She smiled, turning away with a flare of homespun skirt. He glanced at George, wondering if George
could read his mind. But George's attention was on Rachal
as she walked away.

Frank wondered sometimes about Rachal's judgment.
George was the older and half a head taller. Frank considered George by some odds the handsomer, though he could
only guess what a woman's standards might be. He watched
Rachal until she was gone into the small mud-chinked house,
carrying what was left of the milk. Turning to lead his horse
toward the corrals, he noticed two strangers walking toward
George.

Frank slipped the saddle from the brown horse and picked
up a badly worn brush somebody had left under the shed.
Though half its bristles were gone, he rubbed it where the
saddle had been. The horse stood still, enjoying the treatment. Homer said, "Here comes George with two strangers. You reckon he's sore about me tellin' Sam?"

"You don't have to tell *everybody*."

"Now, Frank, you know I ain't no gossip."

George stopped in the corral gate, two tall men beside
him. One was forty or older, his hair and short beard graying. The other was younger, possibly thirty or less. His eyes
had an intensity that cut through Frank like a blade. An
empty right sleeve was neatly folded and pinned above the
point where his elbow should be. Frank guessed he was a
soldier sent home with the scars of that other war.

George said, "Frank Claymore, this is Captain Zachary

of the state troops, and Lieutenant Alex McKellar. They're on scout with their company."

Zachary, the older of the two, shook hands in a free and friendly manner. McKellar seemed to harbor reservations, but he extended his left hand. Frank was self-conscious and awkward, wondering which of his own hands to use.

George said, "I have told them about the Indians."

Zachary nodded. "Since Mr. Valentine heads the militia, I have asked him to go with us in the morning to see if we can pick up their trail. He was kind enough to volunteer your services also, Claymore."

Galled, Frank glanced toward the Wakefield house and knew why George did not want him here in his own absence. He saw Homer grin at his discomfort. "Homer'll be glad to go with us too," he said dryly.

Homer's eyes narrowed in resignation. "Sure thing, Captain."

Captain Zachary smiled, but McKellar did not look as if he had smiled in years. Frank was uncomfortably conscious of the younger officer's eyes measuring him, probably finding fault with his lack of eagerness.

The tall captain pointed with his chin to a rising of camp smoke beyond the compound. "We'll see you at first light."

McKellar kept stride with him as they left, seeming more to march than to walk.

George said, "The captain's lookin' for recruits."

Frank knew what he was driving at. "I'm surprised you didn't volunteer me for that too."

"It crossed my mind." George glanced toward the Wakefield house, then walked off toward his own.

Tiny ribbons of lightning played through the night sky, so far to the north that Frank could hear no thunder as he walked toward the Wakefields' picket cabin. The wind was cold and damp, and he had changed his buckskin shirt for one of rough cotton and a woolen coat. Both were so old that the elbows were patched and the cuffs frayed out. Marks of poverty were no disgrace on the frontier. The longer the war continued, the more common they became.

He heard the laughter of Rachal's younger brothers and sisters as he stopped at the door. He could not pick her voice from the lot. He waited for a lull in the noise, then rapped his knuckles solidly against the rough cedar door. Rachal appeared dark against the flickering candlelight. "Frank?" she asked, trying to be sure of him in the darkness.

He stopped closer to the light. "Wondered if you'd want to walk with me a little? If it's all right with your daddy, of course."

"Daddy's away on a cow hunt. But Mama's here. Come on in."

Frank had never known how to figure Rachal's mother, old before her time, her frowning silence speaking of pent-up bitterness years in building. She had little use for most people in the settlement and even less for Frank Claymore. Anger always showed when she turned her eyes to him, as if she knew very well what Frank and Rachal did when they got away into the darkness by themselves. She probably had done the same herself when she was young, he thought defensively, if she ever had been young. He found it difficult to imagine her enjoying it as much as Rachal. He could not picture her ever having been different than the mean-spirited, used-up shell she was today. Frank reasoned that Mrs. Wakefield saw in him and in all other men here the reflection of her own husband, who had used her like a brood mare and brought her to this rough poverty.

Making an effort toward peace, he removed his hat. She looked away without acknowledgment, sharply telling the children to be still and stop stirring dust from the earthen floor.

Rachal threw an old woolen shawl over her shoulders and picked up a bundle from a bed. "It's all right with Mama."

"We won't leave the camp, Mrs. Wakefield," Frank said. "I wouldn't take her where there's any danger."

The woman did not look at him. Crossly she said, "There's worse dangers here in camp than any to be found outside."

Frank was relieved to be out of the tension-charged shack and back into the cool night air. Outside, the closing door put the couple in darkness. Rachal threw her arms around Frank and pressed eagerly against him. Her lips were warm and hungry. They were forced, in a minute, to pull apart for breath. Fire rushed to his face.

She whispered, "I thought you'd never come."

"It was a long time for me, too."

Arms around each other's waists, they walked across the quadrangle. He let her lead him toward the cow pen, toward a dark shed that would shelter them from prying eyes. The only resistance he offered was to point out, "If anybody sees us, they'll talk."

"They'll talk even if we *don't* do anything. Show me the locket, Frank."

He reached into his pocket and brought out a small silver-looking oval she had given him. She said, "I've been afraid you might lose it."

In terms of monetary value it would be little loss, for it was but a cheap trinket. But its sentimental value was beyond price. He touched a clasp, and the cover opened to a tiny, crudely painted portrait done by an itinerant artist who would better have served the world as a carpenter or a stone-mason. It looked vaguely like Rachal; imagination filled in where artistry had been lacking. "I won't lose it," he said. "I look at your picture twenty times a day."

The cow-pen gate was a series of three bars. She slid the top one aside, then turned as if to ask him to move the others. He did, closing them behind him. She hurried ahead with the bundle and waited beneath the shed, where the raw north wind did not reach her. She threw her arms around him and kissed him again, hungrier than before. He sensed that she was still leading him, that soon she would lead him beyond any stopping.

They had been shy and slow and awkward about it the

first time, weeks ago. Now there was no shyness, no waiting, but a breathless rush by both of them, an eager searching of hands, half-words whispered, a frenzied pressing
together, then a long, warm, silent holding, one against the
other.

She asked, "You love me, Frank?"

"Can't you tell without me sayin' it all the time?"

She shrugged. "You might do this with *any* girl."

"I never have. And I never would."

"You used to talk about marryin'. You ain't said nothin'
this time."

"I've already promised you—first chance we get."

"Preacher Smith is over at Fort Belknap. Captain Zachary's company brought the word. He'll be here tomorrow
or next day. We can get him to marry us; then it won't matter what people say." She pulled away, straightening her
dress. From a feed trough she picked up the little bundle she
had brought from the house.

"Look what I made for you." She let it roll out, holding
the edges so it would not fall. "A shirt, Frank. I spun the
cotton myself. You can't tell in the dark, but it's nice and
white. Just right for a weddin' shirt tomorrow."

"I won't be here tomorrow." He explained that he had
been ordered to ride out with Zachary's company.

She reacted with a minute's stunned silence. "But the
preacher mightn't stay long. Might be gone before you get
back."

"Then we'll have to wait awhile longer."

She began to cry. He tried to put his arms around her, but
she turned away from him, as if it had been his fault.

He said, "Preacher'll come around again. Another month,
maybe two . . . we can wait."

"I can't," she said, sobbing. "I mean, I had my heart set
on us marryin' now. In this awful place, who knows what
might happen in another month or two? I want you *now*,
Frank." She turned suddenly and threw herself against him.
Bewildered, he held her, feeling her shoulders shudder. A

dozen wild possibilities ran through his mind. He considered taking her tonight to Belknap, but the notion was discarded as quickly as it came. Indians might kill them both.

She whispered, "Can't you tell the captain you won't go till after the preacher gets here?"

Tempted, he knew he had to refuse. "Orders. They'd throw me in jail, and we couldn't get married a-tall. Might even make me go east to where the *big* fightin' is."

"Oh, Frank," she cried, "I have a terrible feelin'. If we don't get married now we never will."

He held her gently, love coming over him like a warm, smothering blanket. He never wanted to let her go. "I promise you, we'll get married soon's the chance comes. Till then you just got to have faith."

She ran sobbing to the gate, threw the first rail aside and climbed over. She ran back toward the Wakefield cabin. He stared after her in confusion, wanting to run to her but not knowing what he would say if he caught her.

Something white lay at his feet. He folded the new shirt carefully and tucked it under his arm. At a distance he saw the glow of cookfires in Zachary's camp. A helpless anger welled up at the thought of being hostage to the authority of others.

Why did you have to come today? Why couldn't you have waited?

Frank slept poorly, for Rachal kept coming to him in his mind, the consuming fire of her loving moments, the anguish in her face as she had run from him. Early in the morning he got up feeling irritable enough to take offense if it was offered from any quarter, even by Homer. He pulled on the deerskins, still damp and cold from yesterday, and knew this was going to be an unfriendly day. He put on his boots, stamping to drive his feet all the way into the rough, wet leather. He grunted, hoping to stir Homer. As was his custom, he walked outside to get some feeling for the day's weather. He saw only darkness where the morning star should be. Lightning still flickered in the north. The stockman in him was glad at the prospect of rain; the reluctant soldier did not relish riding in it. He saw movement in Zachary's camp and knew the rifle company was up, seeing to breakfast.

He shouted back into the cabin, "If you want time to eat, you'd better stir yourself. They won't take kindly to waitin'."

The lightning was nearer than when he had gone to bed. Once the earth trembled to distant thunder. He fixed a hasty breakfast of deer ham over a fire Homer had kindled in the small stone fireplace. Leaving, he picked up the woolen coat he had used for a pillow. Threadbare and roughly patched, it would feel good on this trip.

He saw the shirt Rachal had made. He rubbed his fingers over the fabric woven by her own hands, and he touched it reverently to his face. Carefully he spread it out across his bed so it would not wrinkle. One day soon he would wear it.

The captain's men were saddling when Frank and Homer rode to the encampment. Zachary greeted them civilly but invested no time, for he was seeing to it that everybody was ready. A small black boy of twelve or fourteen years brought the captain his pistol belt. It was not unusual for a slave-owning officer to keep a servant with him in the field. "Tobe, is everything packed?"

"Yes, sir, Captain. Got it all tied on the mule."

Lieutenant McKellar seemed everywhere at once, crisply upbraiding the laggards, silencing any protest with his rigid bearing. Frank would wager that he had been the first man packed, the first man a-horseback. McKellar did not allow his lost arm to be a handicap.

George Valentine rode in and reported to Zachary. Then he nodded at Frank. "No hard feelin's, I hope."

There were, but Frank saw no advantage in airing them. He had always liked George Valentine despite his shortcomings, despite the attention he gave to Rachal. As scarce as friends were on this broad frontier, a man couldn't be throwing them away. "No hard feelin's."

When the company was formed McKellar rode in front of it, silently counting. He reined around to face the captain and saluted, not a custom in the state troops. "All present and accounted for, sir." The left-handed salute seemed not a bit awkward.

Zachary's return salute was too casual for regular army. "Claymore, think you can find where you lost your Indians?"

Frank looked eastward, where day's first light put an edge on the trees and brought their shape up out of darkness. Today he should at least be able to see landmarks. "I'll try."

Zachary nodded. "Then plow ahead."

The expression told Frank the captain was a farmer at heart, not a soldier. Turning, he loose-counted about twenty men besides himself, Homer and George—better than a match for yesterday's Indians. Unlike the camp militia, they carried their rifles as if the weapons were a natural part of them. Most had probably been farmers, but they had made themselves into something else. They possessed a quiet purpose, a will.

Zachary seemed to know his thoughts. "These men are the pick of a good crop, Claymore. The rest I sent home." His jaw hardened. "Or buried."

Frank sensed a challenge offered. He saw no reason to respond; his connection with this company would be temporary. He touched spurs gently to the brown horse and set a course upriver to Sam Ballinger's place. He glanced northward from time to time, trying to gauge the weather, the distant rain. The damp chill worked through his woolen coat and leather shirt. He hunched his shoulders, though it did no good.

Zachary frowned at the ruins of Sam's cabin but made

no comment. He had probably seen a hundred places like this. Frank told him about Sam and his vow to come back.

Zachary said, "A commendable spirit, if not good judgment. There is a time to fight, and a time to preserve one's assets." He dismounted to rest his horse. His men followed his example without an order. Most walked to the river and drank their fill. Frank was not thirsty.

Zachary said, "It is a good policy to water out anytime you can. You never know when the next opportunity may arise."

Frank glanced at Homer and George. The three led their horses to the river and drank.

The rest period gave Frank a chance to study the men in good daylight. They were mostly young, prime material for the Confederate Army had they not chosen frontier service. An exception who aroused his curiosity was a spare, gray-whiskered man in grease-blackened buckskins, an ancient Mexican-style hat sagging around his face as if it was too old and fatigued to hold itself up. Frank would not have voiced his judgment, but he thought this venerable gentleman deserved a comfortable rocking chair. He had no business here.

The old man's frame seemed in a state of collapse, in keeping with the brim of his hat, but his pale gray eyes were never still. They caught Frank's and gave him a sense of guilt for staring. "How old you think I be, sonny?"

Frank's face warmed. "I don't know."

The old eyes seemed to laugh. "I never did know myself. As far back as I can remember, I been full-growed."

"I didn't mean you no offense."

"None taken. People been callin' me old for thirty years. But I'll still be a-horseback when most of them are layin' on the ground beggin' for a rest." The gray eyes fastened like claws to Frank's face. He extended his hand. "Name's Beaver Red."

The strength of his grip astonished Frank. He tried to

give back as firmly as was given and saw approval in the time-punished face. "Frank Claymore."

"I knowed yours. Heard it this mornin' early."

Frank hesitated to inquire into a man's personal business but decided to do it anyway. "How'd you come by a name like Beaver Red?"

"Trapped beaver once, out in the Rocky Mountains. Taken furs to Santy Fee and Taos. And my hair used to was red, way back yonder." It still was, amid the gray.

Frank's interest quickened. Santa Fe and Taos were names he had heard, mysterious places far west beyond two or three hundred miles of unknown Indian country. He had never talked to anyone who had actually been there.

He wanted to ask questions, but Captain Zachary swung onto his horse. Lieutenant McKellar glanced at Frank. The order was unstated but clear. Frank mounted the brown, found yesterday's tracks and took his direction.

George rode up once and pointed northward. "Seems to me like we ought to go yonderway."

Frank realized with a start that George had not even discerned he was following yesterday's trail. He wondered sometimes how George would ever make it on his own; he had no feeling for directions. Frank pointed to the tracks. George betrayed his surprise and dropped back.

There were those to whom the land spoke in silent voice. As far back as he could remember, Frank had always heard. Somehow, George never had.

Homer never asked questions. He simply followed, comfortable in his faith.

Once Frank lost the tracks in the tall, wet grass. Quietly Beaver Red moved to the front and helped him search. The old man took but a minute, then pointed to a fragment of track Frank had missed. He dropped back, not asserting himself further.

The heavy clouds allowed only the faintest notion of the sun, but Frank knew it was late afternoon when he came suddenly upon the mass of horse tracks. He felt a prickling where his backside fit against the saddle. This was the place, he thought, or close to it. He reined up, looking for a landmark. He had nothing to go on but instinct.

Homer rode out across a broad opening and turned. "Right here is where we was, Frank. I remember that dead tree. Yonder is where you and that Red Shield faced one another."

A chill played up Frank's back.

The captain said, "Good work, Claymore. Now, who left the field first, you or the Indians?"

"They did. Sort of faded into the mist, yonderway." He pointed northward.

Zachary turned in the saddle. "Beaver . . ."

Beaver was already there. Without questions he started riding a broad arc, studying the ground. He circled his hand over his head, then dropped it to point north.

The wind turned colder as the little company rode directly into it. Frank pulled his woolen coat tighter, wishing he had done a better job of patching. The wind sought out the holes and worried through to the skin. Homer and George wore no wool, only thin deerskin jackets covering rough cotton shirts. He could have told them this would be a cold ride, but they should have thought for themselves.

The heaviest clouds lay eastward. Frank guessed it was probably raining at Davis camp, the kind of cold, steady rain that so often rolled down across the vastness of the open plains and fell upon the settlements ahead of winter's first hard freezes, as the Indians sometimes fell upon them in their last search for horses and glory and blood before retreating to whatever distant lands they used for winter camping grounds.

Rain began slowly, a light mist at first, increasing steadily until it was a driving, lashing force, washing out the tracks Beaver Red had followed. The old man turned to the captain with a shrug of lean shoulders. "Sorry, Thomas. I expect they've got a medicine man in league with the weather spirits."

That was the first time Frank had heard anyone address Zachary other than as *Captain*. He supposed age offered privileges denied even to rank.

"It's time to look for camp anyway," Zachary replied. "Do you know of any sheltered places around here?" The question seemed directed at both Frank and Beaver Red. Frank waited for the old man to reply, then said, "I've hunted cattle up here. There used to be a stone cabin."

"Lead the way."

Frank followed his instinct and tried to appear confident. After a while a cabin's dark shape materialized through the rain. His relief turned to disappointment. The stone walls stood, but only charred and broken logs were left of the roof.

The captain took the letdown in stride. "The Indians are thorough. They allow us no comfort."

There was no comfort, not even dry wood for fires. The men contented themselves with cold bread and a little meat carried over from their breakfast. They shared with Frank and Homer and George. Coffee was a sometime luxury since the early days of the war, and if any man carried some with him he had no opportunity to boil it. Frank heard no complaint; he sensed these men were used to being deprived. The cabin walls seemed to mock them with comfort promised, then denied. The only virtue of the camp was that the stone corral was undamaged, and the horses could be penned for the night.

The men huddled in silent misery against the walls for their little protection from a driving rain. Frank wrapped his saddle blanket around his shoulders and let the cold water run off, making a rivulet past the skinned toes of his old boots and losing itself in the greater muddy mass running down the slope away from the cabin ruins. Zachary saw to his men, then looked down upon Frank and his two companions.

"I am sorry to have brought you to this."

Frank shrugged, bringing cold water down his neck. He glanced at George and lied. "We come because we wanted to."

Lieutenant McKellar stood in the rain, staring down at Frank with a look near belligerence. "Or perhaps you came because you had rather do this than serve your true duty?"

Frank looked up in surprise. "Sir?"

"You appear able-bodied. You could very well be back east defending your country against the northern invaders."

Frank dropped his chin, guarding against a betrayal of his thoughts. "I got no stake in that war back yonder."

The captain said, "Leave him be, Alex. This is no place for politics."

"*Any* place is a place for patriotism." McKellar strode away, his body stiff, ungiving to the rain.

The captain said quietly, "He gave an arm. He cannot see why some of us are not eager to give at least as much."

Frank's eyes narrowed. It occurred to him that the captain himself might be here because his devotion to the Confederacy was less than wholehearted. It was not a thing for a man to ask, or even to talk about. Men had been hanged for no more than suspicion about their loyalty.

Gravely the captain said, "I gave a son. And I gave a wife. She was so weakened by grief that she succumbed to the first fever epidemic that came along. That is more than I owe."

The rain abated before daylight, but the damage was done. Wet, cold, miserable, the tired little company arose to a breakfast the same as evening's supper except even smaller. Captain Zachary rode forward with Beaver Red, searching for any remnant of tracks. The droop of Zachary's shoulders said he expected to find nothing. They rode northward awhile. The company followed, spread out loosely, the men hunched in fatigue.

Frank missed George and looked around. He saw him trailing, talking to Lieutenant McKellar.

Well into the morning Zachary signaled for a halt and dismounted to rest the horses. The dejected set of his shoulders remained. McKellar rode forward to confer with him. In a few minutes the captain motioned to Frank. Glancing at Homer, Frank touched spurs to the brown horse. Homer followed; he always did.

The captain said, "As you have probably guessed, Claymore, we have lost all sign of your Indians. I have chosen to give up the pursuit."

Frank nodded. He could have told them that at daylight.

Zachary said, "As you have probably already seen for yourself, this unit is short of men. The lieutenant has been conferring with your militia officer. He says Mr. Valentine has volunteered your services to us for thirty days."

Frank made a cry of protest and turned in the saddle, looking back angrily. George had shown the good judgment to remain behind with the rest of the company. "I got stock to see after, sir."

McKellar said sternly, "It is in the law that any man exempted from regular military service can be pressed into special duty by the militia for up to thirty days, Claymore. If you had rather, we could see that you are sent to Virginia in short order."

That damned George, Frank thought. "I got personal business, Captain."

Zachary nodded. "So does every man in my company, sir."

Frank clenched his fist; he was trapped.

Homer spoke up. "Am I volunteered too, Captain?"

The captain glanced at McKellar. "If you want to be."

Frank said, "You better stay back and look after our cattle."

Homer shook his head. "Since George volunteered us, let *George see* after our cows."

The captain beckoned to George. He told him Frank and Homer were staying. "These men are concerned about their livestock. I feel confident you will see after their interests while they are gone."

George nodded, smiling a little as he looked at Frank. But Frank did not smile. When the captain and McKellar and Beaver Red rode back toward the waiting company, Frank remained. He managed to hold down most of his anger. "You'll tell Rachal why I didn't come back?"

George said, "I'll explain to her."

"And, George, I don't believe I need to tell you . . ." He could not put it into words, but he felt confident George followed his meaning. "I've always tried to be your friend, George, but damned if you don't make it hard." He put the brown horse into a walk, moving toward the company. Homer followed him, leaving George sitting by himself.

Somewhere to the east, thunder rolled.

2

The courtroom was close with spring's early warmth. Frank Claymore gazed at the windows on the far side, thinking he might be more contented if he could but see through them, if he could but see the rise and fall of the prairie, the high platform of the caprock that edged the Llano Estacado. He wished for the comfort of the wind that moved always down the long valley. A man could die in here, choked for want of fresh air.

The selection of the jury seemed to go on endlessly. Claymore wondered how many more men one attorney or the other would reject before they finally ran out of people; this town wasn't that large. He had stared at the succession of faces and wondered how so many strangers came to be here. They had to live in this valley or they would not be eligible for the jury panel. Yet he could not fix a name to one out of four. Where had they come from? Strangers . . . strangers in *his* valley, strangers who would decide what was to become of Frank Claymore.

He tapped his cane impatiently against the wooden floor until the judge fixed a wicked eye upon him.

Attorney Anderson Avery touched Claymore's hand. He whispered, "Please, Mr. Claymore, do not antagonize the bench."

The hell with the bench, Frank thought, but he stilled the cane. Damned poor outcome, to have survived all the snares a long, rough life had laid for him, then end up in the fullness of his years facing a jackpot like this.

Turning in his straight, heavy chair, he resentfully studied the faces of men who still waited as prospective jurors. *They look too well fed, the most of them, cutting themselves a share of something somebody else built. Where was they when first I come into this country? Where was they when so many good people died to take and hold this land?*

Special prosecutor Elihu Mallard, brought in from somewhere east because of the importance attached to this case, asked the same questions of each man. "Are you personally acquainted with the defendant, Frank Claymore?" Most said they had seen him but had never gotten to know him.

Damned right they don't know me. I never let them . . . Johnny-come-latelys . . . bone pickers . . .

Once the lack of acquaintanceship was established, the prosecutor would press the question of Claymore's reputation. "You are aware, of course, that legends abound of the defendant's exploits in his younger days? No doubt you have heard the whittle-and-spit fraternity's accounts of daring deeds and heroic gestures?"

The answer was usually yes. The prosecutor would then say, "But of course you know that most such stories are idle invention. You know that Frank Claymore is mortal like all other men, subject to the same weaknesses and flaws. In his case, perhaps, more weaknesses and flaws than most men, worsened by an arrogance that makes him feel himself above the average cut of mankind. Now, sir, do *you* believe Frank Claymore has any right to ignore the rules of conduct that must be obeyed by you and me and any other respectable, hardworking citizen of this state?"

The answer invariably was no.

"Very well, sir, I believe you will see your duty, and I am confident that when the time comes to render your verdict, you will act with conscience and courage to show that in the state of Texas no man can regard himself as above the law."

It would then fall to Claymore's attorney, Anderson Avery, to try to purge the seed the prosecutor had planted in the prospective juror's mind even before evidence was introduced. When he felt he had not, he rejected the panelist as predisposed against his client. He had rejected a worrisome number.

The judge periodically held his pocket watch at arm's length, then frowned at the half-filled jury box. He had been in town two days already, and the trial proper had not even begun. He growled, "Would counselor move along with it, please?"

Avery had told Claymore the judge was assigned to this case out of his normal jurisdiction without any enthusiasm on his part. It had been argued by the prosecution that the judge who regularly served this district might be swayed for the defendant in view of their long acquaintanceship, and by the defense attorney that he might be swayed against the defendant for the same reason.

Judge Whitmore Holmes had been forced to give up the comfort of his Dallas home and subject himself to the dubious hospitality of a remote and dust-plagued town that had but one hotel, and that hotel seemed not to offer one bed that did not sag in the center. Nothing would suit him better than to find an acceptable pretext for declaring a mistrial and catching the first mail hack east.

Claymore would admit that Holmes seemed completely impartial; he had no patience for either side.

He leaned toward his attorney and whispered, "Rate this is goin', we're liable to be here till Christmas."

Avery had not smiled in the courtroom since the process had begun. "Were I in your place, Mr. Claymore, I would not be in any hurry."

Claymore looked at the water pitcher on the judge's bench and wondered about the result upon court decorum were he to get up and help himself to a glass. He decided against it. He had been thirsty many a time. It had never proved fatal . . .

* * *

Frank's mouth was dry, his lips cracking from thirst and the relentless cold wind, but he saw no purpose in talking about it with Beaver Red. The scout's own condition was no better. The two men pushed tired horses across a dry-grass prairie that rolled endlessly before them. This was farther to the northwest than Frank had ever been. It was clear that Beaver was also unfamiliar with the land.

Frank felt resentful of prodigal nature. "Don't seem likely it could've rained so much behind us and not spill a drop here."

Beaver told him, "Ain't but one natural law that holds on the plains, and that's the law of gravity. This country's got weather all its own."

Despite his years, Beaver's eyes remained sharp. He was the first to see the mustangs, all of them bay in color. Frank's original thought was that they might be Indians.

"Too scattered," Beaver said, "and not movin' like they had men on their backs. Them's wild horses, comin' out from water."

Frank had difficulty enough just seeing them, much less telling whether they had been to water. Beaver said, "They're pokin' along, stoppin' to graze. Was they goin' to water, they'd move steady."

Water was the reason Frank and Beaver were here, miles ahead of the company. Following a faint trail more than a day, Zachary's men had finally lost it in a region none of them knew. The patrol went into dry camp to wait while Beaver searched for a seep or spring, or even a buffalo wallow that might still hold water from the last rain. The idea of idling in camp had left Frank restive, so he had volunteered to provide an extra set of eyes and a rifle. Usually Beaver demurred when Captain Zachary tried to compromise the solitude of his scouting trips. He always said he had the fastest horse in the company and did not care to hold back waiting for someone else's slow pony if he was faced with a run for his life. Beaver had accepted Frank's company without comment, however. Frank did not know whether this was a tribute to him or his brown horse.

Beaver frowned at the horizon. "You got to always watch this country. It's as apt to kill you as the Indians are, sonny."

Frank would not have accepted the term *sonny* from just anybody. But with Beaver he apologized for his ignorance. The old scout seemed pleased. "Some things you trust to your instinct, and nobody can teach you that. Most is just common sense. This looks like an empty country, but it ain't. It's full of God's creatures, big 'uns and little. Learn to watch them, and they'll show you where the water is at. You see a bunch of wild horses like them yonder, you can figure there's water. If they're goin' to it, follow them. If they're comin' away from it, backtrack them."

They made a wide circle to avoid spooking the mustangs. Frank saw no reason, but Beaver commented respectfully, "They was here before we was."

The first tangible sign of water was a small cluster of mesquite trees, limbs winter bare, a remnant of their summer bean crop lying broken and trampled amid the dry grass at their base. The wild horses had picked up most of them long ago. Frank was disappointed about the water hole, only twelve or fifteen feet across and too shallow to wet a man to his knees. It was still muddy from the mustangs' visit. Beaver dismounted, loosened the girth and let his dun horse drink before he sought comfort for himself. Shame touched Frank, for he had been about to drink first. Beaver handed him his reins and walked around the edge.

"Here's the seep," he said, dropping to bony knees, then flattening on the damp ground, cupping his hand and sinking his chin into the muddy-looking water. After a few long swallows he began to drink slowly, as if savoring, stretching the pleasure.

Frank flopped down and almost choked on his first sip.

Beaver smiled. "You'll drink worse and swear it's mother's milk." He seemed concerned that Frank might not drink his fill. "Water out, sonny. Never leave a waterin' place without you take on a-plenty."

Beaver looked around cautiously while Frank took all he could stand of the muddy, gyppy water. Beaver pitched him half a dozen empty canteens. "I'll be back directly."

Frank felt cowed by the size of this land. He thought he had seen much of Texas by the time he and Homer and George had reached the Clear Fork with their cattle, but he realized now how much more there was. He shuddered at a dark vision of dying out here alone, where a hundred years might pass before another human chanced upon his bones. Yet the land held a fascination for him, as if he were among the first men ever to see it.

Beaver was gone perhaps half an hour. Sitting alone, Frank let his mind wander back to Rachal, to the warm sound of her voice, to the dark nights they had walked together beyond the boundaries of the camp and had taken the pleasures they found, each in the other, at first with hesitation and guilt, then with eagerness and without shame. The wanting arose strongly in him, and he lost himself in a fantasy of lying with her.

Beaver reappeared suddenly and close up, startling Frank. The scout sat on his horse, his patchy old buffalo robe across the saddle, his rifle delicately balanced. Wind pulled at his unkempt gray beard and gave him a wild look that befitted the country. His narrowed eyes held accusation.

"Don't never go to sleep in the daytime, sonny. Even at night, you keep one eye open." He reached down for his share of the filled canteens and slipped their leather straps around the big horn of his Mexican saddle. Frank cinched up and mounted, his face warm despite the north wind's bite.

Beaver let him simmer awhile in his own juice as they rode through brittle grass the color of his dun horse. "At least you don't make excuses. That's a sign you can learn."

He began to talk, not idly and endlessly as Homer might, but with point and purpose about what he knew of this land

and its creatures. He saw the Indian as chief of those, little different from the wolf or the buffalo except that he possessed a human intelligence, for all the good and the bad that fact implied.

Frank gave voice to a point that bothered him. "Somehow I had a notion we'd find Indians livin' all over this country."

"These are horse Indians. They don't live in any particular place." Beaver made a broad sweep with his arm, cold wind lifting the ragged fringes of his buckskin sleeve. "Comanches and Kiowas, they live here awhile, then yonder. They ain't like a white man that builds him a house in one place and takes root forever. It's *all* home to them."

"How can they claim it all? They don't use most of it."

"They use it, but not the white man's way. You might put you a cabin in a place where no Indian has been in years, but he'd see you as a trespasser. Someday he might want to kill him a buffalo right on that very spot, or raise him a tepee and spend awhile. You'd be in his way."

"You sound like you agree with him."

Beaver shook his head. "My side in this war was set the day I was born white instead of Indian, sonny. So was yours. Was I an Indian, the other side would've been set for me the same way. A man may see both sides, but he can't forever be lookin' back, wonderin' if the one he was born into was right."

The men of the company were cooking supper over half a dozen small fires when Beaver and Frank returned. It was faster and more efficient to have several small messes than to equip and carry a cumbersome field kitchen. The black boy Tobe did most of the cooking for the captain and McKellar.

Some of the men sauntered out to meet the returning pair, eager for the water that sloshed in the canteens. Beaver admonished them, "Don't shake it too much. Maybe some of the mud has settled."

Frank knew better. The ride had not been that smooth.

Homer Whitcomb hunched over a small fire, holding a long stick with venison strips wrapped around it. Frank hungrily watched the fat and blood bubble from the meat. His belt fitted a notch tighter since his time with the rifle company.

Captain Zachary walked with Beaver to the edge of camp where they could talk alone. Presently Zachary called, "We'll eat in the saddle, men. The horses need to go to water."

Homer groaned. "This meat ain't half cooked yet. Never cared to eat somethin' that looked like it might get well."

Darkness turned day's chill to night's biting cold. Clouds covered the stars. But Beaver, wrapped in his heavy robe, rode point and held direction as unerringly as if he used a compass. When the water hole was finally reached and the horses had drunk their fill, Frank decided not to trust the picketline tied at the edge of camp. He picketed his horse near his blankets, looping one end of a horsehair rope to his wrist.

Beaver did the same. A flicker of a smile crossed his bearded face. "Sonny, I believe you'll do."

Next morning Zachary broke the company into small patrols, each to ride off and explore in a different direction, to find and map any additional watering places, any hidden canyons that might now or someday furnish sanctuary to Indians. He looked at Beaver Red. "Beaver, would you like to ride west?"

The old trapper nodded as if that direction was his natural choice. Beaver's eyes sought Frank. "Sonny, you wasn't too much of a hindrance to me yesterday."

Frank was pleased to be chosen. "How about Homer?"

Beaver gave Homer a critical glance. "If you can get him to hold his silence."

Homer raised his thin and translucent powder horn against the morning light to appraise its contents. Frank had filled his yesterday from the short supply packed on a company mule.

The captain said, "We'll regroup at this place before sundown."

Beaver touched heels to the dun horse's ribs. Frank trotted to reach his side. Every time Homer spurred up even with Beaver, the scout seemed to urge a brisker pace from his dun. Homer gave up and followed.

The land changed. Though it was not evident to the eye, Frank knew by the brown horse's labor that they were gradually climbing. To the west, the morning sun bathing it with full light, lay what appeared at first to be one wide, flat-topped plateau rising above the rolling plain. Gradually he began to perceive broken patterns and realized that what he saw was a succession of broad, mesa-topped hills rather than a single solid wall. The dry grass bent before a biting wind that strengthened as the morning wore along but lost its chill under the warming touch of a winter sun that lay off his left shoulder.

Even Homer held quiet as the riders crossed a land creased and gullied but blanketed over most of its breadth by a heavy turf of short brown grass. They rode up a steep incline and glanced at one another in surprise as they saw a narrow creek snaking across a little valley no more than a couple of hundred yards wide. The horses nosed at the water and seemed disinclined to drink. Frank saw a glistening of white crystals in reddish sand at the water's edge. The stream was spreading gypsum as it made its slow and easy way toward one of the Brazos tributaries. Beaver dismounted, scooped water into his palm and tentatively touched his tongue to it. He grimaced. "The lord never meant this country for people."

Frank said, "He put a-plenty of grass on it."

Beaver retorted, "A man can't eat grass."

"A cow can, and a man can eat a cow."

Frank saw several black shapes far ahead, lying on the lee side of a hill out of the wind. Beaver said, "We'd be popular in camp tonight if we showed up with some buffalo hump and a couple of hindquarters." Homer slipped the soft rawhide cover from his rifle. Beaver raised his hand. "Not yet. Time enough to pick up a nice young heifer when we turn back."

They struggled up a steep slope and unexpectedly were struck in their faces by a strong plains wind. Even Beaver whistled in amazement.

Frank could not hold back. He spurred until he came to a rock-edged rim from which the ground suddenly fell away. The wind seemed to wrest the breath from him, or perhaps it was not the wind. Perhaps it was the broad, grass-covered valley that spread for miles. Perhaps it was the buffalo, thousands upon thousands, some grazing, some already bedded down and chewing cud in the gentle warmth of a noonday winter sun, some watering in a clear-running creek that came down from the north, where the valley made a long bend. Frank could only guess how far it might be to the head of the creek. He rubbed his eyes, for the wind brought water to them.

"Lord in heaven! Did anybody ever see such a sight?"

He laughed for no good reason. He felt awash in exhilaration. He was sure he gazed upon the world as God had shaped it and meant it to be, not a human mark visible upon it.

Beaver said solemnly, "We're skylined up here. If there's Indians in that valley, they'd be blind not to see us."

Frank barely heard, and what he heard did not register. "No wonder them Indians fight," he declared. "If this was mine, I'd stand against all hell to hold it."

Beaver warned, "We better get down off of this hill." Miles across the valley Frank saw a hill taller than the rim upon which they sat. "Way yonder," he said, stretching his arm. "That point of rocks . . . I want to go over there and see what's beyond."

Beaver growled, "It's noon already; time we turned back. Else we'll be ridin' in the dark."

Stubbornly Frank said, "I don't care if we ride all night. I want to see the other side of this valley."

Beaver gave in. "I reckon I had that look in *my* eye, first time ever I seen the great Rocky Mountains." He began to pick around for the easiest way down.

Buffalo spread apart for the riders. Large bulls, shaggy with new winter coats, snorted and gave alarm. Animals broke into a lumbering run, their humped bodies seeming to rock backward and forward. They would stop and turn to look again, reassessing the danger. Buffalo upwind quickly settled back to grazing or, after the riders passed, eased themselves down upon the heavy turf to rest and chew.

Frank normally had a strong sense of time, but time was of no concern as he pushed the brown horse across the valley, passing Beaver and taking the lead. He stopped when he reached the creek. The brown did not hesitate about dropping its nose into the water. Frank tested it himself, gingerly.

"Sweet," he said.

He would have pushed on, but Beaver took down his canteen and poured out the muddy water from last night's camp. Impatience prickled Frank as he watched the canteen bubbling, filling slowly. But he forced himself to follow the trapper's prudent example.

He bore toward the rock pile he had seen from the other side, a place where slow erosion of time and wind and rain had worn away the soft earth from beneath a large segment of caprock, collapsing the heavy shelf into a jumbled heap like great shards of broken pottery. It stood well away from the rain-gullied wall. It was a tall prominence in splendid isolation on the broad valley floor.

They were three hundred yards short of it when Beaver reined up. "Sonny, these horses need to rest and blow."

Frank still felt the prickling. "My horse is all right."

Homer seemed inclined to press on, but Frank said, "You stay with Beaver. Your horse never could travel as far as mine." He touched spurs lightly and rode on, glancing back once to see the two men dismount and loosen their cinches.

Frank seldom pushed a horse to its limits, but this valley was like a strong liquor stirring fire in his blood.

The wind had turned moderately warm, and Frank had taken off his woolen coat before he reached the creek. Now, unaccountably, a chill touched him. He shivered, glancing north, expecting to see a winter storm bearing down across that mysterious land only the Indian knew. But the sky was clear, and the wind was still warm on his face. Nevertheless, the chill persisted. A sense of foreboding settled upon him like a dark cloud. Staring at the pile of rocks, he slipped the rifle from its case. He considered turning back, for he had always leaned heavily on instinct, but the call that had drawn him was undiminished. He flicked his tongue over dry lips and gently urged the horse forward in a walk. He held the rifle high and ready while his gaze searched restlessly over the rocks. He watched the ground for tracks, for a sign that something or someone might have been here ahead of him. The foreboding clung and tugged. Cautiously he rode around the back side of the tall rock pile. He saw not one track, not of a horse, not even of a buffalo.

Riding to the rough jumble of broken stone and washed earth, he sought a way for the horse and saw none. Dismounting, he tied the reins to a stunted cedar. He worked his way upward afoot, holding the rifle tightly, picking his path with caution because the footing was treacherous. The chill persisted. He remembered a premonition akin to this once when, as a boy, he had come suddenly upon a man several days dead in timber along the Colorado. He paused and tested the air but found no smell except of dust and dry grass.

He took the final difficult steps to the top and was struck by a wind so fierce it staggered him. Cold bumps arose on his sweat-dampened skin. He looked down upon Homer and Beaver, squatted where he had left them. They seemed far beneath him, and more distant than he knew them to be. His gaze moved across the grass-floored valley to the promontory from which he had seen this point of rocks. Beyond, the rolling plains stretched eastward far past sight, to the Clear Fork and on to the Cross Timbers. He turned, searching northward for the beginnings of the creek. It was lost somewhere in the unmeasurable distance, beyond a far bend in the valley. Breathing was difficult. He first blamed the wind but realized the problem was his own awe, the impact of the splendor before him. The cured grass bent and waved, little damaged by the buffalo that grazed it by thousands beyond counting. Frank's exhilaration ran wild and free. Never had his eyes gloried in anything so magnificent.

He did not know how long he remained, watching, absorbing the raw beauty. He became conscious, finally, of Beaver waving his hat, trying to flag his attention. Reluctantly Frank turned and started down, but he stopped, unable yet to leave. He climbed back for a final look, letting his gaze sweep from as far north up the valley as he could see, back south to where detail dissolved in a distant haze. He let the picture burn into his mind. Sadness came over him for the need of leaving.

He knew he had stayed too long. He began a slow and careful descent by a different way than he had come up, his eyes restless and searching. Halfway down he caught a splotch of alien color beneath one of the great broken slabs of caprock. On the underside, protected from the weather, he saw paintings in black and red and yellow, crude figures as strange at first glance as words written in another language. He perceived that some represented horses, some buffalo, some men. He saw circles that he took to be the sun, lines radiating outward. He surmised that a man or men had intended these pictures to tell the past deeds of warriors, or perhaps of ancient gods and spirits known only to people born of the prairie. He rubbed fingers over one of the figures, trying for some sense of its age. The cold feeling settled over him again, as if he had intruded into a house where he was not wanted, a secret place sheltering mysteries meant for other eyes.

Beaver was out of sorts. "Damn it, sonny, we'll be half the night gettin' back to the captain."

Beaver's impatience did not touch Frank. He described the eerie feeling the place had given him, the paintings he had found on stone.

"A medicine hill," Beaver said. "A holy place where the Indians come to make medicine with their spirits. Bad place for a white man."

Solemnly Frank told him, "I'm comin' back here someday. I'll live in this valley."

"Or, more likely, *die* here," Beaver retorted impatiently. "The Indians got a notion this all belongs to them."

"Someday it'll all belong to *me*. Me and Rachal." Frank looked Beaver squarely in the eyes. "Ain't you ever seen a place you knew you had to go back to?"

"A dozen times. Usually I just never managed to do it. Time or two I did, somebody else had come in after me and taken up claim. Nothin' ever looks the same the second time."

"This will," Frank declared. "I'm comin' back."

The company was in its base camp when Captain Zachary decided it was time to release Frank and Homer. Regretfully he said, "You've both done good service for us. I wish you'd reconsider and stay with the company."

Frank shook his head. "We got too much waitin' for us back at Davis camp."

The captain made a faint smile. "So I have been told. I found marriage a most comfortable state myself. But should you for any reason change your mind, you'll always be welcome in this company. You'll know how to find us."

Lieutenant McKellar walked with them to their horses. His eyes bored into Frank's. "Captain Zachary would not beg you, nor will I. I would simply appeal to your patriotism."

"Patriotism to what?" Frank demanded. "I can't think of a damned thing the Confederacy has done for me."

McKellar gave Homer only a glance; he had long since learned that where Frank went, Homer went also. He turned on his heel and strode briskly toward his tent.

Beaver Red had stood back, watching McKellar. "Don't think too bad of him, sonny. He's a hard man to like, but don't you get any notion he ain't game. He didn't lose that arm runnin' away from a fight. Beaver stuck out his hand. "You-all take care of yourselves, both of you. I've rode with worse."

A cold rain set in before they had traveled far, and Frank had to fight his brown horse to force him across a couple of normally dry creeks awash in roiling, muddy water. He spurred into a lope the last quarter mile, once he was able to see the still-unfinished picket wall that marked the camp's boundary. Homer trailed behind him, trying vainly to conduct some kind of conversation. It was one-sided, and Frank had no idea what Homer was talking about. He shouted exultantly as he trotted the brown through the open gate and turned in at the Wakefield house. The horse slipped in the mud and almost went down.

"Rachal!" he shouted. "I'm back."

He dismounted and pounded his fist upon the hewn door, oblivious to the rain that pelted him. The door swung inward. Rachal's father stood there, staring in surprise. Rachal's mother stood behind him, her gaze hardening in recognition.

"I'm lookin' for Rachal," Frank said eagerly.

The farmer, ill at ease, glanced back at his wife. "She ain't here no more."

Mrs. Wakefield said flatly, "She's over at George's house."

That shook Frank a little. But he did not waste time with questions; he wanted too much to see her. "Thanks," he said, and swung back onto the brown.

Homer sat hunched in his saddle, uncomfortable. "You don't need me. I believe I'll go on to our place."

"Sure, Homer, sure." Frank quartered the horse across the quadrangle, stopping and tying him to a post in front of

George's picket house. He had never knocked before opening George's door. He pushed on it and stepped inside.

His knees almost buckled.

George and Rachal lay together on the narrow bed, arms around one another. George rolled over quickly, dropping his feet to the floor. Rachal made a cry and drew up the blanket to cover herself, but not before Frank saw that she was naked.

His face went instantly to flame. His hands trembled. "George . . . Rachal . . . what the hell?" He took a step toward them, then stopped, forcing down a wild impulse to hammer both of them with his fists.

Rachal managed to stammer, "Frank . . . it's not . . . it's not like you think . . ."

Frank raged, "I can see for myself what it is!"

George pulled on his boots and shoved his shirttail into his trousers as he stood up. "I reckon nobody told you, Frank." His eyes narrowed. "You tell him, Rachal. I'll go out to see about the milk cow."

Frank seemed paralyzed as George walked past, giving him room. George pulled the door shut behind him. Frank stared in confusion and anger at Rachal sitting in the bed, the blanket drawn up to cover her breasts. At last she said, "Turn around, Frank. Let me get myself decent."

"Decent?" he half-shouted. "That's some word for it." He faced the door, listening to the whisper of her clothing.

She said, "All right, Frank." He turned to see tears on her flushed cheeks. She told him hoarsely, "We're married, me and George."

The breath seemed to go out of him. Wanting to sit, he felt that he might not reach the chair. "But me and you . . ."

She walked past him to the door, peering out after George. "I had to, Frank. There wasn't no tellin' when you'd come back. There wasn't no more waitin'."

He managed to make the chair and sag into it. "Wouldn't've been much of a wait. Thirty days was all."

"Thirty days?" She seemed surprised, then dismayed. "I

was afraid I'd be showin' pretty soon. Look at me, Frank.
You see anything different?"

He stared, not yet comprehending. "No."

"You soon will. *Everybody* will." Shame in her face, she
put her hand to her stomach.

He understood then. He rubbed a sleeve across burning
eyes. "Mine?"

She seemed hurt that he even asked. "There never was
nobody but you. I wanted to wait for you, but George said
you volunteered. Said you might be six months comin'
back."

His anger swelled again. "That was a lie. George volunteered *me*. And he knew it wouldn't be but thirty days."

She sat on the bed again, tears running. "He wanted me.
I reckon he seen his chance."

Frank looked at her small waist, not yet beginning to
expand. "Does he know about that?"

"No. I'm hopin' he'll think it's his."

"He lied to you. That'd be reason enough to leave him."

"But I'm married now. The preacher said the words and
signed the paper. Ain't no backin' away from that."

"I ought to kill George!"

She began to cry. "I'd just lose the both of you. Then
where'd I be at? It's done now, Frank. We got to live with it.
I couldn't stand the shame no other way."

Her tears were contagious, and he had no intention of crying with her. He made for the door. Rachal called, "Frank,
I love you."

"If you loved me, you'd say to hell with the shame. You'd
go with me."

He stumbled out into the rain. He swayed a moment, then
walked purposefully toward the cow pen. He heaved aside
the three bars. George sat beneath the shed, milking his
cow.

"George," he shouted, "you lied to her." George stood up
just in time for Frank's fist to strike him full in the face. The
half-filled bucket went sailing, showering milk out into the

rain. The startled cow backed quickly from the crude stall, knocking George off his feet. Frank grabbed the front of his shirt and pulled him up, then struck him again, sending him stumbling backward to fall once more.

George came up crying in rage and hit Frank with a fist hard as a hickory knot. Frank fastened his arms around George's shoulders and lunged. George's feet slipped. He fell backward into the mud, Frank on top of him.

George made sounds like some angry animal as they wrestled and floundered and slipped, sometimes on their feet, sometimes on their knees, sometimes one or the other on his back. Frank became aware that Homer and Sam Ballinger had hurried into the cow pen, a weeping Rachal behind them. Homer tried to step in, but Sam caught his arm and held him back.

"It was comin'," Sam said evenly. "All we can do is make sure they don't kill one another."

Frank pounded George in the stomach, in the ribs, in the face, until George lay finally in a sodden heap, breath gone, face bloody, shoulders heaving while those sounds went on. Frank swayed to his feet, almost going down. One eye was swelling shut. But he saw enough. He saw Rachal bend over George in the rain, the hem of her dress soaking up the mud.

Homer took hold of Frank and steadied him. Sam Ballinger looked at first one man, then the other, regret in his eyes. "You better go away awhile, Frank, before this comes to worse."

Frank looked back at Rachal, weeping over the man whose name she had taken. He nodded dully. "I reckon I had."

Sam said, "I'll watch out for your cattle. Homer, you better go and watch out for *him.*"

Captain Zachary had said Frank and Homer would always be welcome in the militia company. Frank knew nowhere else to go. They rode away together in the rain, Frank hunched in the saddle, every joint aching, one eye afire and temporarily blind. He became aware, after a time, that

Homer was unusually solemn and quiet. "You ain't said a word in three miles. You sick?"

Homer shook his head. "Just grievin' a little"

"What *you* got to grieve about? I'm the one that lost her."

"Grievin' over friendship, I reckon," Homer replied quietly. "Losin' an old friendship is like a death in the family."

3

For an hour or more prosecuting attorney Elihu Mallard had recounted what he had been able to learn of Frank Claymore's early years, and much that he had simply surmised, for the most part missing by a mile and a quarter. Defense attorney Anderson Avery leaped to his feet with a regularity that irritated even Claymore.

The judge glared at both lawyers. The protracted jury selection had not improved his disposition toward participants or town. Claymore thought by the look of him that he probably suffered from dyspepsia. That, he had long observed, was a common ailment among men who made a living without having to work for it.

Avery had just objected to Mallard's telling of an old tale he considered irrelevant as well as false.

The prosecutor argued, "Your Honor, the case which brings us into this courtroom is hardly without precedent when we consider it in the context of the defendant's life. Since his youth he has consistently demonstrated himself to be a creature of violence. I believe it is indeed relevant to conduct a full inspection of his past, back to a time when this violent nature first began to manifest itself."

"Objection!"

Claymore found himself dispassionately watching his attorney and wondering how many more times Avery would have the energy to rise so quickly. It had been Claymore's studied opinion over the years that the general run of city-bred men lacked stamina. Life was too comfortable for them. Hardship was healthy; most people did not enjoy enough of it for their own good.

He glared each time the prosecutor turned from the jury and jabbed his finger toward Claymore's face. He whispered to Avery, "How come the judge lets him tell any old lie that runs through his head? When'll it be our turn to tell a lie or two?"

His whisper was as loud as some people's normal conversation. Avery looked around quickly to see who might have heard. "I assure you, Mr. Claymore, our time will come. Court procedure is a little like a game of poker. Right now it is his turn to play out his hand."

"I can't say I fancy his cards."

"Nothing would suit him so well as to goad you into an ill-advised action and prejudice this court. I plead with you to be patient."

"I've always been a patient man. But sometimes it don't take much to be enough."

He leaned back, grumbling under his breath. His rheumatism goaded him almost as much as the prosecutor's words. Just having to sit in that hard, ungiving chair so long was probably part of the punishment, he thought.

Self-reliant as far back as he could remember, he resented his forced dependence upon the black-suited Avery, who seemed to be working himself toward some kind of seizure. Claymore realized he should be grateful, but he hosted a strong suspicion that his attorney's first interest was in his fee, an amount not yet established and likely to be outrageous.

The prosecutor declared, "Your Honor, the record will show that during the late War Between the States, Frank Claymore declined to offer his services to the army of the Southland. He chose to remain at home and see after his own commercial interests. He served even the militia only because the law required it of him, and because in that manner he might legally escape a higher claim which other men accepted as their solemn duty to their country.

"In short, gentlemen of the jury, despite the spurious reputation he has been given in some quarters as an intrepid pioneer, opening this great West of ours, he was in fact a shirker who did only that little which law impelled him to do."

Avery objected, to no avail.

The prosecutor continued. "Now, gentlemen, this brings us to the battle of Dove Creek, in that bitter winter of 1865. The record reveals Frank Claymore to have been a combatant in that shameful incident, condemned by history for the needless shedding of innocent blood. At a time when truly savage Indians roamed the plains with the blood of white women and children dripping from their hands, Frank Claymore and those misguided souls with him fell upon a band which had been noted only for its friendship with the white man. They brutally slew those innocent children of the prairies while the real foe went free and unpunished.

"I submit to you, gentlemen, that just as Frank Claymore willfully participated in that outrage, so he willfully perpetrated the crime—the murder of an unarmed man—which has brought him here to stand judgment."

Anger rushing into his face, Claymore pushed painfully to his feet. He waved his cane vigorously at the prosecutor. "Now, sir, that is the biggest goddamned lie you've told today!"

The judge had been leaning back, staring vacantly at George Washington's portrait on the courtroom wall. He straightened and pounded the gavel. "Order! I will have order in this court. Counselor, you will please restrain your client, or I shall be forced to means of my own."

The defense attorney was on his feet, tugging at Claymore, trying to coax him into seating himself. Avery apologized. "Your Honor, Mr. Claymore has had little experience with court procedures. I am sure Your Honor can understand that a man of his years is confused and justifiably distraught at hearing such wicked falsehoods recklessly flung at him."

Claymore sat down, his rheumatic hip lancing him with pain. He grumbled.

His attorney said, "Your Honor, I must object to the prosecution's repeated accusations. It is true Mr. Claymore was in the lamentable battle at Dove Creek, but it was not of his own choosing. He was under orders, as any good soldier. His only alternative would have been desertion, and he was too honorable a man to consider such a dishonorable course."

Claymore muttered, "I considered it. Hell yes, I considered it."

The judge fixed a stern gaze upon him. "Counselor, in due course you will have time for rebuttal. For now, sir, you will please sit down. And please keep your client in check."

The attorney seated himself, face flushed with frustration. Under his breath he whispered, "Please, Mr. Claymore. You are not helping."

Claymore snorted. "You *said* we was goin' to tell them the truth."

By military standards Zachary's company was lax on discipline and had no precision whatever. By Frank Claymore's standards it was rigid and confining. In base camp those men not assigned to patrol duty went through mounted and dismounted drill daily under the critical eye and sharp command of Lieutenant Alex McKellar. He was always in sight, his back saber stiff whether he sat on his well-brushed black horse or marched beside the men across the open field that passed for a parade ground. He snapped orders and rebuke in a voice that cut like a quirt. Frank never saw the man smile, never saw him betray a sign that he was pleased for even a moment. Frank reasoned that all this strenuous activity was McKellar's doing. The captain showed little interest in it. He seldom appeared for formation except at morning roll call. As a private in the ranks, Frank was not privy to inside information provided to officers, but talk

among the men held that daily mustering was a new requirement passed down from state headquarters in Austin. It
was an attempt to stem the increasing desertions from frontier units as pay and supplies failed to materialize and war
news from the eastern battlefields reflected defeat after
defeat for the Confederacy.

Frank would rather have grubbed up mesquite roots for
firewood than drill for McKellar. He tried to make allow-
ances for the man's being crippled. He reasoned that the sur-
geon's knife that had severed the shattered arm had left a
poison in McKellar's blood. He was glad to get away from
the lieutenant's stern gaze at any opportunity, whether hunting meat for the mess or scouting for Indian sign. Usually
he contrived to take Homer Whitcomb when the choice was
up to Zachary. If McKellar was making the assignments,
the partners were invariably split. This nettling practice was
not confined to Frank and Homer. Talk was that McKellar
felt the men were less likely to desert in the field if separated from close friends and partners.

Despite these precautions, or possibly because of them,
morning muster would frequently reveal unauthorized ab-
sences. Men slipped away in the night to go home, or to ride
south for the neutrality of Mexico. Captain Zachary always
appeared more sad than angry. McKellar would clench his
fist and bear down harder on the men who remained.

Many Indian trails were discovered that early winter, but
few Indians were seen. Comanches and Kiowas in small
raiding parties slipped past the picketline patrols and made
incursions into the thin western edge of settlement, usually
satisfying themselves with the taking of horses and mules,
occasionally spilling white blood when it came at little risk
to their own. They were daring but not suicidal. Almost always they escaped as quietly as they had come, patrols following hopelessly behind and losing the trail as it evaporated
like a morning mist.

But a day or so after Christmas a courier loped into camp
on a sweat-lathered horse. Frank and Homer glanced at one

another in speculation but went ahead with the cleaning of their rifles. It was officer business.

Shortly Captain Zachary and Lieutenant McKellar stepped out of their headquarters tent. The bugler sounded assembly, the notes quavering on the north wind. Homer carefully laid his rifle on his blankets. "You reckon the war is over?"

Frank said, "Not out here."

The men formed into a line ragged enough to make Mc-Kellar frown. Zachary told them to stand at ease, which they already were. "Gentlemen, I've received word that militiamen of Captain Gillentine's company have found a large Indian trail north and west of here. All companies are ordered into pursuit. You will pack your necessaries, catch your horses and be ready to receive marching rations and ammunition in thirty minutes. Lieutenant McKellar will remain until the return of all patrols, then follow us. Any questions?"

Homer usually had one. "How many Indians, Captain?"

The captain grimaced. "Many hundreds, I am advised."

Beaver Red took a step forward. "Thomas, you sure about that report? Comanches and Kiowas don't generally move in that kind of numbers. That sounds like an army, not a war party."

McKellar started to lecture Beaver on military protocol. Zachary waved him off. "It is not within our province to question an order, Beaver."

Beaver shrugged. "I don't question no order, just the report. Most of them militia can't track a furrow in a cornfield."

The chafing McKellar could not hold back. "We are soldiers. It is a soldier's duty to do what he is told."

"*You're* a soldier," Beaver replied. "I'm just a wore-out old fart who wonders sometimes what the hell he's doin' here."

Frank had already determined that military life involved rushing to get somewhere, followed by long and idle waiting.

The Ranger companies were to assemble at Camp Colorado on Jim Ned Creek beyond the lower edge of the Cross Timbers. When Zachary's little command reached that point it was ordered to move southwestward to Fort Chadbourne on Oak Creek. There it found a collection of stone buildings constructed by the Union Army north of the Colorado River more than a dozen years earlier. Captain Henry Fossett, in field command of all the Confederate frontier troops, paced the dry-weedy ground of the old cavalry post and complained about the slow movement of the militia, overdue and nowhere in sight.

For the first time, in the presence of so much authority, Frank sensed the ponderous nature of military command, and he realized how far down that chain Captain Zachary really fit. Morosely, from a respectful distance, he watched the officers gather on the grown-over parade ground before moving into the headquarters building for conference. Unexpectedly he felt resentment for the little deference shown Zachary.

Uneasiness gnawed at Frank. He said, "Homer, if them officers make a mistake they can get us killed. Me and you have got no more say than our horses do."

Homer shrugged. He had been used to following for years. "They're the officers. You got to have faith."

Frank stared moodily to the southwest, to the blue-tinged mountains that stood row on row like monuments. Somewhere in there, he supposed, the Indians moved. He pulled his coat tighter against the cold. "I have faith in myself, and nobody else."

For two days the command waited at Chadbourne for the militia. They killed a few beeves from among wild cattle that had strayed down from north and east. The state troops and their officers grumbled about the undisciplined militia, who should all be home on the plow. At length, with the Ranger companies and a few militia units that had straggled in, the restless Fossett set out southwestward, angling toward the Colorado River.

Frank's uneasiness plagued him like an itch he could not scratch. Though Fossett had scouts, Frank rode along the outside, trusting his own eyes and ears. It disturbed him that Beaver had not been chosen to help explore the terrain. Beaver took his exclusion philosophically. "Many are called, but few are chosen," he said. "I never been this far south."

They rode through a red-clay country, cured grass often tickling the bellies of the horses as they moved across the open flats between the rust-and-gray rock-ledged hills. Other times the grass was ankle short on slopes where soil was shallow and the clay tended to shed rain. An occasional small herd of buffalo would snort and run. Orders had been sent down the line that no shots be fired, lest the Indians be alerted.

The troops came, in time, to the red-stained banks of the Colorado, its waters a few shades duller than blood. It was hard for Frank to believe this was the same river he had known as a boy, hundreds of miles to the east, for there it seemed broad and languid and lazy.

They came upon the Indian trail, so large that any tenderfoot could have found it on a moonless night. Frank had not seen Beaver so agitated. The old trapper did not ask questions or wait for orders. He rode out and inspected the evidence for himself. Frank and Homer galloped after him. Beaver said little, riding along at a walk, looking at the ground. Twice he stepped down to pick up some relic, once a moccasin with a hole worn through its sole, the beadwork salvaged for reuse, another time a tin cup crushed beyond salvation.

"Sonny," he said at last, "this ain't no raidin' party. This is a whole nation, by the look of things. Yonder's where their horse herd went. I'll bet they was a thousand head or more, and that's just the loose horses."

The Indians had evidently camped on the river for some days. Packed rings and circles of stones marked tepee sites, dozens upon dozens of them for half a mile or more along the crimson river. Heads and bones of buffalo and other game lay where they had been discarded. Deer hair, white and gray and brown, was carried on the wind where women had dressed the hides. Frank pointed out some dried coffee grounds.

Beaver's frown settled deeper into his weather-ravaged face. "I don't know what manner of Indians these be, but they ain't like no Comanches I ever seen."

Beaver carried his misgivings to Captain Zachary, who heard him out with gravity. Frank followed as Zachary took Beaver to Captain Fossett. One of Fossett's own scouts was arguing, "There's a good chance they're some of the friend-lies from up in the Nations, sir."

Fossett's eyes seemed masked, blocking out all contrary opinion. Beaver put in, "We ought not to jump them till we get a better notion of their intentions."

Fossett gave Beaver a reproachful look. "*I* will make the decision, in consultation with other officers. These Indians are in Texas. They have no business here, no matter what tribe they are."

Zachary had held silent, his eyes narrowed until they barely showed. "Captain Fossett, I'd ask you to take note of how many they are, and then count *us.*"

Fossett said firmly, "If you are reluctant to show them your steel, sir, I can request Lieutenant McKellar to take over your command."

Zachary stiffened. "That will not be necessary, sir." He turned and walked briskly away, Beaver pushing hard to keep up on his reluctant legs. Frank fell in a step behind them.

Beaver argued, "You can't just let it lay thataway, Thomas."

Zachary shook his head. "This is a military organization. There is nothing more I can do."

"There's one thing. We could pull out and leave."

"That would be desertion. We can only go along."

"Even when we know they're fixin' to make a mistake?"

"Even then. Let it go, Beaver. We did our best."

Beaver stopped, watching Zachary with sadness. He turned to Frank and Homer. "Was I you boys, I'd slip out tonight while it's good and dark."

Frank frowned. "Would you go with us, Beaver?"

Beaver considered, then shook his head. "No, he's too good a man to leave. I owe him too much. You boys don't owe nobody but yourselves. Get out of this while you can."

Frank glanced at Homer. The notion had a great deal of merit, he thought. He considered it seriously but had to reject it. "If you stay, Beaver, I reckon we will."

Frank had lost track of the days since Christmas. He was fairly sure New Year had passed. New Year, 1865. Perhaps this was the year that needless war back east would finally drag to some sort of conclusion.

The command pushed on, scouts riding to the front from custom rather than need. The greenest man in the procession could have followed the trail, the grass trampled or cropped short by slow-moving animals given plenty of time to graze, twin tracks of travois cut deeply into the red soil by the weight of tepee skins and camp goods and children with which they were laden. The track crossed a wide valley and a broad, clear-running river somebody said was the North Concho. There Fossett camped two days, waiting for militia units reported to be still straggling.

At third daybreak the scouts returned with news that Indians had encamped on the south side of Dove Creek, some thirty miles southwest. Fossett gave in to his nagging impatience and decided not to wait for more militia. The men pushed their rested horses and by afternoon reached the broad Middle Concho. Two scouts returned after nightfall. Crisp air carried the sound of argument. Its gist, the best Frank could tell at some distance, was that the scouts were still convinced these were not hostiles. They opposed an attack without at least a parley beforehand.

But too many officers counseled striking first, of using surprise to offset their short numbers. Zachary and McKellar came back to the company with the verdict. Zachary was grim. "We attack at daybreak. See to your ammunition, men. By their numbers, you'll need much of it."

Frank and Homer exchanged somber glances. Frank knew it would take but a word and Homer would leave with him for Mexico, or anywhere. It weighed upon his conscience that he had not chosen to do so.

The sun lost its meager warmth, and night's cold settled hard upon the command moving southward. West of a pair of small, rough peaks that stood together in isolation from other promontories, the horsemen came upon the junction of two clear streams. Scouts pointed to the southernmost as Dove. The command sought a shallow point and crossed Spring Creek, sounds of horses and men almost masked by the music of icy waters splashing against stones near the edge. Fossett moved slowly, giving trailing units time enough to ford. The pack mules fought, pulling back against their lead ropes, some having to be dragged into the water.

The wind was from the southwest, but it bit like a norther. Where water had splashed on Frank in the crossing, the chill was severe. Considering that they were several hundred horsemen, the Rangers and assorted militiamen rode in almost total silence. Whenever a buzz of conversation began, an order for quiet was passed quickly down the line.

Far into the night Frank thought he began smelling smoke. A prickling played along his back, for he knew what the source must be. Homer also sniffed the air but had nothing to say.

The command pushed through heavy stands of towering pecan trees, which sent long roots to feed in the creek's eternal mud. The foliage had long since fallen, but now and again the wind loosened vagrant pecans that had clung past their time, and these pelted the men, startling the horses and mules. In the darkness men rode into tangles of briars that threatened to pull them from their saddles. Horses squealed in protest against the sting of the nettles.

Frank saw no stars and judged the sky to be clouded over. His sense of time told him it was an hour or two past midnight when the command halted. The order was passed to dismount, to unsaddle and rest the horses. Once in a while the wind brought a faint aroma of wood smoke. Frank tied his horsehair rope to the bridle and played out a few feet to give the brown horse room to move around. Looping the other end to his wrist, he rolled up in his blanket and lay on the ground, using the saddle to turn the chilling wind from his head and shoulders. His legs and feet were painfully cold. There was no question of building fires. Sleep would not come. His stomach churned, bringing nausea. He tried not to think about the confrontation daylight would bring, but it would not be pushed aside. His foreboding was heavy as stone. When he forcibly put his mind on other things, Rachal came to him. He made himself think of the valley, and for a time he dozed, though never so deeply that he did not feel the cold. Inevitably the premonition of disaster brought him fully awake. He lay with legs drawn up under his chin, trying vainly to bring his whole body behind the protection of the saddle. Other men must have been having the same problems, because many were up and stirring before good daylight. They talked in low tones, awakening those who might somehow have managed sleep. Frank walked around in circles, trying to stimulate the blood and warm his feet and legs.

Homer unwrapped himself and stood up, stamping, slapping his arms. "It's colder than the grave."

Frank's dread had not lessened with the coming of daylight. "I doubt that." He turned away, not wanting Homer to read the thought in his face.

As the light improved, Frank found that Fossett had camped them in a hollow back away from the creek. A heavy stand of timber shielded them from the south, where the Indian camp must lie. He shivered and wished for hot coffee. He ate hardtack from his saddlebag. He washed it down with water so cold his teeth ached.

Homer's eyes widened as he looked northward. Frank turned quickly, instinctively reaching for his rifle. He saw movement at a distance. Horsemen, he was sure, though he could not make out details. He slipped off the soft rawhide case that had protected the rifle from the damp.

Beaver Red said, "Take your ease, sonny. Ain't nothin' but more flop-eared militia. They've got here just in time to fight."

The riders moved in a loose-jointed line that appeared to stretch a mile. They pretended no military order, no military bearing. They were farmers and shopkeepers and cowmen, millers and carpenters and blacksmiths. They were dressed in every conceivable outfit and carried every kind of weapon from squirrel rifles and shotguns to pistols and a few old-fashioned muskets with barrels that bloomed at the muzzle like a morning glory. They rattled and jingled and plodded.

Captain Fossett and many of his officers rode out to confer with the militia leaders while the rest of the column came forward in its own slow time. After a while Captain Zachary and Lieutenant McKellar rode back to the company, steam playing from their horses' nostrils. Four Tonkawa Indian scouts followed. Frank studied their dark, troubled faces and judged they felt little enthusiasm.

Zachary summoned the company around him. He pointed south. "Scouts say the Indian camp is just below us, on the far side of the creek. There is a steep bank, however, that will make it difficult to climb out except in certain places." He swung his arm. "The horse herd is scattered beyond the camp, along the creek. It is our mission, first of all, to run off the horses. We'll stampede them back in this direction, clear of the camp, and turn them over to the Tonks. While we do that, the other Ranger units will attack the camp. The militia will dismount and flank the Indians through the brush from the east. Once we have the horse herd running, we are to turn back and strike from the northwestern quarter. Any questions?"

They left their blankets and saddlebags and all unnecessary equipage. The captain told the black boy Tobe to stay and watch them. The boy seemed relieved.

Zachary swung his arm and started west, leading the men in a column of fours, quartering into a wind so cold it seared the lungs. They remained north of the creek for a time, its timber screening their passage. A heavy accumulation of old leaves and rotted black pecans rustled beneath the hoofs as the company angled across the floodplain. Frank's right hand was stiff on the rifle cradled across his left arm. He glanced anxiously at Homer. "You watch out now. Stay close to me if you can."

Homer betrayed little of the apprehension that rode heavily upon Frank. "Don't you fret about old Homer. I always taken care of myself."

With help, Frank thought.

He could see excitement rising in the men's faces. Most seemed to look forward to a fight. Some might have wondered about the rightness of it, knowing their captain's doubts, but the decision had been made. Moral questions were put behind them. The only consideration now was to fight, and to win.

Camp smoke lay like a fog amid the creek timber. The Indians were up and stirring, Frank knew. His dread seemed to grow. It was something beyond fear, a foreboding that enveloped his soul.

Just as he saw the loosely herded Indian horses on the south side of the creek, he heard gunfire rattling behind him. Ahead, he saw the Indian herders, boys by the look of them, heeling their ponies into a run, trying to throw the herd together and push for the village. The column of fours broke up as the Rangers fanned out, spurring hard to push around the herd, to prevent its being stampeded eastward into camp, into warriors' hands. Gunsmoke burst gray and pungent on the crisp morning air. Men shouted around him. He bent over the pommel of the saddle and spurred to avoid being left behind. His eyes burned. His vision blurred from the speed and the biting cold. As if in a terrible dream, he

saw the Rangers sweep around the herd. The herders fell
one by one as they tried vainly to put up a defense. They
were boys, not fighting men. He saw an older man, an over-
seer of sorts, waving a white cloth, shouting something that
was lost in the rush and the wind. The man went down, his
horse bolting away. The white cloth caught on a bush and
continued to flutter its lost message in silence.

In minutes the horse herd was running, moving northward as the Rangers intended. Frank galloped along in its
wake, his rifle still cold and unfired. He looked around for
Homer, feeling guilt for not having watched after him in the
charge. Homer was a stone's throw away, shouting at the
running horses.

They drove the herd across the creek in a great splashing and churning, trailing them up a north bank left muddy
by the tiny rivulets streaming from each animal. From
somewhere the Tonkawa scouts appeared and took over.
Captain Zachary waved his arm, signaling the men to drop
back and re-form around him.

As the thunder of hoofbeats drummed away, Frank became aware of heavy gunfire downstream. The Rangers and
the militia were into the village, he judged. His heart raced
as the captain reined around and led eastward in a gallop.
Men reloaded their weapons as they rode.

It seemed only a moment before they were into the
thick of the fire. Frank realized at a glance that the resistance was strong. Defending rifle fire crackled from the
heavy cover of brush and briars. These were not simply
bow-and-arrow Indians; they had firearms, a great many
of them, and good weapons at that. He saw a Ranger jerk
half around and tumble from his saddle. He felt a tug at
his sleeve and found a new hole. His lungs seemed to block.
He leaned low, trying to make as small a target as possible, trying to find something to fire at but seeing only gray
clouds of powder smoke.

From somewhere Captain Fossett came circling in a lope.
He motioned at Zachary to sweep way around, westward

and down. "Move south," he shouted. "They'll be getting away."

Disorganized, without semblance of formation, Frank and Homer and the rest of Zachary's company galloped around the western edge of the camp, plunging through clinging briars, firing, being fired upon. Frank began to grasp how massive the Indian defense really was. He saw a Ranger horse stumble and fall, its rider rolling, losing his rifle. The man scrambled to his feet, fright in his eyes as he shouted for help. A friend reined around and gave him a stirrup to swing up behind him. The rifle remained where it had fallen. The friend who had made the rescue jerked and almost fell. Only the embrace of the man riding behind him saved him from tumbling. The horse, in panic, galloped back in the direction from which it had come.

The company was badly scattered. Zachary had lost control. The southward course was blocked by an impenetrable wall of Indian fire. Now and again Frank glimpsed a dark form moving through the brush, but he could not keep one in sight long enough for aim. He realized in near-panic that he had lost sight of Homer. He had lost nearly everybody. He was surrounded by gray smoke. His ears rang from an incessant firing of guns, the shouting of embattled men, the screaming of women and children.

He found himself in a small clear island amid the heavy brush and briars. He pulled the brown horse to a stop and whirled, searching desperately for a way out. Ahead of him was a single rider, Captain Zachary, spurring toward a tangle of undergrowth. From that tangle half a dozen rifles blazed. A screen of gray smoke rose to be whipped away by the wind. Frank saw Zachary slump, clutching at his chest, then slip from the saddle and fall in a heap into the dry grass.

Frank's first instinct was to rush to help him, but he hesitated. He stared wide-eyed at the brush from which the gunfire had come. For all he knew, the captain was dead. Frank might also be killed if he rode down there. He waited, looking wildly about. He saw no one. No one would see, no one would tell or blame him if he turned and ran away. He whipped the brown around, touching spurs to him, setting him into a run toward the only opening he saw.

But a scalding shame washed over him. *He* would know. However long he lived, a minute or a hundred years, he would know. He turned back. Spurring, he passed the captain's frightened horse racing to safety. He fired one shot into the brush as he neared the fallen Zachary, then pulled hard on the reins and hit the ground running almost before the brown horse was able to stop.

"Captain!" he shouted. "Can you get up, Captain?"

He dropped to his knees as a slug snarled past his head. He saw the flash of a rifle in the heavy briars.

He slipped an arm under the captain's back. Zachary's eyes were open, but the man was confused, his face draining rapidly of color. Zachary strained to help but was too weak to support himself. His heart hammering with fear, Frank somehow brought Zachary to his feet and pushed him against the nervously dancing brown horse. "Lift your foot into the stirrup, Captain," Frank heard himself shouting. "I'll boost you up."

The captain tried to raise his left leg. Frank helped him, fitting the foot into the stirrup. He kneeled, putting his shoulder beneath the captain's buttocks, lifting him. The brown horse took fright at the shooting and jerked loose. He galloped back in the direction from which he had come, carrying the half-conscious captain.

Frank stared desperately after him, an anguished shout rising and sticking in his throat, for he had been left alone, stranded in the midst of hell. He turned in fear toward the crackling of brush. Something struck him with a hard, searing force. Frank went to his knees, gasping for breath, feeling as if a furnace had been lighted in his stomach. His left hand closed over the shaft of an arrow, driven in above his navel. Instinctively he grasped it with bloody hands and tried to wrench it free. He cried out. A great red blaze burst before his eyes.

I am dead, he told himself, wondering that the thought brought no fear. Anything to cool this terrible fire . . .

He was conscious of running horses, of a renewal of gunfire, of men shouting. A blur rushed past him. He blinked heavily and saw Lieutenant McKellar and several men rushing the heavy brush, shooting into it as they rode. He felt rather than saw horses moving around him. Strong hands lifted him. He cried out against a savage pain as they boosted him into a saddle. A pair of strong arms encircled Frank and held him. A familiar voice urged, "You just hold on."

Homer.

Frank felt the horse move quickly into a lope. The arrow shaft bobbed with the motion. The point of it gouged and tore at Frank's vitals with every stride. He seemed to be falling, but he was conscious of the strong arms holding him, of the rhythmic stride of the horse beneath him. All the sounds melded—the distant shooting, the drumming hoofs, the shouts from far behind. All he could sort out of it was Homer's voice, quiet and reassuring, never stopping.

"Don't you go and die on me, Frank Claymore. We'll be at the creek in a minute, and it's safe on the other side. We oughtn't to've ever come here. Them boys back yonder, they're gettin' theirselves whipped real bad. Be damned lucky if most of them come out of this thing alive."

Frank could not grasp half the words, but just hearing them was a comfort of sorts. Homer kept talking, as he might talk to quiet a nervous horse. "It was Beaver Red seen you in trouble. He seen you raisin' the captain into the saddle, and seen the horse come tearin' back without you. And that McKellar! Cuss him if you want to, but he come a-runnin'. Wasn't for him, you wouldn't've made it out of that fix."

Frank wanted to ask if the captain was alive, but he could not form words. He could only groan against the blinding pain.

Then, somehow, he was lying on his back. Through the red blaze he saw Homer and Lieutenant McKellar. He could see what at first seemed a heavy cobwebbing above them. Blinking, he made out the bare limbs of the creek's huge pecan trees, crosslaced one over the other to a point that he could barely discern the leaden gray of the clouds above.

Homer was saying plaintively, "Lieutenant, we got to get that arrow out of him. He'll die if we don't."

McKellar's voice was calm. "Johnson, Cauley, you two hold onto Claymore's shoulders and legs. Whitcomb, you take a good hold on that shaft. Now, straight out—pull!"

Frank screamed, and consciousness left him.

He had no real sense of the time he had lain there. He knew he had passed in and out of consciousness. It was difficult to know what was real and what was dream. Now and again he was aware of a low level of talk, of excited shouts and of orders given. Gunfire rattled in the distance. Occasionally he heard someone cry out. He and the captain were not the only wounded brought to this place.

At times the pain seemed to leave him. Rachal drifted into his mind, and he was with her on the tall point of rocks, showing her the beautiful valley he had found for them to share. Then, suddenly, he would be fighting with George Valentine, rolling and twisting in the rain and mud of Fort Davis.

He tried to raise his right hand but could hardly summon strength to move it. He tried his left. Reluctant, it came up slowly, working its way up his side to his rib cage, his stomach. The arrow was gone. He tried to remember who had pulled it out.

He heard Homer. "Don't move that wrappin', Frank. You done bled too much as it is."

Frank stammered, finally managing words. "The captain?"

"Taken a bullet in his chest. He's in a bad way. You done all you could for him. Now you lay still and take care of yourself."

Frank drifted back into a blurred world somewhere near unconsciousness, knowing only that he hurt so much it would be a mercy to die. When he awakened, it was suddenly. He was conscious of a loud voice. He listened but did not hear it again. "Homer?" he cried out.

"I'm here, Frank."

"I heard somebody talkin' loud."

"It was you. You was talkin' out of your head."

"What was I sayin'?"

Homer hesitated. "You was callin' for Rachal."

Frank blinked until he could see the bare pecan limbs high overhead. He became aware of activity around him, but when he tried to see, the pain grabbed him. He heard a moan that told him someone was dying. "Homer, who is that?"

He had to ask a second time. Reluctantly Homer said, "It's Beaver Red. He's taken hard."

Despite the pain, Frank turned his head. He saw Beaver lying a few feet away. Beaver's face, what part of it showed around the rusty beard, was as colorless as Brazos River mud.

Homer began to talk, his words coming faster and faster as he spilled out his grief and anger. "He taken a bullet deep in his stomach. Ain't nothin' we can do but watch him die. And all for nothin'. Them poor Indians was Kickapoos, Frank. Nobody found out till it was too late, and I reckon it wouldn't've changed nothin'. They was the whole Kickapoo nation, come down out of the Indian reserve to get away from the war. They didn't want to fight nobody; they just wanted to go to Mexico. But they given us an awful whippin'. We got dead and wounded men scattered all up and down Dove Creek. And all for nothin'. They ought to've listened to Beaver."

Frank listened to Beaver. He listened to Beaver dying, and tears scalded his face.

The shattered Texas fighters spent a bitterly cold night along the banks of the creek, its timber affording some shelter against the wind. Frank dozed at times, but he was awake much of the night, listening to the groans of wounded men. Sometimes the groans were his own. He heard Beaver's ragged breath stretch into spasms, turning finally into a thin rattle.

The misery was compounded by a snow that started after dark. By daylight the ground was covered. Heavy flurries continued to fall like a dense white curtain. Homer had built a small fire of deadfall timber near enough that Frank felt its limited but welcome heat against his feet. He could hear the quiet crackling of a dozen other fires along the pecan-covered creek bank, though he could not see them all through the heavy snow. The smell of smoke was pleasant, bringing at least the illusion of warmth.

Homer was unusually quiet, poking fresh but wet wood into the fire. At times it seemed a contest to stay ahead of the falling snow that tried to snuff out the flames.

Frank could not remember when he had ever had to prime Homer into conversation. He asked, "Is Beaver dead?"

Homer nodded, not looking at Frank.

"And the captain?"

"Alive. They dug the bullet out. Way everybody talks, we'll spend the day here, gettin' everything gathered up, buryin' the dead. We'll pull out tomorrow." He still did not look at Frank. "I got to tell you somethin'. We didn't get the arrowhead out. The shaft come loose, but the head's still in you someplace. It's too deep to cut."

Frank imagined he could feel it. His face twisted. "Am I goin' to die, Homer?"

Homer turned away. "I don't know." Frank saw Homer's shoulders shake. He closed his eyes, and they burned.

Frank listened to the volleys of rifle fire as salutes were fired over new graves. He wondered which volley was for Beaver. Some of the dead could not be found in the snow. Many men, particularly of the militia, had pulled out on their own, so nobody knew for certain how many had died and how many had simply left for home.

A general retreat began after dawn. For those men like

Frank and the captain, too badly wounded to ride, long poles were cut from along the creek bank. Two saddled horses would be brought up in tandem, one behind the other. The poles were lashed to the stirrups on either side and the stirrups securely tied beneath the horses' bellies. Blankets were laced to the poles to serve as litters between the horses. Frank was lifted upon such a litter and tied down so he would not fall off. Alarm raced through him as the lead horse slipped in the snow and seemed about to go down. Frank knew he was in danger of being kicked to death if the horse panicked. Homer was there in an instant, bringing the horse to its feet, talking and petting it, keeping it from giving way to fear.

The jostling brought back pain as strong as before. Frank drifted away into a merciful state that was half sleep, half unconsciousness. He was only dimly aware of the long, slow day, the struggle through deep drifts of snow, across patches of icy ground slick as glass. He was aware that more men died, but he was beyond crying. He held onto one thought: to live.

A man named John Chisum had a ranch where the Concho and the Colorado rivers met, far east of the battleground. Riders pushed ahead of the slow procession and drove back some cattle, but they brought no bread, no salt. Frank managed to take hot broth, boiled from the fresh beef. It gave him strength. He felt his fever had broken. The swelling was down a little.

Somewhere inside he imagined he could feel the stone arrow point, lying in wait like some concealed enemy bent on destroying him. With each passing day he realized the chance became smaller that it could be removed. It would remain there, part of him from now on, a reminder that once he had been led by someone else's folly into a place he did not want to go, a reminder that his own judgment had been sound when others' was faulty.

At last the column reached Chisum's ranch. There, for the first time, Frank and Captain Zachary saw each other. The wounded were carried inside Chisum's ranch house, into a room where dry mesquite blazed in a big open fireplace. They were put to rest upon blankets on the floor. As he was carried into the room Frank heard a weak but determined voice. Captain Zachary said, "Place Frank Claymore next to me, please."

Zachary reached out his hand. Frank lifted his to take it. The captain's grip was weak, but the emotion was plain. "Thank you, Frank Claymore. Thank you for my life."

The black boy Tobe had been at the captain's side from the time the wounded had been carried to the banks of Dove Creek. He remained close to him now, caring for him, fetching. But he gave some of his attention to Frank as well. He brought food and hot coffee and fresh blankets not crusted with blood. When Frank asked him why, Tobe said, "For the captain, sir. Wasn't for you, I wouldn't have no captain."

Lieutenant McKellar kneeled at the pallet on which Zachary lay. "I have arranged to borrow a wagon, sir. I am going to send you home to Dallas."

Zachary thanked him. "What about Claymore, Alex?"

"He can't ride. I'll have to leave him here."

"He needs medical attention."

"So do many others. I can't do anything more."

"You can send him with me. I owe him my life."

McKellar stared at Frank. Frank thought it was the first time he had ever looked the man in the eyes and found no hostility. "If that is your wish, sir."

Homer Whitcomb asked, "Can I go with him? I can help Tobe."

McKellar shook his head. "We're badly crippled. We need every man who can ride."

So Frank was forced to tell Homer good-bye for the first time he could remember. Homer tied Frank's brown horse behind the wagon, where Frank lay beside the captain. He tucked a heavy buffalo robe around Frank to keep out the cold air. "Now, don't you fret about me. Old Homer'll take care of himself."

"I know you will," Frank said, though he wondered.

McKellar was on the other side of the wagon. The captain said, "It's your company now, Alex."

"In its heart, sir, it will always be yours." He looked up at the black lad bundled in two heavy old woolen coats. "You had better get started, Tobe. It's a long way."

Frank was afraid the words would not come out properly, but they had to be said. "Lieutenant, I . . ." He swallowed. "I won't forget what you done."

McKellar nodded. "Nor I you, sir. We'll meet again, perhaps under better circumstances."

Frank tried to raise up, looking past his brown horse at Homer and McKellar and the rest of the company as Tobe clucked and flipped the reins and jolted the wagon into motion.

4

The courthouse clock struck four, and the building shuddered. Frank Claymore stopped in the hallway and leaned on his cane while he waited for the reverberations to stop paining his ears. He found Homer Whitcomb at his right elbow.

Homer said, "Seems to me like that judge takes a lot of recesses. Must have a leaky stopper."

Claymore felt a transient annoyance, which he was in some danger of directing at Homer because no other victim stood handy. He looked to the other side and saw the deputy Willis trailing two paces behind, awkward and self-conscious. "Boy," Claymore grumped, "have you got to follow like some pot-lickin' hound?"

Reddening, the deputy glanced hastily behind him to see who might have heard. "I just got my orders, is all."

Claymore grunted. "A *man* don't take orders; he gives them. But if it'll keep your cream from turnin' to clabber, I'll wait out the recess in the sheriff's office. You can *all* watch me."

The deputy sputtered, and Claymore turned away from him, having already granted Willis more time than he thought him worth. He marched doggedly toward the office door, shrugging off Homer's attempt to take his arm and support him. The sheriff, uncomfortable in the necktie mandated by his appearance in court, looked up from his desk in surprise. He was a ranch foreman pressured into running for this job and probably regretting by now that his opponent had not trounced him. The sheriff glanced inadvertently toward the locked rifle rack.

Claymore said grittily, "Give me credit, Ed. I'm an old man, and I got more sense than to try for a gun. I just hope you can show me a chair softer than I had in the courtroom."

The sheriff stood and fetched his own. Its seat was leather covered and stuffed with horsehair. He held it steady while Claymore carefully settled himself. "I never thought, Mr. Claymore. I'll take this one into the courtroom for you." He stood back and regarded Claymore with unreadable eyes that would do credit to a poker player. "Could I bring you somethin' else?" He opened a desk drawer and held up a half-empty whiskey bottle.

Claymore shook his head. "My brain gets slow enough just bein' old. No use puttin' poison in it."

Homer said, "I do believe I'd take a shot of that, Ed, if you don't mind." He tilted the bottle and took one long swallow, then thumped the cork back into it. Claymore watched with disapproving eyes.

Homer said, "It'd do you a world of good, Frank."

Claymore tapped the end of his cane soundly on the floor. "Never seen it do *anybody* any good." He would admit that he had never observed Homer taking more than one or two drinks on any occasion, but he was convinced Homer would be healthier and happier without even that much.

Weakness. Why did good men always seem to cater to one weakness or another? Claymore was glad he never had.

The sheriff pulled a straight chair up to his desk and tried vainly to concentrate on papers. His eyes were both sad and angry. "I never would've believed you'd shoot an unarmed man."

Claymore winced. "I never wanted to kill him. But I've told you from the start, Ed; there *was* a gun."

The sheriff looked away, no nearer believing now than he had been that night.

Claymore's eyes clouded, and he blinked to stop a burning. "Ed, do you think they'll hang me?"

The sheriff made no answer.

Claymore said, "I had a fear when I was a young man. I was afraid I'd die out there on the open prairie, and no one would ever know." He paused, remembering. "Now there's no place I'd rather have them bury me."

The deputy Willis stared out the window. "Ed, them Indians ain't moved. They're still squatted out there under the tree."

The sheriff did not turn. "They make you nervous?"

Willis nodded. "A little. All the Indians was run out of this country before I was born."

Homer put in, "And who do you think run them out? It was Frank, and me, and a lot more like us. If it wasn't for Frank Claymore, there wouldn't none of you be here." He pointed his chin at the window. *"They'd* still have it."

The sheriff turned back to Claymore. "That makes it seem all the odder that you'd count those out yonder as friends."

Claymore shook his head. "The fightin' was done a long time ago. We've made our peace."

Willis said sharply, "Well, *I* ain't made no peace with them. I got half a mind to go out there and run them off."

Claymore tapped the cane firmly. "That's *all* you got is half a mind. Time was, that old one out yonder'd've put an arrow through your brisket and taken your scalp before you hit the ground."

The sheriff's curiosity was aroused. "He ever try to do that to you, Mr. Claymore?"

Claymore glanced at Homer, remembering. "More than once. And he come awful close."

Homer nodded. "One time I thought he had both of us."

The sheriff beckoned to Willis. "Come away from the window if they worry you."

Claymore became aware of a commotion in the hallway. A clerk stopped in the door. "Ed, the judge is about to commence." He noticed Claymore. "I expect you'll want to come too, Mr. Claymore."

Claymore pushed reluctantly to his feet and steadied himself against the chair a moment before he moved farther. "I don't reckon they'd offer me much choice."

As he had promised, the sheriff carried his soft chair into the courtroom and set it in place for Claymore. Judge Holmes watched, frowning. Claymore guessed he had no stuffed chair behind the bench.

The amenities here were nothing like those the judge enjoyed in Dallas . . .

Dallas was not large by the standards of 1865, but it was the biggest town young Frank Claymore had seen. Before the war it had begun to be counted a banking center, an important factor in the growing blacklands cotton trade, rivaling older Clarksville to the northeast along Red River. The Zachary home was out from town near the Trinity River, on a farm the captain had acquired while trading in cattle and cotton and corn. It had four white pillars, like pictures Frank had seen of grand plantation houses, alien to his poverty-dulled Colorado River upbringing. The pillars seemed too large for the modest two-story structure, like massive legs beneath a small table. Frank decided they represented the hope of future prosperity, the house being expected to grow to match the columns. The long war had left its old paint peeling shabbily.

A young girl and a middle-aged black couple hurried down as Tobe stopped the wagon beside the broad front steps. They paid only token attention to Frank at first. They made a fuss over the captain until Zachary told why he had brought Frank here. Then Frank was carried into a guest room on the ground floor, near the kitchen. The captain was taken to the master bedroom beyond the head of the wide staircase.

In his first days Frank made little effort to get up. He was bone weary from the long trip, and every move cut him with pain. A persistent low fever from his slowly healing wound left him little energy. The captain's doctor, reeking of camphor, confirmed prior judgments that probing for the arrowhead was too dangerous.

Frank demanded, "That means I got to live with it from now on?"

The doctor's voice betrayed a tinge of bitterness. "It will remain a constant reminder to you of war's futility."

Frank grunted, for he needed no reminder. He surmised that the doctor and the captain shared political philosophies.

Sometimes Tobe brought Frank's meals on a tray, but more often that chore was handled by Tobe's father or mother, who had belonged to the captain for years. Old Wash daily dressed Frank's wound, his hands gentle and slow. He talked freely, but his wife viewed Frank with misgivings bordering on fear. Despite the inhibiting circumstances of her servitude, she let him know by look and guarded words that she considered him a wild and uncurried frontiersman, advanced but little beyond the level of the hostile Indians.

As his strength began to revive, Frank labored his way to the kitchen for his meals, sitting alone at the plain table. Bess kept her distance, but Wash and Tobe obligingly fetched and carried. When Frank was able to dress, with Tobe's help, and no longer had to cover himself with a robe, he began exploring other downstairs rooms, particularly the parlor. He had always heard about parlors; this was the first he had ever seen. The clothes given him were loose but of store-shelf quality, a luxury he had never known. Wash told him they had belonged to the captain's son, killed early in the war. Bess broke into tears the first time she saw Frank fully dressed. She said, almost resentfully, "It was like Marse Jim come back to life."

Moving with a cane, Frank at last was able to look upon the man-tall grandfather clock he had heard striking away each passing hour. He marveled at the hand-carved beauty of the case, at what he could see of the shining innards, dutifully marking the long years a minute at a time. He moved to the wall shelves and gazed upon rows of books, some thick, some thin, some plain, some glittering with gold letters. He moved his hand slowly along their spines, stopping upon one at random, feeling the brown leather binding with his fingers, then removing it from its long-settled place. He realized vaguely that he had heard the name somewhere: *Shakespeare.* He let the book fall open, and his eyes searched the pages for familiar ground. Many of the words were strange.

A girl spoke behind him. "I didn't know you could read."

He turned half around to face Captain Zachary's daughter Letitia. He had heard her voice often during the long days in this house, but he had caught only brief glimpses. He had decided she shared Bess's misgivings.

Suddenly flustered, he hoped he was all buttoned up. "I can't read *this.*"

She gave him a tentative smile. "I can't either; not well. My mother used to explain it to me."

A picture of the captain's wife was in a gilded frame on a parlor table, alongside that of son James. Both pictures were draped with black cloth.

Frank did not want her thinking him illiterate. Defensively he said, "I can read a newspaper. And I can read the Bible a little, when somebody makes me the loan of one."

She asked, "Do you often get the loan of one?"

His face warmed. He had a notion she was implying that he had not lived the life of a Christian. "I been to preachin' more times than some I know of."

"Bess is convinced you're the devil's disciple."

"I never give her no cause . . ."

The girl shook her head. Frank saw a smile in her eyes, large brown eyes that seemed to look through him boldly and without reservation or shame. Probably she would be a right comely young woman when she got a few more years on her, but she was no more than thirteen or fourteen and badly in need of stern lecturing as to manners.

She said, "You come from out west. Bess figures the

land west of the Trinity River is primitive, and so are the people."

Still defensive, Frank said, "Well, we ain't. Your daddy can tell you there's a-plenty of good folks out there, as God fearin' as any here. We don't have fine clothes, nor no fancy church to go to, but I reckon the Lord didn't either, when He walked the earth."

Defiantly he waved the book at her. "I can *learn* to read this book, and I'll do it!"

She smiled with mischief. "You get mad easily, don't you?"

"When I got somethin' to get mad about, you're damned right."

She started to leave but stopped at the door. "Daddy says you're not married."

Rachal Wakefield flashed into his mind. The memory brought him pain almost as real as that arrowhead.

She said, "Maybe *I'll* marry you someday." Laughing, she disappeared down the hall.

He started to put the book back on the shelf, then changed his mind. He would show that girl; he would show everybody. He would read that book if it killed him. He made his way to a chair near the window, where the light was good. He sat down heavily, tired even by limited exertion. Opening to the title page, he read slowly, his finger following the words as his lips silently formed them one by one.

He fought his way through the book in about a week, though half of it remained as some foreign language to him. He found easier reading in Sir Walter Scott and Charles Dickens, and he related to Washington Irving's *A Tour of the Prairies* because it told of frontiers and Indians.

As his strength built he ventured out of the house to the winter-fallowed garden, to the barns and pens. He watched his brown horse, fleshening on a small-grain field and on liberal portions of dry oats fed by the boy Tobe. One day when the pain had largely left him, Frank persuaded the reluctant Tobe to saddle the brown. Carefully Frank placed his left foot in the stirrup, then pulled up slowly, cautious not to strain against the healing edges of the wound. He rode in wide circles between barn and house. Presently the jolting awakened the pain. He quit.

Captain Zachary, wrapped in a woolen blanket, sat in a straight chair on the gallery and watched. When Frank came back, taking short steps to avoid aggravating the pain, the captain eyed him with concern. Zachary's face was drawn and pale.

"Captain, sir," Frank said, "oughtn't you to be in the house? You could catch your death out here."

"So could you. But I am tired of the smell of sickness up in that room. My lungs need fresh air."

Frank shrugged. It was not his place to advise the captain. Inadvertently he pressed his hand to his stomach, as if that would ease the ache.

The captain asked, "Are you impatient to leave us?"

Frank frowned. "I never did fancy takin' from folks without I earned it."

"You earned it." Zachary's eyes narrowed. "I would not be in any hurry if I were you. People bring me news. I believe if you'll wait a bit longer the war will be over. Then there will be no rifle company for you to go back to."

Frank had heard little news himself, for the captain's visitors rarely shared conversation with him. They were bankers and merchants and planters, a class of men with whom Frank felt no kinship. He said, "I don't reckon our war out yonder will be over."

The captain motioned toward an empty chair. Frank sat. The captain stared across the winter-bare fields. "I owe you much more than you've received here. I would like to help you get on your feet and make something of yourself. The people of this state are in terrible financial trouble; I am myself. I doubt that you could stir up a thousand dollars in gold between here and the Red River. But when the war is behind us, I believe the opportunities will be here for men of imagination and determination. There'll be cotton to sell, and cattle, and many other goods that have been denied a market by the war. I believe I can find employment for you, Frank, that will pay you better than anything you can do out on the Clear Fork."

"You mean you want me to work for you?"

"For me, or with me . . . We could come to terms."

"But you'd be the boss."

"*Boss* is an unfriendly word. I have never liked it."

Frank gripped the arm of the chair. His hands were not yet strong, but his will had never weakened. "All due respects, Captain. If ever I wanted to work under a boss, you'd be the best one I ever knew. But that Indian fight taught me somethin'. My judgment told me better from the start. Your judgment told *you* it was wrong, but you had to answer to somebody else too. We all got drug into it because somebody else was boss.

"Every time I've done somethin' I didn't think was right, I've paid for it. I've come to see that nobody else can judge for me. There ain't nobody ever goin' to tell me what I have to do, not ever again. From now on the only boss for me will be Frank Claymore."

The captain studied him with eyes so clear and penetrating that Frank wished he could quietly pull away. Zachary said, "I understand. But a man can be his own toughest master."

New spring grass was rising green and tender amid the brittle remnant of the old when Frank put Dallas to his back and set the brown's feet upon the deeply rutted wagon road toward Fort Worth, Fort Belknap and west. It wound through round hills gentle and civilized compared to the rough terrain of the Clear Fork.

For weeks he had fidgeted, restless to start, but the pain would strike vengefully as soon as the horse hit its jolting trot. Being idle was the hardest work Frank had ever done. He had read most of the books on Captain Zachary's shelves

and found much of wonderment in worlds far removed from
any he knew. He had mastered even Shakespeare, after a
fashion, though he preferred Scott and Dickens, because
their language was nearer his own. Besides, he knew about
poor folks and had learned of warriors firsthand, while
kings and queens were beyond his ken. When eyes and patience wearied of reading, he would poke around the musty
barn, enjoying the familiar smells trapped in it long ago,
currying and brushing his horse, feeding and helping Tobe
milk the cows. The cattle, though dog-tame, reminded him
of his own, probably scattered to hell and gone.

Captain Zachary exerted every effort to make him comfortable, to draw him into his own circle. Frank was introduced to bankers, lawyers, farmers—well-to-do men before
the war had wrecked them. They talked of the past, not of
the future. They were lean and threadbare now; their glory
days a receding memory. Frank related to them with difficulty, for his thoughts were mostly on what lay ahead of
him, not what was behind . . . except for Rachal Wakefield.

He looked often at the tiny portrait in the locket Rachal
had given him, and his mind dwelled much upon her. He
thought the girl Letty might be responsible for that. Frequently Frank found himself watching Letty and thinking
of Rachal. It was not that she looked like Rachal or that she
aroused a sexual interest. On the contrary, she irritated him
to a point that he would go out upon the gallery or down to
the barn to escape her adolescent coquetry. It seemed to
him she needed the attention of the captain's razor strap,
but her father lavished affection upon her and saw no fault.
Frank could not discern that she received any discipline beyond frequent lectures from the black woman Bess. Those
rolled off unheeded, like quiet spring rain from a good
cypress roof.

The only thing Letty had in common with Rachal, as far
as he could determine, was that both were female. He supposed that was enough to cause him to look at one and see
the other, to relive the torment of a shattered dream.

Upon Frank's leaving, the captain had forced him to accept a twenty-dollar gold piece, though Frank was determined not to spend it. By the time he had traveled ten miles, he realized the captain had been right; he had not waited long enough. So fierce was the pain that he cried aloud and climbed down from the saddle, bending over with arms pulled tightly against his stomach. He considered making his way slowly back to Zachary's, but that would be a tacit admission that he had been wrong. He chose the lesser pain, lying on the ground until the hurting eased, then riding on, westward.

The will was strong but the body weak. Late in the afternoon he came upon a government freighters' camp and was invited to supper. His knees buckled as he dismounted. Two freighters eased him to a bedroll. When he explained how he had come to this predicament and where he was going, they offered him a seat on a wagon as far as Belknap, before the war a military post, now used by Confederate frontier guards.

They had the charity not to inquire about his political feelings. The little they said about the war substantiated what he had heard at the Zachary home: the conflict was grinding to a shuddering conclusion, the South exhausted. The freighters doubted they would ever haul another load for the Texas Confederate government. They doubted they could even spend the paper money paid them for this trip.

One of the freighters hobbled around camp on a wooden leg. He had lost the real one in Virginia. As they spoke of the war he pounded his fist against the piece of hackberry branch that supported him. He said bitterly, "For nothin'."

Those were the words Homer had spoken when Beaver died. Frank pressed his hand against his stomach. *For nothing.*

He made it to Belknap but no farther, not for a while. He became so ill along the road that the freighters feared they might be obliged to bury him. Belknap's doctor, such as he was, said Frank had pushed his luck too far. The arrowhead still worked around in there, looking for a place to rest.

"It's a damned poor piece of luck for you that it didn't come out the day it went in," the doctor frowned.

"Can't you take it out?" Frank asked. "Anything is better than this."

Gravely the doctor shook his head. "I've got nothing but whiskey to give you before cutting, and poor whiskey at that. I've killed three men that way since Christmas."

"Damned thing will kill me anyway, looks like."

"Maybe not. It may find a place to lodge, and the body will gradually pad it. You could carry it and live to be a hundred. Or . . ." He paused. "Now you lie still."

Frank remained in Fort Belknap that night, and many more.

He was sunning himself on the south side of a picket barracks the afternoon a rider loped into the compound and up to the commanding officer's stone quarters. In a few moments the company's captain came out, his face as cold as January. The bugler sounded assembly. When the company was formed into a line, the captain said, "Men, I have news—" His voice broke. He turned his back a moment, regaining control. "The Confederacy is no more."

A heavy, brooding silence fell over the little company. Frank looked at the stunned faces and wondered. How could they have failed to realize this was inevitable? He supposed it was like a slow death in the family, expected but never prepared for.

One of the men began a quiet but bitter, "Damn . . . damn . . . damn . . ."

The officer looked at him with reproach, then with sympathy. "Gentlemen, this is a moment not for blasphemy but for humility and prayer. Would you please bow your heads?" The hats came off. The men stood in silence, heads down. Frank heard a quiet sobbing from the largest and strongest man in the company.

The captain said, "Almighty God, we beseech Thy mercy in our darkest hour. We ask that Thou guide us now. and in the darker days yet to come. We think now of many loved ones, and we ask Thy blessings and Thy mercy for them. We entreat Thee to show us the way out of this darkness and back into the light, for we have strayed so far from Thy teachings. Help us, o God, for we are lost. Amen."

The big man still sobbed quietly. The others stood there a long time. No one had words. The officer went back into quarters, forgetting even to dismiss the formation.

The men began to drift away over the next few days, each in his own direction, without leave or discharge. The authority that had brought them together as frontier soldiers of Texas had been wiped away at distant Appomattox.

One morning the doctor told Frank, "I've done all I can except give you some advice. I doubt that you'll take it."

Frank conceded him little. "I'll listen."

"Don't try to rebuild the whole country at one time. Set a pace slow enough to heal you, not kill you. Do that, and maybe we'll see each other again if your business ever carries you down into Stephens County."

Frank did not want to be the last man to leave Fort Belknap. He made up his mind to ride the brown horse if it killed him. A couple of self-discharged soldiers came through in an appropriated military wagon, bound for Camp Cooper and a reunion with families there. Frank rode with them much of the way, bidding them good-bye when they reached a point he judged was nearest to Davis.

"Well, old brown," he said as he watched the wagon raise a thin ribbon of dust, "I reckon it's me and you again." He swung into the saddle and resolved not to give in to the pain.

His frontier instinct for caution came back quickly, though he had been away several months. He saw whatever moved, heard every bird that proclaimed its territory in the timber. As in earlier times, he ate his supper early, what little there was, then rode awhile in darkness, leaving his snuffed-out campfire far behind.

He knew the green valleys and the rocky hills long before he approached Fort Davis. The nearer he came, the faster his heart beat, and the slower he rode. He stopped beside the corrals at the edge of the camp and sat a long time in the late-afternoon sun, eyes drawn to the rough cabin he had shared with Homer, then to George Valentine's, where he had found Rachal and George lying in each other's arms. Now that he was here, he wished he were not. He considered riding way around and working upriver to the burned-out ruins of the place where he and Homer had ranched before the forting up.

But he could not bring his eyes away from the Valentine cabin. It was idle even to think of leaving without seeing Rachal. He had been compelled here by her memory etched into his soul. He even thought it probable that her image, and only that, had brought him alive through the aftermath of Dove Creek.

Looking at the cabin, he remembered with regret his bruising battle against George. That he had won brought no comfort, for Rachal had been lost to him in spite of it. Any repetition of that fight now might cause the arrowhead to kill him. But he had not ridden this far to turn away. He harbored a hope, however slight, that George might by now have abandoned Rachal, that he had not wanted her so badly as he had thought.

Frank nervously set the brown into a walk across the compound. It was obvious the place was breaking up, the people scattering now that the war was over. The picket cabins deteriorated quickly if no one lived in them. His and Homer's was beginning to lean, much of the roof's dirt covering washed or blown away. But George's roof was recently freshened, and the ground was swept clean in front of the door.

He reined to a stop and flexed his shaking hands as he considered the rough cabin. He swung down and tethered the horse to a post. Frank took a deep breath and rapped his knuckles against the ax-hewn door. "Rachal? George?"

He waited for a period that seemed ten minutes before the door swung inward just a little, dragging the earthen floor. He saw her eyes back in the shadows, peering distrustfully.

"Rachal," he said huskily, "is that you?"

"Frank?" Her voice was strained, trying not to cry. "Frank, I'd made up my mind you died."

He guessed he should have written somebody. "I come to see you, Rachal."

She moved her face to the opening, but she did not widen the door. "You oughtn't to've. George won't like it."

"I didn't come to fight with George. I just want to see you, then I'll go on up the river."

"There can't nothin' come of it," she said, seeming a bit frightened. She opened the door, finally, and stepped out into the light to see if anyone was watching. Frank did not look. He did not care. He struggled against an impulse to crush her.

She was different, some way; he could not say how. She looked older. The life that had always seemed so bright in her eyes was dulled and troubled. "You're thin, Frank," she spoke. "Homer *said* that arrow taken you real hard."

"I'm fine, Rachal," he said. "And you look fine." It was a lie, but he would not have told her otherwise. He gave in to his urge to the extent that he gripped her shoulders. She quickly pulled free, back into the cabin.

Chagrined, he offered, "I'm sorry, Rachal. I didn't come here to cause you grief."

He heard a whimper and thought it hers, then realized it came from beyond her. His eyes accustomed themselves to the darkness. Against the back wall he saw a crib, and a movement beneath a thin blanket. A sudden chill left him cold.

Hesitantly Rachal said, "You want to see him?"

Frank felt more like turning to run. "Wouldn't be no purpose of it." But he was drawn to stay.

"We named him Billy," she said. "Billy Valentine."

He frowned. "Billy?"

"I always liked that name. I didn't think we ought to call him George, and I sure couldn't name him Frank."

Hurt welled up, and the feeling of loss. Frank turned back into the sunshine, staring through a haze. "I still wish you'd told me in time, Rachal. Things wouldn't be this way."

"There ain't no changin' them now."

"You could go with me."

She seemed shocked by the notion. "A woman can't do such as that. It'd be a sin, and we've done sin enough already."

"We love each other. Is *that* a sin?"

She glanced back toward the baby. Almost resentfully she said, "Must be. I sure got punished for it."

He looked at the floor again. "I'm sorry, Rachal. I just wish . . ."

He heard footsteps outside, then a man's stem voice. "I was hopin' I seen wrong, Frank. I was hopin' you'd stay dead, like they first said you was."

Reluctantly Frank turned to face George Valentine. He started to extend his hand but saw in George's cold eyes that the motion would be wasted. "I didn't come for trouble."

"There won't be none if you go."

"I hoped time would change things, George."

George's eyes narrowed for a moment of charged silence. "It has. I want to show you somethin', Frank." He jerked his head. "Rachal, I want to talk to Frank alone."

Rachal's eyes were fearful. Her hands went up to cover her mouth. "George, please don't . . ."

"There won't be no fight without he starts it."

She turned back as if to pick up the baby. George said, "Leave Billy here. I want Frank to look at him."

Eyes stricken, she left quickly, not looking at Frank again. Turning, Frank saw a rifle on pegs against the roughly plastered wall. George stood within easy reach of it.

Frank repeated, "I didn't come for no trouble."

George went to the crib and lifted the thin blanket. The startled baby raised its tiny hands. George said, "Come look at Billy Valentine."

Frank held back, more inclined to leave. But he became compelled by something far stronger than simple curiosity. He walked across the dirt floor, careful not to raise dust that might choke the baby. He gazed at the tiny, wrinkled face. In the poor light the infant resembled an old man more than a child. But Frank felt a warm glow. He wanted to reach down and touch, but he did not dare.

Bitterly George said, "Who do you think he looks like, Frank? Would you say he looks like me?"

Frank's throat tightened.

George's voice was embittered. "Been a lot of people said he looks like his mother. Ain't nobody said he looks like me. I look at him and I see Frank Claymore."

Frank's face went hot. He wanted to leave, but his feet would not move.

George said, "Other folks've seen the resemblance, too. They don't say much to me, but I can tell what they're thinkin'. I can guess what they're sayin' later."

Frank knew denial was useless. His voice came back. "What do you think you ought to do about it, George?"

George was a time in answering. "Nothin'. I'm goin' to do nothin'."

"You could leave her. You could set her free."

George made a bitter laugh. "That's what you'd like me to do—turn away from her so you can have her. And that's one reason I won't do it, Frank. I'm keepin' her, and I'll raise that boy like he was mine."

Frank did not look away. He faced the hostility in eyes that had once shown friendship. "We done wrong, me and Rachal. But part of it was *your* wrong too, George. This wouldn't've happened if you hadn't lied to Rachal about how long I'd be gone. She'd have my name, and so would that baby."

It was as if George had not heard. "I'm tellin' you to your

face, Frank: I'll never forgive you. Any time God shows me the opportunity to raise my hand against you, I will."

Frank tightened his fists. "I can take care of myself. But if ever I hear of you mistreatin' Rachal or that baby, I'll come huntin' you."

George nodded grimly. "We understand each other. Now you better go, Frank, before I break my promise to Rachal."

Frank walked out into the sunshine, his blood cold.

The baby cried, and its voice cut Frank like a knife. He stopped midstride. He had to force himself to walk on toward the horse. With trembling hands he untied the rein. Rachal came to him, her eyes pleading the question.

Frank shook his head. "He's set like a rock. The only way you'll be free is to leave him."

She said, "That'd be shameful. You know I can't never do it."

The arrowhead gouged Frank as he pulled himself into the saddle, but that was the least of his pain. He rode away with his head down. He did not look up until he crossed the river and felt the water splash cold upon his legs. He glanced back once, then picked up the old trail and followed along the Clear Fork. His eyes burned. He blamed that on facing into the rapidly sinking sun.

He rode a long time, only half seeing what was around him as he nursed a dozen deep angers and frustrations, futilely asking himself *What if?* The brown horse followed the trail without guidance.

Frank was startled out of his trance by three horsemen who seemed to materialize suddenly from nowhere. Heart hammering, he reached instinctively for his pistol. He had it half out of the holster when he realized these were not Indians. They were cow hunters, by their look. They hauled up short, watching him warily as he held the pistol half in and half out.

"Easy, friend," said the older of the three, a man with a short beard half gray. "We don't mean you no harm."

Feeling foolish, Frank let the pistol slip back into the

holster. He managed apologetically, "You come upon me with my mind someplace else. I'm Frank Claymore." He extended his hand.

The older man took it. "We've heard the name. I'm Bige Akins. These are my boys Matthew and Mark." The smile widened. "I also got Luke and John. They're over yonderway in camp, with their sister Naomi. I'm afraid the boys ain't as saintly as their names, but we do the best we can."

Frank was not given to quick and easy friendship, but now and then he found someone he liked instinctively, as he had Beaver and Captain Zachary. He felt that way about these men. "You-all must've just lately moved into the country."

Akins replied, "I was off to the war for three years. Come home to Hamilton County and found it overstocked, so me and the young'uns brought the cattle out here and scattered them. Couldn't tell that anybody had a claim on the land."

That was the way it had been since people had first begun moving into the Clear Fork country before the war. Few if any had title or up to now had even sought it.

Akins said, "It's comin' on dark. Be pleased to have you share the camp."

In his dark mood Frank felt he had rather not share camp with anybody, but he realized he had to stop somewhere, and soon. Bige Akins somehow reminded him of Sam Ballinger. He said, "I got mighty little to put in the pot. A dab of flour, some parched corn that passes for coffee."

"You won't get fat on our grub either," Akins assured him. "It'd pleasure us to share the misery with you."

The crude camp was marked by three tattered old military tents, a little something salvaged from the wreck of the Confederacy. Two large boys and a girl stood waiting. The sight of the girl momentarily brought back the pain of his parting from Rachal, but it passed. The horsemen unsaddled inside a crude brush corral thrown together around standing oak trees. Akins said, "We're out to get rich in the cattle business." His joking tone made it clear he never expected such a thing actually to happen. "Looks to me like cattle ought to do good here."

Frank nodded. "Cattle do. Catt*men* don't always."

They hunkered around a little campfire. Frank was uncomfortably conscious of the girl's eyes on him, but when he looked at her, she would glance quickly away. He sensed that she was somehow a little afraid of him. He could understand that. In his mood he probably looked like a thunderbolt hunting a place to strike. He judged her to be around sixteen. She was thin and hungry looking, a mark of the times. She would probably be pretty if he were of a mind to pay attention to such things.

He said, "My old camp's upriver a ways. You-all by chance seen anything of my partner? Name's Homer Whitcomb."

Bige Akins grinned. Matthew slapped Mark's back and laughed. He said, "He come by the day we first made camp. He seen Naomi, and he's been comin' back real regular."

The girl blushed and turned quickly away, telling her brother to mind his tongue if he wanted any supper.

Frank asked, "Is he all right?"

Matthew chuckled. "You'd have to ask Naomi about that. What do you think, Naomi? Is he all right?"

She threw a bucket of water on him. A little of it set the fire to hissing. Matthew jumped to his feet, still laughing, and caught his sister. He wrenched the bucket from her hand and poured the little remaining water on her head. She stamped down on his foot, then stepped back giggling while he hopped around gripping his toes.

Bige Akins watched them, smiling. "I lost my wife while I was off to the war. The kids've been a comfort to me."

They sat up late, talking about old times, about the war, about their hopes and fears for the future. Frank noted that Akins's sons and the daughter stayed near their father, listening to whatever he said. He sensed a love and mutual respect in this family that he could not remember among his own. He warmed himself on the glow of these people, though it awakened in him a sense of pleasures missed, pleasures he probably would never know. He had only tentative and hazy memories of his father, and his mother had lived but little longer. For the Claymore boys the struggle to survive had been so fierce that it left little time or inclination to develop the close family relationships he saw here. The Claymores had been so intent upon the hungry growl of the wolf at their door that they had never heard the birds sing in the timber.

Bige Akins watched thoughtfully as Frank saddled his brown horse after breakfast. "If we can ever be of help to you, Frank, all you got to do is come and ask."

Frank nodded and pointed his chin. "If *you* ever need help, you'll find me upriver."

Carrying a quarter of venison the Akins boys had insisted he take, he came in due course upon his old place. The charred remnants of the cabin looked just like the last time he had seen them. He had hoped to find Homer but did not. The garden was planted, however, its sagging pole fences propped to keep animals out. Perhaps Homer was at Sam Ballinger's, farther on.

He saw the old lightning-struck tree before he spotted the new stone walls rising past the river's known floodline. Sam Ballinger was wise in the ways of the country. He knew a bucket was better used to pack water up to the cabin from the river than to bail the river out of the cabin. A tarp-covered wagon stood near the building site. Frank saw Mrs. Ballinger and the two girls hurry behind the walls as he approached. A rifle barrel poked out between a pair of narrow stone slits.

Frank called, "Hello the house! It's Frank Claymore."

The rifle withdrew. Sam Ballinger's lean frame appeared in the unfinished doorway of the house that as yet lacked a roof. A grin washed across his furrowed, sweatstained face. He walked hurriedly. "Git down, boy!" Joy was in his voice.

They howdied and shook with some violence. Mrs. Ballinger and the girls and the little boy ventured from behind the walls. The girls were country-shy, but the boy Sammy had not learned fear. He stood within touching distance and stared up into Frank's face. The woman, bonneted but nevertheless burned by sun and wind, kissed Frank on the cheek and welcomed him as a son lost, then found. She stepped back and studied him up and down. "Sam, we've built wall enough for this day. Frank needs a good feedin'."

He protested against their making a fuss, but they would hear of nothing less than their best, which was not all that much. The coffee was ready first, made over an open campfire near the wagon. Frank could not guess where they had obtained coffee, and he would not ask. He sipped the strong black brew from a tin cup, savoring it long and lovingly, wondering how anybody could prefer whiskey to such as this.

Pride was in Sam's eyes as he looked at the half-built house. "We're puttin' her up strong, two stories tall. I'm buildin' me one the Indians can't burn. Stone plumb to the eaves, and I'll keep dirt on the roof so they can't catch the shingles afire. They won't run us off again, not me and mine."

"You're a long ways from help."

"I'm buildin' this one strong enough we oughtn't to *need* help. But you'll be settlin' back where you was, won't you, you and Homer? I watched your cows till Homer come home. Branded your last calves with a C Bar W for you. If I hadn't, I expect George Valentine might've got them. He's put his iron on everything he could catch."

Frank flinched at the mention of George's name. He glanced at Sam, wondering if he knew, but he saw nothing in Sam's eyes.

He refilled his cup. Studying the place, he decided Sam had put first things first. He had planted his garden and his field before he had undertaken the new house. "Goin' to be hard-scrabble awhile. What a man can't build or raise, he'll have to do without."

Sam replied, "We got us a milk cow and some chickens.

Turned some shoats loose downriver a ways. Still plenty of deer in the thickets. They'll play hell starvin' us to death."

He heard the rattling of a wagon and pushed to his feet. Homer Whitcomb drove into camp with a fresh load of stone for the house. He threw his arms around Frank and fiercely bear-hugged half the breath from him. Frank pushed Homer away to arm's length and stared happily at that welcome face, its grin wider than a wagon hoop. "Homer, I was afraid some Indian had put you under."

Homer slapped him on both shoulders. "Ain't I always told you? Old Homer can take care of himself."

5

The judge had told the people in the courtroom to hold their places a few minutes while he retired to the clerk's office to investigate a point of law. Claymore's attorney leaned forward, talking in a voice he hoped would not carry to the prosecutor. Claymore put his hand to his ear and strained for hearing.

"It occurs to me, Mr. Claymore, that we can use that arrow wound to our advantage. It should help gain juror sympathy."

Claymore grumbled, "I never asked for sympathy in my life, and sure not from the likes of *them* coffeepot polishers." He gave the jurors a dark and disapproving study. "Catchin' that arrow in my gut never got me much sympathy in the old days. Anyway, I never was proud of the fight. I'd of thought a lot more of it if Old Red Shield had done it to me."

The attorney let his exasperation show. "This is no time for pride, Mr. Claymore. You are on trial for your life."

Stubbornly Claymore said, "I ain't never begged, nor put on a show."

"I am not asking you to grovel like a mendicant showing off a stub of a leg. But I do say that if you were in close combat with an Indian and your rifle failed to fire, you would use your pistol. If your pistol did not fire, you would use your knife. And if your knife's blade was broken, you would pick up the first stick that came to hand. No weapon would be beneath your contempt."

"I ain't beggin' them people to feel sorry for me just because somebody else's foolishness once put me in the way of an arrow."

The attorney wiped his glasses with a handkerchief, doing more violence to them than necessary. "At least we should mention it. That might take the edge off of the prosecutor's claim that you shirked your duties."

Claymore mused. "I reckon I *would've* if they had let me."

The judge reentered through a door behind the bench. Claymore thought he looked more relaxed. Some people found comfort in the Bible. Perhaps the judge found relief in law books.

"Is the prosecution ready to proceed with further witnesses?"

It seemed to Claymore that half the people in town had already testified.

Prosecutor Elihu Mallard stood up. "I am, Your Honor. I would like to call to the stand Mr. Isaac Farraday."

Claymore twisted in his chair and looked back, frowning. He had never heard the man called anything except Rusty. After all these years it came almost as a surprise to learn he bore a Christian name. Farraday had become a heavy man, the excesses of his life bearing down hard with punishment. Always ruddy, his face now was florid from chronic high blood pressure and the strain of being called to testify before a crowd.

Homer, sitting directly behind Claymore, said loudly enough for everyone to hear, "Won't do them no good to swear him. Son of a bitch ain't told the truth since he fell out of his crib and claimed he was pushed."

The judge gave Homer a glare that would touch off gunpowder. Homer slumped a bit lower in his chair, but his attitude did not remain long subdued. He passed a similar remark as Farraday held up a big, puffy hand and swore to tell the truth, the whole truth and nothing but the truth. The judge pointed his gavel sternly at Homer. "If I hear one more such comment, sir, senility will not be accepted as a defense."

Claymore's attorney whispered, "What is Farraday likely to say that will hurt us?"

Claymore shrugged. "Anything that comes into his mind, truth or lie."

Homer declared, "He wouldn't know the truth if it come up behind him and bit him on the butt."

The judge beckoned the sheriff, then pointed toward Homer. "Will you please escort that gentleman out of this courtroom? If he attempts to reenter today, I want you to place him in the meanest cell you have, sir."

Ed Phelps took Homer gently by the arm. "Sorry, Homer. You heard the judge."

Homer looked sorrowfully at Claymore. "Have I got to, Frank?"

Claymore glanced bleakly around the courtroom. With Homer gone he could count his friends in this courtroom on one hand. "You better do what he says. You ain't ever been in jail."

Laughter rippled across the courtroom as the sheriff led Homer to the door. The judge rapped the gavel and recovered control.

The prosecutor stared a moment at Frank Claymore, then turned back to Farraday, hunched nervously in the witness chair. "It is my understanding, Mr. Farraday, that you have known Frank Claymore a very long time."

Farraday nodded, his heavy jowls wobbling. "Yes, sir, a lot longer than I'd've wanted to."

"Has he ever threatened your life?"

"Yes, sir."

"How many times, over the years?"

Farraday considered, his red face twisting. He counted on the tips of his fingers. "Well sir, to have him come right out and say it, not many. But to look like he was figurin' about it, quite a bunch."

Mallard smiled thinly. "Tell us about the first time."

Farraday squirmed. "Well, sir, it was that first summer after the war broke up. Me and some other boys was helpin' George Valentine work a bunch of his cattle. Frank Claymore and Windy Homer Whitcomb—that's him the sheriff just throwed out of here—and old Sam Ballinger come a-ridin' up. About the first thing he done—Frank Claymore, I mean—he pointed his rifle in my direction and tried to provoke an excuse to kill me."

The defense attorney turned quickly to Claymore, his eyes asking if the story was true. Claymore grumped, "Damned shame I didn't know enough to go ahead and do it . . ."

Frank had never owned more than a few dollars, so he was probably more hardened than many for the long, hungry summer that followed the war. He did not tell Homer about the twenty-dollar gold piece Captain Zachary had given him. He wrapped it in an old scrap of leather, put his back to a corner of their burned cabin and took twenty paces toward the Big Dipper. There, while Homer slept, Frank buried the coin for safekeeping.

Homer was in favor of rebuilding the cabin first, but Frank had other priorities. They put up a brush arbor, covering it with a molding layer of canvas Homer had found on an abandoned, broken-down wagon. They threw green branches and leaves on top to keep it from blowing away. A heavy rain would leak through, but rains were a seldom thing on the Clear Fork.

After making that minor concession to comfort, they rode out searching for cattle that had strayed far from home. It was not entirely a futile effort, but the number they found and pushed back to their own range in that first month of hard riding seemed little compensation for the effort. They came across a few of Sam Ballinger's and drove them where they belonged. Considering cattle's almost total lack of cash value, Homer questioned the purpose in so many long days of work.

Stubbornly Frank said, "They'll *be* worth money one day. When they are, we'll have somethin'."

He had spoken more sharply than he intended; he seemed to lack patience anymore. But he did not apologize.

He and Homer lived mostly on game, for it was almost a religious principle with him that cattle were to raise, not to eat. When Homer broke the leg of an unbranded yearling— not altogether an accident, Frank suspected—they butchered it at once. They carried part of it to the Ballingers, part to Bige Akins and his family. Homer quickly ran out of conversation with the Akins men, but he seemed to have plenty to say to the girl Naomi when the two sat in the comforting shade of a big live oak tree, away from the others.

In return for the beef, Bige Akins gave Frank a sack of coffee beans and a little news. "Federal troops are movin' in to the east of us. Folks talk like they're more interested in keepin' down the old Southern boys than in the Indians."

Frank said, "They got no interest in me. I never raised a gun against the Union."

As he and Homer rode back toward their place on the river, they heard cattle bawling. It was not the call of one cow to a strayed calf but the concentrated complaint of many cows and many calves being gathered or driven. This was not Frank's range, and he realized he and Homer would finish their ride in the dark if they did not keep moving. Nevertheless, curiosity got the better of him. In a clearing he found half a dozen horsemen pushing cattle into a small herd. The man in charge was giving instructions by hand and by holler. Frank recognized him and almost turned away.

Homer said, "That's George Valentine. We ought to at least say howdy. Maybe he's got over bein' mad."

Frank tried to tell Homer that George would *never* get over it, but Homer did not understand a grudge.

George did not acknowledge Frank beyond a long, dark study, mercifully interrupted when a cow decided upon a break for freedom in the direction she had last seen her calf. George did not chase her himself; he shouted to one of the young horsemen, a kid of fourteen or so. Frank doubted that George could afford to pay help. They were probably living on promises and hope, like everybody else.

Homer tried to be friendly, but George gave him only a quick, uneasy word, holding his eyes on Frank. Frank rode slowly around the cattle, reading the brands. He found none of his own, but he spied a cow wearing Sam Ballinger's. A big, unmarked heifer calf stayed close to her side. Frank said, "That one's Sam's."

George showed his annoyance. "If Sam wants her, Sam can come and get her. I've got no time . . ."

Frank rode into the herd and eased the cow and calf out from the others. He gave them a push westward, then reined around. "Me and Homer'll take them to Sam."

George's voice crackled. "Ain't you got enough to do without holdin' up *my* work?"

Unwillingly Frank began to host a suspicion. That heifer was old enough to wean. George might have put *his* brand on her, knowing she rightfully belonged to Sam. The George Valentine of old had had his faults, but he would not have been a thief. Frank was not sure he knew *this* George of the smoldering eyes.

The cow kept looking back as Frank and Homer drove her. It was easier to drive twenty cattle than two.

The longer Frank thought about George, the more he worried. By the time they shut the gate on the tired cow and calf in their own pens, he had made up his mind. "Soon's we take that pair home to Sam, me and you are goin' to make a sashay through George's country. That's one place we've never hunted for any of our cows."

Homer was not given to looking at the negative side, but once in a while even his smiling visage could be corrupted into a frown. "You sure it's the cows that's got you frettin', and not Rachal?"

Frank had never struck Homer in anger, though he had been tempted on occasion. He left the arbor to Homer that night and slept wrapped in his blanket by the river.

Sam Ballinger was grateful for the return of the cow. He could identify his on sight and could describe most from memory. He had not seen this one in a year or more. She had probably weaned off a previous calf without his ever branding it.

"It's probably packin' *somebody's* brand," Frank said.

Sam's eyes became troubled when he learned Frank's intentions. "My corn don't need hoein'. I'll go with you."

Frank argued, "Me and Homer can take care of any cattle we find."

"It ain't the cattle that concerns me."

Something in his eyes told Frank: *he knew.* It was probable that everyone knew. But Sam offered no advice, no criticism. He accepted a man as he was.

Frank said, "You sure you want to leave your family alone?"

Sam replied, "Ain't been an Indian seen in six months."

He waved to his family as he and Frank and Homer rode across the broad patch of ground he had cleared so visitors— Indians or otherwise—could not ride up to the house unseen. "You-all watch sharp," he called back. "Don't stray from home."

They spent two days riding in a switchback pattern, slowly and carefully looking at all the cattle they came across. They found none bearing their brands, though they saw cows of brands unknown to them. Some were trailed by calves with George's brand burned on their hips.

"Stray brands," Frank said. "Cattle drifted in from God knows where. George don't see much chance of a real owner showin' up. If he waited till the calves weaned theirselves, *anybody* could brand them."

Sam remarked, "At least there ain't none of them ours."

"None we've *found,*" Frank said.

Toward the middle of the third day they heard cattle bawling. Frank said, "Let's have a look."

Sam suggested, "Let *me* have a look first."

Frank disregarded him. He touched spurs to the brown horse and set out in the lead. He did not look back at Sam and Homer.

He saw the cattle first, then the riders. George was the only grown man. The rest were boys, mostly the same ones Frank had seen the other time. He rode past them without a nod.

He felt a moment of hostility as his eyes met George's. George said, "Am I ever goin' to be shed of you, Frank Claymore?"

Frank offered no answer. "I want to look at the brands."

"I've already looked at them."

"Won't take but a few minutes for me to look at them too. Then we'll *both* be satisfied." He did not wait for further argument. A broad-shouldered boy with rough, freckled face and a thick mop of rusty-red hair moved belligerently toward him. Frank said, "Back away, boy. I wouldn't want to hurt you."

George said, "Get back, Rusty." Reluctantly the boy pulled aside. Frank glared until the boy could not match his stare and looked away. He moved the brown slowly to avoid stirring the cattle. They were range stock, not used to close handling. They would run at any excuse.

He had half expected what he found, but he had not expected to find it so quickly. The familiar droop of a horn led his eye to a spotted cow he remembered driving up all the way from the Colorado River. He remembered every calf she had ever had, except the one that stood beside her now. "That cow's mine." He edged her toward the outside.

George signaled the boys to close in behind him, and he blocked the cow's exit from the herd. "I don't see your brand."

In a more objective frame of mind Frank might have admitted that the hair had grown over to a point of almost obliterating the old burn. In a more congenial atmosphere he might have suggested clipping the hair to reveal the scarred hide beneath. But now he had no such intention. "She's comin' out."

"Like hell," declared George. He reached for the rifle in a scabbard beneath his leg.

Frank moved faster, laying his own rifle across the pommel, aiming it more or less at George. George hesitated, his weapon not clear of the scabbard. His eyes were sober.

The red-haired boy had a pistol in his waistband. He inched his hand toward it. Frank stopped him with the rifle's muzzle. "Boy, is George Valentine any kin to you?"

The boy was slow to respond. He shook his head negatively. Frank demanded, "Is he blood kin to *any* of you boys?"

No one spoke. Frank held his eyes to those of the red-haired boy. "He's in the wrong here. If he's payin' you, you owe him your work. You don't owe him your lives. And it'll be the life of anybody who tries to stop me!"

None of the boys made any further move, though Rusty still seemed to consider it. Frank shifted his gaze back to George. "You know she's mine. If you intend to stop me, pull that gun."

George did not take his eyes from Frank's rifle. He spoke in a strained voice, "You boys'll bear witness. He's takin' that cow by force."

Frank would not have clipped the brand for George, but he wanted the others satisfied. "Homer, would you and Sam stretch that cow? I don't want nobody to hold a doubt."

Homer managed to work a rope over her head, Sam her heels. While Frank and George sat on their horses and watched each other, two boys grabbed the cow's tail and jerked her down. One cut away the hair with a sharp knife. No doubt remained about the brand.

Frank nodded in satisfaction. "Sam, you and Homer better finish lookin' through that bunch."

They found no more of their own, though several cows had brands Frank did not recognize.

George could not hold his eyes to Frank's. "I reckon I was wrong about that cow."

"No you wasn't," Frank told him. "You was wrong about *me*." He leaned forward a little, voice rising. "You never was much of a cowman, George. You wouldn't make much of a thief!"

He held a minute to see if George might arouse himself to another challenge. He did not. George looked away as Homer and Sam pushed the cow and calf farther from the herd. Frank turned and rode after his friends. Glancing back, he saw the red-haired boy still watching him, still looking as if he might fight.

The three men covered at least a mile in a silence as oppressive as an oncoming storm. Sam finally said, "You went too strong, Frank. I don't think George knew that was your cow."

Frank did not reply.

Homer could contain himself no longer. He turned on his partner with a challenge Frank had seldom seen from him. "My God, Frank, you'd've killed him—or got yourself killed."

Frank nodded grimly. "If it'd come to that."

"For one old droop-horned cow and a knot-bellied calf? The two of them together wouldn't fetch two dollars, if you could find somebody who *had* two dollars."

Impatiently Frank declared, "It ain't the money that matters, it's the *takin'*. You let somebody take what's yours, even if it's somethin' little, and sooner or later they'll come back to take it all. That cow was mine."

Hurt came into Homer's eyes. "I kind of had a notion she was part mine too."

Frank felt a nudging of conscience, but he did not let it

soften his voice. "Nothin' stays yours very long if you don't stand ready to fight for it."

Sam looked Frank squarely in the eyes. "It wasn't the cow you challenged him for."

Sam said no more, but even in silence he was a nagging conscience, as uncomfortable as a boil on the backside. Frank was glad when they got home.

They branded the calf the next morning, then turned it and the cow out of the brush pen. Watching the pair trot toward cattle upriver, Frank said, "I laid awake half the night thinkin' about the stray cattle George's been gatherin'."

Homer still fretted over yesterday's incident. "That old heifer could've got both of you killed."

Frank ignored the invitation to argument. "I remembered when we set out toward that fight down on Dove Creek, and we come across a bunch of strays on the Colorado River. Them cattle tromped through my head all night. They belong to whoever goes down there and takes them."

"Even if they've strayed, they've got owners someplace."

"Any grown cattle without brands belong to the first man who puts an iron on them. Whatever branded cattle we pick up, we'll write to the county courthouses east of us and tell folks where they're at. Not many'll come and claim them. Whatever increase we raise'll be ours. Give us five years, Homer. In five years me and you'll have more cattle than anybody. We'll make George Valentine look like a milk peddler."

Homer still frowned. "You doin' all this for us, or *against* George?"

"George has got nothin' to do with it."

Homer sniffed. "And where we goin' to graze this mighty herd? We don't even own the ground under that brush arbor."

"From here yonderway"—Frank pointed his chin west— "is open range. Except for Sam and his family, there ain't three people west of us that don't wear feathers in their hair. It's free for the first man who turns stock loose on it."

"Free if he can hold it. But there'll come others, and maybe they'll want what we've got."

"We'll have to ride longer, work harder and be meaner."

Homer grimaced. "How mean do you intend to be, Frank?"

"However mean I *have* to be." He pressed his hand to his stomach. Every once in a while that arrowhead still grabbed. "A man's got to watch out for himself. He can't always worry about what other folks think."

"You goin' to always ask me what *I* think?"

Frank did not make promises he might not keep. "I'll do whatever seems best at the time."

Homer was not satisfied, but that was the best he was going to get. "When you reckon we ought to start?"

The nearer their horses carried them to the red clay of the Colorado River, following landmarks well remembered from December's campaign, the more somber the mood that settled upon Frank. The country looked different in many ways, summer green instead of winter brown, but the flat-topped mountains were the same, and the old military trail seemed to point them inexorably toward Dove Creek. At times, when the warm south wind bent the low cedars, he could almost hear the tramping of the long column, and more than once he turned in the saddle as if expecting to see Beaver Red loping up. It would be good, he thought, when they began working cattle; perhaps he would not have time to remember.

The trouble with high expectations, he had long since decided, was that they were almost never lived up to. He avoided disappointment by drawing a firm distinction between hope and expectation. The stray cattle he and Homer jumped out of the cedar thickets were less numerous than he had hoped, and a great deal wilder. The ones they managed to gather represented a substantial investment in sweat, strain and blood, paid by themselves and their horses.

Frank had never seen cattle so completely reverted to nature. These had taken on the fleetness and man-fear of deer. There were bulls five and six years old, lifelong fugitives from iron and blade. There were first- and second-calf heifers never earmarked or branded. It was to these that Frank and Homer most often gave chase, for if they could be caught, claimed and driven to a more manageable range, there would be no question of ownership right. The older cows, those that wore brands, were usually easier to catch, but any claim would be tentative. As for the bulls, they had no cash value. Frank deemed them unworthy of the risk to man and horse. He harvested a few young ones for beef and for hides to cut into strips and braid into raw leather ropes.

When a cow or heifer was finally run to ground, it usually turned sullen, tongue lolling out, head shaking, offering fight. Usually, after she was branded, she was granted the dubious favor of a short tie rope, by which one of her legs would be drawn up out of all use or dignity and securely anchored by two or three firm wraps around her horns. No matter how strong her attachment to liberty, she exercised it poorly on three legs.

Two weeks of strenuous effort wore the horses to the bone and failed to profit the two partners by as many cattle as Frank thought the blood and labor to be worth. On one particularly poor day they netted just one heifer. They had to forfeit an unbranded cow that led them a twisting chase through a succession of thickets much of the afternoon, finally breaking her leg in a desperate effort to descend a stony bluff. Frank had no choice but to cut her throat.

Homer showed more patience than Frank thought the occasion justified. "Frank, I been wantin' to make a recommendation."

Shoulders heaving from heat and exertion, Frank loosened his cinch to let the brown horse breathe easier. He looked down at the wasted cow and offered up a few strong words he had sometimes found to offer pacification. "You've waited almighty long with your advice."

"I didn't figure you'd listen till you was sorely vexed and about to pop a gut. Looks like you're there."

Frank gritted his teeth. *If he gives me that grin, just once . . .*

Homer said, "We need some help."

Frank swore. "We got no money to hire anybody."

"We could offer them an equal share of what we catch."

"Workin' by ourselves, we keep *all* of it."

That damned grin broke through, as Frank had known it would. Homer said, "Yeah, count them. At this rate, a thousand days, a thousand cattle."

Like some of the cattle they had caught, Frank sulked, turning away and nursing his frustrations. He was scratched and bruised in forty places. His clothes hung in ribbons. He realized Homer was right, but to admit it would be to concede his own error. "Very well," he said finally. "If you're such a damned poor hand that you can't do for yourself . . ."

They took several days driving the cattle home, pushing them hard at first to wear down whatever inclinations they might still have to run, then slowing to let them fill on the late-summer grass. A few wild ones made much of the trip on three legs, the fourth tied up. By the time they reached the Clear Fork, they were chastened and tractable.

Sam Ballinger leisurely rode his tall bay horse through the newly arrived cattle scattered along the river. His leathered face was smiling as he reined up where Frank and Homer sat in the shade of the brush arbor that by now looked as if it would have to shelter the partners through winter. It was difficult, in late, hot August, to imagine how cold November would be.

Frank tried not to show how much he wanted Sam's help. "There's more down yonder where these come from. We thought you might want to go with us the next trip, you and maybe some of the Akins boys. It'd be share and share alike."

Sam rubbed a big hand through several days' growth of black and gray whiskers. "I'm cattle-poor already." But his gaze went back upriver to the scattered livestock.

Frank said, "Cattle-poor today may mean cattle-rich in times to come."

"I'd hate to leave the missus and the kids . . ." Sam kept looking at the cattle. "But, still . . ." He turned back, eagerness in his eyes. "When you figurin' to go?"

Frank shrugged. "Week, maybe. We need to recruit our horses a little first. Sure wish we had us some extra mounts." He thought of the wild ones he had seen on that scout with Beaver Red. Maybe in the winter, when there wasn't much else to do but sit around and cuss the cold . . .

Sam did not ponder long. "Come by when you're ready."

Frank and Homer did some gathering from their garden and shelled out dry corn to carry. They could parch it or pound it into coarse meal and make rough hoecakes. A man would not take on weight, but he could subsist.

When the necessities were met, Frank and Homer rode down to the Akins camp. A picket cabin was almost finished, though Naomi still cooked on an open campfire. Her face brightened at the sight of Homer, and Homer's grin was so broad Frank thought it must pain him.

Bige Akins showed an interest in Frank's proposition, but he was also concerned. "There's already about all the cattle this grass will support. Come winter, we'll have cows with their hipbones stickin' out like my elbow."

"There's room west of us," Frank argued. "Me and Homer, we're pushin' ours thataway, out past Sam Ballinger's. Seems like a shame for that good country to go to waste, nothin' on it but sometimes the buffalo."

Bige frowned. "There's a reason. That's Indian country."

Frank said, *"Everyplace* was Indian country once. Somebody'll lay claim to that land. It might as well be us."

Akins watched his daughter take dried clothing down

from a thin rope line. Homer helped her. "The price could be high."

"You ever see anything cheap that was worth the havin'?"

Like Sam, Akins decided quickly. "I'll take the two oldest. Luke and John had best abide, work on the house and watch out for their sister. Now, stay and eat with us, won't you?"

Frank nodded, pleased he had been able to persuade two men years older than himself, men of competence and good judgment.

The morning they were to start, Frank and Homer caught their horses before daylight. Their saddles carried a heavy load of freshly braided rawhide rope for catching and tying. They reached the Ballinger stone cabin just as the rising sun bathed it in brilliant orange. They helloed the house as a precaution before riding across the open space in front of it. Sam's gaunt frame appeared in the doorway. He laid his rifle back inside when he was sure of his company. "You-all come in to breakfast."

Frank saw a lad of sixteen or so, an orphan named Bobby Baxter who had hung around Davis, living with first one family and then another. He surmised that Sam had gotten him to come out and stay with his womenfolk.

Because Sam had turned hogs loose on the river, he and his family were blessed with pork and plenty of lard for cooking. Mrs. Ballinger and her daughters bustled about, feeding the men. Sam's small son Sammy pulled his short bench up to the table, proudly allowing the women to wait on him. Frank sensed that he had been begging his father to let him go.

Homer said, "Now, button, you eat all your fixin's so you'll grow fast. First thing you know you'll be takin' your daddy's place on these cow hunts."

"I want to go now," Sammy persisted. But he accepted with dry eyes when he saw it was not to be. Sam kissed his wife and hugged his two daughters. He picked up the boy and carried him outside, hugging him an extra time before he set him on the ground. "You're the man here till I get back. You watch out for your mother and sisters."

The boy nodded sadly. As the three men rode away, he walked after them, so far that it looked as if Sam might have to turn back and admonish him. The boy stopped and watched them go on.

Sam said, "I wish we could've had the boy first. I wish he was the oldest instead of the youngest."

Frank said, "If you're uneasy, maybe you better stay."

Sam shook his head. "Bobby'll be here. I been gone before."

The last time Frank looked back, the boy Sammy still watched.

Bige Akins waited at his brush corral, upward of midday. His four sons materialized quickly from around the camp. Bige shook hands with all three visitors. "Girl's about got dinner ready."

Naomi's outdoor kitchen had been hidden from view by her tent, which had a long canvas flap extending forward to shade the ax-carved table upon which she prepared the food. The cook fire was in the open, far enough that the flap did not trap smoke or catch sparks. She poked at burning wood beneath a blackened coffeepot. A pot of beans was set on a thin layer of coals and ashes to stay hot. Venison simmered in a skillet.

Homer busied himself fetching more wood for her, though she no longer needed it. Bige and Sam fell easily into conversation, while Bige's sons gathered close to listen. It pleased Frank that Sam and Bige seemed to have the same spontaneous liking for each other that Frank felt toward them; it bore out his own judgment.

The second roundup went faster and easier because six men were working instead of two. Watching the Akins boys, Frank learned things he had not known about handling cattle, especially roping them. The boys had grown up around Mexicans, who had brought their skills northward from below the Rio Grande. These Mexican styles of cow work had as yet made little impression in the northern sections of Texas, where stock handling was still modeled after methods brought in by small-herd settlers from the Deep South and the middle states. Good enough for farmstead cattle, these ways were hardly a match for longhorns reverted to the wild. Frank watched how the Akins boys formed loops in their rawhide ropes, how they swung them over their heads until the feel was right, then sailed them out to snare the runaways.

Though Frank would not have admitted it, he could see that Homer had been right about looking for help. The six found far more cattle and let few get away. In a week they had as many as they thought they could handle or the grass up on the Clear Fork could accommodate.

The only thing that bothered Frank on the trip was Homer. For the first time he could remember, Homer was silent for hours at a stretch. Several times Frank inquired after his health.

Homer said, "I just ain't got nothin' to talk about."

That had never stopped him before.

Frank felt relieved when Homer finally got through some nervous, silent lip-chewing and asked, "That girl Naomi—would you say she's got blue eyes, or gray?"

Frank could not remember.

Homer said, "Somewhere in between, I think they are."

Though they did not recognize it at the time, the first sign of trouble was a camp they came across on one of the southern tributaries to the Clear Fork. While the others paused to water and rest the cattle and horses, Frank rode up to a half-dugout to pay his respects. He wanted also to apologize for any damage the herd might have caused cutting across the corner of a garden, breaking down the dried cornstalks. He found unwashed plates on a rough table, the food dried to them. A coffeepot appeared to have boiled itself out over the fireplace. The ashes were gray and cold.

Folks left in a right smart of a hurry, he thought.

Approaching the Akins camp, Frank saw that the roof was nearly finished on the new picket cabin. Bige Akins drew his horse over beside Frank's. "Boys been makin' good time. I hope Naomi can cook us a meal inside. I'm tired of sand in my beans."

Like the other, the camp was awesomely quiet. Frank had not let the first one worry him, but now a foreboding came over him.

Bige called, his voice straining. "Naomi! Luke! John!"

Matthew Akins walked into the nearly finished cabin. He came out waving a piece of paper. Bige glanced at it, then gravely passed it to Frank.

It said, *Everybodys gone to Davis camp. Indiens.*

Frank tried to calm the anxiety he saw boiling up in the others.

"They'll be safe enough at Davis. We better turn the cattle loose and go see what's happened."

Sam said worriedly, "I better get on to my family."

Frank argued, "They'll be at Davis by now. Whoever warned the Akinses would've gone on and warned your folks."

They rode in a lope much of the way, against Frank's better judgment, for they might need to push the horses farther than just Davis. But he understood the fear that tugged at Bige and his sons, and he read much from Sam Ballinger's tightly drawn mouth. As the riders spurred down into sight of Davis, Frank could see many wagons there, many horses penned in the oak-log corrals. Rachal had been much on his mind, but the sight of such a gathering eased his concern. This was a safe haven.

Naomi Akins came running out to meet them at the bank of the river. Bige Akins was down from his horse before it stopped. He grabbed her in his arms. "Where's your brothers? Everybody all right?"

She nodded quickly. "They was, the last I seen of them. They went off with some others to give warnin' to any that hadn't heard. It was a big Comanche raidin' party, Pa. Killed some folks, taken a bunch of horses."

Sam was on the ground in an instant. He took the girl's thin shoulders with his big hands, frightening her. "Is my family here?"

She shook her head. "I don't know your family, Mr. Ballinger. There's been a lot of folks come."

Sam swung back upon his horse and began a circle of the compound, shouting his wife's name.

Frank saw Rachal hurrying out from her house, the baby in her arms. His heart came up into his throat. He looked for something in her eyes, but all he saw was fear. She glanced back over her shoulder at Sam Ballinger. She said excitedly, "Frank, Sam's family never has come in."

A coldness dropped over Frank. "Did anybody go for them?"

"George and a bunch of others."

Bige Akins rode hurriedly across the compound after Sam. Frank sat on his horse and looked at Rachal. He asked, "Everything all right with you?"

She nodded, tight-lipped. "Till this Indian business." The baby seemed fitful, perhaps sensing the excitement. She rocked it in her arms. "If you see George, tell him to please come home as soon as he can. We need him."

Frank blinked at a burning in his eyes; all these people were stirring a lot of dust. "I'll tell him."

Homer was standing with his hat off, talking to Naomi. As Sam and Bige came back in a long trot, Frank shouted, "Come on, Homer. We're ridin' to Sam's."

They crossed the river, and Sam set spurs to the bay horse. The others had a hard time staying up. The horses were flagging badly as the riders came to Frank and Homer's camp. A glance showed Frank they had had visitors. The arbor lay in blackened ruins, only a couple of posts still standing. Homer's eyes met Frank's. It was just as well they had not gotten around to putting up the cabin.

Sight of the charred wreckage brought a wild, cornered

look into Sam's eyes. He gave the place only a moment's attention, then used the spurs harder. Frank was half afraid the horse would not finish the trip, though he knew of no stronger on the Clear Fork.

In a while Frank began to see the roof of Sam's tall stone house above the timber. His first reaction was of relief, for he saw no damage. Several horses were in Sam's corral. Half a dozen men stood in front of the house.

Then Frank's heart began to sink, for he saw two men up the slope from the house, digging. Sam's shed had burned and fallen in. The house's front door had been smashed. Frank glanced at Homer and knew by the stricken expression that he had seen too. Frank could not bring himself to look at Sam.

George Valentine stood beside the door, his face grim.

Sam read it all in an instant; it was clear in the manner of the men who had come here ahead of him. He swung down from the saddle and made several quick strides toward the house. George hurried out and threw his arms around him.

"Sam, don't go in there. For God's sake, Sam . . ."

Sam pushed him aside and hurried into the building he had vowed would never burn. Dismounting slowly, not wanting to get down at all, Frank heard Sam's cry of anguish. He felt the hot rush of tears and wiped them with his sleeve.

The enmity between Frank and George was set aside, at least for this moment. George said, "His womenfolks are in there. The Indians surprised the Baxter boy out in the field. Things couldn't be no worse."

Sam's tall frame lurched into the doorway. His eyes were wide and wild. "My boy! Where's my boy?"

George turned quickly. He put his hands on Sam's quivering shoulders. In a breaking voice he said, "We've hunted, but all we've found was his hat. It was out yonder a way, on the trail the Indians made when they left here."

Homer said, "They taken the boy with them?"

George nodded. "Looks that way. They do that some-times."

Sam turned back to the cabin but did not go inside. He dropped to his knees at the doorway and broke into a cry like an animal mortally hurt. Homer turned away, took off his hat and bowed his head.

Frank put a hand on Sam's shoulder. He wanted to talk, but his throat was blocked, even if he had the words.

The younger Akins boys had been up on the slope, dig-ging. They came down and stood beside their father and the two older brothers. No words passed between them; none was necessary. Rusty Farraday was with them, quivering in shock.

Sam pushed to his feet, a stranger. In his eyes glowed a fearsome look Frank had seen in men at the battle on Dove Creek. He seemed to look through everyone. He said, al-most calmly, "I'm goin' after my boy."

Frank managed, "How long a start you reckon them Indians have got, George?"

George Valentine shook his head. "Most of a day, at least. This was the last place they hit before they went yonder." He pointed northwestward, toward the rolling plains.

Sam swung onto his lathered horse. Frank cautioned, "It's comin' on night. Let's rest the horses till first light."

Sam said sternly, "I've got to find my boy." He started off alone, not looking back to see if anyone followed.

Frank glanced around. "Homer?" Homer was already mounting his horse. So was George. Bige Akins told his two younger sons to go on with the burying, then hurry back to Davis and see to their sister. He looked at his other two. "You boys are old enough to decide for yourselves."

They glanced at each other. "We'll go with you," Mat-thew said.

Rusty Farraday hung back. "If you-all go out yonder, there won't a one of you ever come home. George, you ain't goin', are you?"

George was.

The trail was clear enough, in the beginning, and easily followed until darkness. No one had come prepared for this eventuality, so they had nothing to eat. Matthew and Mark rode into the timber about sundown. Frank heard a shot, and the boys were soon spurring to catch up. Matthew carried a young spike buck across his saddle. Frank would have preferred there be no shooting, but he reasoned that the Indians were too far to have heard. That night, in a dry camp, the men singed the venison over a fire hole gouged deeply into the earth to hide its flame from unfriendly eyes.

As first light touched the distant hills, Sam was saddling his bay horse. By the look of him Frank guessed he had not slept. Frank had slept little himself, for he had kept seeing that boy standing alone, watching them ride away. A hundred times during the night he wished he had never suggested the cow hunt, had never encouraged Sam to leave his family. Perhaps Sam's presence at home might have made the difference. But probably not. Frank knew it probably would only have meant he would be dead now with his wife and daughters.

Sometime in mid-morning the tracks became more difficult to follow. Partly it was the terrain, a harder ground that stubbornly hid its secrets. And partly it was, Frank realized, that they had lost some of the Indians. Somewhere, somehow, a party had broken off. Now it was anyone's guess which group had Sam's boy. Frank looked into Sam's eyes and saw the torment of decision. Sam stolidly set out following the tracks that he could see. The others trailed silently.

It became evident as morning wore on that Sam was not a good tracker. He was a farmer and a stockman; trailing men was not part of his natural element. At times he lost the tracks and had to circle back to pick them up. Usually Frank found them first. After a time Frank was riding beside Sam, helping him hold to the trail. He remembered things Beaver Red had taught him and wished he had listened more carefully to the rest.

Sam would not stop for the sake of the men, but he was forced to consider the horses. They reached a creek where Indian sign was strong, though evidently hours old, and Sam called a short halt to rest the mounts. That gave the men a chance to roast more of Matthew's deer. Frank crossed the creek to examine the tracks. Fewer horses had come out on the north side than had entered on the south.

Sam showed no change of expression when Frank told him. His face was blank, but his eyes smoldered with a wild light. He pointed his chin upstream, then got on his bay horse and started in the opposite direction. Frank rode against the current, watching the north bank for evidence of horses leaving the water. Homer came after him. Frank said, "Go back. Your horse needs a rest."

"He's as strong as yours."

Frank did not argue. Together they rode two miles, three. Not a sign did they see, though they found several places where the banks were gravelly enough to have let horsemen ride out without making tracks. At each such place Frank would make a wide circle to the north, hoping to cut some sign.

He wanted to weep. "I'm not good enough, Homer. I'm just not good enough."

Sam had returned ahead of him. He did not speak, but his eyes told Frank he had done no better. He chewed on half-cooked venison, his brooding gaze fixed across the creek. When he pushed to his feet and wiped greasy fingers on his trousers, George said regretfully, "Sam, our horses are done in. Even if we found the Indians, there just ain't enough of us."

Sam broke a long silence. His voice was solemn and without rancor. "You're right. Go back. You'd just as well *all* go back." He swung into the saddle and spurred the bay horse across the creek, pointing him northwestward along the diminishing trail. George and three others remained behind as Frank, Homer and three Akinses followed Sam. Frank looked back once, resenting them for Sam, because Sam would not.

All afternoon they rode, the trail dimming. At times it disappeared, and they would lose half an hour before Frank or Sam found it again. The timber was well behind them. They were into the rolling plains, into a land none of them knew. The prairie seemed to swell and fall in successive waves until, far in the distance, heat melded the horizon into a brassy sky. Frank turned in the saddle from time to time, looking for landmarks that might guide their return. He saw none, for each mile was like the one ahead and the one behind. They rode through curing grass a foot tall to stirrup high.

Somewhere, far yonder, lay the broad valley that had haunted Frank since the day he had found it, that had called to him ever since he had turned his back upon it and ridden away.

Sam ignored any suggestion that they stop and rest, that the horses were tired. He looked at no one, not even Frank, who rode beside him much of the time. His eyes were on the trail, or on the distant rising ground. Not until dark did he stop, and then only with bleak reluctance.

There was no question of building a fire, and no reason to do so. The venison was gone. No one had coffee. Frank felt a stirring of hunger, a thing he could usually put aside.

Sam sat apart, staring northward into the night. Hesitantly Frank squatted beside him. "You got any kind of a plan, Sam?"

Sam shook his head. He did not otherwise answer.

"If we ride up on them Indians, they're apt to kill the boy first thing. Then us, more than likely."

Sam's shoulders trembled. "I been a sinful man at times, Frank. But why couldn't He of just punished *me*? Why did He put it on my family?" He began to weep.

Sam was an older, wiser man. Frank felt helpless to do or say anything that would comfort him.

"God has got nothin' to punish you for. You're a good man, Sam Ballinger, as good as walks. It's just a thing that happened."

He could only sit and watch Sam tear himself apart. At length Frank said, "You try to get some sleep, Sam. The rest of us'll take the guard duty."

Sam shook his head solemnly. "*I'll* take the first tour. You-all get yourselves some rest."

Frank knew argument was useless. "You wake me, then, when you're ready to be spelled."

Much later he awoke with a start, rising and looking around him in the moonlit camp. His first thought was that Sam might have gone to sleep. He could see the horses; each man had picketed his own where he slept. Relief washed over him as he realized the camp had not been violated.

"Sam," he said quietly. "Sam, where you at?"

No answer came. Frank made a quick circle. A gnawing uneasiness turned to certainty. He counted the horses. Five. Sam's big bay was gone.

Frank stood frozen, realizing gradually that he could do nothing. He decided against waking the others. He had just as well let them finish a needed night's rest. He sat in the grass, arms braced around his knees, and wept silently for an old friend gone.

When daylight came, Homer and Bige Akins discussed the possibility of following Sam's trail.

Frank shook his head. "He don't want to be found. He figures it's his search, not ours."

Homer argued, "He's just one man. What can he do?"

Frank shrugged. "What could six of us do?"

He tarried longer than necessary about saddling up and turning south. Taking a long chance of being seen by hostile eyes, he rode up on a tall swell on the prairie and stood in his stirrups, searching the long miles that stretched before him. Far to the northwest the morning sun struck an illusion of gold upon a distant line of hills. He saw no sign that men had passed this way; not recently, not ever. The prairie was awesome in its size, its openness, its appearance of emptiness. A thousand men could lose themselves upon the vastness of it. He knew he would never find one man, if that man did not want to be found. A dark and heavy sadness descended upon him as he tugged the reins and brought the brown horse down from the little hill. He pointed him in the direction of the Clear Fork.

Homer pulled in beside him. The others took places behind.

Homer asked, "You reckon we'll ever see Sam again?"

Frank had no answer.

6

Claymore's attorney Anderson Avery frowned as he listened to Farraday recount his first meeting with Frank Claymore. He leaned toward Claymore with a tone of reproach. "I wish I had known about this incident beforehand. You should have told me."

Claymore's jaw jutted forward. When he was paying a man, he should not have to accept criticism from him. "Never thought of it. What happened that day didn't seem all that much at the time. Seems like a lot less now, thinkin' back on it."

"The jury may not agree with you."

"They wasn't there."

Prosecutor Mallard was asking Farraday, "Now, sir, you chose not to accompany the defendant and George Valentine and the others on the search for Mr. Ballinger's son. Would you please tell us why?"

Farraday looked at the floor. "Seemed like a real good chance to get slaughtered by the Indians." He glanced across at Claymore, then looked back at the floor. "Besides, I didn't want to go nowhere with Frank Claymore. I figured he was as apt to kill me as the Indians was."

The defense attorney jumped to his feet. "I object. That is malicious speculation on the witness's part, totally without substance. Mr. Claymore's motives on that expedition were humanitarian. I submit that he would have welcomed the help of Mr. Farraday, and any and all others who would have volunteered. I submit that Mr. Farraday's reason for not

going was cowardice—his terror of the Indians and nothing else."

The prosecutor voiced his objections, and the ensuing argument took up several minutes, during which Farraday
sat fidgeting, fearful and confused, glancing apprehensively
at Claymore but looking away when their eyes met. Claymore watched him without sympathy. If Rusty Farraday had
not been the direct cause of many problems over the years,
he had at least been instrumental in them. Claymore
clenched his fist.

I'll bet he could tell what happened to that gun.

The judge attempted to put half the room between the two
attorneys. It looked almost as if they were coming to blows,
but Claymore knew the incident was a show to impress the
jury. Come tonight the two worthies would probably meet
in a bar or a hotel room and enjoy drinks together. At least
in the old days when two men had a fight they set out to
draw blood, not to draw a crowd.

Even Rusty Farraday had more bottom to him than
that.

When he wearied of the contest between the attorneys,
Claymore let his attention wander to three city newspaper
reporters who sat together at a long table, scribbling at a clip
that he thought must eventually wear away the flesh and
leave only the bone to show for their fingers. He knew they
had roasted him daily in their dispatches, for he had seen
some in print and had heard about others.

One reporter troubled him. He was heavy-jowled, hair
gray and wild, where he had any hair left. He wore heavy-
rimmed glasses and had a complexion not unlike Rusty
Farraday's, leading Claymore to speculate upon the proba-
bilities of a misspent life. Something about him looked
vaguely familiar. That worried Claymore, for he knew no
reason he should have met such a man. He had had little
truck with reporters, and wanted none.

The attorneys finished their jousting with one another.
The prosecutor turned back to the sweating witness. "Now,

Mr. Farraday, I presume you comprehend the meaning of cross-examination?"

Farraday blinked. It was evident he did not understand altogether, but he was reluctant to admit ignorance. "Yes, sir."

"When I have finished questioning you, the right honorable defense attorney, Mr. Avery, will endeavor to compromise your credibility, to diminish the jury's acceptance of your testimony."

Farraday asked, "He'll try to make a liar out of me?"

"Precisely. He will also attempt to persuade the jury that the actions and attitudes of Mr. Claymore in those early times were no more extreme, no more contentious, than those of others under like circumstances."

"Oh, he was contemptuous, all right. Them days he never looked back for nobody. Still don't, for that matter." Farraday tried to look at Claymore but could not keep his nervous, whiskey-reddened eyes still. "Only difference in him then and now is that he walks slower. If he finds a man down, he still goes out of his way to give him the toe of his boot."

Claymore declared, "I never gave you the toe of my boot, Rusty. Many a time I should've."

The defense attorney pulled at Claymore's sleeve. "Please. We'll have our chance at him eventually."

"I'm just thinkin' of the chances I already had at him and didn't take."

The prosecutor smiled, for Claymore so far was perhaps the best witness he had. "Now, Mr. Farraday, you are a state's witness, under protection of this court. You need not fear Frank Claymore."

"Not here, maybe, but later."

"There will be no *later*. It is the purpose of these proceedings to see that he never again is allowed to trample on justice, to victimize those weaker than himself."

Claymore's attorney rose to object, then changed his mind and began to scribble notes on a pad.

Farraday mumbled defensively, "He ain't no better than

me. Never was. I always been a poor workin' man, tryin' hard to get ahead. Claymore was forever comin' along about the time I was fixin' to climb up out of the hole, and pushin' me back in. A dark and angry man, he always was. Pity the Indians didn't kill him. A lot of people in this country would've had more than they've got today. And one more good man would still be alive . . ."

The sight of the Ballinger roof high beyond the timber brought back a brooding darkness that had ridden with Frank most of the way down from the rolling plains. The place had the quiet of a graveyard. The men who had done the grim job of burial had returned eastward to their own families in the heavier-settled country. Frank saw four crude wooden crosses on the slope, but he did not ride up there. He looked at the smashed front door.

"We'll come back and fix that, Homer, so cattle won't get into Sam's house."

Looking toward the graves, Homer replied, "Sure, Frank." His tone said what he would not put into words: it would be for nothing. He asked, "What about Sam's herd?"

"We'll take care of them till he gets back."

Homer did not speak his thought, but it was clear enough.

They talked little, riding downriver. Even Homer held his silence. In a while they came to their own camp. Frank gazed bleakly at the charred remains.

Bige said, "Winter'll be on us before you know it. Me and the boys'll help you put up a cabin."

Frank shook his head. "You got your own work to do. Me and Homer can scratch a dugout into the hillside. It'll keep us warm of a night." He expected to spend little daylight time in it.

Bige seemed hesitant. "You could use Sam's cabin. I think he'd want you to."

Frank sternly rejected the suggestion. "He'll need that when he comes back. A dugout'll do us fine."

The two younger Akins boys and Naomi waited anxiously in front of their new picket cabin, the cedar stakes naked where an ax had shaved off the rough brown bark. The riders trooped in, shoulders drooped, beards gray with dust. Bige dismounted heavily and hugged his daughter. Homer watched, not taking his eyes from the girl.

Naomi seemed to read the story in the men's weary faces. "You didn't find the boy."

Bige said, "No." He glanced up at Frank, still in the saddle. "We lost his daddy too." He responded to Frank's silent argument. "You'd just as well make up your mind to it, Frank. He's gone."

Frank looked off into the distance. "Sam's the nearest thing I've had to a father. He'll be back; I can feel it." He realized his voice sounded angry. He had not intended that. Naomi stared at him with faint resentment. He had observed her strong protective attitude toward those she cared for. He felt he should apologize to her, but he said nothing.

He saw how her eyes softened when she turned to Homer. "Hello, Mr. Whitcomb. I expect you're hungry."

Homer gladly admitted that he was near starvation.

As Frank dismounted, his failing knees told him how exhausted he was. He leaned heavily against the brown horse. A sharp pain ripped his stomach. It had been there in a petty, nagging way for days, but he had forced himself to ignore it. Now it was too strong to ignore. He turned his face away so no one would see.

Homer saw, nevertheless. "It's my fault, Frank. If I hadn't been so clumsy pullin' that arrow out, maybe I'd of got it all."

Frank shrugged. "It was my fault for bein' where I was."

He was too sick to his stomach to eat. He watched Homer fill his plate three times with venison and beans and corn bread, lauding Naomi's skill at the hearth. She cooked in the new stone fireplace, pots suspended from an iron bar or set on coals and hot ashes.

Bige remarked that Frank did not look well. He had

known little of Frank's trouble, but Homer obligingly told him all he probably wanted to know, and more.

Naomi stared unflinchingly at Frank. "Is that what makes you so irritable all the time, Mr. Claymore?"

Bige protested, "Daughter . . ."

She offered no apology. "A smile wouldn't do your face no permanent harm, Mr. Claymore. Try it sometime."

Frank would have tried smiling for her if he felt better. He got up from the rough bench and walked out into the crisp night air of autumn. He leaned against the uncured oak pickets of the cabin wall and pressed his hand to his stomach.

The Akins girl reminded him uncomfortably of Captain Zachary's daughter Letty. There wasn't three cents' worth of good manners in either of them.

He felt guilty about letting Homer do the heavy pick and shovel work in constructing the dugout. Frank tried but had to confine himself to dragging up oak timbers with the brown horse. He paid a penance of sorts because he was a captive audience as Homer explained in full detail the intricacies of building a dugout, though this was his first. When the job was finished Frank admitted to himself, though not to Homer, that it was a good piece of work. Homer had the ridge pole solidly supported. The front wall of pickets, extending beyond the side of the hill, looked sturdy enough to outlast them both.

Its being on the hill's lee side protected it from the force of the season's first blue norther. A small blaze in the mud-and-stone fireplace kept the tiny room warm if not very cheery. For a window Homer had contrived a small door on rawhide hinges, just large enough to let in some light or, if worse came to worst, serve as a rifle port.

On bad days Frank rested in the dugout. On prettier days he did whatever light outside work his busy imagination could come up with. When Homer was away seeing after the cattle, Frank repaired the corrals, rebuilt the fence around the garden and rigged a little platform over the edge of the river so he could dip a bucket into deep, clear water without getting his feet wet. Homer constantly lectured him about his need for rest, to pacify the arrowhead. Frank ignored the lectures.

Winter's cold brought chilling rains and occasionally snow. Cattle ribs showed through rough hair dulled by stress and hunger. Homer kept pushing the cattle farther west, onto grass no one had claimed. Homer protested, but Frank began going with him, bundled against the raw, cold wind.

Winter passed, and with it Frank's pain. He supposed the arrowhead had finally lodged and had again taken on a protective padding of some kind. He was able to ride the brown horse formidable distances.

"Homer," he said, "we need some more horses."

"Horses cost money. We ain't seen a dollar since the war."

"There's wild horses up on the plains. Comin' out of the winter they'll be weak. Our horses been eatin' corn."

Homer's face was always a mirror of his mind, and it was saying no. But he recognized the futility of arguing with Frank. "We'll need help."

Because it was yet too cold for spring planting, and because Frank argued that the hunt might yield strong horses trainable to wagon or plow, Bige Akins consented to let Matthew and Mark accompany Frank and Homer. He cautioned, "Ain't no horses worth as much as my boys. Any sign of Indians, you-all hightail it home, you hear me?"

Naomi Akins was not inclined to hide her feelings about anything. She told Frank distrustfully, "It's dangerous out there, and you're takin' my brothers."

Frank sensed that she would not be cowed, and he knew denial would settle nothing, so he kept his mouth shut.

Homer put in, "I'll watch out for your brothers."

She turned to Homer with a look part anger, part anxiety. "And who'll watch out for *you*, Mr. Whitcomb?" She looked at Frank again, setting her belligerence aside.

"Please, Mr. Claymore, you take care of my brothers. And my Mr. Whitcomb."

My Mr. Whitcomb. Frank nodded solemnly, feeling somehow empty, somehow left out. No woman worried about him that way.

The four riders led one extra horse, upon which they packed such meager supplies as they had and a generous quantity of rawhide ropes and hobbles. As soon as they were out of their sister's hearing, Matthew and Mark began singing a raucous ditty of which she would not have approved, and that might have been embarrassing if they had had to explain where they had learned it.

Frank had little use for that kind of frivolity. It had been discouraged in his family, both by the elder brothers who set the tone and by the poverty that allowed little time or attention to anything beyond survival.

The younger, Mark, was by all odds the better rope hand. Where Frank had spent his boyhood, few knew how to cast a loop and catch an animal at some distance. Most men simply tried to get up next to their quarry and slip a noose around its neck, sometimes no easy matter. Frank watched intently as Mark shook a loop into a rawhide reata, swung it almost lazily and sailed it over a clump of bunchgrass. He was too reticent to ask the boy how he did it, but Homer was not. As the miles passed beneath the horses' feet, Homer practiced. He had always had manual dexterity. He caught on quickly.

Matthew asked Frank, "Why don't you try it?"

Frank shook his head. He knew he would miss, and he did not want to appear inadequate against two boys much younger than himself. But he watched Mark's style and resolved that when he was alone, where his dignity would not be compromised, he would learn the method.

Once they left the scrub timber and ventured upon the rolling plains, Frank had to rely upon memory and his instinct for direction. Every so often he looked back for anything that might guide their return, but one dip in the horizon

looked like another. At a different time of day, in different
light and shadow, it would not appear the same. Used to being closed in by hills and timber, he felt a renewal of the
awe these open plains had brought him before. He felt exposed, vulnerable. Yet he felt an intoxicating liberty, a par-
adox he accepted but could not understand.

Frank had never caught a mustang. He had helped break
young horses to saddle or plow, but those had been farm
raised and tractable, not mustangs following the stormy instincts that came from generations of wild blood. He asked
Matthew and Mark, "You-all ever gone mustangin' before?"

Matthew said, "Nope. We're figurin' on you teachin' us."

Frank nodded as if it were nothing new to him and began trying to devise a strategy. He saw no purpose in un-
dermining the other men's confidence by admitting his lack
of experience.

He was aware that mustang hunters in the lower country
built strong brush corrals at or near the water and tricked
the horses into them, but on the plains a man was lucky to
find wood enough to boil his coffee.

They came, in time, upon fresh horse tracks. Frank's first
thought, voiced quickly by the others, was that they might
have been left by Indians. Recalling what Beaver had told
him, Frank soon decided they had been made by mustangs,
grazing casually. The winter-dry prairie grass was so brittle that its stems broke beneath the cutting hoofs and drifted
on the wind. Rain had been scarce. Frank had not seen even
a buffalo wallow holding recently caught water. The mustangs had to go to a living spring or seep to drink.

He recognized the little stand of mesquite trees clustered
around the seep. Mud at the edge was pocked with horse
and buffalo tracks, locked into semipermanence as runoff
water from fall rains had gradually dried out and the depression was reduced to the output of the slow seep.

"Look for moccasin prints," he warned.

The Akins boys were dismayed by the water's gyppy
taste. Frank said, "Time we've been here a week it'll taste

like mother's milk." It came to him that the words were Beaver's, and he felt a fleeting moment of sadness. "You-all unload the packhorse. I'll make a circle."

He rode out from the seep a mile or so, then began a long arc, watching tracks. He almost rode upon a small bunch of wild horses before his brown pointed its ears forward. Alerted, Frank leaned low to present less profile. He was met by a bay stallion with a stringy black mane and a bushed-out tail that dragged the short grass. Trailing were fifteen or eighteen mares, mostly the same color, many followed by colts from newly born to weaned yearlings not yet kicked out of the band. Frank expected them to run but realized he was downwind. He edged down on the off side of his horse, left leg over the saddle Indian-style as he peered at the mustangs from under the brown's neck. The stallion pranced, head high, nickering a challenge. He was perhaps twenty yards away when he seemed suddenly to realize something wasn't right. He snorted. The trailing mares turned and broke into a run, the colts struggling to keep up. The stallion remained behind them, in their dust, head and tail high as he bent his neck at intervals to see if Frank was in pursuit. Gradually the horses made a wide circle in the general direction of the water hole.

Frank formed the beginnings of a plan. He told the others, "We'll camp here and keep them off of the water. In two-three days they'll be thirsty enough to come up close."

Mark said, "That's cruel."

Frank said, "If they're dried out, the chase'll be shorter."

As in the Ranger service, he found it tiresome to idle around camp. He felt content only when he could watch the wild horses on the prairie, trailing in toward water, stopping short and testing the wind. Always as they scented or saw the men, they would break away in a run. After a little they would circle half around and stop, strung out in a line. Sometimes they would run again. Other times, especially as want of water weakened them, they would make a wide arc, remaining in distant sight, reluctant to leave. By the third day they were coming closer before turning back in frustration.

Had Frank ever known any professional mustangers he might have been better prepared, but he was reasoning out his plan as he went along, based on what he knew about the general nature of horses. He had identified three sets of mares, each led by a mature stallion. In addition came stragglers, mostly young stallions ranging from big colts to two- and three-year-olds, driven out of the bands in which they had been foaled and not yet old enough or aggressive enough to stand their own against the harem keepers. They tended to follow the mare bands at a respectful distance, out of harm's way.

These, Frank reasoned, were the most likely to be useful.

The fourth day the men had their mounts saddled and waiting as the first band ventured up, their need for water beginning to outweigh their natural fear of the man smell.

"We'll get them to circlin' the water," Frank said. "We'll run them in relays till they get good and tired. Homer and me'll take them first, then you boys come out and spell us so we can water and rest our horses. We'll run them spraddle-legged before ever we put a rope on them."

Nearing the first band, Frank spurred into a lope. The stallion snorted an alarm. The mares broke to running. Four big stud colts had trailed like orphans but joined the others in flight, fearing the horsemen more than they feared the old stallion. The rushing wind burned Frank's eyes. He pulled his hat down snugly against his ears to keep from losing it. Fear reached for him as he realized what might happen if the brown stumbled. But this fear gave way to a wild exhilaration at the speed, at the excitement of the chase. He worked to the outside and turned the horses slowly. The water hole lay a mile or so toward the center of the circle the horses were making. Homer shouted, waving a coiled rawhide rope.

Before the first big circle had been completed, some of the mares with young colts were dropping behind. Frank signaled Homer to let them go. He had no wish to run colts to death.

The brown horse was lathering when the Akins boys angled across to take up positions. Frank and Homer dropped back to let the horses run free of them, then turned toward the water hole to make sure none of the other bands drank. Breathing heavily, Homer wiped his sleeve across his face, streaking sweat and dust. He grinned. "A feller could get to enjoyin' that."

Though he had the same feeling, Frank replied soberly, "We didn't come here for fun."

He had always gone by the theory that if a man enjoyed his work he probably was not doing it right.

Homer regained his breath and began to talk excitedly about the horses, giving his appraisal of their individual prospects. It bothered Frank that Homer had observed them more closely than he had. Homer might exercise his jaw too much, but he kept his eyes open.

By the time the wild bunch had finished the wide circle, the four young studs were in the lead, the mares and colts flagging badly. The big stallion remained behind, trying always to put himself between the band and the riders. Frank and Homer rode out and fell into an easy lope beside Matthew and Mark. The young men were enjoying themselves. Frank took that for a bad sign.

He asked, "You-all think your horses have got it in them to go in there and pick up one of them big colts?"

Yelping, Mark spurred out and sailed a rawhide loop around a young bay stallion. He slowed gradually, avoiding a sudden impact that might snap the rope. The big two-year-old plunged and pitched, fighting feverishly against the frightening unseen thing that had snared him. "Matthew," Frank said, "you stay with your brother. You may have to heel that colt and throw him down."

Frank nodded at Homer. They hazed a colt out to the edge, away from the rest. "Now, Homer, try your hand."

Homer missed the first loop. Frank was tempted to try

but did not want the others to see him miss. Homer rebuilt a loop that turned into a figure eight and lay across the colt's neck and ears. Just when Frank thought it would fall away, Homer managed to flip it a little and manuever it over the head.

The more the colt fought, the tighter the rawhide bound its windpipe. A terrible wheezing came from its mouth and nostrils as it labored desperately for breath. Frank felt compassion, but he told the alarmed Homer, "He'll go to the ground pretty soon. We'll hobble him and let up on the rope."

It took longer than he expected for the frightened, oxygen-starved colt to collapse. As soon as the horse was on the ground, Frank ran forward with a short length of rawhide. He looped an end around one forefoot, then caught the other forefoot and wrapped the rope around it, tying a firm knot while he dodged the colt's efforts at pawing him.

"You watch out there," Homer shouted. "You'll lose a mouthful of teeth, and maybe stir up that arrowhead again."

When the hobbles were tied, Frank threw himself upon the colt's neck and called for slack. He loosened the loop that had choked the animal, drew a half hitch to prevent its tightening again, then threw a coil around the nose.

The young horse heaved, eyes wide and frightened as it began to refill its lungs. It made another run against the rope, and Homer came near losing it before he managed a double wrap around his saddle horn. Matthew and Mark came along shortly with their catch, its forefeet hobbled in the same manner. It plunged and fought against a rope tied around its neck, firmly but with enough slack to allow breathing.

"Well," Homer said, "we got them. Now what we goin' to do with them?"

Frank replied, "Stake them to mesquite trees at the water hole till they learn who the boss is."

Homer shook his head. "*I* ain't sure who the boss is."

The four men rode out once more in pursuit of the band

and, shortly before sundown, returned with the other two young stallions. These they tied like the first, giving them only a few feet of rope to run against, lessening the likelihood of their breaking the rawhide and getting away. They repeated the process the next day, running another band, picking up six more.

Frank was skeptical about the look of the mustangs. He was used to higher-bred stock.

Matthew Akins said, "They ain't much for pretty, but they're hell for stout. Folks used them a lot where we come from."

Mark said eagerly, "I'm sure anxious to throw a saddle on these."

Frank frowned. The newest broncs still gave fight to the rawhide ropes that held them within pawing distance of the mesquites. "Your daddy might not like it. Wait till we get home and he says it's all right."

He was not eager to break the horses out here on the prairie any more than was necessary to get them back to the settlement. The initial problem was to teach them to lead or be driven.

Days, he was too busy to let his mind wander beyond the work at hand. Nights, he had leisure to remember. Sometimes when the wind came gentle from the northwest he would walk out into the darkness and stand with the breeze touching his face. He imagined it was coming from the valley he had seen with Homer and Beaver. His skin would itch with an urge to go.

There came a day, when they had about twenty young horses snubbed to the squatty timber, that he decided to act upon the growing compulsion. As the four men bent over a thin breakfast of venison and gyp-water biscuits, Frank said, "You-all keep pullin' the horses around, teachin' them to lead. I'm takin' my leave for a little while."

Homer frowned. "I've felt this comin' on like a bad cold. You think we ought to be goin', Frank?"

"*We* ain't. Just me. You stay and help the boys."

Homer's frown deepened. "You don't know what's up there."

"My valley's up there." Frank gave Homer no time to raise a stronger argument. He cut his breakfast short and saddled the brown horse. He took a little bread and venison in a sack. "I'll be back by tomorrow night."

Homer's eyes were narrowed. "And if you ain't?"

"Then get yourselves home in a hurry."

He looked back once before he lost sight of the camp. Each of the Akins boys had his own horse saddled and was leading a bronc at the end of a heavy rawhide rope. The mustangs still fought, but they would lose.

Frank raised up in the stirrups and tested the wind. The valley's call was there, like a woman. No, stronger than a woman. Stronger even than Rachal had ever been.

Rachal. Times he had been able to put her out of his conscious thoughts for hours at a stretch, but always at some unguarded moment she would be there, she and that baby, like an unexpected shout in the night, startling him at first, then leaving him with that haunting pain of loss.

He saw no landmarks, but some inner sense told him he was following the same track he had made with Homer and Beaver Red, riding over the same rolling hills, dropping into the same little swales and tiny valleys where floodwaters occasionally ran when it remembered to rain. He knew he and the brown horse were slowly climbing, though the ascent was not evident to the eye. He came upon buffalo grazing in an old watercourse where last year's remnant of bunchgrass had begun a tentative greening at the base, though the nights were yet chilly enough to impede its growth. The buffalo flushed like quail. They were scarcely more startled than Frank or the horse. He lectured himself on vigilance. They could as easily have been Indians.

His excitement built. It was an effort not to spur the brown to more speed than endurance might properly tolerate.

Ahead, he saw the distant flat-topped hills. He crossed the gullied land and came to the little creek of the red-sand bottom and the sparkling white crystals of gypsum. The brown horse nosed the water and seemed reluctant.

"Wait," Frank said. "There's better water ahead."

The brown ignored his advice and drank, though sparingly.

He came upon more buffalo, the herds small and dispersed. In places they had eaten the grass almost to the ground. In others they had let it grow rank and tall until it was unpalatable, and allowed it to waste. Frank reflected that they had some human perversities.

He came finally to a long slope he believed would lead him up to the east rim of the valley. He spurred the brown into a fast trot though the climb was taxing. He broke out into the open and felt the battering force of the north wind.

There it lay as he had carried it with him so long . . . his valley.

Shouting with the joy of rediscovery, he gazed across the wide floor at the expanse of grass reawakening to spring's first warm promise. He had harbored a nagging fear that it would not be as he had remembered it, that he would be somehow disappointed. That fear had been for nothing. The valley was just as he wanted it to be, untouched, unspoiled.

He sat a long time, letting his gaze slowly sweep from as far south as he could see, upward past the tall point of rocks—the Indians' medicine hill—on the opposite side, then northward to a place where the river and the valley made a long bend and were lost to sight. He was startled to see what he first took to be a dwelling. A quick anger arose at the thought that someone might have beaten him here to claim a prior right. He pulled back the skin at the edges of his eyes to sharpen his sight. He made out finally that what he had seen was but shadow lying in a shallow wash. He gave a long sigh of relief.

It was awhile before he sobered enough to realize how

visible he must be to anyone down in the valley. He saw no sign of human activity, however. The buffalo grazed peacefully. He became aware of distant gray forms skulking through the winter-brown grass. The buffalo had their constant grim companions, the lobo wolves, watching always for a chance to pull down a calf or a cripple or an old one unable to defend itself. He reached for his rifle before he thought better of it. Even if he killed a wolf or two, it would change nothing. Nature provided each being for a purpose of its own. She would send more wolves to replace any he eliminated. Powder and lead were too hard to come by to waste them trying to foil nature.

But when he brought his cattle up here someday, certain things would have to change. He must eliminate the wolves lest they prey on his calves. Even the buffalo would have to be driven out because they would compete for grass his cattle needed. He reasoned that compromise had to be accepted. Nature must not stand in the way of man's needs. But he promised himself he would preserve what counted. He would keep what truly belonged—except for the wolves, and the buffalo, and perhaps certain other varmints. The valley would remain as he saw it today . . . except those things he had to change.

After one more long and careful look, he eased the horse down a buffalo trail that led to the valley floor. He considered riding directly to the medicine hill on the far side but elected to quarter northward and investigate the upper region he had not been given time to explore on the earlier visit. This time no one was pushing him. His stomach complained, but he had more urgent interests than hunger.

He took particular notice of the grass. Though spring had barely begun, he thought the heavy clumps showed more green at the base than he had seen on the higher ground. The high walls protected the valley to some degree, blunting the winter winds. That would explain the concentration of buffalo. Whatever was good for buffalo must also be good for cattle.

He let the horse water at the clear-running creek and paused to slake his own thirst, unnoticed until he saw and heard the whispering water and remembered how good it had been. He rode upstream, noting the varying width of the floodplain, watching always for a place where he might someday build his headquarters. His heartbeat quickened as he found where the creek bent back almost to the west wall. There large cottonwood trees laid their shade across the edge of the water, afternoon sun glistening through the first pale leaves of spring. The great branches, swaying gently, seemed to beckon him. An old memory came unbidden—a vision of his mother calling him to supper.

He had a strange sensation of coming home.

Before he even reached the trees, he chose the site for the main house, the bunkhouse, for the barns and corrals. In his mind's eye he had already built them. He could see his cattle milling and bawling in dusty pens and scattered across the valley in numbers as great as the buffalo. He rode through the trees and thought how restful it would be to sit beneath them in the cool of evening when a day's work was done, listening to a benign wind exploring their leaves, to the music of the water that was life to the valley.

Southward, he could see the distant hill standing like a sentinel. Yet from this peaceful grove he perceived that it was somehow out of place, out of time, a lone remnant of an earlier age, dying gradually with each rain that brought a little of its substance down from the heights and spread it across the grass. Frank reasoned that the valley had been created in this way, from the slow, measured destruction of the high walls. Nothing in nature was immune to change, not even the mountains.

He gave in to the insistence of hunger and ate from the cold bread and venison. He staked the horse to let it graze while he walked out the area adjacent to the cottonwoods, measuring in long strides the dimensions of the barn he would someday build, the working corrals for handling his cattle. He wasted no time upon the house site, for that interested him little. A house was simply a place to sleep. The time that mattered would be spent outdoors.

Indians were always in the back of his mind, but when they appeared they were a surprise. Riding toward the medicine hill, intending to survey the valley again from that great vantage, he saw them as they moved up out of a gully, four riders perhaps three hundred yards away. His hair bristled.

The Indians stopped, as startled as Frank. His breath came short. He brought his rifle up from its scabbard, but he was not strongly tempted to try it at this distance. That their intentions would be hostile he had not the slightest doubt, but he was not sure of his marksmanship. He did not want to waste powder and lead that might be put to more effective use at closer range.

The brown horse nickered, wanting to join the others. Frank reflected darkly on the intelligence of horses.

From the violent motions of the Indians' hands, Frank surmised that they were arguing. At length one rode northward up the valley, looking back over his shoulder as if sent against his will. The other three moved toward Frank, their mounts held to a walk. He sensed that the fourth had been dispatched to fetch help, probably on the suspicion that Frank was not in the valley alone. These three would stalk him.

Frank glanced quickly at the far side of the valley. He put down an impulse to spur the brown into a run. There would be time enough for running, and he would save the horse's strength for it. With luck he might make a good shot and reduce the odds. Damned if three Indians were going to chase him out of his valley like a thief. He turned the brown southward, holding to the same gentle trot that had brought him this far. The Indians moved to the same pace, not trying to close the gap.

As he watched them over his shoulder, his mind forced him back to the fight on Dove Creek. He remembered the deafening shots, the screams, the smell of powder, the numbing fear. He had made up his mind long ago never to give himself to that kind of fear again. He held it down but could not put it away.

He came to a small stand of hackberry trees and waited for the riders to come up within good range. If he could put them out of action, he should be able to leave the valley before the fourth man returned with help. But the Indians disappointed him by stopping short, at a distance that would sorely test his marksmanship. He gauged the little grove's value as a defensive position and judged against it. The point of rocks would afford him better protection.

He decided to give the Indians some discouragement before he went on. Tying the brown, he braced his rifle against a hackberry. He held his breath and squeezed the trigger.

An Indian horse went down. Another, a black, danced in sudden excitement. The downed Indian was quickly on his feet. Frank fired another round and missed. The Indian afoot jumped up behind the man on the black, and they rode off in a run. Frank made a glad shout, thinking he had scared them away. But that hope died as the Indians stopped after a hundred yards. They intended to trail him until help came. Muttering, Frank climbed back up on the brown horse and set him into a long trot.

He had no plan beyond reaching the medicine hill. Protected by its great rocks, he might hold out against three Indians, one already afoot, until he could trim the odds further and get away. But if they held him until more arrived, the only question would be how long it might take them to finish their work.

The Indians began running, trying to cut him off from the rocks. He put spurs to the brown and called up the speed for which he had conserved its strength. He stopped quickly at the base of the promontory, dismounted and steadied the rifle on a boulder. Seeing his intention, the Indians drew up too late. He fired, and they had only the black horse left.

Frank reflected on the trouble he and Homer and the Akins boys had undergone in catching the wild horses they might or might not be able to use, and on the waste to which he had just put two likely looking mounts. It seemed a shame that good horses had to suffer for men's mistakes.

The Indians pulled back to a longer range, conferring a long time while afternoon shadows lengthened. Frank led the horse around the base of the rock pile until he reached a point from which he could see most of the valley. He ate a bit more venison and bread and sat on a small boulder to take his rest. He had a notion he would need it.

After a time one Indian rode toward him on the black horse, his shadow stretching far behind him across the grass. The other two stayed, watching. Puzzled, Frank raised the rifle but did not fire. He would soon have a clear shot from better range. Three Indians afoot would be no running match for the brown.

Long before the lone Indian reached the hill's base, he was waving his bull-hide shield above his head, shouting words Frank did not understand. Frank studied the black. He had always had an eye for horses, and he was sure he remembered this one. He could see the shield clearly now, crimson in the last flush of sunlight. Recognition somehow brought no surprise. This was the same horse, the same Indian he had seen that cold, misty day above the Clear Fork when he and Homer and George had chanced suddenly upon a Comanche hunting party. He began to make out features of the warrior's dark face and found that they were already indelibly etched in his memory.

He sensed that Red Shield was going to offer the same proposition as before: come out and fight, knife to knife, man to man. Frank's blood went cold.

Despite his precarious situation, he felt a grudging admiration for the warrior's nerve. The words were alien, but the challenge was plain. Frank stepped from behind the boulder that sheltered him. He raised the rifle, knowing that unlike last time, if he killed the Indian, the others were too far away for vengeance. He sighted on a small leather bag that hung from the Comanche's neck, and in that moment he felt a power he had never known. The Indian did not flinch. He looked Frank squarely in the eyes.

Frank could not squeeze the trigger. He blinked, for the front sight seemed hazy. His hands were wet and cold on the rifle. He could not bring himself to fire, to kill a man who willingly put himself into this jeopardy for nothing more tangible than honor. He lowered the rifle and made a sweeping motion with his hand. "Go on," he said firmly, hoping the Indian would understand the meaning. "Get the hell out of here!"

The Indian stood his ground. Frank took a couple more steps. He raised the rifle as if to shoot the horse, then moved the muzzle aside and pulled the trigger. The black horse shied away, its eyes wide at the noise and the fire and smoke. Frank reloaded quickly, knowing the Indian could be upon him in an instant if he chose.

"Damn it, Red Shield," he declared, "I don't want to kill you. But I will if I have to. Now git!" He made the motion again, then backed toward his own horse, tied in the protection of the boulders.

Red Shield followed him a few steps, until he was at the base of the hill. There he stopped, looking past Frank, looking higher up toward the rocks large and small, scattered without form or pattern. Frank saw something in his eyes, fear perhaps, or awe. He sensed that the rock pile had meaning to the Indian, some call to wild blood. He remembered the chill he had felt the time he had climbed it, a prescience he could not understand.

He felt that chill come over him again.

The shadow of the wall began to reach across the valley. If he was to leave, he had better do it now. He untied the brown horse and swung into the saddle. He worked his way down the slope toward Red Shield, who watched in grim silence. Frank held the rifle's muzzle toward the Indian. "Now, friend," he said with a calm that surprised him, "I'm fixin' to go home."

Red Shield held his ground as Frank rode past him. He

began to follow at twenty paces, bow in hand, arrow fitted to string. Frank shifted in the saddle to watch him, keeping the rifle pointed. He let the brown stay in a walk. If he broke into a run, the Indian would probably be after him in an instant, and the arrow might fly truer than the bullet.

It was a long, unblinking contest of nerve. Frank did not remember that he had ever let anyone stare him down, but the stakes had never been this high.

He held the walk all the way to the creek, and Red Shield maintained the distance. Neither man looked away from the other. Frank put the horse in and walked him across, half expecting the Indian to rush him in the water. Red Shield stopped at the creek's edge, making no effort to cross. Frank kept the brown walking, though his skin prickled with a terrible urge to spur into a run. He continued looking back, watching the lone horseman who remained, the sky a blazing red behind him.

To the north, from a low-lying cloud Frank had not noticed before, came a distant roll of thunder.

He rode much of the night, not expecting pursuit but not willing to gamble. When he quit it was to spare the horse. He staked the mount and rolled up in his single blanket on the ground, resting his head against the saddle. He did not sleep. The confrontation had left his nerves raw and electric. He had not understood why Red Shield did not break at some point and make an attempt to kill him. He sensed something holding the Indian back but knew it was not fear. He lay with eyes closed, trying to find rest. His mind moved in a run and would not slow.

Weary, the want of sleep heavy on his stomach, he rode into camp at mid-afternoon. Dully he made a rough count of the horses tied to the trees and found the numbers increased by two during the time he had been gone. The three horse hunters walked out to meet him as he slowly dismounted, holding to his saddle until his feet felt solid beneath him. He saw that Mark's arm was bound against his chest.

"What happened to you?" he demanded.

Mark sheepishly looked at the ground.

Homer said, "One of them broncs throwed him off. Cracked his arm."

Frank grimaced. He could already imagine the anger he would see in the eyes of the girl Naomi, blaming him.

Homer grinned. "You ought to've seen him ride, Frank. He done real good till that long-headed one yonder caught him with a spin. Yes, sir, Frank, you missed all the excitement!"

Three days later they drove the captured horses into the corral at Frank and Homer's camp. Frank was surprised to see a buggy in front of the dugout. When the gates were closed and the mustangs were running dusty circles inside the corral, Frank turned the brown horse up the hill. Even at the distance, recognition was easy.

"Captain Zachary! Tobe!" Frank shouted.

Zachary was thinner than when Frank had first met him, and his hair had turned almost completely gray. But his eyes glowed with life, and with pleasure. He pumped Frank's hand.

"You look well, Frank, better than I expected. Have you finally gotten rid of that arrowhead?"

"Arrowhead?" Frank lied, "I've plumb forgot about it."

Zachary stood off at arm's length and studied him, smiling. "I'm glad, because I think you and I can do some business."

Frank had never been bothered by the dugout's cramped dimensions until he and Homer shared it with Zachary and Tobe. The opinions of most people were of no consequence to Frank, but he wanted the captain's approval.

Zachary's gaze traveled along the rough earthen walls and up to the ceiling of timbers, covered by an old piece of canvas and topped by a sod roof. "Many a night with the troops I wished for a snug shelter like this."

Homer was pleased at the credit, but he had reservations. He still paid extra deference because to him the captain remained an authority figure. "It's bull-stout, but it ain't nothin' for an officer. No fit place for a woman, either."

Frank said, "Won't be no woman comin' here."

A fleeting smile played across Homer's face.

The captain did not let the coffee come to a boil before he got down to business. "Frank, I came out here to ask you to buy some cattle for me."

Frank's mouth dropped open. He had not seen a dollar paid for a hoof of any kind since the war.

The captain said, "An old business associate of mine has come back to Dallas from the North. We've made use of my connections and his money to buy cotton. Now he has a market for Texas cattle in Missouri. Naturally I'd expect to give your own cattle first preference, Frank. I'll pay you a commission for whatever additional cattle you buy for us, gathered and delivered to the Trinity River."

The captain wanted up to a thousand head, steers if possible. He could accept dry cows—those without calves and not looking as if they were likely to calve along the trail.

Frank and Homer went out into the darkness and tallied on their fingers. Frank said, "We could sell sixty-seventy of our own."

Homer nodded. "The Akinses could sure stand to lay their hands on some Yankee silver."

"So could a lot of folks. We can find more cattle than the captain can pay for."

Homer looked off into the night. "What about George?"

Frank tightened. "What about him?"

"He's got more cattle than anybody, and I expect he needs money about as bad as any."

Frank felt an old anger rising. "Then let him drive his own cattle to Missouri."

Homer argued, "You-all used to be friends."

"Used to be. It was him made the choice, not me."

"Then forget about him and study on Rachal, and the baby."

Sharply Frank declared, "There's damned little I've ever demanded of you, Homer, but I'm goin' to now. I don't want you to ever mention them to me again."

Homer was silent a moment. "All right. But not talkin' about them don't change nothin'. They're still there."

Frank took the captain to the Akins place next day in the buggy. The scene there set the pattern for a dozen others as they rode together, negotiating for cattle at three dollars a head. Frank introduced Bige Akins, who shook the captain's hand so hard that Frank worried about the frail Zachary. "I'm mighty pleased to meet you, sir. I've heard some of what you done durin' the war."

"Old history, Mr. Akins," the captain said. "Nobody cares anymore what happened yesterday. They want to know what's going to happen tomorrow."

As they left, after shaking hands on a deal, Frank looked back to see the stocky Bige dancing a happy little jig.

He and Zachary visited many small ranches and farmsteads over the next three days, leaving joy in their wake, and a little silver for down payment against delivery of cattle. One old settler told Zachary, "Captain, you've come to the rescue of this country before, but you was never more welcome than you are right now."

On their return the fourth day, Frank saw Homer and Tobe in the corrals, working with the young mustangs. But his attention was drawn to a strange wagon sitting near the dugout, and a man who squatted in the wagon's shade. Frank squinted, then frowned upon recognition. "If you'll pardon me, Captain, there's somebody up yonder I'd rather not have on this place."

He handed the captain the reins to take the buggy on down to the pens. He felt an automatic defense rise as the red-haired youth, Rusty Farraday, lazily pushed himself to his feet. Seeing the challenge in Frank's firm stride, Farraday raised both hands in a gesture of truce. "I didn't come here because I wanted to, Claymore. I come because I was told to."

Frank had more challenge to offer, but Homer came running, half out of breath. He leaned with his hands against the wagon and gasped for air. "Frank, *she*'s up there." He pointed his chin.

Frank glanced up the slope. "Who you talkin' about?"

"Her! The one you didn't want me to call the name of."

"Rachal?"

"You said her name; I didn't."

Frank glanced uncertainly at Farraday, who seemed not eager for a fight, though he probably would not back away. "You brought her here. What for?"

Farraday shrugged with a hint of insolence. "I just work for wages, if I ever get paid. I didn't ask the lady no questions."

Frank stared toward the dugout, half eager, half in dread. It took him a minute to build up his nerve. He pushed against the door and walked in, leaving it open for propriety. Rachal arose from a rough chair of Homer's. She held the baby.

Frank asked, half hopefully, "Did you leave George?"

"No, Frank." She seemed startled by the question. "I thought we settled that before."

"I just couldn't figure another reason for you to be here." He remembered happier times. He wanted to reach and touch her, but he had learned better control. Even so, he did not know what to do with his hands. "You look fine, Rachal. How's Billy boy comin' along?"

"Growin' fast," she said, turning the baby so Frank could see him better. Frank looked, then made himself draw away. He wanted to touch Rachal, and he wanted to touch the baby. He shoved his hands into his pockets.

"If you ain't left him, why did you come to me?"

"I hear you been buyin' cattle for Captain Zachary. I was hopin' you still need some."

Frank felt a sharp disappointment. Of all the reasons he might have considered for her coming here, this would not have occurred to him. "Fact is, we've bought all he can pay for."

She stared at the dirt floor, gathering courage. "We need the money, Frank."

"Everybody needs money."

"But not like we do. If we had a little money we could leave here . . . go where nobody knows anything about us."

Leave! That was something else he had not considered. "What do they know about you here?"

"Everything. About me and you, about how I come to marry George."

He angered a little. "Anybody says anything, you just let me know. I'll—"

"You'd make it worse, and shame me even more. When Billy gets old enough to understand—"

"No matter where you go, he'll know someday."

Her voice toughened. "I didn't come to you for advice, Frank. I come for a chance to get us some money, to get me away from this place and all these gossipy people."

"Does George know you're here?"

"No. I figure on tellin' him after you say you'll buy some cattle from us."

Frank's stubbornness began to take hold. "If he wants to sell me cattle, he can come and tell me himself."

Tears came to her eyes. "You know he won't do that. He's bent backward with pride, Frank."

"I've got pride too. I didn't start this fight. *He* did, when he lied to you about how long I'd be with the Rangers. Whatever's happened since, he's brought on himself."

"You owe me, Frank. You brought this shame on me."

"Leave him and I'll marry you."

She seemed about to weep but stopped herself. "I never would've thought you could be a mean man, Frank."

"I ain't, but mean things've happened to me."

"I come to ask, not to beg. But I'll beg if it'll make you happy." Bitterness crept into her voice.

"You tell him to come. I'll buy if he'll come."

"Then don't you wait, Frank." Her eyes had a touch of flint he had not seen before. "The snow'll be four feet deep here the Fourth of July before George'll ask you for anything. Or before I will, ever again."

He stood in the dugout door, watching her walk stiff-backed down to the wagon. He wanted to call to her, to soften his stand, but compromise was like gall to him. His jaw firmly set, he watched Rusty Farraday hold the baby while Rachal climbed the spokes of the wheel and seated herself. In a minute the wagon was on its way down the dim river trail. Frank clenched his fists and thought of all the things he should have said, but he knew if she were suddenly to return he would not change a word.

She did not return. He sensed that she never would.

He felt a sourness in his stomach that he could not blame on the arrowhead.

The captain went back to Dallas to make arrangements while Frank and Homer and the two younger Akins boys received the cattle from eager sellers and shaped them into a trail herd. Homer stayed to watch after business on the Clear Fork while Frank made the long, tiresome drive with Luke and John and a couple of other young men whose fathers were newly blessed by the possession of some authentic U.S. specie.

Captain Zachary met the herd on the west bank of the Trinity, near Fort Worth. He brought a crew of eight drovers—hardy ex-soldiers every one, from the look of them—to take charge of the trail-broken cattle. The sights and noises of civilization were boogery to the animals at first, and they would have required little provocation to set off a stampede.

Seeing that the cattle were in capable hands, Frank left them for the first time to ride his brown horse out and shake hands with the captain. Zachary looked rested and cheerful, better than when he had left the dugout on the Clear Fork.

"Frank," he said, "I want you to meet Abel Babcock, my partner in this enterprise. Abel, Frank Claymore."

Frank learned that the tall, slightly overweight Babcock was a native Texan who had remained loyal to the Union and had escaped early in the war at considerable risk to fight for the other side. Babcock had an open and honest way of looking a man in the eyes and gauging him as he shook hands. Frank took that for a favorable sign, though he had never felt much in common with men who spent their lives beneath a roof.

The captain motioned toward another man, tall and thin, older than any of them. "This is J. J. Brooks. He will take the cattle to Missouri." Brooks had the rangy, weather-ravaged, rawhide look of a man who had spent his life on horseback. Frank instinctively felt at home with him.

Frank asked worriedly, "Captain, you ain't figurin' on goin' to Missouri with the cattle, are you?"

Zachary glanced at Babcock. Regret was in his answer. "Abel has persuaded me that my health is not good enough."

Frank decided he approved of Abel Babcock.

A decision was made to go ahead and count the cattle. Frank knew exactly how many there were, but he sat on his horse behind J. J. Brooks and watched the man count with motions of his hand as the cattle passed him in a narrow column, pinched down by the drovers. Brooks held several small stones in his right palm. Each time he came to a hundred he transferred one to his left. Frank had not mastered the art of counting large numbers, but he intended to learn. He intended to own twenty times this number of cattle before many years passed.

Brooks's count exceeded Frank's known tally by just one. Frank advised the captain of the discrepancy. He dismounted and untied his saddlebag. "You left me more money than it took to pay for the cattle. I'd be obliged if you'd count this."

The captain glanced at Babcock. "That won't be necessary. I know it's there. You may consider the herd delivered. Now, let's go across the river. I wager you would like a bath and some new clothes before supper."

Frank saw no pressing need for either, but he had always liked to please the captain. He hardly knew how to buy clothes from a store shelf, but he managed. He took a haircut and shave and a long, restful soak in a wooden tub at the back of the tonsorial parlor and emporium. It seemed a shameful extravagance, but it left him with a satisfied glow. He could almost feel at ease with the captain's moneyed friends.

The captain had taken rooms for Frank and his crew in a small frame hotel. Frank considered it excessively elaborate because it had curtains on the windows. He warned the boys not to expect this kind of treatment in the future.

He heard a knock on the door. The captain called, "We're going to the dining room for supper. You-all come on when you're ready."

Luke Akins, prideful in a new suit of clothes that still showed the wrinkles of the store shelf, said, "I've been ready for a week."

Frank took one more glance at the mirror. His new outfit was wrinkled too, and he supposed that was the way the rich folks looked. It proved the clothes were not homemade. Self-consciously he made his way down the warm, narrow hall, the boys trailing behind him. He stopped at the clerk's desk beneath the stairway and asked, "Which-away's the dinin' parlor?"

The clerk seemed somehow amused, which touched off a flare of resentment in Frank. The man pointed with the slightly condescending air of one who knows more than is good for him. Frank never completely gave up command. "Come on, boys, it's yonderway."

He stopped in the door to search for Zachary, and he stared in surprise. A right pretty young woman sat beside the captain. Frank had to look a moment before he realized she was Letitia Zachary. The captain stood up, smiling. "Frank, I almost didn't recognize you, all dressed up. You remember Letty, of course."

"Sure I do," Frank responded uncertainly. He didn't remember her like *this*. She seemed a grown woman, almost, filled out some from the last time and wearing a lacy dress that looked like something out of a picture book.

She said, "My, my, Frank Claymore, you look almost civilized."

He decided quickly that her manners had not improved. He grunted. "I'll get over it."

She reached out her hand, and he shook it briskly, as he had shaken the hands of Abel Babcock and J. J. Brooks. The captain motioned toward an empty chair. "Frank, you sit down by Letty. I'm sure she'll have many things to ask you."

Poor manners or not, she was a woman, and Frank found he was shy and uncomfortable sitting next to her. With the exception of Naomi Akins, who had never aroused any sexual interest in him whatever, he had not been this close to a young woman in a long time. The room was close and hot. Frank could sense the body warmth from Letty, which made him feel even warmer. He wanted to go raise the windows higher, but he knew everybody would be looking at him. He had an uncomfortable feeling they would all see and know the scandalous thoughts running through his mind.

Red Shield had not scared him as badly.

The captain and Babcock talked of the drive and the Missouri market. They talked of their confidence in Brooks, who had taken herds in that direction for Zachary before the war.

Zachary said, "You'll be interested to know, Frank, that they are running a railroad across the continent. We hear the rails will soon be into Kansas."

Frank nodded as if the news were of great interest. He could see no way that rails through Kansas would be of any benefit to him out on the Clear Fork.

Zachary said, "That means we'll soon be able to drive

cattle to Kansas instead of Missouri. That will be much shorter, and much easier because we won't have to pick our way through so much settled farming country. It means a bigger outlet for Texas cattle. It means opportunity for you, Frank, and for me."

Frank's interest sharpened. "How do you mean, me?"

"You were telling me about your valley. If you are willing, Frank, I'd like to work up a partnership with you. You can find and buy cattle. I'll arrange to have them driven north. You've made yourself a little nest egg, gathering the herd you delivered today. You may be surprised at how soon you'll be able to claim your valley."

Letty said, "And I may decide to marry you and live there."

Face reddening, Frank told himself he had been right; she still had no manners.

He did not have a good night's sleep during the trip back to the Clear Fork. He lay awake far into each night, excitement rolling like a river in flood, his dreams for the valley taking precedence over his need for rest, though he knew they might be years in coming to pass. He bubbled with anticipation, planning how he would tell Homer.

He did not even stop at the Akins place, letting Luke and John drop out, then spurring on. A mile short of the dugout he heard cattle bawling in a thicket. Homer hailed him and rode out to intercept him, waving. He asked how the drive had gone. Frank assured him it had been completed without a serious hitch and asked, "Any news around here?"

Homer shrugged. "Not much. George Valentine heard the Yankee army's got a bunch of Indians penned up on the Pecos out in New Mexico and needs beef for them. He's gathered a bunch of his own and got some other fellers to go in with him. They'll be headin' their cattle west pretty quick."

Frank mused. "West? Sounds risky."

Homer nodded. "But he says if you can drive cattle east, he can drive them west. He didn't ask me for no advice."

"Any other news?"

"Circuit-ridin' preacher come by, is about all."

Frank reined up suddenly as he came within sight of camp. He saw the two older Akins boys setting big picket posts into the ground fifty paces from the dugout. It was obvious they were building a cabin.

"What happened?" he demanded. "Did the dugout cave in?"

Homer's grin spread wider than Frank had ever seen it. "I told you the preacher come by lookin' for work. Me and Naomi Akins, we let him marry us."

Naomi stepped through the door of the dugout and shaded her eyes with her hand. The wind lifted and waved her apron. Even at the distance Frank could see flour on her hands.

He felt as if a horse had kicked him. Not once had he considered the possibility of living close to that sharp-tongued young woman. "This is one secret you kept real good, Homer. I never expected such a thing."

Homer said, "You know a lot about cattle and horses, Frank, but you don't pay much attention to people. If you've got a failin', I expect that's it."

7

Frank Claymore slouched in the hotel room's big, soft horsehair chair and reluctantly yielded to the pain of his bad hip. He watched with irritation the dark spiral of smoke in the lamp's glass chimney. Homer Whitcomb was talking, and defense attorney Anderson Avery was engrossed in Homer's story. Neither paid attention to the lamp. Claymore considered getting up and turning down the wick, but he hurt too much. Maybe if the room went dark Homer would quit talking.

Damned small chance, he thought.

Homer was saying, "I felt real bad about it when Comanches hit George's herd at Horsehead Crossin'. Taken his horses and most of his cattle. It's hell to be afoot on the Pecos."

Claymore said grittily, "I could've told him it was a fool notion to go."

Homer was like a conscience that never slept. "If he'd've asked, you wouldn't've told him nothin'."

Claymore growled. "He was a grown man."

Anderson tried to break up the beginning of a disagreement. "I knew the Indians were great horse thieves, but I never realized they stole cattle."

Homer nodded. "Years later we found out they swapped the cattle to Comanchero traders out of New Mexico for guns and powder and stuff. I talked to some of them New Mexico people, when we was all too old to prosecute. They said the Indians had a fair notion of the cow market."

Claymore grumbled about the morality of men who would buy booty and encourage the theft. It had been a long time ago, but some old angers never died.

Homer said, "Maybe if George hadn't fallen on such hard times, things would've turned out different. He blamed Frank for his troubles."

Claymore commented, "Mighty few men ever blame theirselves."

An infernal grin slid across Homer's face. *Peculiar,* Claymore thought irritably, *how Homer can point a finger without moving it.*

Avery made an effort to edge Claymore into a kindlier direction. "During the time George Valentine's fortunes were failing, *your* luck was on the ascendancy, was it not?"

Claymore frowned. *Why can't the man use plain English?* "Wasn't no luck to it. Hard work is what it was, and stickin' to business." He glanced at Homer. "Me and Homer *worked.*"

Homer said, "Me and Frank put in the sweat. Captain put in the money. Hard work is all right, but money sure helps."

Claymore frowned. "Money wouldn't've done it either if I hadn't wore out twelve good horses travelin' like a whiskey drummer, buyin' cattle for the captain to send up the trail to Kansas. I kept back good young cows to put on our own country. Money don't grow by itself. You've got to water it with sweat."

Avery nodded. "As I understand it, Captain Zachary was a full partner in your ranching venture."

Claymore started to answer, but Homer took it from him. "He owned half of it. Me and Frank, we owned the other half."

Claymore said firmly, "But I ran it. I was the boss. From the day I left the Rangers, I never taken orders from nobody. That was my agreement with the captain. The day ever come that I didn't run it, the partnership was finished."

Homer put in, "Frank and the captain agreed that if ever they *couldn't* agree, the one who made the highest bid could buy out the other. Didn't seem likely us and the captain would ever fall out; he was a prince of a feller." Homer smiled. "Thing was, though, the captain had a princess."

Stiffly Claymore said, "These walls are as thin as paper. You're talkin' to the whole damned hotel."

Avery kept trying to keep Claymore diverted from points of friction. "It was a full ten years after the war, wasn't it, before you were able to come and claim the valley?"

Homer answered again, like a fast-running poult grabbing a bug from under a rooster. "We could've come a lot sooner except for the Comanches. It was the winter of '74 that Mackenzie and his cavalry drove them to the reservation. Me and Frank decided to gather our cattle and take the valley before anybody else could. Captain fixed it with officials down at the state capital so we could buy or lease the land that had water on it. Without water, the rest of it was no good to anybody else." Regret came into his eyes. "Too bad it couldn't stay that way."

Claymore nodded grimly. "They ruined it. They taken this beautiful valley, and they ruined it."

Homer shook his head. "*We* ruined it. We come into a paradise and didn't know better than to change everything." He looked wistfully at Avery. "I wisht you could've seen it the day we brought the first herd. It was a sight that stays with a man the rest of his life, long after he's lost it . . ."

Frank rode point at the head of the C Bar W herd with the leathery old trail driver J. J. Brooks, who had brought several drovers to help. Frank's rump prickled against the saddle, for they had not many more miles to ride. The rising ground before them promised the valley beyond. Its grass would be the fresh green of a generous spring. Winter had been wet and cold, severe enough to drive holdout Indian warriors to the shelter and rations offered them on the reservation beyond Red River. The wetter the winter, the greener the spring.

Frank turned in his saddle and looked back at the herd stretching a mile and more behind him—cows with calves, young heifers, bulls, steers—long of leg and horn, sporting all colors known to man. "They'll be home for supper."

Brooks frowned at the westering sun, beginning to work its way under his broad hat brim. It would soon be in his weather-pinched eyes. "A damned late supper." He did not quite share Frank's enthusiasm. It was not his herd, or his land.

Frank had inspected the valley late in the winter, firmly resolved to drive out anyone who might have arrived ahead of him. He had found buffalo crowding the range, badly abusing the old grass. By now, he reasoned, most should have migrated up over the caprock and back out upon the high plains. The grass should be on its way to recovery under the healing warmth of a May sun. His valley should be far better grazing than the overstocked ranges along the Clear Fork, hard pressed to accommodate the ever-growing herds brought by new settlers responding to the hope of cheap land and the promise of protection by federal troops at Forts Griffin and Richardson and, farther south, Fort Concho.

Many new arrivals brought land titles, a fine point of law some old settlers had ignored. The sight of surveyors' tripods aroused the kind of fear that an unidentified horseman had brought in the Indian times. There seemed more call for lawyers now than for soldiers.

He hoped it would never happen in the valley. The state allowed individuals such as Claymore and the captain to buy only limited acreage, which they concentrated along the living water. It willingly leased them the rest but held fast to its title for release at some unspecified time in the future. Preserving those leases would require constant vigilance by the captain and his friends in Austin officialdom.

Frank looked back upon his crew, scattered the length of the herd. He had brought Naomi's younger brother Mark, a working straw boss for Frank and Homer in recent years.

Mark had accumulated a set of competent young hands who
spent what Frank considered an inordinate amount of time
making sure they looked right, and wore big-roweled spurs
of Mexican extraction that jingled altogether too much. The
hands called themselves cowboys.

Cowboy was a new term to Frank. He had heard it only
recently and was not sure he approved. It sounded somehow belittling. If they wanted to be known by such a name,
he supposed it was all right, but he would not tolerate its
being applied to *him*. He had stopped being a boy when he
had left his brothers on the Colorado River. He did not take
the hands to task, however, at least not within Naomi's hearing. She was as protective of them as of her children. She
filled their stomachs, washed their clothes and nurtured
their individual dreams.

Frank and Brooks startled a dozen or so buffalo bedded
down in a hollow's tall grass, sheltering from the wind. The
animals snuffed and snorted and broke into a run. Frank's
frightened horse almost turned out from under him, and
Brooks grabbed at his saddle horn. At his age that act of
self-preservation brought no shame.

Frank turned quickly to be sure the buffalo had not frightened the lead cattle and chased them back against the rest
of the herd. Relentless meat hunting had eliminated buffalo
along the Clear Fork. Most of these cattle had never seen
them.

Frank heard a horse gallop up behind him. Homer's oldest boy, now about six, shouted excitedly as he reined his
paint pony to a stop. He was dwarfed by the wide, droop-
ing brim of his hat. "Was that buffalo, Uncle Frank?"

Frank declared impatiently, "Jimmy, I've told you not
to come to the point of the herd. You go back to your
wagon." Jimmy, named for his old grandfather back on
the Colorado, seemed not to hear. He took advice like his
mother.

Brooks put a brown-spotted hand on the lad's thin shoulder. He had raised several boys of his own, years ago. "Yes,

young'un, them was buffalo. You'll see more of them ahead. They might scare your mama's team, so you better go back. She'll need a man's help."

The boy grinned over the responsibility and for a moment looked like his father. "I sure will, Mr. Brooks." He put his pony into a run, skirting the edge of the herd. Even at his young age he knew better than to frighten the cattle. He stuck to the saddle like a burr, his soft hat brim flopping to the rhythm of the pony's stride.

Frank's eyes followed the boy. "That hard-headed mother of his . . . I tried to get her to stay behind till we got settled and made sure the valley is safe. She said her place is with Homer."

"My wife always done the same," Brooks said, disagreeing without making a point of it. "Naomi's good cookin' ought to make up for any frettin' she causes you."

"Not enough," Frank said.

Jimmy reined in beside his mother's wagon several hundred yards back, on the upwind side of the herd. Anytime now, Frank suspected, Naomi would push her way up here, wanting to know when they would camp so she could start supper for family and crew. She would throw a fit if she knew how late that was going to be.

In the boy's place came another horseman, spurring harder than Frank liked to see an animal used. "Here comes that damned newspaperman again," Frank grumbled. "I wish you could've lost him before you ever reached the Clear Fork."

Brooks looked back disapprovingly. Like Frank, he had little tolerance and no understanding of people who did not make their living a-horseback or with their hands. "As I told you, the Dallas paper belongs to an old friend of the captain's. This boy wants to write about the frontier while it's still got the hide and hair on it."

The reporter loped his horse up beside the point men. He slid him to a stop more abruptly than was necessary, and Frank told him so. The bespectacled young man seemed not to hear. "Gentlemen!" he exclaimed. "Look behind you. Isn't that a splendid sight?"

Frank glanced back. All he saw was cattle and horses and wagons. "What?"

"That," Jeffrey Singer declared with a sweep of his hand. "The great milling herd."

Frank corrected him impatiently, "If they was millin' they'd be goin' in a circle, and we'd be losin' time."

"Semantics," the young man said, eyes shining with the excitement of a high adventure. "A figure of speech."

Frank had no idea what he was talking about, and no curiosity. "Don't you do nothin' that might *set* them to millin'."

Singer seemed happily oblivious to Frank's resentment. "I only wish that I were an artist, so I could do this scene justice. I am afraid you gentlemen are too close to it to appreciate its importance." He gave both men a look of pity and spurred forward, up the long slope that led to the rim of the valley. Frank called after him not to go too far by himself. The words were lost on the wind that bent the new grass. Jeffrey Singer stopped his horse at the edge and stared. Frank could see, even at the distance, that the reporter was writing on a pad he had carried in his pocket all the way from the Clear Fork. He had taken enough notes, Frank judged, to write a book.

Singer rode back, awe in his face. "Gentlemen, this will be the high point—the stunning climax—of my story."

Frank said, "Climax, hell. We ain't half started to do things yet."

"The climax of the pioneering phase," Singer said. "From here on the exploration is over, and the building begins. That is never as exciting as the pioneering."

Frank replied, "It's a damned sight more peaceful."

They rode together to the rim, Frank's heart quickening. A cool wind came sweeping up from the valley floor, bringing the scent of spring's eternal renewal.

Brooks whistled softly. "Frank, you told it true."

The valley was the greenest Frank had seen it. In that respect he was pleasantly surprised. In another he was disappointed, for buffalo by the hundreds were scattered all the way to the distant point of rocks.

"I'd hoped they'd be gone north by now," he said.

Brooks warned, "They'll be trouble. Cattle and buffalo won't mix."

"We'll have to run the buffalo out."

Brooks frowned. "They been here forever."

"So were the Indians. You want *them* back?"

Brooks looked over his shoulder. The lead cattle were almost upon him. "You comin', Frank?"

"Directly. I'll watch here awhile."

Singer spurred recklessly down to the valley floor and quartered across it by himself, joyously scattering buffalo.

The cattle began dropping off the crest and spilling down a steep buffalo trail. They followed Brooks and the lead animals, shadows long in the late-afternoon sun. Mesmerized, Frank lost track of time until Homer came up behind him.

Homer said, "I'm anxious for Naomi to see this."

The spell was shattered. The last thing Frank wanted was an argument with Homer's strong-willed woman. He started down the slope, following the easiest course along with the cows.

He was well into the valley when he sensed excitement among the cattle and heard a clatter of hoofs. Twenty or thirty buffalo stampeded toward the herd. Behind them, the source of their fright, the newspaper writer came spurring desperately. Singer lost his hat but made no effort to stop for it.

Frank waved his hand and shouted, "Hold up! Don't run them buffalo into the herd!" The words were wasted against the wind.

Frightened by the lumbering black buffalo, the cattle in their path broke into a run that Frank knew would scatter them from hell to breakfast. Leaning forward, he put spurs to his horse's ribs, racing to join Brooks at the lead. He shouted at the running cattle.

He did not see the prairie-dog hole. Suddenly he was sailing, striking the ground hard, rolling in the grass. Instinctively he pushed to his knees, scrambling to get out of the horse's way if it should roll forward. The horse missed him, but the cattle did not. He threw his arms over his face as the first wild-eyed cows struck him. Normally they would cut around to avoid him, but pressed by their panic and the animals behind them, they came right over him. Hoofs hammered his ribs, his legs. He was knocked in one direction and another, then sprawled facedown while the breath was pounded from him. He put his arms over the back of his head. The weight of a running cow flattened his face against the earth.

He never quite lost consciousness. When the stampede had passed, he carefully, painfully brought his arms down and tried pushing himself up onto hands and knees. His eyes were full of dirt and burned like the hinges of hell. His shirt hung in strips. His back was afire. For a moment his mind wandered, and he could not remember what had happened. He only knew that he needed to get to his feet but could not.

He heard Brooks's calm voice. "Don't move, Frank. Be still till we know if you're busted up."

Frank only half comprehended and kept trying to rise. He felt Brooks's supporting hands, strong despite the man's age. Brooks said, "Easy now. You look like a side of beef."

Frank wheezed and struggled for breath and decided it was not important to stand after all. He settled back to the ground with his forehead against his knees. "Damned greenhorn!"

Eyes still blurry, he saw Singer and his horse as vague shapes coming through the dust. Singer jumped awkwardly from the saddle. "Are you hurt, Mr. Claymore?"

Brooks did not wait for Frank to answer. He launched a lecture that would have peeled bark from an oak tree.

Defensively Singer said, "But didn't you-all see the Indi-ans?" He turned and pointed.

Brooks said, "All I seen was you runnin' them buffalo into the cattle."

"I saw Indians. I was running to warn you."

Frank declared, "You sure warned *me*, all right." He felt a throbbing in his hip and suspected a bone was cracked. His hand sought the point of pain and found it. Grumbling, he made another effort to rise and decided against it.

Homer Whitcomb loped up and hit the ground running. "You all right, Frank?" He made a quick, clumsy examina-tion. "I'll bet that hurts."

"Hell no," Frank said caustically. "It feels good."

The greater part of the herd had not involved itself in the runaway. It plodded along into the setting sun, paying scant attention to the men, raising dust the north wind seemed to drift into Frank's face as extra insult. He blinked dirt from his eyes. The cattle that had run were easing into a long trot most of a mile away. They would stop at the creek.

He shrugged. "I figured we'd turn them a-loose down there anyway."

Singer talked earnestly to each rider who approached, trying to convince him he had seen Indians. Frank watched him with narrowed eyes. "He was probably imaginin' things, J. J., but you might take a couple of men and make a circle."

Homer said, "Yonder comes Naomi, Frank. You better ride with her in the wagon. I'll tie your horse on behind."

Frank eyed the oncoming wagon with reluctance. That woman would counsel him like a schoolmarm all the way to the campground. "I'll ride if you have to tie me to the horse."

Singer tried to assist him, but Frank scowled him away. Homer and one of Brooks's drovers gently eased Frank to his feet. Frank put his weight on the right leg to test the hip. It felt for a moment as if it might give way, but he sternly commanded it to hold, and it did.

Homer said, "I'm surprised the poundin' didn't jar that arrowhead loose in there somewhere."

Singer was aroused to questions about the arrowhead. Homer gave him a full accounting. Frank forced himself into the saddle as Singer furiously wrote notes.

Naomi pulled up in the wagon and briefly showed genuine concern before she reverted to her normal adversary posture. "Did anybody think to examine the horse?" she demanded. "He might've been hurt."

Brooks and a couple of his drovers were gone for an hour or more. By the time they caught up at dusk, Frank and Homer and the rest of the crew were scattering the herd along the creek. Brooks said, "All we found was buffalo and a few antelope. He probably taken the antelope horns to be feathers. Feller has got to have a good imagination to write for a paper."

Frank nodded dully and turned his attention to a flash of lightning somewhere to the north. He felt as much as heard a roll of distant thunder.

Let it storm, he thought. *I'm in the valley now. Ain't nothin' goin' to move me!*

He was forced to remain afoot for the better part of a week. His body was a mass of black and blue welts, his back and legs lacerated. His right hip felt as if he were driving a nail into it with each step he took. Homer constructed a crude crutch, but Frank stubbornly refused to use it. He hobbled painfully, making the same stern demands upon himself that he made upon the people around him. Be damned if he would show the feather because a few cattle had stomped on him.

While most of the crew made certain the cattle settled themselves in the valley and showed no inclination to drift, Frank impatiently surveyed the place he had decided to build his headquarters, in and around the grove of cottonwoods on the creek north from the point of rocks. He marked off the outlines of the corrals, driving stakes to locate barns and sheds.

Immediately he ran into a quarrel with Naomi. She wanted her house at a place he had decided was perfect for a horse barn and saddle shed. She had gained a good many pounds since her marriage to Homer and the birth of two sons, but in Frank's view she had not gained in patience or in understanding of men's business.

Naomi declared, "People are more important than horses. The shade of these trees will be a good place for the children to play in the summertime. You can build your horse barns farther south, so the wind will carry the dust away from us."

She did not voice it as a suggestion; it was a command. Dryly he said, "And I suppose you want us to start buildin' your house before we do anything else?"

"I do. I am not partial to livin' out of a wagon. If you expect me to cook for this outfit, Frank Claymore, I'll expect *you* to put a roof over my head. I will not cook in the rain."

Frank started to limp away but stopped after a few steps. Stubbornly he said, "This is where the horse pens go."

She ignored him, dragging her toe in the sand, marking the outlines for her house.

By the time Brooks was ready to get back to Fort Worth and start a new drive for the captain, Frank was fairly well recuperated from the trampling. The healing scars itched, and his hip gave him hell, but he considered himself in good shape.

Brooks and the four drovers he had brought saddled their horses in the corral a hundred yards south of the place where Naomi's rock house was going up, in the location she had chosen. The newspaperman, Singer, seemed eager to start the trip east, to begin putting into print all he had written. He had kept himself staunchly insulated against Frank's best efforts to belittle him. He had a great story, he said, and all other considerations paled against that.

He promised, "I'll make you a famous man, Frank Claymore."

Frank grunted. He saw no gain in being famous. Rich, now . . . that might be all right.

He watched Brooks and the others cross the creek and head eastward across the valley until they were specks amid the cattle and the scattering of buffalo that had refused to be driven out. He wished he could have talked Brooks into staying, for the old drover had forgotten more about cattle than Frank expected ever to learn. But Brooks felt an obligation to Captain Zachary, and Frank respected obligations.

When finally he turned, he saw Homer and Naomi and all the hands standing there. "Well," he said gruffly, "what's everybody waitin' for? Let's get this woman's house finished so we can move on to *important* things."

On their way out Brooks and his drovers must have encountered the captain's surveyors, who came to the valley with their wagons, their instruments, stakes and chains. It was their purpose to measure and mark the metes and bounds of the leased and deeded lands, to keep them safe in original hands.

Naomi Whitcomb's face fell as she counted the men in the surveying party. She made no comment, but she looked with dismay at her pots and buckets and Dutch ovens, at the open fire pit where she had been cooking with only a stretched tarp for shelter. She was much relieved to find the men had brought their own cook and planned to feed themselves. In visiting with the crew their first night in the valley, however, she almost wept with joy at finding the chief and one of the others had come from her own home area in Hamilton County. They talked far into the night about mutual acquaintances. She gasped in proper shock over scandals that had occurred since her leaving, and enjoyed them every one. Soon she was cheerfully cooking for the survey crew in addition to the ranch people. She declared that their cook scorched even his wash water and was fit only to carry a chain for a workman who knew what he was doing. When Frank suggested that her extra efforts were unnecessary, she replied that men could not accomplish a decent day's work when their stomachs were wrestling with the indigestible.

Through spring and summer the ranch crew spent more time with axes, shovels and posthole-digging implements than a-horseback, building corrals and sheds at the headquarters and auxiliary corrals at extreme ends of the valley. All this was done after Naomi's rock house was finished, of course. Frank and the bachelor hands slept on the ground through the summer, deferring their comfort to more pressing needs. Along about August, however, knowing a colder season was coming, Frank gave grudging consent for the men to take time from better chores to begin construction of a crude stone bunkhouse, long and narrow. It was Spartan and without artistic pretensions, for in Frank's opinion anyone who saw it in the daylight was shirking his duties. By lantern light, looks would not matter.

It was only Naomi's insistence that made him take notice of Sundays. Frank assumed the Lord had provided seven days in each week so a man could get more work done. Naomi firmly declared that the Sabbath was for rest and worship, and forbade any man to put his hand to labor that was not a requirement of nature. Frank's requirements were of no importance on Sunday. There being no known minister nearer than the Clear Fork, Naomi led the singing, and her brother Mark did Bible readings in the shade of the cottonwoods. Frank was surprised to find him as knowledgeable about the Book as about cattle and horses.

Mark took a wagon to Fort Griffin for supplies. He brought back a minister to conduct proper services. Frank would have been more pleased if the minister's place on the wagon had been used for an extra barrel of flour, but there was no point in making an issue after the deed was done.

"Any news back on the Clear Fork?" he asked Mark.

"Stock's in good shape."

Damn it, Frank thought, Mark ought to know he wasn't asking about the stock. "Did you see Rachal?"

Mark frowned. "Seen George Valentine, and the boy Billy. They was grubbin' stumps out of a new field."

"Grubbin' stumps?" Frank warmed to a quick indignation. "That's too heavy a work for a boy his size."

"He's comin' up on ten, I believe."

"He ain't no ox. George ought to know better." George probably *did* know better; he just didn't care. "You didn't see Rachal?"

"Nobody sees Rachal. She don't show herself."

An old hurt stirred Frank. George didn't want her in public, he figured, didn't want her reminding people of a long-ago shame.

The minister led services in a manner Naomi found pleasing, and he promised to return from time to time to help her and Mark establish a redoubt of Christianity in a far outpost of civilization. It was Frank's reluctant privilege to lend him a horse for his return to Fort Griffin. Frank figured if a man needed a minister to keep reminding him of his religion, his brand wasn't burned very deeply. But Naomi was unusually agreeable for a couple of weeks, and Frank accepted good fortune wherever he found it. She did not even complain about being asked to cook buffalo and antelope meat so they wouldn't have to butcher partnership beef.

The grass cured, and the days became noticeably shorter. One day Frank looked up to watch a large flight of geese noisily passing. When they had moved on southward in the direction of Mexico, he let his gaze sweep up the valley to some of his cattle. They had summered well, he thought with satisfaction. They carried good flesh to ease them into winter. More, they had left an adequate stand of old grass to keep filling their bellies when cold blue northers moved down from the high plains and howled off the canyon wall. The captain would be proud.

A movement caught his eye. A buggy worked its way slowly down the east rim and out upon the valley floor. The minister, he thought, and sought Mark Akins. "Your sin catcher," he said, pointing. "Why don't you go meet him? You can advise him of all my transgressions before your sister gets the chance."

Mark smiled. He derived a certain harmless entertainment from Frank and Naomi's frequent set-tos.

Frank busied himself with making a couple of cowboys redig a posthole and straighten out a bowed section of corral fence. He paid the buggy no more mind until he heard the jingle of chains. He turned to speak to the minister and shouted in surprise. "Captain Zachary!"

Thomas Zachary was not alone. His daughter Letty held the reins, and the young black man Tobe trailed behind on horseback, with Mark. Letty wore a broad-brimmed hat with a veil to keep dust from her face. She lifted the veil over the brim. "You could say hello to me, too."

Frank became conscious that he was covered with dirt from the fencing job. He started to slap off some of it with his hat but saw that the sudden move made the buggy team nervous. What the hell? This was not Dallas, or even Fort Worth. Let her accept him as he was.

"Hello to you, too," he said, struck by the warmth of her smile but knowing that behind it was a tongue as sharp as Naomi's. "I didn't expect you-all."

He cut his attention back to the captain. A second look alarmed him. Zachary was rail thin, face pale, eyes without luster. "Captain," Frank said, "you don't look well." That was an understatement.

Zachary shook his head. "Just tired is all. It has been a long trip."

Tobe dismounted quickly and reached up to assist the captain's shaky descent. Letty said, "You can help *me,* Frank Claymore." She reached out her hands, and he hesitantly lifted her down. For a moment she stood against him. He felt an unexpected stirring he thought he had put behind him years ago, after losing Rachal. She kissed him lightly on the cheek, which went to flame.

"What did you do that for?" he asked, flustered.

"Seemed like a good idea," she said and smiled. "I thought it might sweeten your dour disposition."

Self-consciously he drew away from her and faced the captain. "Mark, you'd better take them up to Naomi's house. It's the only place here fit for company." He tried not to show his concern. It was hard to believe how much the captain had broken. "Me and Tobe will put the team away."

Zachary's steps were short. Letty put her arm around him, partly from affection but partly to give him support, Frank realized. He watched, sadness sweeping over him.

The black man declared, "Doctor says it's his heart. Miss Letty tries, but she can't slow him down much."

The captain looked better by evening, after resting awhile. At supper he brought several newspapers out of his bag. "I want to thank you folks for the hospitality you showed that newspaperman."

Homer said, "We showed him a lot of things." He glanced at Frank. "Hospitality wasn't always at the head of them."

The captain gave part of the newspapers to Frank, part to Naomi and Homer. "His stories created a stir in Dallas. I am surprised you haven't been overrun by adventurers."

Frank slanted the paper toward the lamplight, frown deepening as he read. When the fictionalized account of the cattle drive became too much, he flung the newspaper to the packed-earth floor. "They actually pay a man to write such lies as that?"

Homer laughed and read aloud the part about the band of hostile Indians who stampeded the buffalo and set off the cattle run that resulted in Frank's fall and trampling. "Hell's fire, there wasn't no Indians in the valley that day, nor none since."

Naomi said sternly, "We can do without the profanity, Mr. Whitcomb."

The captain said, "What is important, Frank, is that he speaks of you in the most glowing terms. True or not, that story can do us a great deal of good in the state capital. And in Dallas you could probably obtain financial backing for anything you wanted to do."

"All I want to do is stay in this valley. I don't need nothin' else."

The captain nodded thoughtfully. "Perhaps." He pushed shakily to his feet. "Let's go outside, Frank. I would like to take a little of the night air before bed."

They walked in silence, Frank taking slow, short steps to avoid pushing Zachary. At length the captain leaned against a corral post and stared into the night. "You said you don't need anything else, Frank. I wonder about that."

"Time," Frank said. "Time is all I need now."

"You'll have that, years and years of it. I wish *I* did."

"You been workin' a way too hard, sir."

"Because there was so much to do and so little time to do it. Now my time has almost run out."

Frank tried to argue, but the captain waved him down. "Even if the doctor hadn't told me, I'd know. I wouldn't mind, but I've left some things undone, and I'm afraid I won't be able to finish them. I may need your help."

"Anything you want, you just ask me."

"I'm concerned about Letty. I had hoped to see her married to a good man and her future secure before I had to leave her."

"She's a nice-lookin' woman. A little forward, and plain-spoken at times, but I reckon some wouldn't mind that. Can't she decide on a man?"

"She decided on one a long time ago, I think."

Frank stiffened. "You don't mean *me*, Captain?"

"She's always had an eye for quality, Frank."

Heat came to Frank's face. "There was only one time I ever felt like marryin', Captain, and one woman."

"I know about her. I also know that affair is beyond remedy. There comes a time when you have to close the book on the past and look to the future."

"That's easy said."

"In any case, I'd like to know you'll at least look after Letty's interests when I'm no longer around."

"She's got a strong mind of her own, but I'll try."

"That's good enough." The captain reached out, and Frank shook his hand.

During the next two days Frank took the captain and Letty over the valley in the captain's buggy. The more Letty saw, the more enthusiastic she seemed about the place. "Papa, if you would forget all your other business and move out here, I think you could regain your health."

"You'd like to live here?"

"I could stay in this valley the rest of my life."

The captain glanced at Frank. Frank diverted the conversation to land and cattle.

He thought at first Letty might have mellowed, that she was not going to burden him with advice. He was wrong; she simply saved it up to be dispensed all at one time. The third night she scolded, "Naomi Whitcomb is a fine woman, Frank, and you're asking altogether too much of her."

"I can't remember I ever asked anything of her."

"*Told* her, more than likely. She's cooking for this whole outfit on an open fireplace. She needs a good big stove. When I get back to Dallas I'll ship her the best one I can buy."

"We been doin' all right," he argued.

Letty said, "On second thought, it's high time this company hired a regular cook. I'll ship *two* stoves, and a man to come with them. You'd better get busy building a cookhouse."

Frank declared that she would do no such thing, but she paid no attention. "Naomi needs to be relieved of the burden. After all, she is in a family way again."

Frank stammered. "I didn't know she was—like that."

Letty sniffed. "If she'd been a cow, you'd probably have noticed." She began figuring aloud what else would be needed in the way of pots, pans and general utensils. Frank's words of protest went over her head and drifted off down the valley.

The morning of the Zacharys' leaving, the captain waited beside the buggy for Letty to say her good-byes to Naomi Whitcomb. He said, "Frank, I always knew you could do anything you set your mind upon. But this valley outshines anything I dreamed of."

Frank said, "I wouldn't be here if it wasn't for you. You backed me when I needed it." A thought came. "I still owe you a debt, Captain."

"A debt?"

"That first time I left Dallas, near the end of the war, you gave me a twenty-dollar gold piece. I've still got it."

"Keep it for luck. Perhaps now and again it will serve as a remembrance of me."

"I won't need a gold piece to remember you by, sir. But I'll keep it. Kindness don't come as easy to me as it does to you. Maybe someday when somebody needs help from me, I'll look at that gold piece and remember a man who was kinder to me than even my father was."

Frank had just begun the early-spring branding when a messenger brought a note from Letty. Even before he read it, he saw where a teardrop had smudged the ink, and he knew what the message would be. He crumpled the paper and closed burning eyes. Homer walked across the branding pen and silently took the note. He scanned it, then turned away toward the bawling cattle. He stood in unaccustomed silence and blew his nose.

At length he said, "You'll be goin' to Dallas, I suppose."

Dully Frank shook his head. "Captain's already buried. I reckon there ain't no use in hurryin' now."

"Letty says she'd like your help in gettin' her business affairs straightened out."

"Ain't much I know to help her with except this ranch."

"It might be she just wants some comfort right now."

"I'm not the one to give her that. Every time we get together, we end up in an argument."

Homer seemed out of patience with him. "I just wisht sometimes that you knew a little less about livestock and a little more about human people."

Tobe saw him coming and stood waiting for him in front of the tall white columns, before the steps that led up onto the porch. He reached for the reins as Frank stepped down from the saddle. "I'll take care of your horse, Mr. Frank. Miss Letty's in the house."

Frank studied the grieving eyes of the young black man who had spent his life in the captain's shadow. He placed a hand on Tobe's shoulder to say what he could not put into words.

"Lord, Mr. Frank," Tobe pleaded, "what'm I goin' to do? Who'm I goin' to belong to?"

Frank said, "You don't belong to nobody except yourself. You've been a free man ever since the war."

But he knew that in his mind Tobe had never been free. The slave dependence clung like a leaden weight to many who had grown up in it, even as at times Frank himself occasionally awakened suddenly from a bad dream, shuddering over an illusion that he was back on the Colorado River, a boy in rags, hungry, wondering if the day would yield him enough to eat. Old fears might be locked away out of sight, but they were never destroyed.

Head down, Tobe walked toward the barn, leading the horse. Frank looked up the steps to the double front door. He saw the slight figure of Letty Zachary standing just inside. Wondering what he could say, realizing he probably could say nothing, he started up the steps. She met him on the porch and put her arms around him. He held her a long while, neither speaking.

"I came as quick as I could get free," he managed finally.

Her cheek was pressed against his chest. "I've watched for you every day. It'll be easier now that you're here."

"I don't know much I can do to help."

She looked up with shining eyes. "Just be here."

Abel Babcock had remained the captain's partner on many ventures and his chief adviser on legal and financial matters. He came to the Zachary house as soon as he heard Frank had arrived. He was silver haired now and corpulent from a full enjoyment of his harvest years, but Frank sensed that he had lost none of his considerable mental capacity. He shook Frank's hand with a surprisingly strong grip. "Frank Claymore, it is great to see you, even under such sad circumstances. After those newspaper articles, a lot of people around town have looked forward to meeting you."

The thought of becoming a public display was unnerving. Frank said, "I just come because of Letty. She wrote that she wanted help gettin' the captain's business straightened out."

"Thomas Zachary put his affairs in good order before he died. About all Letty has to do is sign legal documents transferring ownership over to her."

Frank said in some confusion, "I don't know what she needed me for, then."

Babcock's eyes seemed to smile. "My expertise, if I have any, is in law and finance. My good wife will readily testify that I have little in the field of human relationships."

One day of accompanying Letty and Babcock convinced Frank that he had made the trip needlessly. Supposedly he had come to protect a vulnerable young woman from any who might exploit her ignorance of commerce. He was quickly disabused of that misconception. Letty knew her father's business as thoroughly as Frank knew his valley. She could tally to the bale how much cotton she had in storage, what had been paid and what the market would bear today.

She knew the real estate trades, the land parcels involved and their probable value with no more than a cursory glance in the ledgers she carried. When Frank stole a look at the books, he recognized that most of the notes were in a fine feminine hand—Letty's hand. He realized she had been her father's principal bookkeeper.

He told Babcock, when Letty was out of hearing, "It was a waste of my time comin' to see that nobody beats her out of anything. It's them she trades with who need a guardian."

Babcock smiled. "I knew that years ago. I am surprised you are just now coming around to that knowledge."

It became evident to him within a few days that Letty was methodically disposing of her father's trading ventures, none at any sacrifice.

"How come you're sellin' everything?" he asked her. "You could carry on with the business just like your daddy did."

"Not from way out at that ranch," she replied.

His jaw dropped. "The ranch? You ain't goin' out there."

"Why not? It's half mine."

"But you're a woman—a *single* woman."

"I don't expect to remain a single woman forever. Sooner or later, Frank Claymore, you are going to ask me to marry you."

Frank flinched as if she had bitten him. "You're crazy."

"Probably. But you will."

Face afire, he stomped back and forth, mustering his arguments. "I won't allow you to live at that ranch."

"I don't believe you have that much say in the matter."

"My agreement with the captain was that I am the boss of the ranch. I have the say."

"That agreement was with my father, not with me."

"You don't intend to live up to it?"

"I'll review the partnership contract. Whatever is in writing, I'll honor."

"That part wasn't written down. We just shaken hands on it, a gentlemen's agreement."

Her smile returned, wicked and calculating. "I am not a gentleman."

"And damned little of a lady," he exploded, stalking out of the house.

He went to Abel Babcock, who listened with a mixture of sympathy and amusement. Frank omitted the part about marriage. He said, "I have it in mind to buy her out. You think I could get the backin' here in Dallas?"

Babcock's wide brow slowly furrowed. "There is not enough financial backing in all of Texas if she does not care to sell."

"She might listen if *you* told her she doesn't belong out yonder."

"I'll not try to tell her where she belongs. She belongs wherever she wants to be." Babcock eyed Frank sternly. "You're both too strong-minded for your own welfare. If I were you, I'd be careful how I made the offer to her."

"I thought I'd take her to a nice restaurant and feed her a big supper."

"She once emptied a pitcher of water over a young man's head in a restaurant here, in full view of a hundred people. His proposal was somewhat different from yours, of course. At least I believe your intentions are honorable."

"She wouldn't dump no water on me. This is business."

Babcock suppressed a smile. "Just the same, I would have the waiter bring the water a glass at a time. I would not let him leave a pitcher on the table."

Frank read the prices on the menu and swallowed hard. He could spend half the value of a steer here on one meal. Much of the wording was strange.

"French," Letty told him. "It gives the place refinement."

Frank grunted. "Knew some Frenchmen on the Colorado when I was a button. Wasn't nothin' refined about that bunch; they couldn't hardly talk good English. Menu's just fixed to fool the public into thinkin' they're gettin' extra."

She was smiling. "Nobody fools you for long, Frank."

Her smile bothered him; it was as if she knew some secret joke on him and was laughing to herself. Abel Babcock had promised secrecy about their conversation, but now Frank wondered, for Babcock's first loyalty was to the Zacharys.

She said, "Well, *partner,* I am not often fooled either."

He hoped the warmth in his face did not show. He ran his finger down the menu, looking for a familiar word. He told her, "Get anything you want."

"I usually do," she said.

He stole a look at her eyes and wished he had not. His face was too warm now for the color not to be showing.

She said, "You had just as well get used to me, Frank. I have never been one to hold anything back."

True words if ever I heard any, he thought, warily glancing at the water pitcher the waiter had left without asking. He tried to plan a conversation that would lead her in the proper direction without being obvious. He looked around the high-ceilinged, white-painted room, its tall windows covered with elaborate curtains, the furniture looking too fancy for people actually to sit in.

"A place like this fits you like a hand in a glove," he observed. "Ain't nothin' like this in the valley, or even on the Clear Fork."

She caught him with her eyes as she might catch a fish on a hook. "How much, Frank?"

He drew back. "How much what?"

"You're leading up to trying to buy my half of the ranch, aren't you?"

Flustered, he demanded, "Did Abel Babcock tell you . . ."

"Abel Babcock told me nothing. *You* did. Your manner is transparent. You didn't bring me to this place just because you wanted to do something sweet. So tell me, how much?"

Frank stammered, "Well . . . I ain't figured on a price, exactly. We'd have to tally up what the cattle are worth, and the land." He tried to hold his eyes to hers but could not. "I wouldn't cheat you. I'd pay you a fair price."

"You don't have the money. You'd have to borrow it."

"I'll bet I could."

"Do you think you could raise more money than I can, Frank? You'd have to, you know."

He felt a prickling on his backside, a warning. "What do you mean?"

"The agreement was that either partner could buy out the other. The valley goes to whoever makes the highest bid. Think you can outbid me, Frank?"

He had a sense of being trapped; this turn of events had not crossed his mind. He felt the building tremble and thought it was his emotion playing tricks. He saw a flash through the lace curtains and heard thunder. The storm brewing outside was small compared to the one in Letty's determined eyes.

He said, "I didn't figure you'd feel that strong about it. I thought I'd be doin' you a favor, takin' that ranch burden off of you."

"You started this, Frank, and you can't back out now. I fell in love with that valley."

"But I found it. It's mine."

"Not if I exercise my option."

Stunned, he slumped in his chair and stared at her, hoping she would smile again and tell him it had all been a joke. Not since the battle on Dove Creek had he felt so boxed in. "Letty, you wouldn't take my valley . . ."

"Wouldn't I? You were going to take it from *me*."

"Not take it, *buy* it, and at a fair price." He looked across the room at people sipping wine. Right this minute he wished he were a drinking man. Anger began rising out of his helplessness. "You don't know nothin' about a ranch. There ain't no way you could take that valley and make it work."

"I could if I had the right kind of husband."

Frank listened to the thunder. The air seemed electric, about to explode, "Are you askin' me to marry you?"

"No. I'm waiting for you to ask *me*. I had rather you asked me of your own free will, but if coercion is necessary, I am not above that." Confidently she counted on her fingers. "Let's see . . . you now own a quarter of the ranch, and Homer owns a quarter. Marry me and you would own three quarters. *Don't* marry me and you own none."

He pushed angrily to his feet. "That's blackmail."

"It's business." She smiled, but the smile had a sharp edge. "Each of us wants something. All each of us has to do is agree to an honest trade."

He turned on his heel and almost knocked down a waiter carrying a tray. He dug into his pocket and came up with twenty dollars. "For the lady's supper," he said curtly. "That's all she's goin' to get from me!"

He stalked outside and was momentarily blinded by a flash of lightning. Tobe waited beside the buggy, looking up worriedly at the dark sky. "You-all done eatin', Mr. Frank? Maybe if we hurry we'll git home before the rain commences."

"Miss Letty'll be goin' home by herself."

Tobe blinked. "You ain't fixin' to walk with that storm comin', are you? You'll chill yourself to the bone."

"I've already taken a chill, in yonder." He set out walking, not sure where he was going, just sure he wanted to put Letty behind him. The thunder rattled windows. Lightning flashed in his eyes. The rain started, a quick sprinkle, then a downpour that went through his clothes and left him trembling from cold. He walked aimlessly, the wind-driven rain lashing at him. He talked angrily to himself, vowing to find a lawyer and fight her through the courts, though he realized after some consideration that her resources would surely beat him.

He became aware of a vague shape beneath a porch roof. A uniformed policeman watched him suspiciously. A gruff voice said, "You've had a bit too much to drink, haven't you, bucko? If you've got no place of your own to go to, I think I can find the place for you."

Frank angled across to the other side of the street, hands in his pockets, water pouring from the collapsed brim of his hat. He stopped just inside the big open door of a livery barn. The old familiar smell of the place brought him a feeling, for a moment, of being home. Fingering the locket Rachal had given him long ago, he shivered, watching the driving rain, the long muddy streets revealed in flashes of lightning. He wished he had stayed in the valley. In his frustration he cursed aloud, and someone grumbled sleepily in a pile of hay.

Much later he stood on the gallery of the Zachary home. Through an oval window he was surprised to see a candle burning in the front parlor. All decent folk should be in bed asleep. Hesitantly he rapped his knuckles on the door. The candle moved out of the parlor and into the front hall. The door opened, and the light flickered on Letty's face. She was still dressed as Frank had left her in the restaurant.

"Hello, Frank. I was hoping you might still come around."

He said, "You know I don't love you."

"You can learn. I have nothing more important to do than teach you."

"You know there's another woman. You know I've got a son. How can you want me when all that stands between us?"

"You love that valley. Did it come easy to you?"

"I worked like hell, and fought when I had to."

"Then *I'll* work like hell, and fight when I have to." She set the candle on a hall tree, reached up and placed her hands upon his cheeks. She stood on tiptoe, pulling his head down. She put warm lips against his and held them for a long moment. She whispered, "Don't tell me you don't feel *something* from that."

He would be a liar if he said an old wanting did not surge

in him. But he remembered another time, another woman. The wanting had been the same, but much else was different. "There's a word for it," he said, "but it's not love."

"Love will come," she whispered. "Give me the chance."

The wedding crowd was small, friends of Letty and her father able to come to the church on relatively short notice. When the services were over and well-wishers clustered around, the old minister said, "Young lady, I almost despaired of ever performing this happy duty for you. I rejoice, for I know you are the luckiest couple in Texas at this moment."

Frank tried to force up a smile. The ordeal of shaking hands with all these strangers was almost as formidable as having the cattle herd run over him. Abel Babcock was the last in line. He kissed Letty as he might kiss a daughter. "Your father and I worried a great deal about you, Letty. Now I can ease into my old age without that concern." He studied Frank, looked around to be sure no one else would hear, then said, "I know your reservations, Frank. But the time will come when you will look back and know this was the best day of your life."

Frank could think of no reply.

It was full dark when he pulled the buggy up in front of the Zachary home. Tobe and his parents had sat quietly in the rear of the church according to custom, and they had had more than time enough to be here ahead of Letty and Frank. Nevertheless, the house showed no light.

Letty said, "I sent the folks visiting. They won't be back for a couple of days. There'll be just us in the house, Frank, you and me." She touched his hand, asking for a response. He gave none.

He said, "Then you'd just as well climb down and go on in. I'll put up the team." He sensed her disappointment, though she said nothing until she had climbed the steps. At the front door she declared hopefully, "It is customary for the groom to carry the bride over the threshold."

"It is customary," he said flatly, "for a weddin' to be the groom's idea." He put the team into a trot toward the barn.

He took his time, dreading being in that house alone with Letty, wishing he could put down his lingering resentment. *My God,* he thought with a sense of despair, *how can I face the whole rest of my life with her if I can't even face the first night?*

When he could defer no longer, he entered the house through the rear door. Letty sat in the kitchen, waiting, still wearing the white wedding dress long kept in a cedar hope chest. He stopped short, staring at her as if for the first time today. He would not have told her, but here in this place, in the lamplight, in that dress, she was the most beautiful woman he had ever seen. A forlorn thought brought pain.

Why couldn't you be Rachal?

She asked, "Are you hungry? Bess cooked us a nice supper. It might have to be warmed a little."

"No need. I've eaten many a cold supper."

"But you shouldn't always have to remember that you ate one on your wedding night."

"Wouldn't be the worst thing that's happened to me today."

She grimaced. "I'll go put the jewelry away now."

He shrugged. "Do whatever suits you." He watched as she walked out, regretting that he was so cold to her, wishing he could tell her how beautiful she looked in that dress. He turned to the stove and kindled a fire. She was right about that supper. A lingering touch of winter was in the air, and there was no sense in eating the food cold.

Silence lay heavy between them all evening. Still wearing the white dress, Letty played the piano awhile, the music mostly slow and sad. When the tall grandfather clock at last struck eleven, she arose. She picked up the lamp, and he saw her hands tremble a little. She said, "I guess it's time."

He nodded reluctantly, wishing he knew what to do next. Seldom had he confronted a situation in which he could not see an answer somewhere. He saw none here. He stood up, and she handed him the lamp. She started up the wide stairs, taking a few steps, then looking back to be sure he followed. Quietly she opened the door to her room and stood while he brought the lamp.

He set it on a dresser and surveyed her bedroom. It was simpler than he had expected, though it had lace on the curtains, upon the arms of the chairs, upon the bedspread. He was profoundly aware of a faint and arousing suggestion of perfume. His heartbeat quickened, though he tried not to respond.

She said, "There's no need to be nervous. It's just me, and you've known me for years."

"I thought I knew you," he said. "In here you're somebody else, a stranger." He sat on the edge of the bed, trying not to be obvious as he looked at it.

"Papa always kept a bottle of brandy in his room. A drink of that might relax you."

"I'm relaxed," he lied, his heart pumping faster.

She walked behind a dressing screen in the corner. He could see only the top of her head as she removed the wedding dress and draped it carefully across the screen. She came out wearing a flowing nightgown cut precariously low in front. He turned away self-consciously, but he still saw her in his mind. She put her arms around him from behind, pulling his head back against the softness of her breasts.

"Do you sleep with your boots on?"

He blew out the light before he undressed. He slid between the blankets, shying away from the first touch of his leg against hers as if she might burn him. He lay looking up toward the ceiling, his breath short, his nerves wound tightly as a clock spring. It might have been less difficult had he simply slept in the captain's room tonight.

Letty's hand, warm and gentle, moved upon his chest. She raised up on one elbow and leaned over him, kissing him high on the cheek, then on the lips. "I know it's awkward for you," she said. "It's awkward for me too. But Papa taught me from the time I was a little girl that the best way to handle a problem is straight on. Get at it, he said, get it done, and it will be easier the next time."

She kissed him again. He felt fire in her face. She whispered, "I've wanted you for a long time, Frank. And whether you believe it or not, I'm going to make you want me."

Her wanting was strong, and he could not resist her long. His arms were soon around her, his hands roaming eagerly over the body that urgently pressed against him, answering his every move with one of her own. His resentment was lost somewhere in the rising insistence of a need long denied. She whispered his name and slid beneath him as he turned. It mattered not where he was or who she was. The years seemed to roll away, and he was once again in old Davis camp with another woman, in another time.

She clung to him with a desperation he had forgotten a woman could have, until at last she gasped and spoke his name again, and he answered, "Rachal . . . Oh, Rachal . . ."

8

Frank Claymore had lain awake much of the night, staring into the empty darkness at long-ago faces, long-ago scenes. In recent years memories had become his refuge from the increasing ugliness and contention in his valley. His listened to Homer's snoring in the other bed across the hotel room and wondered how his old partner could sleep so soundly while the world tumbled down around him.

He reached for his pocket watch lying on a small table. It was too dark to read the time, and striking a match might awaken Homer. Claymore was in no mood to listen to Homer talk from now until court took up. He rose stiffly, his hip giving him its morning lecture about the follies of youth and the penalties of age. The east window betrayed no sign of dawn, but lamplight shone from a small frame building across the street. Old Dutch-oven Devers was probably firing up his stove and putting on the coffeepot in his little chili-joint café.

Them old wagon cooks are always the first ones up, he thought. The habits of a range life were hard to break, even after a man admitted his years and moved to town.

He glanced across the dark room toward the vague shape that was Homer's bed. He wished Letty were here instead. But he had advised her not to attend the trial, fearing it would upset her. There was nothing she could do, except fret over him.

He put on his hat, then his shirt and trousers, and lastly his boots. His fingers, always stiff of a morning, gave him trouble in pulling the bootstraps. He fumbled for his cane, then quietly made his way to the door. It was not locked. That somebody might have the temerity to break in and attempt harm to him was a thought too outrageous to consider.

He almost stumbled across the deputy Willis, sleeping on a bedroll in the dark hallway. Anger came near making Claymore take a swing with his cane. *Still afraid I might run away,* he thought resentfully. *There ain't no trust in anybody anymore.*

He considered which would be the meanest, to awaken Willis from his sound sleep or to let him find out later that his charge had slipped past him. He chose the latter because he did not want the sneaky little son of a bitch trailing after him.

He made his way downstairs and through the lobby, where a night lamp burned dimly. The street was dark and quiet. He paused to take a long breath of the early-spring air. He could almost pretend the town did not exist, a condition he devoutly wished were real.

Devers's front door was unlocked, a fact that brought reassurance. Some people could endure town life without losing all their old virtues. A gruff voice called from back in the kitchen, "Coffee ain't ready yet. You'll have to wait."

A square-jawed man with belligerent mustache and three days' growth of whiskers appeared in the kitchen door, ready to fight the whole awakening world. He blinked in surprise, the challenge fading. "Mr. Frank! You all right?"

That he said Mr. *Frank* instead of Mr. *Claymore* was a favorable sign. Devers had cooked at Claymore's chuck wagon many years, until cold northers and hot summer sun became more than he wanted to face.

"Couldn't sleep," Claymore told him. "Don't ever let them put you on trial, Dutch-oven. You won't enjoy it."

"If they ever try me it'll be for singin' too loud in church. That's about all the sin that's left in me, these days." The cook frowned. "I hear the prosecutor's pounded you hard."

"You ain't watched any of it?"

Dutch-oven shook his head. "I *seen* a circus once. This one ain't even got an elephant."

"Yes, they have, and I'm it."

The cook returned to the kitchen. Through the door Claymore saw him dump a cup of water into the boiling pot to settle the grounds. He poured coffee into two cups and seated himself at the table with Claymore. Claymore saucered and blew on his. He marveled at Dutch-oven's ability to sip the scalding coffee without waiting. The cook had probably drunk enough of it in his time to flush the creek from one end of the valley to the other, Claymore thought. He must have a cast-iron mouth.

The two men sat in silence. Friendship did not require talk. Friendship was a rarity for Claymore in this town. He made an admission he had not voiced to anyone else. "They're fixin' to convict me, Dutch-oven."

The cook looked him in the eyes. Anyone else, even Homer, would have denied it and tried to soothe his feelings. Devers accepted the world the way it was, beauty and warts alike. He said, "That's the talk I hear."

Claymore could appreciate honesty, even when it went against him. "Did you hear the shots that night?"

Devers nodded.

"Did they all sound like they came from the same gun?"

Regret pinched Devers's eyes. "I wisht I could say somethin' to help you. At the distance, with the echoes and all, one gun would sound like another."

Claymore stared at his cup, dreading the day. When he looked up, the hotel across the street was emerging from darkness. "I'd best be goin'. When your regular customers start showin' up, I won't be good for your business."

"The hell with them," the old cook said with a snort. "If it's any comfort to you, Mr. Frank, I don't let them cuss you in my place. They all know where I stand."

"Thanks, but you better take care of your own business.

A man can get awful lonesome, speakin' up for an unpopular cause."

"I worked for you many a year, Mr. Frank. I seen you do things I didn't agree with, but I never seen you do nothin' little or mean. Whatever you done, I figure you had cause."

A minority opinion, Claymore judged, but he was grateful. He reached into his pocket for a coin. Dutch-oven motioned for him to keep it. "You don't owe me; I owe you for all the years you put up with an ill-tempered old reprobate like me."

Claymore said, "If you hadn't made good coffee, I'd've kicked you out of the valley years ago. One ill-tempered old reprobate is enough, and I'm him."

As he reached the door he almost bumped into a customer coming in. He blinked, recognizing the heavyset reporter with the thin gray hair, the one who had vaguely troubled him ever since the trial began. "Don't I know you from someplace?" Claymore demanded.

The reporter had a slight stoop to his shoulders, and he made an effort to straighten them. "You don't remember me?"

"I do and I don't. Why am I supposed to?"

"I am Jeffrey Singer, Mr. Claymore. I accompanied you when you brought your first herd to this valley."

As Claymore studied him in the dawn's brightening light he saw remnants of the young man, but time had not been kind. "Sort of let yourself go to seed, ain't you?"

"We've all changed, Mr. Claymore."

"Your stories damned sure have. Them you wrote about me a long time ago, they made me sound like Sam Houston and Davy Crockett and Kit Carson, all in one. Them you're writin' now make me sound like Satan's stepbrother."

Singer shrugged his heavy shoulders. "Readers change, too. In those days they wanted heroes. Today they are looking for villains. I am a writer. I write what they will read." He nodded. "Good morning, Mr. Claymore," and went on into the little café, where prices were cheaper than across the street. Claymore frowned after him, resentment churning the coffee he had just drunk. He would bet that when Singer listed his expenses, he put down hotel prices for the meals.

He limped back to the hotel, turning on the gallery to see the first color rise over the motley collection of frame and rock structures that had so long cluttered the lower end of the valley. Daylight would not improve them.

He walked up the stairs, taking his time. In the hallway Willis still slept while the world awakened around him. A malevolent urge took possession of Claymore, and he poked Willis in the stomach with the point of his cane. Willis awoke with a start, eyes wide. He flung aside his thin blanket. He had been sleeping in his clothes, even his boots.

"Where do you think you're goin', Claymore?" he demanded. "If you thought you'd sneak past me, you're wrong. You don't even blow your nose unless I'm there to watch you."

Claymore said dryly, "I ought to've known I couldn't put anything over on you. If I was you, I'd hit Ed up for a raise."

He found Homer sitting on the edge of his bed, pulling his boots on. Homer grunted, "I hope you slept better than I did. I laid awake all night, rememberin'. What makes the old times always seem better?"

Claymore replied sadly, "They *was* better. We was always happy, then."

Frank had not expected to return from Dallas to the valley at the head of a caravan. But to his chagrin the buggy pointed the way for four wagons, two loaded with lumber, one with some of Letty's household goods, one carrying carpenters and stonemasons she had hired. He rode in silence for the most part, occasionally breaking the quiet with an impatient grumbling as he looked back at the wagons unable to keep up the pace he insisted upon setting.

Letty smiled too much. When Frank attempted perversely to provoke her into argument, she declined the bait. "If you're trying to make me turn back, Mr. Claymore, you are much too late. I am Mrs. Claymore now, and Mrs. Claymore I shall remain."

He grumbled, "It wasn't my idea."

"But it isn't as bad as you thought." She leaned her head against his shoulder. "You haven't complained about the nights."

He looked back quickly to see if the servant Tobe or one of the other three men on horseback was within hearing. Some things a couple did not talk about in the presence of others. Some things were not proper even to discuss with each other. He could not evade some feeling of guilt because he did not want to enjoy going to bed with her, but he could not help himself.

"I never saw such a shameless woman."

"I am shameless only with you, sir."

She had seemed but briefly disturbed by the fact that in an irresponsible moment he had called her by another woman's name, that in his heart he had been making love to someone else. The second night as she moved beneath him she bit his ear gently and whispered, "This is me—your wife Letty—and I am not going to let you forget it, ever again."

At times he still did. Letty stirred him in ways he was ashamed of, and Rachal remained a third person in their bed.

The string of wagons pulled into the whiskey village of Fort Griffin, whereupon half of the crew, tired after several arduous days on the trail, proceeded to get staggering, falling, laying-down drunk. Frank resorted to profane extremes to no avail. There would be no moving this outfit for at least a day or two.

"I never could understand why men let a bottle make slaves out of them," he declared with exasperation.

Letty said patiently, "Every person has some kind of weakness. Mine is you. What is your weakness, Frank?"

"I never had one."

He detested this town, which had begun its existence as

a parasitic growth beneath the high hill upon which the army had built its fort of the same name, overlooking the Clear Fork of the Brazos River. It maintained a precarious existence at first, peddling cheap liquor at high price to the soldiers, providing them abundant opportunity to lose their meager pay over a card table or in the beds of coarse-mouthed women who washed their guts with whiskey more thoroughly than they washed their skins with water. Frank had long enjoyed an ungiving contempt for all such self-destructive activity. A man ought to be out yonder working and saving, building something for himself, not squandering his time and resources on something so transient and profitless, he had always declared. If a man worked hard enough, exhaustion would protect him from such nonsense.

Of late, since Colonel Mackenzie had driven the Comanches and Kiowas to the reservation, Fort Griffin town had become headquarters for an army of buffalo hunters who earlier had turned the Kansas prairies into a boneyard. Now they had begun the slaughter of the Texas herd. The wind carried a nostril-twisting stench from long ricks of dried buffalo hides piled in traders' yards. Spring had given life to millions of flies that followed the hide wagons in from the buffalo range. Fanning them away from his face, Frank said to Letty, "Let's get out of this pesthole. We'll go visit the Akins family till your damned drunks swill their fill and get ready to work."

"*Our* drunks," she corrected him. "It will be your house too."

"Bunkhouse was good enough for me."

After waiting for a tandem pair of hide-laden wagons to move past, trailed by their full complement of flies, Frank swung the buggy team around and started down the dusty street toward the Clear Fork road. Another wagon came to meet him, carrying a load of hay from last fall's cutting.

"At least the farmers are makin' somethin' out of this," he said, trying to find some saving virtue for the town.

As the wagon neared he muttered under his breath. The

driver was George Valentine. Frank's attention shifted to a boy of ten or eleven who shared the wagon seat. His stomach drew into a knot as he reined his team to a stop.

Letty sensed his sudden change. "What is it?" She looked at the oncoming wagon and went quiet. It was almost scary, the way she seemed to read his mind.

George Valentine appeared to look for a place to turn his wagon and avoid meeting the buggy, but there was no side street. Coming up even, he said reluctantly, "Howdy, Frank." He glanced toward Letty with some curiosity. "Been a long time."

Frank's attention remained with the youngster. "Didn't figure to run into you, George." The boy had been a baby in Rachal's arms the last time. But Frank knew the face, in many ways a mirror image of his own when he had been this age.

George brought his fingers to the brim of his hat for Letty's sake. "Howdy to you, lady."

Frank remembered the proprieties. "George, this is my wife Letty. You remember Captain Zachary. Letty's his daughter."

George nodded. "Pleased to meet you, ma'am. Sorry about your father's passin'. He was a good man."

Letty uneasily murmured her thanks.

George said. "This here is Billy—my son."

It seemed to Frank that George put an unnecessary emphasis on the last part. Billy's blue eyes were fastened upon Frank. They were sad eyes, Frank thought. The boy's clothes were threadbare, though George's were also. Billy's hands were big and rough from hard work.

His son, or his slave? Frank wondered darkly. He doubted the advisability but had to ask, "How's Rachal?"

George's eyes narrowed. "Tolerable. I'll tell her you inquired." He looked once more at Letty. "I'll tell her about you too, ma'am."

Billy studied Frank in brooding silence as the wagon moved on.

Frank sat a moment before putting the buggy team into motion. He kept exploring that unhappy young face in his mind.

Letty said, "He's a good-looking boy."

Frank knew no way to respond.

She said, "Perhaps someday we'll have one like him."

Frank avoided Letty's eyes. He flipped the reins and spoke to the team.

Their return to the valley as a married couple did not surprise Homer and Naomi as much as Frank thought it properly might. He suspected collusion, at least between the women. He could not accuse them without tacitly admitting that he had been entrapped. He would not consider such an admission.

Watching Naomi and Letty hug each other, Frank pondered their similarities, and their differences. Both had a strong tendency to speak their minds whether they offered sense or not. Physically, Naomi outweighed Letty by at least thirty pounds. Naomi had never lived in a town, and she labored over reading a newspaper. By contrast, Letty was city raised and educated. Naomi, despite her critical tongue, had a country-woman sense of proprieties, an almost militant modesty that sometimes made Frank wonder how she and Homer had managed to produce their two sons and the pregnancy that now was becoming obvious. Letty was forward and bold, delighting in fetching a blush to her husband's cheeks.

Naomi told Letty, "You and Mr. Claymore will take the boys' room. The baby can sleep with me and Homer, and Jimmy's big enough to stay in the bunkhouse with Mark and the hands."

Letty shook her head. "We've brought a large tent. We'll board up its sides and be as cozy as two bunnies in a burrow till the men get our house built. Won't we, Frank?"

He always expected her to put the most suggestive connotation to whatever she said. His face warmed. "We'll get by."

Naomi insisted that she at least share her kitchen until Letty's own was ready. Frank would not say so, but he approved of that arrangement. He had not yet learned if Letty was any kind of cook, but he knew Naomi was as skilled a one as ever touched steak to skillet. For that great virtue he had long overlooked her irritating tendency to intrude in his business.

Frank beckoned to Homer, and they walked toward the barns. He said with a hint of accusation, "I hoped you'd be more surprised."

Homer grinned. "That girl wanted you, Frank. Any blind man except you could've seen it. I don't suppose you'd want to tell me how she roped and tied you?"

Frank said nothing. Homer muttered, "I didn't much figure you would."

Frank gazed at the expanse of spring grass. "Anything happened here?"

Homer shook his head. "Been some buffalo hunters come by, wantin' to know if it's all right to kill them in the valley."

Frank grimaced. The buffalo were a nuisance to him, but those great ricks of hides in Fort Griffin had sent a cold shudder down his spine. "What did you tell them?"

"To wait and ask you."

Frank considered, then said reluctantly, "If you see any more, tell them to go ahead and do it. Buffalo get in the way of the cattle. And tell them I'll expect them to shoot any wolves they come across. I hate losin' calves."

Homer's silence indicated he did not like the decision any more than Frank did, but progress carried its price. At length Homer's old grin returned. "Captain'd be glad to know you brought his daughter here to stay. And I'm glad for *you*, Frank. The right woman can give a man a lot of good things. That Rachal ain't worth you wastin' your life."

Anger rushed over Frank. With difficulty he restrained

himself from grabbing Homer by the collar. He choked back words that might have set a breach between them for the rest of their lives. "I don't want you to ever say nothin' bad about Rachal. Not now, not ever again."

Homer swallowed, but he did not look away. It was Frank who had to divert his eyes, ashamed for his outburst, though he would not say so.

Homer said soberly, "I thought you'd finally put the past behind you. If you married that little woman just to be a substitute for somebody else, I reckon this is the first time I was ever bad disappointed in you."

Frank watched narrowly as Homer walked back to his house. He could not recall that Homer had ever spoken to him that way, no matter how Frank might on occasion have abused him. The realization left him cold.

Frank was supervising the carpenters in boarding up the sides of the tent when one of the young cowboys rode in from the north, looking nervously back over his shoulder. He carried his rifle across the pommel of his saddle. Sweat showed that the horse had been run.

"Mr. Claymore!" the rider shouted before he was within talking distance. "Mr. Claymore!"

Frank had caught a carpenter sawing boards off short to fit the temporary tent, boards he had frugally expected to reuse in building the house. He was already shy of patience. "You don't have to holler," he replied curtly. "I'm right here."

"So's somebody else, sir. I seen a couple of horsebackers up yonder."

"Who were they?"

"I don't know. Soon's I rode toward them they pulled away. I'm afraid they're probably Indians."

Frank looked quickly toward the carpenters. The last thing he needed was an Indian scare that might stampede them back to Dallas. He motioned the boy toward the barn, out of anyone else's hearing. "Ain't been an Indian here since Mackenzie. Maybe they was buffalo hunters. Maybe they taken *you* for an Indian."

The boy gazed up the valley with a lingering of fear in his eyes. "One sure looked like an Indian to me. Other one, I couldn't tell."

Frank wondered. Indian times were passing, and now every young man who had never seen one suddenly wanted to, before it was too late. The boy was probably exercising a rich imagination. Still, it hadn't been that long.

Frank thought of another possibility. Now and again the valley was visited by the long-rider breed, outlaws looking for a place where memories were short and lawmen scarce. Frank had hired a couple of these, figuring they would do him no harm so long as they drew their pay. Their presence was a deterrent to other outsiders, for they were not men to mess with.

"All right," he said quietly, "go see how many hands you can bring here to me. Don't say nothin' about Indians."

He went into a corral and saddled a horse while the boy Joe hunted up half a dozen men, including Homer and Mark. Quietly Frank told them, "Joe claims he run into a couple of suspicious riders. Anybody else seen anything that didn't look right?"

The men looked blankly at each other. A young hand punched Joe and grinned. "Was one of them a girl?" he asked hopefully.

Joe replied defensively, "Not unless she was an Indian." He caught Frank's critical stare and looked down.

Frank said, "I don't want to excite people here without cause, so don't nobody else mention Indians. It's probably just buffalo hunters, or squatters hopin' for a place to light. We'll split up in pairs. If it's hunters, tell them they're welcome. If it's squatters, tell them to camp a night and move on. This valley is taken."

They searched most of the afternoon, but Joe was unable to show Frank anything that substantiated his report. The horse tracks they found might have been left by anyone, including the ranch's own riders.

Joe's face reddened as Frank expressed his reservations.

"I'll swear on Jeff Davis's grave, Mr. Claymore, they was here."

Frank's recollections of the Confederacy led him to expect better collateral. "Maybe. Let's go to supper." The rest of the horsemen fell in with them as they rode back across the valley. Joe brought up the rear in solitary discomfort.

In truth, Frank was strongly inclined to accept the boy's account, and it occurred to him he probably should tell him so. But he held his silence because of the chance Joe had been victim of an active imagination. It was easier to withhold praise than to withdraw it.

The search and its lack of results continued to bother him, though he said nothing of it to the women. They had just as well assume the afternoon's scout had been a cow hunt. He lay in bed, staring into the tent's darkness, knowing he must go back out tomorrow and search again. Letty's warm hands gently tickled and teased him, but he did not respond. He worried not only about possible intruders in the valley but also about the probability that any sounds he and Letty made would carry beyond the thin canvas to eavesdroppers. He did not trust those lewd-mouthed city carpenters.

He became dimly aware of movement outside the tent, and he sat up in bed. Homer's voice called, "Frank! You awake?"

Frank swung his bare feet to a cotton rug Letty had laid on the ground as substitute for a wooden floor. "I am now."

"Light a lamp. You got company."

This time of night? What in the hell? Frank quickly drew on his hat, then his trousers. He was buttoning his shirt when he opened the tent flap. He saw two vague shapes. One he took to be Homer. The other was much smaller.

"Can we come in?" Homer asked. "I mean, I wouldn't want to embarrass Letty."

She was sitting up in the bed, a blanket drawn around her. "It's all right, Homer."

Homer ducked to pass through the low opening. "Come

on, boy." A lad followed timidly. Frank lifted the lamp to shine full in the boy's face. His knees went weak.

"Billy Valentine!"

Homer nodded soberly. "That's who he is, all right. You can imagine how surprised I was when he showed up at our door, lookin' for you. He naturally figured the *big* house would be yours."

The boy stared boldly at Frank. Frank studied him a minute before demanding, "How'd you get here, son?"

The boy said, "You're my real daddy, ain't you? Folks say you are."

Frank avoided looking back at Letty. "Folks say lots of things. What do your mama and daddy tell you?"

"They don't tell me nothin'. Papa told me never to talk about it."

Frank demanded, "What're you doin' here, boy?"

Hesitantly Billy Valentine replied, "I come to live here."

Letty had wrapped a robe around herself. She bent before the boy. Her voice was compassionate. "Surely, young man, you didn't come all this way by yourself?"

The boy nodded. "Yes, I did. I followed the tracks of your wagons most of the way. I never got lost till I come off into this valley. That's when the man found me."

Frank glanced at Homer. "What man?"

Billy shrugged. "He didn't tell me."

"What did he look like?"

"An old man. Drawed up and thin, with a white beard. Looked kind of crazy when he first come up to me. I tried to run, but he caught me, him and that Indian."

"Indian?"

The boy's eyes went wide as he told it. "I thought for sure I was killed and scalped, but the old man told me not to be scared. Said he'd been huntin' a long time for a boy like me. He asked me who I was and what I was doin' way out by myself. Seemed real surprised when I said I was Billy Valentine, and I was lookin' for *you*."

"He knew your name . . . and mine?"

"Said he knowed there was people in the valley, but he didn't know you was one of them. Then he brought me here."

Homer asked, "What about the Indian?"

"He went on by himself. Just the old man fetched me."

Frank stared at Homer, wonder changing to possibility, possibility to conviction. His blood ran cold. He pushed quickly through the tent flap, out into darkness.

"Sam!" he shouted. "Sam Ballinger!"

Homer came out of the tent and stood beside him. "Sam Ballinger's dead, Frank. It's been years . . ."

"He's alive. That was him brought the boy. It had to be him."

He called again: "Sam Ballinger! It's me, Frank Claymore."

He had awakened just about everybody in camp, but that did not matter. He trembled from the night's chill, only a thin and half-buttoned shirt to protect him, but that was of no consequence either. He walked farther from the tent, the rough ground cutting at his bare feet.

He called once more, and from down the creek came a cautious reply. "That you, Frank Claymore? That really you?"

Frank's eyes burned. "It's me, Sam. Come on in here where I can see you."

From out of the darkness a man came timidly on horseback. Twenty feet away he halted, hands high to give assurance that he presented no threat. "You sure you're Frank Claymore?"

Frank's voice broke. "As sure as you're Sam Ballinger." He walked out to the horse and raised his hands. "Come down from there, Sam. You're home."

Hesitantly Sam said, "I hope I done right, fetchin' the boy. For a minute when I found him, I thought . . ." He rubbed one hand over his eyes, then slowly dismounted. Frank threw his arms around Sam and felt the gaunt shoulders racked with a quiet sobbing.

Homer finally said, "Everybody'd just as well come on up to the house. Ain't nobody goin' to sleep anymore tonight."

The boy Billy was bewildered by the excitement. He stuck close to Frank's side as Frank and Letty hurriedly dressed. He walked with them to Homer and Naomi's house, where lamplight glowed yellow in the windows.

The only thing he said was, "You goin' to let me stay?"

Frank did not answer.

Naomi made coffee. Sam Ballinger caressed the cup between his hands and smelled the steam with the look of a man standing at the gates of heaven. He had always been spare of flesh, and now he looked poor as a whippoorwill. His hands were thin and frail-looking. His eyes, sunken and burned out, stayed on the boy Billy.

Frank knew why. "Ever find any trace of *your* boy, Sammy?"

A heavy sadness weighed in Sam's face. "Never so much as a word. I reckon over the years I visited near every Indian camp from here to the big mountains. I've looked at a hundred captured young'uns—white and Mexican and Indians of enemy tribes. I've talked to just about every Comanche that walks. Never a one owned up to seein' my boy."

Homer said, "We figured you was killed by the first bunch you come upon."

Sam looked at him with haunted eyes. "I taken roundance on them for a long time, and studied the camps from a ways off. They'd come huntin' me, and I'd slip away. After a while they decided I was crazy, and they left me alone. Got to where I could ride into a camp bold as old Lucifer. Once they knowed what I'd come for, seemed like most of them kind of wanted to help.

"Taken me awhile, Frank, knowin' some of them had likely been the ones killed my womenfolks and taken my boy, but I got to where I made friends amongst them. They ain't bad people, when you know them. They just look at things different."

Naomi was frying steak. The aroma carried to Sam, and he lifted his head like an animal might to sniff out a scent. "Don't seem possible you're that little girl of Bige Akins's. You wasn't much bigger than a minute, nor older than a pup."

She was considerably bigger than that now, well along in the carrying of her third child. She loved to cook, and she loved to eat. She said, "You don't look like you've had a full meal the whole time you was gone. But I'll fix that."

Letty was making up a batch of biscuits. She had never known Sam Ballinger, so she watched him now with curiosity and a touch of fear. Frank thought he could read her mind. She was thinking the Indians had been right in their first appraisal: Sam was a bit crazy.

Sam said, "Most trouble I had was after the Indians was driven to the reservation. Army and agency people didn't like white folks messin' around; figured they was whiskey runners and horse thieves. I dodged soldiers more than I ever dodged Indians."

Frank glanced at Billy. "Boy said an Indian was with you."

Sam nodded. "Comanche. This used to be his runnin' grounds. When he come into manhood he talked to his spirits down yonder on that pile of rocks. Now he's got him a wife, and she's turned sickly carryin' his child. He wanted to see if he could get his spirits to help her. We figured this country'd be swarmin' with white people by now, and maybe I could keep them from killin' him. I had no idee this was your valley till we come onto the boy."

Frank asked, "Is your Indian at the rocks now?"

Sam's eyes were suddenly guarded. "You wasn't figurin' to do somethin' to him . . ."

"I've got no quarrel with Indians anymore, long's they got none with me."

"He's callin' on his spirits . . . if they didn't all leave when the white man came."

"We'll pass word to the hands to let him alone."

Sam seemed considerably relieved.

Frank said, "Sam, you'll stay here with us, won't you?"

Sam pondered. "I'm an old man. I couldn't do enough work, hardly, to pay my keep. And I ain't got a nickel."

"You're wrong about that. We finally had to sell your cattle, but the money's drawin' interest in a Dallas bank. I always hoped you'd come back."

Tears ran down Sam's cheeks and disappeared into the unkempt white beard. The boy Billy stared at him in wonder, as if he had never seen a man cry. Sam reached out, and Billy went to him. Sam gripped the boy's shoulders with thin hands. "How about you, boy? *You* goin' to stay here?"

Billy said, "Yes, sir, I am."

Frank put in reluctantly, "I'm afraid Billy has run away from home. His mother'll be worryin' herself to death. Soon's he's rested, we'll have to be sendin' him back."

Billy cried out in protest.

Frank had to shove his hands into his pockets, for he wanted to crush the boy in his arms and never let him go. His right hand closed on Rachal's locket. If George Valentine were the only consideration, Billy could stay here forever. But Frank had to think of Rachal. Because of her, he could never acknowledge his son.

He said, "When you're of age, Billy, you can come here and stay. For now, your mother needs you."

The boy turned away from him and ran crying to Sam. Frank could only look at the floor. The cry cut like a knife.

Naomi took Billy into the room where her own boys slept. There, with Letty's help, she spread a pallet for him on the floor. During what was left of the night, the adults sat and looked at each other. Frank and Homer took turns drawing out Sam on his experiences during those long, lost years. Often Sam used strange words Frank assumed were Indian, words that fit a situation better than the English Sam had used so little during his exile.

A notion took Frank by surprise. *He's turned half Indian himself.*

More than once Sam brought the conversation back to Billy Valentine. "If my boy Sammy was still alive, he wouldn't be but a few years older than Billy. This is a boy with a lot of trouble on his shoulders, Frank. You could help him." Sadness lay deep in his eyes. "I'd like to help you help him."

If he just knew how bad I want to do that, Frank thought. "Best help we can give him is to send him back to his mother."

Letty touched Frank with gentle hands. "Maybe if we just let him stay a little while . . . We could send word . . ."

Frank looked at his wife in surprise. He wondered that she could consider such a thing, knowing who Billy Valentine was, knowing his presence would be a constant reminder of another woman. "He might get to likin' it here, and I might get to likin' for him to be here. Longer he stayed, the harder it'd be to leave. Better he leaves now."

Naomi was not often inclined to grant him the final word. "I wisht I was like you, Frank Claymore . . . always right." Her voice was heavy with sarcasm. Frank tried not to take offense but to blame it on her pregnancy. There had been times, in the past, when he had doubted himself. He seldom did anymore. "The boy goes home."

At first sign of daylight the women began breakfast. Sam slumped in a chair, nursing yet another cup of coffee. Frank said, "Me and you and Homer better go see to your Indian. Wrong people come across him, they might do him harm."

As they rode, Frank was surprised to learn that Sam knew this valley well. He told of coming here once to see about a blue-eyed boy said to be riding with a hunting party of Comanches and Kiowa allies. The boy had turned out to be simply an Indian with a dark birthmark blotched across his face.

"Boy carried strong buffalo medicine though," Sam said. "The party couldn't find a buffalo in the whole valley. He climbed up on that point of rocks and talked to the spirits, and they sent more buffalo than the whole nation would've needed for winter rations." Sam's eyes narrowed. "You don't believe that, but you can see strange things if you look with more than just your eyes. White man don't see, and he don't hear, but that don't mean the Indian spirits ain't out there just the same."

When they neared the medicine hill, Sam raised one hand. "I better ride up there by myself and put his mind at ease." He rode ahead. Once he had been one of the strongest men on the Clear Fork. Now a brisk wind might blow him away.

Frank said, "I had about given up on ever seein' him alive."

Homer murmured, "Are you sure he is? He ain't the Sam Ballinger we used to know."

"We've all changed."

"Not like him. He left more in that Indian country than just tracks. He left a part of his mind."

After a time Sam hailed them from the foot of the great rock pile. Frank saw another man on horseback, a blanket wrapped around his shoulders. As Frank made out the dark features and the black eyes that studied him distrustfully, recognition chilled him.

"I know this man," he declared. "This is Red Shield!"

Sam argued, "No, that ain't what he's called." He spoke the name, but the sound was alien to Frank.

Frank said, "*I* called him Red Shield because he carried one. Him and me, we met each other twice—one time right where we're at."

Studying Frank intently, the Indian spoke in a quiet voice, as if revealing a secret. Sam nodded at Frank. "He says you've changed a right smart, but he remembers. Says you were a man he couldn't scare."

"I damned near wet my britches."

Sam spoke in the Indian's language, adding a few hand signs Frank easily followed. A slow smile came to the Comanche. It had never occurred to Frank that Indians had a sense of humor.

Sam declared, "Red Shield says the war days are over. It's time for old enemies to be friends."

Frank extended his hand. Red Shield took it hesitantly. Frank said, "Tell him I hope he finds his spirits. Tell him to stay as long as he wants to. When he's ready to start home, we'll send an escort to be sure nobody messes with him."

The next day Sam volunteered to take Billy Valentine back to the Clear Fork. He said he wanted to see his old homestead anyway. Frank suspected he just wanted to be with the boy awhile longer. Billy did not cry, but he looked back over his shoulder as long as Frank stood watching him.

Rusty Farraday appeared in the valley that winter with several wagon loads of supplies. By the time Mark Akins and a couple of the cowboys discovered him far down in the south end, he had already constructed a rude dugout into the side of the high west wall. Frank rode there with half a dozen men and found Farraday had just as many, Fort Griffin toughs who looked as if they would spill blood for the pleasure of it, whether it paid them a dollar or not. Several wagon loads of goods were lined up on either side of the dugout. Clearly, this was meant to be a trading post.

Farraday stood in front of his dugout, rifle in his hands, red-veined eyes full of whiskey and fight. He had matured from the boy he had been the first time Frank had seen him, but age had brought no improvement. "I got every right to be here, Claymore. George Valentine sent to Austin to see what you have a right to and what you don't. You never had more than a Winchester claim to the bottom end of this valley. Now it's me and George's, and he's got the papers."

"Papers don't mean nothin' out here. You're a long ways from Austin."

"But not from Griffin. You give us any trouble and we'll fetch the law out here so fast you'll think a blue norther has come down and froze you. We're settin' up a hide-buyin' station, and there ain't one damned thing you can do about it."

Frank's face was afire. "There never was a time I couldn't whip the likes of you, Farraday. I'll give you three days to load up this mess and clear out. If you're still here, we'll see about that whippin'."

Letty was disturbed. She said, "I'll go to Austin and talk to my father's old friends. Perhaps the climate there has changed, and they can help us find a way to get title."

Frank declared, "Politicians! The only way to fix this is to meet George and Rusty face-to-face, and stop them right now. If we let them keep even a foothold, we'll be fightin' them from now on."

Letty was still pleading with him the morning he rode south, flanked by almost every man who worked for the ranch. They passed the medicine hill in somber silence and traveled on down the western side of the valley, near the high wall that sheltered them from the cold winter wind moaning across the rimrocks. Frank was not surprised to see that the number of wagons had increased. A horseman at the edge of camp spurred toward the dugout. A dozen armed men fanned out in a broad line to face Frank and his riders. Frank scowled, knowing the two in the center. Rusty Farraday had been joined by George Valentine.

A third man stepped out in front and walked with firm stride to meet the riders. He was tall and thin and carried himself like a soldier. He wore a pistol on his left hip.

Frank discerned, to his surprise, that the man had but one arm. Recognition was jarring.

Alex McKellar stopped to wait for the horsemen, his gaze locked on Frank. He pulled open his unbuttoned long coat. A silver badge glinted on a woolen jacket beneath. McKellar gave Frank a moment to see it, then let go of the lapel. He had changed little since the last time Frank had seen him except that he was a decade older, a decade grimmer.

"Hello, Frank Claymore," he said calmly. "I have not seen you since Chisum's ranch, after the battle on Dove Creek."

Frank wore two heavy coats, but the cold seemed to bite through. He shivered. "Lieutenant McKellar! This is the last place I'd've expected to see you."

"Given my choice, those men back there would not be my preferred company. Nevertheless, I am here as a Texas Ranger. I am charged to see that the laws of this state are upheld. Farraday and his crowd are a motley lot, but it is their right to be where they are."

"It's my valley, Lieutenant."

"Not *lieutenant* anymore, just *sergeant*. But the full authority of the state stands behind me. I must ask you to withdraw."

Frank's back stiffened. "Where's the rest of your Rangers?"

"I am the only one here. I came with faith that you would respect the law."

"What kind of law takes land away from honest people and turns it over to the likes of those? Hide-tradin' post, they call it. Whiskey camp is what it'll be, like Griffin."

"I do not like it, but the law is clear. We fought side by side once, Frank. I would not wish us to fight face-to-face."

Frank looked with bitterness past McKellar to George and Farraday and the toughs who waited almost eagerly for a fight. *We could take them,* he thought. *It would be easy.* But he would have to overrun Alex McKellar to reach them.

That he would not do.

He asked, knowing the answer, "You're sure about the law?"

McKellar nodded gravely. "I'm sure, Frank, and I'm sorry."

Frank grimaced. "If it wasn't for you, Lieutenant, I'd've died at Dove Creek. I'd have to hurt you bad, maybe kill you, to get past you here."

McKellar said flatly, "You would."

Frank glanced at Homer and Mark and the other men who stood willing to do whatever he asked of them, regardless of cost. This he could not ask.

Reluctantly he said, "You're in bad company here, sir. I think you'd find our place more to your likin'."

McKellar sighed in relief. "It would pleasure me to go with you."

Frank tried at first to keep the buffalo hunters' wagons out of the valley as they hauled half-cured flint hides to the rough outpost for sale or trade, but after a time he saw that was a futile effort. While he was turning back one, two more would pass him on the far side. By midwinter he acknowledged the inevitable. The best he could do was forbid his working hands from having any contact with Farraday's hide camp and the people who infested it. He skirted the place occasionally to view it from afar and test his suspicions. The first time he found a fresh grave a couple of hundred yards from camp. The second time the number had grown to three. Bad whiskey, bad company and absence of accountability mixed like gunpowder and flame.

The third time he came suddenly upon Rusty Farraday and one of his station hands, riding to intercept a string of wagons. The meeting was as much a surprise to Frank as to the others. Farraday was caught sober, without the bracing effect of whiskey to stiffen his backbone. He watched Frank with anxiety and eased his hand down toward the stock of the rifle beneath his leg. Frank leaned forward in his saddle, and Farraday jerked his hand up empty, eyes betraying his fear. "We're doin' no harm, Claymore. You owe us the road."

"I owe you nothin'," Frank said, fists clenched. "But I owe Alex McKellar, and I made him a promise. Now I'll make *you* a promise, Farraday: I'll leave you alone if you leave me alone. But if ever you let harm come to me or mine because of that hellhole you've got down here, Alex McKellar and a whole company of Rangers won't be able to protect you."

He backed his horse away, letting Farraday and his helper pass. Farraday watched over his shoulder, the anxiety still with him. Frank derived some satisfaction from that.

Naomi's third baby came according to the marked calendar, without complications. By the time the spring grass began to rise, Letty was starting to show. Frank was uncertain at first what attitude to take toward her pregnancy. His initial reaction was that it would be damned inconvenient, even embarrassing. He had tried hard not to allow Letty, much less anyone else, to see that a growing feeling for her was making it difficult for him to sustain his old resentment. He seldom opened Rachal's locket anymore to look at the picture. The fact of Letty's pregnancy was proof for all to see that he could enjoy her as a woman, no matter how indifferent he might appear.

Remembering Billy Valentine, he began looking forward to having a son he could openly claim. He began to think of the valley in terms of a son who would grow up to take it over someday. He began looking at the ranch in terms of what it would be twenty-five years from now.

Pregnancy had never been any challenge for Naomi, and Frank never seriously considered that it might be one for Letty. By summer, however, he sensed that something was wrong. He had had no close experience with expectant women, but he had observed the condition in cows enough to know that all was not as it should be. One day Naomi sent her boy Jimmy spurring out to the herd Frank and Homer and others were working. The excited boy told Frank he had better hurry to the house, and told his Uncle Mark his mother said for him to ride to Fort Griffin for a doctor.

Frank came near killing the horse, pushing him so hard. The animal stood trembling, head drooped and sweat dripping, as Frank hurried up the steps to the house. Naomi met him at the door. He knew from her eyes that she had wept, but the tears were dried now. "It's over," she said gravely. "She miscarried."

Frank had to turn away, toward the outdoors so she would not see what was in his face. He looked out upon the land his son was to have owned, and the distant blue rimrock seemed to dissolve. He rubbed rough fingers over his eyes. "She goin' to be all right?"

"I think so, but she's down in her mind." Naomi folded her arms. "Kind words don't come easy for you, Frank Claymore, but if you've got any saved up a-tall, now is the time to use them."

Letty looked at him for only a moment as he hesitantly pushed through the bedroom door, then she turned her face toward the wall. She crushed a handkerchief in a small hand and tried vainly to speak. He did not know what to say; it always seemed that when he should tell her how he felt, the words would never come to him. He sat on the edge of the bed. Letty began to sob. He put his arms around her and held her with a gentleness he did not know he had. He wished for the proper words, but they would not come. He wished he could cry with her, sharing the grief openly and without shame, but some ungiving reserve refused to release him. His crying was held within.

He managed to tell her, "There'll be another child."

The doctor from Griffin said otherwise. The damage had been beyond any ability of his to repair.

Letty became a second mother to Naomi's sons, especially the baby. She managed to smile brightly and make a happy fuss when she was with company, but Frank sensed the anguish she felt and could not share.

He *had* a son. She never would.

9

Frank Claymore wondered idly if the county was paying Rusty Farraday for his time on the witness stand. He could not recall Farraday ever doing much without hope of reward. Claymore had recognized few virtues in the man, and certainly not generosity.

Prosecutor Mallard led Farraday through a recounting of the trading post's establishment near the lower end of the valley, on the edge of the buffalo range, and a caustic observation that Frank Claymore had always exhibited strong opposition to progress for people other than himself and his friends.

The prosecutor changed the subject abruptly, catching even Farraday off guard. He declared, "It has been said that Billy Valentine was one of the worst outlaws on the Texas plains. Would you agree, Mr. Farraday?"

Farraday's red-rimmed eyes widened in surprise. "I didn't know none of the others."

Claymore's attorney objected that the question improperly solicited a personal judgment, and that it was not germane to the case at hand. Judge Whitmore Holmes sustained the objection on the basis of the first grounds and asked the prosecutor how he intended to demonstrate relevance.

The prosecutor said, "I contend, Your Honor, that Billy Valentine's outlaw career was a direct result of the lawless climate in which he found himself when he fell under the influence of Frank Claymore. I contend that the character of Billy Valentine was in its own pitiable way an extension of the character of Frank Claymore. Certainly Your Honor recognizes that the character of Frank Claymore is the reason for our being in this courtroom today."

Judge Holmes frowned. "I am inclined to grant you the benefit of the doubt, for the moment. But please bear in mind that we are here to ascertain the facts about a recent incident in which a man's life was taken. We are not here to study the history of outlawry in Texas."

Mallard nodded. "I believe Your Honor will become satisfied with the propriety of my direction. After all, sir, the events of recent months have their roots in old rivalries, old enmities . . ." He looked directly at Claymore. "And—old scandals."

Claymore burned him with his eyes. The prosecutor turned back to the witness, who tugged at his unaccustomed tight collar. Claymore could not remember ever seeing Rusty Farraday wear a necktie before. He thought, *Noose would fit him better.*

Mallard asked, "Mr. Farraday, you knew Billy Valentine all his life, didn't you?"

"Yes, sir. He was a babe in his mama's arms first time I seen him. I helped raise him, you could say, to the day he rode off to Claymore's ranch huntin' a cowpunchin' job."

"Would you say that until that point he was a peaceable, law-abiding boy, at harmony with the world?"

"He was taken now and again to fightin' a little, like most boys. But he was a hardworkin' button. He done what he was told."

"You saw no sign of the lawlessness to which he was so tragically to succumb?"

"He never done nothin' you could really call bad. One time when he was a young'un he run off to Claymore's. That was a worry to us. It was common knowledge Frank Claymore was his natural daddy." Farraday braved a defiant glance at Claymore. "I was always afraid the Claymore meanness would crop out in him someday. There was a wildness in his blood." Farraday could not hold his gaze on Claymore.

Anderson Avery objected. Judge Holmes admonished Farraday to adhere to the known facts and not to speculate upon the relative merits of heredity and environment. Farraday clearly did not comprehend what he was talking about.

The prosecutor said, "And I believe you were on the scene the very day Billy Valentine killed his first man?"

"I was. I could've reached out and touched Billy with my hand, I was that close. But I didn't; he might've shot me too, the state he was in. His eyes was wild, like Frank Claymore looked the night he murdered—"

"Objection!" shouted Anderson Avery.

"Sustained. Jury will disregard."

Farraday seemed confused by the restrictions. "Well, they was," he said defensively. "Billy taken a pistol, a forty-four it must've been, and shoved it in that feller's face. Bullet come out the back of his head and tore away a chunk of skull as big as this." He held his hands apart to demonstrate and went on with graphic detail until the judge bade him desist.

Claymore painfully closed his eyes, remembering. *I wish it had been me done it instead of Billy.* But it probably would not have changed the eventual outcome, he knew. A devil had been riding on Billy's shoulders. He had carried with him the sins of his father, and only fire would ever free him.

Frank had hoped the hide camp would die out as the buffalo declined in numbers, but it did not. Instead it developed a new clientele and flourished, largely under the ambitious drive of George Valentine. George had built a small fortune on buffalo hides. The dugout in which Farraday sold liquor and supplies to the hunters was replaced by a rock building, a general store serving the ever-increasing settlers who claimed lands on the rolling plains south and east of Claymore's valley. The establishment bore a big, bold sign: GEO.

VALENTINE MERCANTILE. In the beginning George hired someone to operate it for him while he continued farming on the Clear Fork. Eventually he hired his farming done and spent most of his time at the more lucrative store, though several years passed before his family joined him there. The store gave birth to a village, the village to a town. When that town became large enough to support a school, George fetched Rachal and their children from the old settlement on the Clear Fork.

Rusty Farraday had a tendency to drink up his profits before they were made. Nevertheless, with George's financial backing, he put up a frame building a respectful distance from the store and there continued to dispense spiritous liquors to any and all who brought hard cash. Gamblers plied their trade in the saloon, and it was said Farraday could point a lonesome traveler to pliable feminine companionship. He never married, but he seemed always to have one woman or another cooking his meals and keeping his bed from being cold.

Frank avoided the town except in urgent need. He confined his major trading to Fort Worth until the Texas & Pacific Railroad built its tracks west. Then he sent his wagons down to new Colorado City for supplies, skirting George's settlement as if it threatened smallpox. At first he entertained some hope that withholding the support of his large ranch might cause the settlement to dry up and blow away, but that community thrived and grew, even taking pride in not needing his blessing or business.

George mailed printed pieces all over the country, extolling the virtues of his town and the countryside around it, urging settlers to take up the unclaimed state lands, to bring the open prairies to blossom and yield to each man the fortune that was his birthright in this land of opportunity. It seemed to Frank, observing from afar, that the biggest fortune in sight was George's.

From time to time he inquired discreetly about Rachal and Billy. George had built for Rachal the largest house in town, but it had to be accepted on faith that she lived there. She was never seen upon the streets. Neighbors saw her only as a formless face peering out from behind the shutters, or a shadowy wraith upon the gallery, taking the cool night air when darkness served as a curtain against curious eyes. Some whispered that she was crazy, like Old Man Sam Ballinger, who lived on Claymore's ranch. Others said the only thing wrong was an aversion to the society that whispered about her.

Rumor said Billy had whipped every boy his size or larger in town. The fights usually started with someone wickedly suggesting that he did not look much like his younger brothers and sisters. Reports were that Billy was not much liked in town, was even feared a little. George tried to keep him out of trouble by giving him plenty of heavy lifting at the store and by sending him back to the farm during the summers, away from his antagonists.

George don't need to buy any workhorses, Frank thought darkly. *He's made one out of that boy.*

The valley had changed much in the years Frank had been there, most of the changes to his liking. Buffalo had given way to cattle. The only Indian seen in almost a decade was Red Shield, who came once a year in defiance of reservation regulations to pay respect to his spirits among the great rocks of Medicine Hill. Frank's major concern, besides the growth of George Valentine's town and the farming community, was that the grass seemed shorter than it used to be. Perhaps he had entered the valley in an unusually benevolent time and should not expect those conditions as a constant blessing.

He talked about it with Letty on occasion. That was one thing they could discuss openly and freely: the ranch. As she had done for her father, Letty kept the company books. At any given time she could tell Frank how many cattle and horses they owned and where they were, how much money the ranch had and where it was deposited, how many hands were on the payroll and what they were being paid. Letty and Naomi were always bedeviling Frank for not paying more to such a hardworking crew. One winter Letty raised the cowboys' wages five dollars a month, and Frank did not find out about it until spring. He tried to explain to her that winter was a time for cutting wages, not raising them, because plenty of hands were usually out of work at that time. For a business-minded woman, he found her unreceptive to sound reasoning on this matter.

As a business partner, she was a comfort to him. As a woman, she remained in many ways a mystery. She came less often from her pillow to his, and eventually she moved into another bedroom. He wondered if she sensed that during lovemaking he occasionally thought half-guiltily of Rachal. Letty still seemed to enjoy their sexual relationship, and he suspected that much of her enjoyment came from his having to initiate it, of his going to her instead of she to him.

Increasingly she found her satisfaction in managing the business side of the ranch. She built a serenity and a reserve that saddled him at times with a nagging frustration. He knew he could buy physical relief in town, but he regarded that as another weakness to be sternly shunned, as he shunned whiskey. A man could do without, if he had to . . . if he kept himself tired enough from honest labor that he slipped easily into sleep at night and did not trouble his mind with needless distractions.

Homer suggested they plow out a hayfield to provide emergency winter feed. "No sir," Frank told him firmly. "It might work, and every farmer from here to the Trinity River would be grabbin' for a share of this valley." The state would not sell him more of it than he already owned but seemed willing to sell it to smaller settlers.

Homer argued. "I don't know why you've turned so bitter against the farmers. You always got along with them on the Clear Fork."

"The Clear Fork wasn't mine."

Faces changed. Cowboys came and went. One evening Mark Akins—now far into his thirties—knocked on Frank and Letty's door, hat in his hand. His eyes were troubled. "Frank, I need to talk to you."

Frank had sensed something in the air, for he had seen Mark and Homer in earnest conversation more than usual. At Frank's approach, they had always gone silent. Frank escorted him into the parlor and pointed him to a chair. Letty brought coffee.

Studying the hat he abused in his strong hands, Mark said nervously, "I'm fixin' to go and find a ranch of my own."

Frank's first reaction was displeasure because Mark's leaving might cripple the ranch operation. But he realized that was selfish, and the feeling vanished. Mark Akins had given much to the development of this valley. Frank said, "I wouldn't give a hoot in hell for a man who had no personal ambition."

Mark smiled shyly at Letty. "It's no secret, I reckon, that I been seein' a young lady down at Colorado City." Letty's answering smile said it was indeed no secret. Mark's sister Naomi had no conception of what *secret* meant.

Mark went on. "I've saved my wages over the years. Her and me, we figure we'll make a start of our own."

Frank nodded, becoming more pleased as he thought about it. "You got a place picked out?"

"Not yet. Of course we won't find anything like this valley."

Frank suggested, "There's good land vacant to the north of the valley. I've tried to buy or lease it myself, but them silk-hatted politicians claim I've got too much already. With Letty's connections, I'll bet she could help you get it."

Letty nodded confidently. "We'll take you to Austin, Mark."

Frank said, "It'd be helpful to have you to the north of us. You'd protect the headwaters of the creek from George Valentine's friends. They want to plow up all of creation and put it in cotton. How big do you figure on startin'?"

Mark told him how much money he had saved. Frank frowned. "That ain't enough even to buy saddle horses." He looked at the twenty-dollar gold piece Captain Zachary once gave him. He had placed it in a picture frame on the parlor wall. "Letty, we're goin' to lend him enough to start him off in style."

She said, "What we can't lend, we can co-sign for. I still know who's got the money in Dallas."

The constant influx of settlers kept Frank on the defensive. With Mark's new ranch as a pattern, he helped several good hands acquire state lands and set up ranching operations of their own, whether they had money or not. He placed them in strategic positions, co-signing so many notes that Letty warned him he was walking on thin ice and flirting with financial danger. Frank shrugged off her warnings and their gratitude. The only thing that made him uneasier than criticism was praise.

A relentless tug-of-war grew between Frank Claymore and George Valentine to determine who could settle the most land with his own kind. In terms of land area, Frank was the more successful. In terms of people, George led him by far.

One day Frank and Sam Ballinger were trying to pull a cow out of a drying mud hole in which she had entrapped herself. Sam hunched on his horse, a rope dallied on his saddle horn, the other end around the cow's horns and a foreleg. Frank, to his knees in mud, twisted her tail, trying to give her enough pain and push to bring her up and out of the bog. A horseman approached, but Frank was too busy to give him more than a glance. He assumed him to be some young hand Homer had just hired. When he became aware that the man was just sitting on his horse and watching, he shouted irritably, "I could stand some help here, if you want to earn your pay."

"I ain't *gettin'* your pay," came the answer.

"And you never will, thataway."

The rider edged in closer. He looked familiar, but all

young cowboys appeared alike to Frank until he had time to know them. They had to spend awhile under the wing of some old veteran like Homer or Sam before they made a hand. Frank had no patience for the teaching.

The boy said, "You promised me a job one time. I come to see if you meant it or if it was just talk."

Frank sensed an air of belligerence and responded in kind. "*I* promised? I don't even know you."

"You said when I come of age, you'd make a place for me. I'm Billy Valentine."

In surprise, Frank let go of the cow's muddy tail. Something happened to boys when they passed fourteen or fifteen; they changed from childhood to manhood so rapidly that everything about them seemed different overnight. But he could still see, now that he looked for it, a little of himself in the boyish face, the challenging eyes. He found his voice. Though he would have wished otherwise, it held no compromise. "I don't remember no promise. What can you do?"

"What do you *want* done? I'm good at anything."

Favors himself, Frank thought testily.

Sam smiled, staring at the boy. "I heard Homer say just this mornin' that he wished he had a couple more good hands."

Frank gave the cow a hard shove. One foot came loose, then another, and Sam's horse quickly dragged her out to the dry bank. Frank held his grip on her tail so he was pulled along with her. As Sam rode forward, slackening the rope, Frank took the loop from her horns and dropped it so she could free the forefoot with a step.

Gratitude is not one of a cow's better points. Her most frequent response to rescue is hostility toward the nearest thing that moves. Frank did not move rapidly enough. She raked a sharp horn across his ribs, then turned for another try. Frank ran toward his horse, but the horse did not favor the cow's looks and trotted away. Sam's age slowed his move to intercept her. Frank ducked behind Billy's horse, and she came around looking for him.

"Do something!" Frank shouted.

Calmly Billy said, "I ain't workin' here yet."

"Damn you, you've got the job."

Billy grabbed her tail and pulled it across his leg as he turned the horse away. The cow rolled ignominiously. Sam brought Frank's horse. Frank mounted without much dignity to be out of harm's way when the cow regained her feet. She shook her head in threat but did not charge.

Billy smiled with a brittle humor. "Cow can't tell rich man from poor. She'll charge whichever one gets in her way."

Frank responded grittily, "Damned little help you was. I could've got a horn jobbed in me."

"I didn't see where I owed you anything, not till you hired me. You feel like I owe you somethin'?"

"You owe me an honest day's work for an honest dollar."

Billy's eyes cut into him. "I thought maybe you felt like you had more comin' to you, seein' as we've got so much in common."

Frank felt as if Billy had kicked him with a spurred boot. The boy had come here looking for a fight and had found it before the *howdies* were said. Frank grumbled, "There's been men fired off of this place, but I don't remember one ever bein' fired the same day he was hired."

The look between them was like an electrical charge. Sam Ballinger broke into it. "Fellers, you're hot and bothered. Ain't no use havin' things said that you'll both be sorry for. Frank, how about me takin' Billy and gettin' him settled?" Sam did not wait for Frank to answer. He placed a bony hand on Billy's shoulder. "Remember me? I was the one found you lost that night and taken you to your—to the headquarters. I'm Sam Ballinger."

Billy's eyes softened. "I remember, Sam."

"I knowed you when you was a baby, over at old Davis camp. Knowed your mama, and George, and all them folks. I had a boy myself, once. He wouldn't be a lot older than you if he was still here."

"Yes, sir," Billy responded. "I've heard." His voice trailed away as they rode off together. Frank hung behind, wanting to ride with them, wanting to take back his angry words but knowing he could not. Apology was something he had never learned.

He did some quick arithmetic. Eighteen, Billy would be now. Eighteen, and carrying enough anger to set green grass afire. God, what had George done to him?

All the way to the house, he wondered how he would go about telling Letty, for he had no wish to hurt her. Billy's presence would surely be awkward. Frank fell back on his usual artless strategy, just speaking straight out. "Billy Valentine is here."

She nodded. "I've already spoken to him." Her eyes smiled at his surprise, then softened. "He looks like you a little, like you did the time Tobe brought you to our house in Dallas."

"It goin' to trouble you, him bein' around?" He knew she needed no reminder of Rachal. Though Letty had never seen her, hardly a day passed that Rachal did not rise up between them like some malevolent ghost.

"Do you think it should trouble me?"

"I can see where it might."

"He's your son. That makes him mine too, in a way."

"Damned if I see how you figure that." He could not see how she figured lots of things; she didn't always think in straight lines as he did. He said, "It might be just as well if you give him roundance. He's carryin' a chip on his shoulder the size of a choppin' block. There ain't no use you gettin' your feelin's hurt."

"If my feelings were fragile, they'd have been shattered a long time ago."

He frowned, suspecting that remark was pointed at him. Defensively he declared, "I leave you alone to do whatever you want to. I never ask you for anything."

A suggestive smile crossed her lips and was quickly gone. "Never, Frank?"

"Not that I can think of." He grunted, glad he was able to cut off this little exchange before it could develop into misunderstanding. "Don't you be babyin' him. Naomi Whitcomb will do more than enough of that. Anytime a boy on this ranch scratches his finger, he runs to have her put a wrappin' on it for him."

"I won't baby him. But if he needs someone to talk to, I'll want him to know I'm here."

Frank shook his head. "If he needs to talk, let him come to *me*. I always listen to everybody."

He had long since delegated the hiring to Homer because he recognized that his own abrasive nature would keep the place perpetually shorthanded. He told Homer ruefully, "I overstepped my bounds today. I hired a man without askin' you."

Homer shrugged his acceptance of the encroachment. "The boy'll earn his keep. What he don't know, Sam'll teach him."

"I don't want to put a burden on Sam. He's not strong."

"A burden? Sam's walkin' taller'n I've seen him since old times on the Clear Fork. It's like Billy's the boy he's hunted for all these years."

Frank said worriedly, "That kid's eyes worry me. He's got a lot of anger in him."

"Life's dealt him a bad hand. He's paid heavy for somethin' he had nothin' to do with."

Frank glanced up quickly. "But I *did*?"

"You and Rachal and George . . . all of you. There ain't nobody without some blame to carry. Except that boy, and he's been totin' the load for everybody."

As Homer had suggested, Sam Ballinger adopted Billy Valentine for his own. Wherever one went, the other followed. Some of Sam's years seemed to fall away, and he became more like the man Frank remembered on the Clear Fork. He walked with purpose and carried his gaunt shoulders high. He could not shelter Billy from the hazards of the occupation, like pitching horses and horn-swinging cattle, but he was there to save the youngster from falling if he could, or to pick him up if he did fall.

Billy took pains to keep distance between himself and Frank whenever possible. He cottoned early to Naomi Whitcomb—all the cowboys did—but he watched Letty with suspicion, and usually from afar.

It was cheaper to break broncs than to buy trained horses, so Frank and Homer had built a round corral for the purpose, its posts outside the rails to lessen the risk of cowboys getting their legs crushed if a horse ran into the fence. Bronc-breaking usually attracted onlookers. Frank was sure they must have something more productive to do, and when he was in a properly sour mood he sometimes told them so.

He had been dubious about a certain wild-eyed sorrel colt's being assigned to Billy Valentine; he felt the ranch was paying a couple of bronc stompers more likely to meet the colt's challenge. But Billy insisted to Homer that he could handle the horse, and Frank usually left Homer the final decision in matters dealing with employees. One Sunday after the bronc had been sacked out a few times and staked to a heavy log to teach him about the unyielding tyranny of the rope, Billy decided to mount him for the first time. The dust-raising preliminaries drew a crowd, Letty and Naomi among them. Letty's eyes were concerned.

"Frank, that pony looks a little crazy. We don't know how good Billy is at this sort of thing."

Frank did not want to admit to the same worry. "He come of age when he grew his first whisker."

A couple of young hands held the bronc while Billy saddled him. One bit down on the horse's ear until Billy mounted and said, "Turn him a-loose."

The cowboys jumped back, and the horse went straight up, squealing his outrage at being so badly used. He pitched an arc across the big round corral while Billy began to show a little more daylight between himself and the saddle with every jump. The bronc slammed into the fence, and Billy came off over his neck, his head striking the rails. He tumbled like a wounded bird and hit the ground on his stomach while the horse pitched back toward the other side of the pen.

Sam Ballinger reached him first, sternly preventing the younger men from moving Billy until he was satisfied no bones were broken. He turned Billy over and sat him up against the fence. Blood trickled down Billy's cheek. As Frank and Homer got there, Sam said tightly, "Skinned his face against the fence comin' down. Got half the breath knocked out of him. Otherwise, he done good."

Letty rushed down to the creek and dipped a handkerchief into the cool water. She hurried back. "Here," she said, shoving her way between the gathered men, "let me wash his face and see if there are any bad cuts that need fixing."

His breath recovered, Billy pushed against the fence and shakily regained his feet. He waved her away. "I'm all right. Somebody catch that bronc for me."

Letty said, "Let me wash off the blood. You may be hurt worse than you think."

Billy snapped, "I already got one mother. I don't need two." He turned away. "Somebody goin' to catch me that bronc?"

Sam said quietly, "Don't you worry, Letty. The boy'll be all right."

Letty's eyes touched Frank's for a second, and he shared the hurt he saw there. He touched her arm before he thought. He said, "You can't pet a coyote pup. They'll bite you every time."

Ridicule was one thing against which Sam's protection was no shield. If Billy thought he had left that in town, he was mistaken. It followed him. Every person on the ranch, excepting perhaps Homer and Naomi's youngest, knew or thought he knew the true story of Frank Claymore and Rachal and Billy Valentine.

One night Frank heard horses running excitedly in a corral and hurried out to see what might be frightening them. It had been years since a stray Indian had made an attempt at the remuda, but now and again some four-legged varmint found its way up the creek. Last spring Homer and one of the hands had shot a mountain lion, well north of its usual range.

From the angry sounds in the darkness Frank knew this was no lion, no bear. Men grunted and coughed and cried out in rage, and one or another would impact against a pole fence.

"Hyannhh!" Frank shouted, before he was near enough to see who it was. "Stop that right now. Don't you know you're liable to run a horse into the fence and break its leg?"

Sam Ballinger stepped out of the darkness. The black man Tobe was with him. "Might ought to leave them alone, Frank. Let them get it out of their system."

"If they have anything that needs gettin' out of their system, let them *work* it out. Ain't half enough hard work done around this place as it is." Frank waded into the middle of the fight and pushed the two men apart. One, he found to none of his surprise, was Billy Valentine. The other was a cowboy named Wart Allison, who had been on the ranch a few months longer than Billy. Both breathed hard, and even in the moon's pale light Frank could see they had bloodied each other. "I said stop it! There's enough people snipin' at us without us fightin' amongst ourselves. What's this all about?"

Neither combatant spoke. They only wheezed and struggled for breath.

"You know my orders against fightin'," Frank declared. "I ought to whip both of you off of this place with the double of a wet rope." He glared at first one, then the other. "Who started it?"

Sam said with concern, "It's between them two."

Frank was not often inclined to accept unsolicited advice, even from Sam. "I reckon I *know* how it started." He thrust his chin at Allison, a little the older of the two. "Go see Homer Whitcomb and draw what you got comin' to you."

Billy stepped in front of his opponent. He seemed ready to transfer his anger to Frank. "I fight my own battles. If he goes, I go."

Frank was caught off guard. "Boy, I'll be damned if I can figure out what you want."

"I just want to be left the hell alone."

Frank glared. "Go on, both of you, and clean yourselves up. You look like hogs that've been rootin' around in the dirt."

The cowboy Allison asked with some doubt, "You still firin' me, Mr. Claymore?"

"I never say anything I don't mean. You're fired." He glanced at Billy. "Both of you are fired. Now, shake hands and I'll hire you back."

Sam remained as the two young men wearily trailed down toward the creek in the moonlight. "You better watch out, Frank, or folks'll be sayin' you're as crazy as I am."

Frank leaned against the corral, studying his words. "You may be gettin' too close to him, Sam. That boy's got black powder bottled up in him. If it ever goes off . . ."

Sam's voice held pain. "I reckon you ain't seen the scars on his back. Old whippin' scars, from a long time ago."

Frank slammed a hand against the fence. "George! That goddamned George!"

Sam said, "Have patience with the boy. He's lost, the way I was lost. If you'll give him room, maybe Sammy'll find what he's lookin' for, the way I did—right here."

Frank trembled with a sudden chill. *Sammy!* That was the son Sam had never found.

He said, "The name's *Billy,* Sam."

"Sure it's Billy. Didn't I say Billy?" Sam looked confused. "I'd best go see that them boys stay peaceful. Good night, Frank." Sam walked off after the two cowhands.

Letty waited for Frank on the porch, her arms folded, a sign she was concerned. "What was it?"

Frank kept his eyes from her. "A couple of broncs."

She followed him into the house, studying him in the lamplight. "Was Billy hurt?"

Frank shrugged. He never had been able to lie to her and make it stick. "Not enough to teach him anything. I oughtn't to've let him stay."

"You'd just as well make up your mind that he'll never be a tame one, Frank. He's you all over again. I'll go see if he needs attention."

Frank shook his head. "You've got no business at the bunkhouse. Nobody ever made a fuss over *me* when I was his age."

"They should have. You'd be the better for it. I'll get some clean cloth and some antiseptic."

Her solicitude for Billy was a frequent source of amazement to him, and guilt. "Sam and Tobe'll see after him. He's not yours to worry about."

"He's yours. That makes him as near mine as I'll ever have."

Frank followed her to the bunkhouse, protesting with every step, wondering where she had gotten that intolerable stubbornness. He had just as well talk Comanche to a mule. As she pushed through the door, some of the young men in their bunks quickly pulled up blankets to hide their long underwear.

Sam and Tobe had the two young fighters seated near a kerosene lamp, washing their faces. Letty said sternly, "Tobe, couldn't you find a cleaner rag than that? Move back and hold the lamp."

She stepped to the door and threw out the contents of the wash pan, then refilled it with fresh creek water out of a bucket. Using a clean cloth she had brought with her, she began washing Billy's face even as he protested. "Wart's in worse shape than I am. See after *him*."

"You're both in bad shape," she countered. "I'll get to him in a minute." Billy tried to pull away from her, but she caught his collar and held him. "My brother used to be just like you two—always getting himself into a fight. Never once proved a thing. I used to try to clean him up so our mother wouldn't find out. It never worked. She always seemed to know even before she saw him."

Billy gave up and let her wash his face. She poured some evil liquid into a dry, clean cloth and touched it to the cuts and scrapes. He sucked in a long breath and cringed against the burning. Done with him, she repeated the favor for Wart Allison, who appeared more embarrassed than hurt.

She backed off a step to look at them. "If you two fight again and undo all this work, I'll be mortally ashamed of you both."

Billy stared at her with puzzlement. "Sam and Tobe could've took care of this."

"With dirty rags and dirty water? I worry over you boys."

Billy glanced furtively at Frank, who stood back watching, barely in the light. Billy asked, "Mrs. Claymore, don't you know who I really am?"

"Of course I know who you are. You're Billy Valentine, son of George and Rachal Valentine. If you were at home, your mother would take care of you. You're not, so I will."

Big ways and small, Billy Valentine had a knack for getting under Frank's hide. Frank never knew whether Billy was going to laugh or turn sullen. Either way, he let Frank know he merely tolerated him, and nothing more. He managed to get along with the hands and made a particular friend of Wart Allison once their bruises and contusions healed. Like most of the other cowboys, he would have stuck both feet into a bucket of coals if Naomi Whitcomb had asked him. Naomi had become the foster mother of every homesick hand on the place. They called her Mother Whitcomb, which always set a smile upon her round face like a reflection of morning sunshine.

Billy was courteous to Letty, though standoffish and shy. Sam Ballinger and Tobe were the ones to whom he was closest, along with the Whitcombs' oldest son Jimmy. Sam became Billy's friend, adviser, teacher . . . even his father, after a fashion. In unguarded moments the old man called him *Sammy,* and Billy never corrected him.

Mother Whitcomb put it into words. Watching them walk across the big ranch yard together, she lamented, "Two lost souls. It's God's mercy they found one another."

Frank turned away, hiding his face. *It should've been me.*

One afternoon late, Billy and Sam and Jimmy came riding in together from the south. Frank was at the barn, as usual, quietly counting in the hands and looking over the horses for signs of injury or abuse. He noticed that Jimmy and Billy each carried a handful of wildflowers. Naomi Whitcomb stood outside the corral, waiting to see that her son did not tarry too long at the barn and let supper go cold. Letty was with her.

Jimmy rode over to his mother and held out the flowers. They were a mixture of red and white and blue. "We found these by Medicine Hill," he told her. "Billy said I ought to bring some to you."

Nobody had ever picked flowers for Naomi Whitcomb, certainly not her husband Homer. She hugged her son.

Billy stared uneasily at Letty Claymore, then moved his horse over to her and held out the flowers he carried. "Didn't seem right for Mother Whitcomb to get flowers and you miss out. I don't know what they're called, but they're kind of pretty. Don't have stickers on them, either."

She accepted the bouquet with a warm smile and touched Billy's hand. Flustered, he drew the hand away, then eased his horse toward the saddle shed. Letty turned to Frank, tears in her eyes.

Frank said, "He still didn't tell you he's sorry."

"He's too much like you to say it in words. But he told me."

Over the years Frank had found it fostered smoother running of the ranch if he let Homer supervise the labor. Homer never gave a direct order. It was always, "Would you mind seein' if you can ride the rough edges off of this bronc?" Or, "I'd appreciate it if you'd take a swing down through that draw and pick up anything without a brand on it."

Frank's manner was more to command than request, and to make the command a challenge. When Frank let himself become too closely involved with the day-to-day direction of work, Homer was usually obliged to look for new hands.

Frank tried to keep a respectable distance and silence insofar as Billy Valentine was concerned. He purposely avoided any special show of interest that might cause other hands to suspect discrimination. He kept so much distance that Homer asked if he was shunning Billy.

Homer said, "You got reason to be proud of him. He knows what he's doin', and he works like a horse."

Frank growled, "George made him work for every bite that went into his mouth."

"Bothers me, though," Homer said. "Whatever task I put him to, he wades into it and fights it like an enemy. That boy's got thunder and lightnin' locked up in him."

"Give him plenty of work, and maybe he'll wear it down. A man can't keep fightin' all his life."

Homer's eyes narrowed. "I know one that does."

Frank said musingly, "I've gentled with age."

"An outlawed bronc *never* gentles."

Frank saw much of himself in Billy, but Billy had habits that distressed him. Like most of the other young men, he seemed to take an undue pleasure in rolling and smoking cigarettes. In Frank's early years tobacco had been too troublesome and expensive to come by. It had been just one of many things he could comfortably live without. He tolerated it in others because it was so prevalent that stopping it would have been like stopping a blue norther from whining down off of the caprock and across his valley. Nevertheless, he wished Billy weren't given to it.

Billy was a gambler, too. He seemed to have no regard for his money, uncaring how hard he worked for it. Frank had gambled all his life against drought and storm, against the Indians, against the markets, but he had never gambled across a card table and intended never to do so. With weather, with the vagaries of nature, a man had a fighting chance. Against professional gamblers he had none.

It was a rule of the ranch, though Frank knew it was often broken, that its hands stay out of George Valentine's town. He could not apply the rule to Billy because Billy's mother lived there. Each time Frank watched Billy take his wages and ride south, he felt a guilty envy for him. Billy would be seeing Rachal. Frank had not seen her in seventeen or eighteen years.

He knew something else. Billy was still getting into fights when he went to town. The town dreaded his coming. He was taking his wages over to Rusty Farraday's dramshop and playing them away against men who knew more about cards than Billy knew about horses and cattle. Invariably Billy came back to the ranch broke. It was as if the money—or perhaps its source—was a symbol of shame, and he wanted to be rid of it.

Often Frank found Billy looking at him, but the eyes carefully veiled whatever thought lay behind them. If any filial affection existed there, it was well hidden. For a long time Frank could not bring himself to approach Billy, but he gave the boy ample opportunity to approach him. Billy did not.

One day he knew Homer had set Billy and a couple of other hands to building a set of working corrals against the canyon wall far up the valley. Frank found an excuse for himself—he needed none to satisfy anyone else—to ride in that direction. He found Sam there with Billy, though Sam had taken a hard fall from a horse and Homer had advised him to stay at the headquarters and rest. Two hands were hauling pickets and posts from a timbered header up the canyon while Billy dug postholes, sweat running down his face and soaking his shirt. Frank watched silently as the other two unloaded their wagon. He said, "Go with them, Sam. I'd like to talk to Billy."

He had no call to give Sam an order. Sam held the status of an old pensioner on this ranch and could do what he damn well pleased. It pleased him to stay close to Billy. But he took no offense. "Sure, Frank. Now, Billy, you be civil."

Frank listened to the wagon rattling away. Billy paused but a moment, then attacked the posthole as if he intended to kill it.

Not sure how to begin, Frank said, "Hot job."

Billy granted him but a fleeting look. "I'm gettin' paid for it."

"Are you mad like this all the time?"

"I never see you bust *your* face smilin'."

"Life ain't all that funny. But it don't have to be a constant fight, either."

"That's all it's ever been for *me*."

"You've got friends who'd like to help you."

Billy set down the diggers. "Like who?"

"Well, like Homer and Mother Whitcomb. Like Sam Ballinger. Like Mrs. Claymore and me."

"You? I don't remember anything you ever done to help me. Left my mama when she needed you. Left me with a face and a name that don't match. Left me to fight every time somebody snickers and makes a remark. Now all of a sudden you're my friend. Where was you eighteen years ago?"

Frank's face warmed, not with anger but with remorse. "Didn't anybody ever tell you how it was? They made me go off and fight the Indians. When I got back, it was too late."

Billy's eyes showed he did not believe. "If a man wants somethin' bad enough he can find a way. You just didn't want my mama bad enough, and you sure didn't want *me.*"

"I did want your mama, boy. You don't know how bad. But when I found out about you, George had done stepped in."

Billy hammered even more fiercely at the bottom of the hole. Frank watched him in confused silence, his face still aflame. He wondered what lies George must have told this boy all those years.

At length he brought himself to ask, "How is your mama?"

Billy stopped working, but he did not look up. "How long since you've seen her?"

"Since you was a baby in her arms."

"And now all of a sudden you want to know how she is? Kind of late showin' an interest."

Frank struggled to say what he felt and not have it come out backward, as such things had a tendency to do. "I always had an interest in her welfare, son."

Billy wiped a sleeve across his face and fixed an angry stare upon Frank. "You never let it get in your way. Got yourself a big ranch, ten-twenty thousand head of cattle. Taken care of *your* welfare, all right."

Frank picked up a rock and hurled it savagely against the canyon wall. "Damn you, boy, I didn't come here to fight with you. I come to talk."

"Well, we've talked. And now I reckon I'm fired."

Frank studied him in frustration, wanting to walk to him, to put his arms around him and ask forgiveness for all those lost, mean years. But he stood where he was. "I wish we could understand one another, son."

Stiffly Billy said, "I think we do." He slammed the diggers into the hole.

Frank swayed between staying and leaving. He wanted to say something that might mend the breach, but at such times a perversity in his nature always seemed to take precedence. All that came from him was a critical, "Looks to me like you're diggin' that hole crooked."

The foreboding had been with him long before the crisis came. A merchant from George's town, a man Frank knew from old times in Griffin, arrived at the ranch just after daylight, his sweat-lathered horse mute evidence of a long, hard ride. The man's eyes told of trouble before he summoned courage to speak.

"I'm sorry to bring grief to your door, Mr. Claymore, but you've got a cowboy dead in town, and one that's hurt."

Behind him, Frank heard a gasp from Letty. A chill shuddered through him as he stood in his open door, staring out into the dawn. He knew Billy was one of the two.

"Who's dead?" he asked fearfully.

"I didn't hear the name," the merchant said, twisting his hat in both hands. "But they took Billy Valentine to his daddy and mama's house with his head caved in."

Letty gripped Frank's arm. She whispered, "Thank God he's alive."

George's town. George's damned town. "How'd it happen?"

"Trouble over a card game at Farraday's. That's killed more than one in the past."

Farraday's. Frank clenched his fists, and the merchant took a step backward, fearing violence to the bringer of bad news. "What shape is Billy in?"

The man shook his head. "He was unconscious when I left George's house. Way I heard it, Farraday laid him out with a bungstarter to stop the fight and keep him from gettin' killed like his friend."

"The law been notified?"

"For what good it does. Old Constable Wilcox has never arrested anybody that wasn't already too drunk to crawl. Nearest real law is in Griffin."

Homer had seen the visitor and sensed trouble. He came in and heard enough. Frank demanded, "Anybody gone besides Billy?"

Reluctantly Homer said, "Wart Allison."

Frank turned toward his fireplace and lifted down a rifle. "Round up the crew, Homer. We're ridin' in."

Letty watched him load the rifle. "Frank, the time is past for that kind of response. It doesn't work anymore."

"It still works when all else fails."

The merchant swallowed. "Mr. Claymore, you ain't fixin' to kill somebody, are you?"

"Depends on who I run into that needs killin'."

Letty stopped Frank at the door, her eyes still begging. "Frank, please leave the rifle."

"I won't use it if I don't have to."

"You can't use it if you don't take it." She held out her hands for the rifle. "Please."

He came near giving in, but in his mind's eye he saw Allison dead and Billy Valentine bleeding. "I've warned them more than once to leave me and mine alone." He brushed past her and walked briskly down to the barn where the hands were saddling their horses. He handed the rifle to a grim-faced Sam Ballinger to hold for him while he caught his own mount. Saddling quickly, he swung up and retrieved the rifle. He turned the horse toward the open gate and saw Letty standing in the middle of it, a pistol in her hand.

Stiffly she said, "Frank, you're not going to do it."

"Move aside, Letty. It's got to be done."

She said, "If you ride in there with all these armed men, there'll be more killed. You've already lost one. That's enough."

"What would you have me do?"

"Go unarmed, and just take a couple with you—Homer and Sam. See after Billy and bring the other boy home so we can bury him. Let the law take care of the rest."

"You know the law won't do anything. It never has."

"Then work on getting more law, but don't set yourself against it this way."

"Move aside, Letty. We're leavin'."

She brought up the muzzle of the pistol. "No, Frank."

"You wouldn't shoot me."

"No, but I'd shoot your horse."

"I'd get me another. How many horses can you shoot?"

"How many can you afford to lose?" The pistol did not waver. She had it pointed at the horse's chest.

Homer leaned in. "Frank, she means it."

Frank did not have to be told. He had seen that determination in her eyes before, but never over a pistol.

Homer declared, "She makes sense, Frank. Let's just me and you go in."

Sam said anxiously, "And me. I got to see about my boy."

It was Sam more than Letty who reached through Frank's anger. Frank could see the anguish in Sam's eyes. Sam knew, better than anyone, what it meant to lose a son. Reluctantly Frank turned in the saddle and told the riders behind him, "Get down, boys. You're stayin' here."

Letty lowered the pistol but reached up with her left hand. "Your rifle, Frank."

He gave it to her. She seemed to sag under its weight. Her eyes softened. "I'll pray for Billy."

He realized later he should have thanked her for that. But he had seldom thanked her for anything.

The three of them rode into town abreast. They passed a frame building that bore a large signboard: LICKQUORS AND TABLES. R. FARRADAY, PROP. Rusty Farraday stood on the porch, shotgun in his hands, face grim as he quickly but quietly looked for weapons. He eased when he saw none. Then his eyes met Frank's, and he cringed from the burning contempt. Farraday dropped his gaze.

He seemed surprised that the three men passed without stopping. Frank's first concern was to see about Billy. He rode on down the street to a large frame house that stood a story taller than anything else in town, a gray structure with gingerbread trim and oval glass in the double front doors, the badge of financial leadership in a one-horse town.

The doors swung open, and George Valentine stepped out onto the broad gallery. Frank had not seen him in several years. George was heavier, dressed in the manner of a businessman, looking like a Dallas banker except for the black boots on his feet. He had grown a dark and heavy mustache, befitting his age and position in the community. But his eyes were the same as they had always been. They bored holes in Frank.

"Your cowboy is down at the barber's, Frank. They're buildin' a box for him." His eyes touched Homer and Sam.

"I'm relieved. I thought you'd bring your whole bunch to town and raise hell."

"I thought about it," Frank said evenly. "I changed my mind." He saw no reason to tell why. "What about Billy?"

"Billy's my responsibility. He always has been."

"You didn't answer me, George. Do I have to go in that house and see for myself?"

George stiffened at the threat. "This is my house. You have no right."

Frank saw a movement behind George. Billy Valentine walked unsteadily through the open doors and stood beside George. His head was bandaged. The side of his face was swollen and blue.

"I'll live, Mr. Claymore. But Wart Allison is dead."

Frank felt limp with relief, seeing Billy on his feet. He heard Sam Ballinger make a glad cry and push his horse forward. Sam declared, "Boy, we was almighty worried."

Billy softened, looking at Sam. "I wouldn't've caused you concern, Sam, not for the world." He looked back at Frank, the softness gone. "Constable says it was self-defense. I say it was murder. You goin' to do somethin' about it, Mr. Claymore?" The question was put in the manner of a challenge.

George gripped Billy's arm. "Let's not have more trouble. We can't undo what's already been done."

"That gambler's still here, thinkin' he owns the world. We can make him pay for it, and the next one'll think a long time before he shoots some poor cowboy dead." Billy stepped back into the house. When he returned he wore a cartridge belt and pistol.

George tried to stop him. "Billy, don't . . ."

Billy lurched free of George's grip and walked stiffly down the steps, each stride bringing pain to his eyes. "Lend me your horse, Sam?"

Sam glanced at Frank for help, then reluctantly stepped down. Billy swung into the saddle. "Anybody wants to side me is welcome to come. Anybody wants to stop me had bet-

ter stay out of my way." He put the bare heels of his boots
to the horse's ribs and set him into a trot.

George called after him in vain, then looked at Frank.
"Can't you do somethin'?"

"It's your town," Frank replied sternly. "You should've
done somethin' a long time ago."

He turned his horse and followed after Billy. A movement
at an upper window caught his eye. A hand pulled back a
curtain. Behind that curtain he saw only a shadow. But he
knew who it had to be.

Frank said, "I'll try to stop him, George. Not for you, but
for him. And for *her.*"

He did not look back, but he knew Homer and Sam followed closely, riding double. Spurring into an easy lope, he
caught up to Billy at the front of Farraday's saloon. Farraday was no longer in sight. He had evidently decided trouble had passed him by. But he had not seen the fury in Billy's
face. Frank could see it, and he felt cold.

"Give me that pistol, boy," he commanded.

"You come and take it away from me."

Frank did, moving so swiftly that even he was surprised.
He shoved the pistol into his waistband.

Billy growled, "If I wasn't hurt, you wouldn't've done
that. You'll never do it again."

"I will if I ever have to." Frank grabbed Billy's arms.
"Listen to me, boy. Killin' a man is easy. Livin' with it can
be damned hard."

"That son of a bitch shot Wart in cold blood. I'd've killed
him then and there, but Rusty Farraday clubbed me to the
floor."

"The only decent thing he ever done," Frank said sternly.
"Probably saved your life, like I'm tryin' to do. Now, we'll
go in, but we'll go in sober, and without a war."

Frank led the way up the steps, Billy one pace behind
him, Sam and Homer trailing Billy. They pushed through
the doors. Rusty Farraday's mouth dropped open. He moved
behind the bar as if for protection.

He half shouted, "The constable's already talked to everybody here. Hawkins done what he done in self-defense. That's the truth of it, and the end of it." He kept inching farther along the bar. Frank reached it in three quick strides, for he knew within reason that Farraday kept a weapon there. "You'd best stop where you're at, Farraday, and put both hands on the bar where I can watch them."

Farraday could have reached the shotgun if he had dared, but he looked at Billy's pistol in Frank's belt, and he stopped.

Frank declared, "The constable's a drunken old fool. Billy says it was murder."

"Billy's a minor. His word won't stand up against the men who were here last night. He shouldn't've been here himself."

"But you let him." Frank pointed his finger and jabbed it across the bar into Farraday's chest. "I told you once, Farraday, I would tolerate you and your place so long as you didn't hurt me or mine. Well, now you've hurt mine." He turned to Billy. "The man who killed Allison—is he here?"

He knew the answer before Billy replied, for Billy's gaze was fixed in hatred upon a man who sat at a table alone, a half-empty bottle and a glass in front of him. Frank had seen his type in Griffin in its hell-roaring days, men soft of hands and pale of skin but quick with cards and a gun.

Billy said, "This is him."

The man had the bluster of one who had bluffed his way out of many a scrape and shot his way out when he couldn't bluff. As Frank started toward him, he quickly reached into a coat pocket. "Now look here," the gambler Hawkins said. "Everybody who was in here will tell you, that cowboy reached for his gun. I simply defended myself."

Frank mirrored Billy's hatred. "How many other men have you killed, defendin' yourself?" He moved closer. "Don't you pull that gun. You might kill me, but there'd be twenty men howlin' in here from my ranch, and you wouldn't live to see sundown."

The gambler's eyes wavered. He eased his hands back to the table. Frank reached into the man's coat pocket and brought out a small palm gun.

Billy raged, "That's the one he killed Wart with. Wart didn't do a thing, except say Hawkins fished a card out of his sleeve."

"Sayin' a thing like that is enough to get a man killed," Frank replied. "Did *you* see him draw a hideaway card?"

Billy hesitated. "No, but Wart said he did."

The gambler eased, for Frank seemed to be coming around to his side. "That cowboy was a bad loser," he said defensively. "He wanted back what I'd won fair and square. He went for his gun, and I had no choice."

Frank stared hard into the man's eyes, and he knew within reason that the gambler lied. But he knew also there was no way to prove it. He said, "Hawkins, I want you gone from here. Out of this valley. Now!"

The gambler tried to stare him down but looked away.

Farraday protested from behind the bar. "You got no say in this town, Claymore. You got no right to tell anybody to leave."

Frank declared, "I'm *takin'* the right." He punched his finger against the gambler's breastbone. "Not tomorrow. Not tonight. *Now!*"

Billy cried out in protest, "You just lettin' him go?"

"Nothin' more we can do."

"Like hell there's not!" He moved too swiftly for Frank to counter him. Billy grasped the pistol from Frank's belt and pulled it up almost in the gambler's face. He drew back the hammer with his thumb.

Hawkins screamed, "No!"

The pistol roared. Half hidden by smoke, Hawkins pitched backward upon the floor. His hands reached up and twitched, then dropped as if weighted.

Frank felt paralyzed. He looked down at the gambler and knew the man was dead.

Billy stood with the smoking pistol, his eyes searching desperately for anyone else who might take up the fight. No one moved.

Frank heard a voice gasp, "My God!" and realized it was his own.

Sam Ballinger was the first to break free of the shock. "Billy," he said with amazing calm, "they'll be on you. You've got to get away from here."

Billy came out of his trance. He took a step backward, still holding the pistol ready for anyone who offered him a challenge. "You're right, Sam."

"I'll go with you, Billy. I know a hundred places where a whole army couldn't find you."

Billy looked as if he would argue the point, but suddenly he was sick and confused and vulnerable. He backed toward the open door. Sam stayed close beside him.

Billy said, "I'm takin' your horse, Mr. Claymore. I'll leave him at the ranch when I pick up mine."

Frank followed them out onto the porch and halfway down the steps. Billy mounted Frank's big horse and put the heels to him. Sam hung back a moment. "Don't you fret about Billy, Frank. I'll take care of him. When the trouble is over, I'll bring him home." He spurred away.

Frank stood trembling and watched them gallop out of town together.

When the trouble is over.

This kind of trouble would never be over.

Mother Whitcomb had described them: two lost souls.

Homer stood in the door. For once Frank wished he would say something, and Homer offered not a word.

Frank walked inside again, not wanting to accept, but the reality was overpowering. The gray gunsmoke had cleared. Gambler Hawkins lay on his back, as dead as he would ever be.

Rusty Farraday's face, usually red, was almost the color of ashes. "Good God. Two killin's in two days. In my place."

Farraday's voice, thinned almost to a wail, brought Frank

back to cold anger. "Yes, Farraday, your place. You and your bunch all lied to protect that gambler. Will anybody lie now to protect Billy?"

He saw the answer in the faces of the saloon crowd. They regarded Billy as belonging to Frank, not to George Valentine. This time they would tell it as they had seen it. Billy Valentine would be an outlaw, hunted for murder.

Methodically Frank walked to a lamp on the end of the bar. It was cold, but he took a match from his pocket and lighted the wick. He waited until he knew the flame would stay alive, then he heaved the lamp with all his strength at the wall behind the bar. The glass splintered, and kerosene splattered. The flame burst instantly into a furious blaze.

Frank turned on his heel and sought out the horrified Farraday. "That," he declared, "is for me and mine."

He walked out hurriedly, for he wanted no one to see the tears that scalded his eyes.

10

Defense Attorney Anderson Avery leaned close to Claymore's ear. "It is not helpful when I keep receiving these surprises in open court, Mr. Claymore. You should have told me about setting Farraday's establishment ablaze."

Shrugging his tired shoulders, Claymore held his eyes on the witness chair and the florid face of Rusty Farraday. "It didn't amount to nothin'."

"It did to him. The place was burned out, I assume."

After all these years the thought still brought gratification. "To the ground."

"Don't you realize this incident probably bears upon the depth of his feeling against you?"

"I intended for him to take notice."

"Farraday is the principal and most damaging witness. The depth of his feeling is certain to be sensed by the jury, and possibly transferred to them."

"Everybody knows he's a certified liar."

"Has he told any lies here so far?"

Claymore pondered. "Probably hasn't got his stride yet. I've figured all along that he's the one hid the gun. When you goin' to ask him about it?"

"Upon cross-examination. That is the proper time."

"It was him that done away with the pistol and put me here. It had to be."

Avery looked away. "Perhaps."

Frank's skin prickled as he stared at Avery. It came to him suddenly as a dead certainty that even his own attorney did not believe him. *My God!* he thought, his stomach going into a knot. *If he don't, who will?*

Prosecutor Mallard paced the floor, allowing full time for Farraday's account to register upon the jury. "Your Honor, if anyone doubts the details as cited by this witness, I have on yonder table a transcript of depositions taken by the grand jury some twenty years ago. You will find it in good accord with the recollections of Mr. Farraday. The record will show that an indictment was returned against Billy Valentine, charging murder in the first degree. It will also show that Frank Claymore was cited as an accessory and further charged with the wanton destruction of Mr. Farraday's property. I should add that the cases never came to trial because Billy Valentine was not apprehended, and because Mr. Claymore brazenly refused to submit himself to the custody of the authorities. He simply retired to the fortress of his ranch and would not allow the service of documents against his person."

To his attorney's questioning glance, Claymore said, "It was just that old Constable Wilcox. Nobody else even come. The *real* law over in Griffin knew how things really stood."

"Fort Griffin is gone," Anderson Avery said. "This is the court that matters now."

The prosecutor continued, "Aided and abetted by Frank Claymore and his coterie, Billy Valentine managed for three years to evade capture and to pursue a career of outlawry which brought shame to his mother and to the good and unselfish man who had reared him as his own—a career which still stands as a blot against the history of this good town.

"Little wonder, then, that with this for a background, Frank Claymore stands waiting for your judgment here today. The pity is that he did not stand here twenty years ago. We find ourselves belatedly correcting the omissions of the past."

Claymore slumped in the sheriff's soft chair and stared at the beaded wall, listening to the dramatic rise and fall of the prosecutor's voice playing upon the emotions of the jury and the crowd with the skill of an actor in a Dallas opera house. It occurred to him that actors and lawyers probably attended the same school, for they had so much in common.

He's right that I made a mistake, he thought. *Billy might have got off free if I'd made him stay, if I'd seen to it that he was judged in Griffin. by right-thinking men*. That idea had come too late, when the first excitement was over and Claymore had had time to reason things through. By then Sam Ballinger had led Billy to Indian Territory, where neither friend nor enemy could find them. As Claymore looked back upon it now, the rest seemed inevitable. The sapling was bent. The tree had but one direction to grow.

He became aware that Prosecutor Mallard was pointing at him again. "I need not recount further the misadventures of Billy Valentine. His punishment was left to heaven. But there sits the man, arrogant with power and blinded by greed, who by example and deed pointed his own begotten son upon the forbidden road where violent death was the only possible end. We need not leave his punishment to heaven."

Claymore heard a stirring in the courtroom and saw a solemn nodding of heads. This was George's town. They had waited a long time to drive him into a corner like this.

Hell of a thing, he thought, *to realize you've outlived most of your friends, and all that's left are your enemies*.

Friendship was seldom inherited. Hatred almost always was.

For a long time after Billy's leaving, there was only silence. Frank would have preferred even bad news to the waiting, the not knowing, for imagination conjured up specters worse than anything real.

Letty worried too, though she seldom mentioned Billy. She was attentive as never before to Naomi and Homer's sons. That said more to Frank than any words from her. He wanted to turn to her for comfort, and he sensed that she wanted him to, but he could not bring himself to do so. He had never learned how to share his troubles with her, or even to admit them.

For some time he had become increasingly concerned that the valley no longer grew the grass it once had. He suspected that weather patterns had changed; it no longer rained as it used to. He had observed this phenomenon before; as civilization moved into a virgin area, the range gradually deteriorated. It must be that human activity somehow caused a lessening of rainfall, he reasoned. Homer had suggested that the trouble might be too many cattle for the country's natural capabilities, but Frank remembered the thousands of buffalo once scattered the length of this valley. If the land had supported the buffalo, it should support his cattle, he argued. Homer's answer was that buffalo were migratory, while cattle remained forever in one place. Frank did not see the difference.

Mark Akins brought a possible solution to two of Frank's worries. A mature man of sound judgment, a heavy mustache and twenty-five more pounds than when Frank had first known him, he arrived one day from his ranch to the north and debauched himself shamelessly upon his sister Naomi's dried-apple pie—a delicacy Mark's own young wife had never mastered—then gave Frank and Homer news from the Indian Nations.

"They're leasin' Indian lands to Texas cattlemen. I hear Burk Burnett's taken some grazin' above the Red River. We could ease the load on our grass by movin' steers up yonder to grow them out. They'd be that much closer to the Kansas shippin' points."

Frank glanced at Letty, then stared into a cup of coffee turning cold in his hands. A thought set the hands to trembling. "Are Comanche lands included?" He had assumed from the first that Sam Ballinger would hide Billy in Comanche country.

Mark nodded. "Old Chief Quanah Parker is in charge of

Comanche leases. He used to scalp the white man with a knife. Now they say he's learned to skin him with a pen and stretch his hide with a contract."

Frank's pulse quickened. "I been afraid I'd arouse suspicion if I went up there to hunt for Billy. Now I could tell them I'm lookin' for grass."

Homer frowned. "Could be Billy don't want you to find him."

"I've got to know what's happened to him. It'd look less suspicious if you-all went with me."

Homer and his brother-in-law hesitated but a moment. They nodded at each other. "We'll go," Homer said.

Letty reached out for Frank's hand. He let her take it, and she smiled. But the smile was forced. Behind it, deep in her eyes, he saw anxiety, even fear.

Though Indian hostilities were long buried in past defeats, Frank felt the hair rise on the back of his neck as he and Homer and Mark waded their horses across Red River at a shallow ford and trailed water up the north bank into the Territory. A remembered caution returned, as if only yesterday he had ridden with a rifle across his lap, his eyes and ears keened. The first Indians they encountered were a family standing in front of a small frame house built like white-man dwellings to the south in Texas. Beside it, a buffalo-skin tepee showed evidence of steady use. Surrender had not been unconditional. Frank rode in with misgivings.

These Indians wore white-man clothes. But for their dark, round faces, they could have been Texas farm people. Those faces, especially the man's, made Frank nervous. He had seen such faces through a haze of gunsmoke not all that many years ago. He imagined a veiled hostility, a natural carryover from an earlier time.

Mark had not participated in the battle at Dove Creek. He had no such vivid memories to stay him. He moved out in front and asked directions. The Indian man stood silently as if he did not comprehend, his unreadable expression never changing. The answer was delivered by a boy of ten or twelve, who spoke a creditable Indian-school English.

Riding away, Frank shuddered. "I had a feelin' that old man remembered other times, and wished he could've met us with a gun. Probably did, once."

They came, in time, to the place where they had been directed. Quanah Parker was away, they were told, again by a young man who had been to school; but he would return soon—a day perhaps, or a week. The visitors were invited to share the hospitality of the village and wait. Frank still imagined a latent hatred.

"Tell them we'll be back," he said. "We'll look over the country."

They had ridden through good grasslands, and Indians to whom Mark talked assured him more was to be had. It struck Frank that they had learned commercialism in a hurry, until he remembered that the Indians had always been traders with each other and with the white man, bartering the yield of the chase for goods they could neither raise, manufacture nor take by conquest. It stood to reason they would not be long in learning the value of currency. They had observed that the white man killed for it

Whenever the three cattlemen rode into a village, they attracted a crowd. When they found an interpreter, he was invariably a boy or a very young man. One explained that the older Comanches were too proud to learn the white man's language. If the white man wanted to talk to them, they said, let the white man learn Comanche. Otherwise let him belittle himself by talking through a boy of no rank or recognition.

Frank always made it a point to inquire about a young white man and an old one. At times he suspected the people knew, but he discerned a distrust, a reticence not allayed by his assurance that he was the young man's father.

They had been in the Comanche country a week when they rode into a new village and found a lad in his teens who acknowledged that he spoke English. When Frank asked his usual question, the boy stared at him long and silently as if trying to see beyond his eyes and into his mind.

Frank said, "The boy I'm lookin' for is named Billy. He'd call the old man Sam."

The young Indian considered Frank and Homer and Mark. "You are not from the soldiers?"

"I am the boy's father."

The lad led them to a small frame house beside which stood the inevitable tepee, its buffalo-skin exterior covered by painted designs and by drawings depicting hunts and battles. He said, "I will ask my father." He ducked through the tepee's open flap, which faced to the east. From inside came the dull exchange of quiet voices. In a moment a middle-aged man emerged and took a few steps toward the three visitors.

Frank's jaw dropped.

Homer laughed aloud. "I've always said there's got to be a reward someday for livin' a clean life."

A smile cut across the deep-lined face of Red Shield like a gully quartering a broken field. He spoke his welcome in words Frank would never learn and reached out his big hand. The surprised boy translated. "My father says you have often honored him as a guest. He says you are welcome in his lodge."

Frank dismounted, as did Homer and Mark. Beaming, Red Shield shook hands vigorously with each in his turn. Through his son he invited them into his tepee to smoke a pipe in friendship. Frank followed him. The Comanche turned to the left upon passing through the flap and made a semicircle before taking a position behind a pit where a fire had burned down to glowing coals. Frank knew nothing of the customs but judged it expedient to model after the host. He was amazed how much larger the tepee looked inside. It was a repository for implements of the hunt and of war, relics from a way of life destroyed almost overnight.

Frank asked again about Billy Valentine. The boy said, "First my father will want you to smoke with him."

Impatiently Frank submitted to the ritual, taking several choking puffs from the pipe. He had no idea what the Indian used for tobacco, but it was infinitely more potent than the sacked stuff cowboys carried in their shirt pockets and always seemed to be rolling into cigarettes just when Frank needed them to undertake some task of importance.

Red Shield thanked him profusely for allowing his annual visit to the medicine hill to commune with his spirits among the rocks. He said the son whose natal difficulties had first taken him there with Sam was the healthy youth who now conveyed his words for him. His Christian-school name was Josiah. Red Shield assured Frank that the point of rocks was a potent place for prayer. The spirits were many there, and powerful.

"Tell your daddy he's always welcome in our country," Frank said to the boy. "And then ask him about Billy."

Red Shield betrayed no surprise. He seemed to have sensed Frank's reason for coming. His face drooped into deep, sad lines, and he talked at some length, using his hands much. Frank's backside itched with impatience as he waited for the boy to translate.

"My father says tell you that Billy was here with the old man Sam. They stayed hidden back in the rough hills. But the soldiers found out—there are always people who talk too much—and there was trouble. A soldier was hurt. Billy and Sam went that way." He pointed westward.

Frank chewed on a bitter disappointment. "Did they say where they intended to go?"

The boy talked with his father. "No. They said they would go where there are not soldiers."

Frank closed his eyes. West. That could mean anywhere from the Texas Panhandle to California. "Were they all right—Billy and Sam—when they left here?"

"Only a soldier was hurt. He bled much, but he did not die." He glanced at Red Shield. "My father was disappointed."

Red Shield spoke again. The boy translated. "Now my

father wants to show you some good grass, then take you to talk to Quanah Parker. He says he will see that you have the best grass for your cattle."

Frank thanked them both.

The boy continued, "My father has something else for you." He arose. At his father's direction he searched through an old rawhide packet and found a clay pipe of obvious great age. He packed some of that pungent tobacco into a leather pouch. "My father says you should take this pipe to the hill of his medicine and offer smoke to the spirits. He says they helped him with his son. They will help you find yours."

The older Indian talked at length, demonstrating how the pipe was to be lighted and used, how smoke was to be offered to the earth and the sky and the four winds, and how one must sit and wait in patience for the spirits to appear.

"My father says always when he went to the hill of his medicine, his spirits would come. He says you are a good man even though you are white. He believes the spirits will come to you."

Frank was embarrassed, but he knew he would wound Red Shield's pride if he did not accept the pipe and the tobacco with the same grace with which they were offered. Glancing uneasily at Homer and Mark, he thanked the Comanche and promised he would seek guidance from the Indian spirits.

As they rode south, Homer said, "I don't see where it could hurt anything to try."

Frank did not look him in the eyes.

The three had been gone nearly a month. Mark's ranch was the first they reached, so Frank and Homer spent the night there to rest and eat woman-cooking, a welcome change from trail grub. Frank observed the happy welcome Mark received from the pretty Colorado City girl fetched from the T & P Railroad. They had one child, and if Frank's eyes did not play him false, they would have another not too many months from now. Mark had not told him, so it would be improper to acknowledge the obvious by commenting upon it.

Homer told the young woman that the extra weight looked good on her.

Later Frank watched chubby Naomi Whitcomb throw her arms around her husband and hug him so hard that Frank felt some concern for Homer's ribs.

Letty stood on her gallery, waiting. Frank yearned to open his arms as he climbed the steps, but an old reserve would not yield. He leaned to brush her lips with a quick kiss. Her hand rested a moment on his arm, then slid away. He ached with a wanting he did not know how to show.

"I saw you coming," she said quietly. "There's coffee."

He followed her into the house. She had done much to decorate it through the years; it strongly resembled her old home in Dallas. But with just the two of them there, it had none of the rumpled and lived-in character of the Whitcomb house. It was more a display than a home.

He asked, "Anything happen while I was gone?"

She frowned, hesitant. "There've been rumors about Billy."

He spilled the coffee he was pouring. "What rumors?"

"There's talk that he and Sam were in Tascosa. There was a fight, and a man was killed. Billy and Sam disappeared."

Frank slumped heavily into a chair at the table and spilled more of his coffee. Closing his eyes to hide their pain, he told what he had learned in Indian Territory.

Letty placed her hands gently on his shoulders, and he started to reach up to touch her, but he did not follow through.

She said, "It's just rumor. There may be nothing to it."

"It fits," he said bleakly. "It all fits . . ."

Even Letty's quiet attempts at reassurance had to give way when Ranger Alex McKellar came to the ranch. He remained unchanged except for the added years. He was an unsmiling man, his tall frame stooped a little but his eyes still severe. Frank came home from a hard day of working steers to be driven to the newly acquired grass in Indian Territory. He found McKellar waiting in the big house. The Ranger had shared coffee with Letty, talking of war and her father.

Company usually brightened Letty's eyes, but they were dulled by trouble as she met Frank at the door.

McKellar extended his hand, the gesture formal and made without pleasure. Frank accepted it in the same manner. Dread worked his stomach into a boil. "Has Billy been caught?"

McKellar said, "I'd have no reason to come here if he were."

A small measure of relief was followed by even deeper misgivings. That the authorities had assigned Alex McKellar to the case meant they had become deadly serious. McKellar had built a reputation for staying on a trail until he captured his man or killed him.

Grimly McKellar said, "Billy Valentine has become my mission, Frank. For a time I was able to beg off because of my past relationship with you. Now circumstances have built to a point that I have no option. I hoped you might help me."

Frank closed his eyes. "Deliver him to you? You know I can't do that."

"I am charged to take him dead or alive. I had rather he be alive."

Frank dropped into a chair. "I don't know where he's at." He rubbed his hand over his eyes. "Alex, you know what happened with that gambler Hawkins. If Billy was to give himself up and we could get him tried someplace away from here, don't you believe an honest jury would see why he done it and turn him a-loose?"

"It has gone much further now. There is a federal warrant against him for a shooting in Indian Territory. He is alleged to have been involved in a Panhandle killing, and cattle theft in New Mexico. He has taken to running with lawless men.

"There was a time when he might simply have been a good boy who committed a crime of passion, and a court might have been lenient. Now he has traveled beyond any turning back. He will be stopped. The only question is how."

Frank reached for straws. "When a boy gets in trouble, folks blame him for everything that happens. Like as not he didn't do half what he's accused of."

"If he's done even half . . ."

Frank pinched the bridge of his nose as if that might relieve his burning eyes. "Maybe he's got word to his mother. You talked to her?"

"No, but I talked to George Valentine. He swears they've not heard from him."

"I blame George for all this. He tricked me a long time ago so he could marry Rachal. It's his fault Billy's carried the wrong name, and that name has brought him grief all his life. If it'd been me married Rachal in the first place . . ." Frank saw the hurt in Letty's eyes, but she had always known, and truth was not to be denied.

McKellar's dark gaze followed Letty as she turned away. "Perhaps. Then again, some people seem to be born under an ill star. Its light follows them whatever road they travel." He apologized to Letty for bringing grief into her house. She asked him to stay the night, but he demurred. "Someday, under happier circumstances."

Frank followed him onto the gallery. McKellar raised his hand as if to touch Frank's arm but withdrew it. "Should the opportunity present itself, Frank, try to reason with him. Alive is better than dead, even if it means the penitentiary."

It hurt Frank to admit, "He never once asked my advice. I doubt he'd take it, if I had it to offer."

He sat in silence that night, staring at dying embers in the fireplace. Letty tried to make conversation about business matters but could not reach him. She arose, finally, and put more wood on the fire.

"What's that for?" he asked.

"If we're going to sit up all night, there's no need in our being cold."

"You go on up to bed."

"I couldn't sleep, thinking about Billy, thinking about you sitting down here grieving. I'd just as well stay with you. My mind would be here anyway, and my heart." She kneeled in front of his chair and took his hands. "We've never talked much about Billy. We've talked all around him but never *about* him. Perhaps it would help now if we did."

In the firelight, as flames eagerly licked at the new, dry wood, she looked little different from the night he had taken her to her home in Dallas, after the wedding. Her hands were still as warm, as caring.

He felt himself melting. His feelings began to find their way into words as they never had before, certainly not with Letty. Now they came, raspy, uncertain, from the heart and not the mind. "You're too good a woman, Letty Zachary, to be saddled with an ungrateful old bull like me. You ought to've shot me a long time ago and left me for dead."

"The thought came to me, from time to time." She smiled faintly and brought one of his hands up to her lips. "But I never cared much for guns."

He leaned forward and kissed her forehead. "I never deserved you. I don't know why you put up with me all these years, knowin' there was another woman on my mind."

"I always thought I would beat her someday. I intend to, even yet."

"And Billy . . . you tried to be a mother to him . . ." The anger and the hurt and the despair came rushing. He leaned down into Letty's arms and held fast to her while it ran its course. He said brokenly, "I don't even know how to tell you I'm sorry."

"You don't have to. I know." She pushed to her feet, finally, and tugged at his hands until he stood up. She lighted a lamp and put her arm gently around his waist, easing him toward the stairs. They walked up side by side. At the top he started to turn toward his room. She held his arm. "No. Mine."

He made no argument but let her lead him. When he had undressed, he found her in bed, waiting. He blew out the lamp. The sheets were cold against his skin, but her body was warm as she moved to meet him. She folded loving arms around him. The old fire came back as it had not been in years, and Rachal did not once enter his mind.

He slept awhile, awakening in the darkness, startled momentarily at finding Letty sleeping peacefully beside him. He studied her profile in reflected moonlight, and a glow came back over him. He wanted to touch a hand to her cheek but knew that would awaken her. It surprised him, somehow, that he felt so concerned. He stared into darkness for a time, Billy Valentine heavy in his thoughts. He left the bed carefully, picking up his clothes and carrying them into his own room. He closed the door and lighted a lamp.

As he dressed, his fingers touched upon Rachal's locket. He had carried it so long that much of the original design had worn off the cheap metal case. He opened the locket and held it to the lamplight. He had not seen Rachal in so many years that his mental image of her face had become the image in the tiny painting. He realized that apart from this poor likeness, he no longer remembered what she looked like.

He glanced toward the wall that his room shared with Letty's. He warmed to the thought of the woman whose bed he had just left. Shame came over him, and a sense of wasted years. He closed the locket, opened a large wooden chest and dropped it in.

He made up his mind never to carry it again.

His gaze went to a blanket-wrapped bundle. He removed the covering and ran his fingers over the clay pipe Red Shield had given him. He stood up straight, feeling foolish for the sudden thought. Carefully he restored the bundle to its place and closed the chest. But he stopped at the door, looking back. The thought would not leave him. He pondered a long time, took the bundle from the chest and went out to the corrals to saddle one of the night horses.

As the sun broke over the eastern horizon he was climbing Medicine Hill, carrying the bundle beneath his arm. It took him longer to reach the top than it used to, and his breath was about gone. His hip was afire. He tried to remember the ritual Red Shield had told him. He spread the blanket upon the ground and stiffly lowered himself to a sitting position upon it, facing east into the rising sun. He lighted the pipe with difficulty, for the fierce wind kept blowing out his matches. The first puff of smoke almost choked him. He came near calling off the whole thing, because it seemed childish and superstitious for a grown man. But he remembered the faith in Red Shield's eyes, and his promise to the Indian that he would try. He blew one puff of the bitter smoke skyward, one toward the earth and one to each of the four winds, though here the north wind took it all. He sat then and waited . . . and waited . . . and waited.

No spirit came. No one ever came except Homer. From as far back as Frank could remember, Homer had seemed to have an uncanny knack for knowing what was in Frank's mind.

Early one morning Frank walked into the dark barn to fetch his saddle and was startled by a sudden move in the shadows. He dropped the saddle. He stood motionless a moment, his mouth dry, then struck a match. The flickering light showed him the sad, drawn face of Sam Ballinger.

"I didn't go to booger you," Sam apologized. "I didn't think I ought to come here in the daylight."

Frank looked around hastily, his heart quickened. "Is Billy with you?"

Sam's voice was tight. "I ain't seen Billy in months. I've hunted for him everywhere."

Frank took Sam by the arm. "Come on up to the Whit-combs' and get you some breakfast. You look starved out."

Sam did not deny that. But he worried. *"They're* lookin' for Billy too. And they may be lookin' for me."

Frank assured him that no one had asked about him, not even Alex McKellar. Sam came near crying. "Billy's done some bad things, Frank. I done all the talkin' I knowed to do, but he got to a point he stopped listenin'."

Sam looked too brittle for the hug Mother Whitcomb gave him. Homer had a hundred questions as his buxom wife and Letty rushed to fix breakfast for Sam. The Whit-comb boys clustered around, all eyes and ears.

Sam looked as forlorn and lost as the last time he had come back. His eyes brimmed when he studied the faces of old friends. He cradled a coffee cup in trembling hands and told about the trouble in Indian Territory. "We followed the Canadian River over into the Panhandle, clear west to Tas-cosa. One night there was a row, and a man got killed. Billy said he had to leave me for my own good.

"I trailed after him, but he stayed ahead of me . . . over into New Mexico, back into Texas. About the time I'd think I'd found him, I'd lose him again. It wasn't hard to tell where he'd been; there was generally trouble. And always there'd be them that was bayin' after him like he was some wild animal. It ain't right, Frank, for them to hound him so. He's a good boy, like my Sammy was. There ain't no real bad in him."

Frank reached for Letty's hand and clasped it tightly. "No, Sam. There's been a lot of bad done *to* him, is all."

As he could feel the winter coming while the wind still blew warm, Frank felt the showdown coming for Billy Valentine. Twice a posse swarmed into the ranch headquarters and searched the buildings over Frank's angry but futile pro-tests. From that, he knew Billy must be somewhere in the country. He heard reports from town that a constant guard was posted on the Valentine house in case Billy made an attempt to see his mother. A train robbery was aborted down on the T & P, and some said a robber who fled looked much like Billy Valentine. Frank wondered resentfully how they could think they knew. Billy would be seen Monday in El Paso, Tuesday in Fort Worth and Wednesday in San Antonio, if all the reports were to be believed. Every criminal who had no name was given one: Billy Valentine.

If the stories brought pain to Frank, they bore even heavier upon Sam. The life had flickered and died from his eyes. His step was slow, his frame bent and so thin that once the Whitcomb boys' playful dog knocked him off of his feet. He did not often ride out with the cowboys. He stayed at headquarters, watching the north. At times he talked of Billy, at times of his Sammy. Often it was difficult to know which was on his mind; they seemed one and the same.

Alex McKellar came one morning with the season's first bitter blue norther, three half-frozen Rangers riding with him. Frank and several cowboys were saddling horses in the corrals. McKellar motioned for the three Rangers to remain behind. He passed one his reins and walked to Frank, the wind whipping at his coat. He did not extend his hand. Frank knew from his face that he was on the trail; he had borne that look before the battle on Dove Creek.

McKellar stared into Frank's eyes, probing before he spoke. Frank gathered his full determination and stared back, not blinking. McKellar said evenly, "He was in town last night. He tried to slip into his parents' house, and a deputy shot him. He got away in the dark, but he's carrying lead."

Frank's heart sagged. He heard a cry from Sam, who had walked up to listen. Frank held his eyes to McKellar's. "If he was here, I wouldn't tell you. But he ain't been here, and that's the truth."

McKellar nodded, satisfied. "If he comes, remember he'll probably die unless he gets medical attention." He gave Sam a moment's silent study, then looked over the cowboys. To them he said sternly, "For your own safety, I would urge you-all to remain here today. There are armed and nervous men out yonder who should not even be trusted with a pocket-knife." Leaning into the cold wind, he walked back to his horse.

Sam desperately grabbed Frank's arm. "Frank, what're we goin' to do?"

Frank turned away from him and cried in a stricken voice, "For God's sake, how should I know?" He caught hold of the saddle horn and leaned against his horse, hiding his face in his arms. The moment passed. Bitterly he declared, "Even if he's out there, we'd have no idea where to look. Like Alex said, we'll stay at the house."

The cowboys unsaddled without comment, leaving Frank to deal with his sorrow in privacy. He dropped his saddle to the ground and turned. Homer stood at the fence, not intruding but letting Frank know he was there if he needed him. He had always been there when Frank had needed him.

Frank asked, "What's the fastest horse we've got?"

Homer pondered. "That sorrel you just pulled the saddle off of is as good as any."

Almost in a whisper Frank said, "Let's leave him in the corral, just in case."

He tried to force himself to remain in the house, but he listened to the cold wind challenging the eaves, and it was like the voice of a boy, crying. It was a voice he remembered, a cry he would never forget. Letty watched him worriedly, but she was helpless to comfort him. His skin prickled with impatience, until he was compelled to put on the heaviest woolen coat he owned and climb partway up the canyon wall on an ancient game trail. There he could see across much of the valley. The raw, cold wind burned his eyes and brought tears that burned even more. When he blinked them away he observed horsemen scattered in a broad picket line like cowboys dispersed for a roundup. It would be dangerous for a lone stranger to cross the valley, even one who had never heard of Billy Valentine.

He remained on the canyon wall most of the day, until he trembled uncontrollably from late-afternoon's deep-driving chill. He started down, finally, when the leaden clouds of the norther turned dark and he could no longer see the far side of the valley. His legs were so stiff he had to force them into movement. His feet were without feeling, so that he stumbled and slid and fell part of the way. He picked himself up and found his hand lacerated, his clothing torn. He bled, but he did not feel it.

Letty's eyes were soft with concern as he entered the silent house, but there was no need to speak her mind. He knew. She took his half frozen hands and led him toward a blaze she had kept in the fireplace. "You've had nothing to eat all day."

He shook his head and leaned toward the warmth of the fire. She said, "I'll put some supper on the table."

Bleakly he told her he was not hungry, though he was. She set about stoking the kitchen cookstove. She brought him coffee, and he sipped it in front of the fire, the cup slowly warming his stiffened fingers. She called him a third time before he made himself rise and go into the dining room. Letty ate little, watching him until he pushed back his plate and lowered his head into his hands.

"He's out there someplace," he cried, "cold and hungry, maybe dyin'. I don't know one thing I can do to help him."

She put her arms around him and held him gently. She said, "There isn't anything. There never was."

Frank did not go to bed, for he knew he would not sleep. He sat with Letty before the fire, now and then adding a twisted mesquite root to ward off the pervasive cold that sought its way around the window facings and beneath the doors. Staring into the flames, he remembered a girl at old Fort Davis. He remembered a baby that cried the first time he saw it, a boy who had come to his place for refuge and had wept because he was not allowed to stay.

Sometime past midnight he heard a gentle knock. He saw fear leap into Letty's eyes. He trudged heavily to the door.

Homer Whitcomb stood shivering in the wind. He made no move to enter. "Get your coat, Frank," he whispered urgently.

Frank grabbed his hat and coat and hurried out into the night, matching Homer's brisk pace toward the barn. Letty trailed hopelessly behind. Two saddled horses stood in the corral, one of them his sorrel. In the gloom, beyond the barn door, he made out the shapes of three men. Two were Sam Ballinger and Tobe. The other was bent, leaning against the wall of the barn.

"Billy?" Frank whispered.

He stretched out his arms. Billy Valentine fell against him and clung with a desperation for which Frank was unprepared. "Boy," Frank cried, "you're hurt bad. Come up to the house and let us see what we can do for you."

"I got to keep ridin'," Billy rasped. "They're everywhere."

"They'll kill you out there. Here we can protect you. We can see that you get to town alive, that you get a fair trial."

"And then they'll hang me. You know they'll hang me."

"We don't know that," Frank argued, but he did. It had gone too far.

Sam Ballinger said, "I'll go with him, Frank. I know how to hide him, like before. If we can just get out of this valley, they'll never find us."

"It's hopeless, Sam," Frank said, but he knew he wanted Sam to make the try.

He held Billy in his arms with a despair he had never known. "Son, there's so many things I've wanted to say to you . . ."

Billy clung to him and cried. His crying tore at Frank as it had torn the first time he had seen Billy in his crib.

Billy saw Letty. He pulled away from Frank and grasped Letty's hands. "I'm sorry," he said. She pulled him into her arms.

"God go with you, Billy Valentine," she whispered.

Billy broke free and stumbled toward the sorrel horse. Tobe and Homer helped lift him into the saddle. Frank thought for a moment Billy might fall. The young cowboy gripped the saddle horn and planted both feet firmly in the stirrups. Sam asked, "You ready, boy?"

Billy could only nod.

Sam leaned down and touched Frank's shoulder with a thin, bony hand. "I'll stay with him, Frank. No matter what, I'll stay with our boy." They rode out the open corral gate and disappeared into the howling wind.

Frank stood there until Letty put her arm around him. She trembled from cold, or something. He took her to the house. He slumped into his chair before the fire. Letty sat at his feet, cradling her head against his knees. The fire gradually burned itself out because Frank did not get up to replenish the wood. He was staring hollow-eyed into dying coals when he heard a gentle knock on the door and knew it was Homer's. The sense of disaster weighed heavily upon him. He did not dare look at Letty.

He saw anguish in Homer's eyes, then looked beyond to Alex McKellar and a dozen horsemen. Behind McKellar stood two riderless horses, one Frank's sorrel, the other Sam's favorite bay, much like the one he had ridden years ago. Across the saddles, two blanket-wrapped bundles were tied. Tobe stood with head bowed and aimlessly rubbed his hand against the shoulder of Sam Ballinger's horse.

McKellar said regretfully, "We sighted them at daylight, Frank. They made a stand. After we got Billy we tried to spare the old man, but he seemed to go crazy. He squalled like a Comanche and made a run at us, firing as he came. There was nothing else we could do."

Frank clung to Letty, and she to him. He could no longer see, for the cold wind brought tears that flooded his eyes. He said in a breaking voice, "Leave Sam here; we'll take him to the Clear Fork and bury him amongst his own. You'd best carry Billy home to his mother."

11

The judge had fidgeted for some time, and when prosecuting attorney Elihu Mallard began leading Rusty Farraday toward a recounting of the offense for which Frank Claymore stood trial, His Honor Whitmore Holmes declared the sun was over the yardarm. He recessed court for the day. Claymore's hip ached from sitting so long, even in the soft chair borrowed from the sheriff. He pushed to a stand on his cane, shrugging off Homer's attempt to help him.

Deputy Willis elbowed through the heavy, noisy crowd. His voice was demanding. "You fixin' to go outside, Mr. Claymore?"

Claymore did not see that his kidney functions were any business of this meddlesome upstart. "You got to supervise *everything* I do?"

Willis took an uneasy step backward, bumping against someone trying to beat the main crowd out of the room. "Orders of the court, Mr. Claymore. Anyway, I thought if them Indians out yonder are really friends of yours, you'd want to know they've hitched up their wagon. Even they know you're whipped."

Claymore bit off an intended sharp reply and looked at Homer. "Want to help me get through all these people?"

Spectators pulled aside. Claymore avoided looking into their faces. He had seen enough of hostility. Most of this crowd would probably come to his hanging whether sent an invitation or not. Willis remained close, pushing people aside with the imperious air of one granted more authority than is good for him.

Red Shield's son Josiah was helping his father toward a weathered farm wagon near a gate in the courtyard fence. The old Indian took short, cautious steps that bespoke pain. Claymore moved not a great deal faster. "Run ahead yonder, Willis," he commanded, "and tell them to whoa up."

Willis's authority wavered. "I don't talk Indian."

"The young one talks better English than you do. Let's see you trot a little." He waved his cane for emphasis.

Willis yielded to the domination in Claymore's voice and began to sprint. Realizing then that he was under no obligation to obey, he slowed to a walk but glanced back uncertainly. A wave of Claymore's cane might set him into a run again. "Hey, you Indians!" he shouted. "Wait a minute."

Josiah was defensive at the sight of Willis's badge, then eased as he saw Claymore and Homer crippling their way toward him. The old Indian looked around in some confusion, for his eyes were failing him.

It did not occur to Claymore to thank Willis for his exertion. He extended his hand to Red Shield. "Old friend," he said, "you wasn't fixin' to leave without us seein' you again, was you?"

Josiah translated. Red Shield had never compromised his dignity to learn English. He spoke in a voice quavering with age and, Claymore realized suddenly, illness. Josiah said, "My father must leave this place."

Dismay was in Homer's eyes, for Red Shield's condition was obvious. "Your daddy ought not to be travelin' *anywhere,* except to a doctor."

Claymore did not ask; he ordered. "Willis, you go fetch a doctor over here."

Willis stiffened. "For an Indian?"

Josiah shook his head. "He has seen the white-man doctors. Now he wants to go to the medicine rocks and talk to his spirits."

"I tried that one time," Claymore said. "They never answered me."

"They are not your spirits," Josiah replied, "and they are not mine. But they are *his.*"

Claymore frowned. Faith was all right, in its proper place, but in a crisis he preferred more tangible weaponry. He said with an edge of criticism, "He shouldn't've made this long trip in his shape."

"What my father wants, he does." Red Shield grasped Claymore's hand. The grip was weak, but his gaze did not waver. He spoke, then looked at his son. Josiah explained, "My father says not to be troubled about him; his spirits are kind. He will ask the spirits to help you too."

"Tell him thanks. I need all the help I can get."

Red Shield spoke again, gravely. Josiah put the words into English. "We have fought many enemies, you and me, and their ponies have never run us down. But time is an enemy we cannot defeat."

Claymore studied the furrowed face and realized with a deep sadness that for Red Shield the enemy was about to prevail. *How far behind will I be?* he wondered. He gave the old man's hand as good a grip as he had. "Tell him I'm glad that when we were young we had the courage to face one another, and the good luck not to kill."

Red Shield directed him a long look in silence, then turned away. Claymore cleared his throat. "Willis, you help lift him up into that wagon."

Willis gave the Indians a sharp look of distaste. "I don't work for you, Frank Claymore."

A firm voice declared, "But you work for me. Go do what he said!" Sheriff Ed Phelps had walked up. He made no attempt to hide his puzzlement as the old Indian slumped wearily on the wagon seat and his son put the horse team into motion. Josiah looked back, but Red Shield did not.

Willis watched the departing wagon with resentment and rubbed his hands vigorously on his trousers. The sheriff grunted. "Tryin' to get the Indian off of him."

"Won't do him no harm," Claymore remarked intoler-antly. "He'll never be half the man that old Comanche is."

The sheriff said, "Willis has his uses. Just can't afford to give him too much rope." He looked at the wagon drawing away, obscure beyond a thin veil of dust. "I still don't fig-ure it—an old Indian fighter like you, an old warrior like that. How could you ever be friends?"

Claymore leaned heavily on his cane. A regret nearly forty years old came over him with the weight of a winter wind. "Things change, Ed. Old enemies turn into friends . . . old friends turn into enemies. That's how come they're tryin' me . . . for killin' an enemy who was once my friend . . ."

The raw blue norther that swept the valley at the time of Billy Valentine's death was not the worst of that winter; it was but the beginning. Again and again, with a fury pent up through several benign seasons, nature seemed bent on destroying Frank Claymore and everything he owned. The high west walls of the canyon offered but little protection when the north wind found an open path down the valley and drove snow into banks deep enough to bury a standing horse. Cattle froze in the drifts, and others suffocated when wind-whipped snow blocked their nostrils.

Frank watched with a curious sense of detachment at first, for after Billy's death this seemed the smaller tragedy. But after a time his stockman's instincts and the suffering of helpless animals reached through his grief, bringing him to a full realization of the calamity.

Spring's melting of the deep drifts revealed death losses on a scale he had not imagined. Warming weather raised a stench reminiscent of the buffalo slaughter. For a mile or more upwind of headquarters, carcasses were heaped into piles and burned with dry brush dragged in from distant draws and headers. At first cowboys tried to salvage what they could by skinning the dead cattle, but it was a sicken-ing task. Frank called a halt when Homer warned him half his working force was about to roll up their bedding and leave. So many cattle were dead from the high plains down to the Cross Timbers that the hide market had gone to hell anyway.

Even Homer had little to say that spring. He occasionally managed a brief, weak smile, but the hurting never left his eyes. Naomi Whitcomb and Letty Claymore began a winter routine of being at the barn with a pot of hot coffee when the hands rode in from a hard day that ran into the dark of evening. Letty would walk to the house with Frank, her arm around him. There had been a time he would not have let her do it for everyone to see, but now he drew strength from her, and hope. He did not care who saw, or what they thought.

They never spoke of Billy Valentine, but always he walked with them, as strong a presence now as when he had lived.

Through Letty and the contacts she had inherited from her father, Frank had recognized in the early years the importance of friendly politicians in Austin when the time came for renewal of grazing leases from the state and from school districts to which the income had been allotted. He usually left the butter-spreading process to Letty and Homer. Letty would disarm them with her smile, and Homer would wear them down by telling them the history of Texas. Frank would sit in awkward silence, trying to hide his distaste for dealing with people toward whom he felt contempt. He regarded politicians and bureaucrats in the same light as he regarded screwworm medicine: an unpleasant necessity. He always supported Dalton Everhart for the state legislature because Everhart kept the proper wheels greased and turning.

But political practitioners sow seeds of enmity as well as of favor, and when enough thorn seeds bear fruit, politicians find themselves unwillingly retired. Frank knew George Valentine and most of his townspeople were backing Everhart's opponent, but he was far more concerned about

winter killing a third of his cattle than something as tri-
fling as an election.

He was unprepared for the bankruptcy of two cattleman
neighbors that spring when the full extent of the death loss
was counted, and for the breaking up of their ranch lands
into farming tracts that to Frank were a blemish on the lower
part of the valley. Their loss was his loss too, for against
Letty's firm advice he had co-signed some of their notes.
He was reduced to borrowing money for the first time in
years.

He was even less prepared for the state's rejection of his
application to renew leases Captain Zachary had arranged
so long ago that they seemed almost sacred. Beaten legisla-
tors, he found, had no influence over the state bureaucracy.
As Frank moved cattle off the lost lands, George Valentine
moved settlers in. Suddenly George seemed to know the
land-office staff by first names, while Frank found himself
hardly able to get past a stern secretary who stood guard
nearest the outer door. He was informed by acquaintances
who had no ax to grind that new state policy regarded him
as a cattle baron whose privilege on public land must be
broken.

He grumbled, "They used to stand in line to shake my
hand."

Letty said, "That was a different generation. We'd better
go to Austin and see what we can salvage from the wreck."

Frank had rather take a whipping with a wet rope. In Austin, it seemed to him, half the people had their hands out
with palms up, and the rest extended them in the form of
fists. He took Homer and Naomi on the long ride in the
ranch buggy, Homer to help Letty soft-talk the appropriate
people and Naomi to keep Homer from being lured off into
God knew what by the city's lights.

Their first day in town, Frank had to restrain himself
from punching a smart-aleck young bureaucrat in the nose.
Other men could resort to the comfort of strong drink, but
Frank had never allowed himself that luxury. At the ranch

he sought out work that was hard, nasty and mean when he needed a purgative. Trapped in Austin, he could work off his boiling anger only by stomping the streets like a penned bull, walking briskly down Sixth's saloon row or up Congress toward the new state capitol building that towered on a knoll, an angel of some kind roosting way up on top of the dome.

"Damned sure ain't no angels under the dome," he declared to a startled Mexican boy who carried a crude wooden boot-blacking kit on his shoulder. The boy hurried down the street.

Letty came to the hotel later with Naomi and Homer and said she thought they had managed to patch up some of the damage, but it would be helpful in the future if Frank would become a deaf mute while inside the Austin city limits.

"You're a proud man, Frank Claymore," she said. "You ought to recognize that other people have pride too."

"A town full of midgets," he snorted. "What have they got to be proud about?"

He found his name in the next day's local newspaper. It said he was a wealthy landholder trying to retain an unjustified hold on grass that belonged to the people.

He slammed the newspaper against his leg. To Letty he declared, "I'm people. What do they mean, wealthy? They ain't counted our dead cattle. I've always paid the state everything it asked for, one year after another."

Letty calmly reminded him, "Dalton Everhart always saw to it that they didn't ask too much."

"It's George's doin'," Frank declared. "He's nibbled at me a bite at a time. Now he's tryin' to take it all."

As the four of them prepared to leave the hotel for supper, Frank unexpectedly came face-to-face with George Valentine at the lobby door. Frank froze, one hand on the knob. Mouth open, he could only stare into George's time-punished features. Remembering the young man he had partnered so long ago on the Clear Fork, he searched in vain for a vestige of that youth. George seemed an old man now, lines set deeply under eyes wounded by looking upon much that was bitter.

George brought himself to say, "I'd be obliged, Frank, if you would yield me the door."

Frank did not move. A residual of anger remained from the morning's newspaper. It bubbled to the surface and spilled over. "You've yielded me damned little."

Frank had beaten George once in a fistfight but was not at all sure he could do it now. This George was a much older man, but he was stocky and strong. George said, "You've got more than you need. It's only justice that you give up some of it to smaller men."

Frank's eyes pinched nearly shut. He stepped aside and held the door just half open. "Come on in, George. It don't take much room for a small man."

George met his challenging gaze. "It won't take much for you, either, Frank, not near as much as you've thought."

Captain Zachary's foresight in buying the sections along the creek remained Frank's principal salvation. Without access to living water, which Frank controlled, much of the land lying away from the creek was not desirable for farmers and small stockmen. Neither George nor the state found new takers for dry tracts when leases came up for renewal. Frank was able to salvage a goodly part of his valley lands while waiting for a change in the Austin climate. Nevertheless, as each parcel was taken from him, Frank felt they were cutting off his arm a finger at a time. He grieved over every loss and hunched his shoulders a little more when each stranger built house and sheds and put a plow into grasslands Frank had considered his own.

Windmills were not new. In his travels Frank had seen them for years, their tall wooden towers holding wheels into the wind to pump cool water from unseen streams moving beneath the earth. He had not felt their need in the valley because the creek had never failed him, and cattle could walk to its clear waters from anywhere that the land bore his name. He had forbidden the digging of wells for fear the notion might prove contagious. It might awaken new demand for state lands that were currently useless to anyone else.

He might have known George would bring windmills into the valley. Frank would not belittle himself by riding down for a close look at the drilling rig, but he climbed slowly and painfully to the top of Medicine Hill and viewed from afar the horse team plodding a monotonous circle, providing power that slowly chewed a hole an inch at a time down into the water-bearing sands. He watched sourly as a shining pool slowly expanded in a shallow depression gouged out of grass near the well. He could no longer depend upon his ownership of the creek to protect the outer tracts from encroachment A settler who could afford a windmill could sink his roots anywhere he chose.

Frank forced his gaze away from the well drilling and studied his long valley. He saw it in memory as he had seen it the first day . . . vast, beautiful, its thick grass winter cured, grazed by so many buffalo that he would never have believed they could be annihilated in a few brief years. To the north he saw cattle now where the buffalo had been— his and Letty's and the Whitcombs'. They were fewer than the buffalo had been, but they kept the grass grazed short. In places the ground had turned chronically bare. Wind whipped away the loose soil, leaving scars that stirred his conscience each time he looked upon them. To the south lay the farms that crept steadily in his direction as George's machinations robbed him of one lease after another and the state or school districts sold the land to someone else. This was a defacement, in his sight, an invasion by unworthy men who thoughtlessly fenced and plowed and plundered, who did not realize the enormity of what they had done because they did not share his memory of this valley.

He could not sleep. He lay staring at the ceiling, listening to the announcement of the hours by the old grandfather clock Letty had inherited from the captain. He left his bed, finally, and hobbled down to the parlor. He slumped in his soft chair and mumbled to himself. He would welcome even Homer's incessant conversation if he knew how to awaken his partner without arousing Mother Whitcomb and setting off one of her finger-pointing lectures about how he was abusing the poor cowboys with long, hard hours and nig-gardly pay. She never had gotten it in her head that she was an owner too.

The wooden stairs creaked. Lamplight danced on the walls in rhythm to Letty's slow tread. She stood in the door-way, long white nightgown almost touching the floor. In pale lamplight, when he could not make out her features, she looked the same as the day he had married her. She had gained not a pound in all those years, and her eyes were as alive as they had ever been.

She said, "I thought I heard you arguing with somebody. Are you all right?"

He reached up and touched her hand, then let it go. "I was over to see George Valentine's well."

"And that woke you up? It must be a noisy thing for you to hear it this far."

"If George can drill a well, anybody can. They don't need our creek anymore. They can take over everything we don't have a deed to. They can swamp this valley and ruin it."

Letty set the lamp on a table and took a rocking chair she had long favored. "Nothing stands still. You've changed. I've changed. Even our part of the valley's not the same."

He stared at the framed gold piece given him long ago by Captain Zachary. "I've run too many cattle too long, but I've never scarred it with a plow. I've never grubbed it up by the roots. I could still take it back to what it used to be. When *them* people change it, it'll be gone forever."

"Thirty years is a long time to hold something like this. We're old. The country's young. We can't stop the inevita-ble."

"It's not inevitable. It's George! Forty years, damned

near, he's been hackin' at me. Why don't he just get old and die?"

Letty put a finger to her lips. "You shouldn't say such a thing. Don't even let it cross your mind."

At the turn of the century the State of Texas entered what came to be known as its four-section homestead period. Officials considered Oklahoma's land rushes and decided against a reckless spectacle that matched homeseekers by the hundreds and thousands in a wild horse race for land. They chose instead a course that seemed more orderly and civilized, accepting applications on a specified date—first come, first served. The concept appeared simple enough, and often it was. But in counties where choice land parcels were in strong demand, the reality could be chaotic. At Eldorado, at Sherwood and other county seats, applicants arrived early by hours and even days to establish positions in the waiting line. Pushing and shoving led to slugging. Sheriffs and deputies could do no more than keep the violence from flashing into murder. Bruises, abrasions and broken noses were the price of remaining in contention. Victory went more often to the strong than to the swift.

Frank knew the die had been cast when surveyor teams began blocking off school lands on which his leases were soon to expire. He chased them away, sternly declaring that they had no right so long as he held the lease. They returned with a court order and the sheriff. Regretfully the lawman said, "You can fight it out in court, Mr. Claymore, but in the meantime you'll have to leave the surveyors be. Time old judge hears the case, your leases will be up and gone."

Frank tried not to impose his anger on Ed Phelps. He had a feeling the sheriff was inclined in his direction; he was a cowboy at heart, not a farmer. "Looks like George and his bunch have got me rimfired."

The lawman studied him critically. "They'd probably turn me out at the next election if they knew I told you this.

They've set the date to sell off these lands at the courthouse in tracts of one section and up. Just about anybody can qualify for one tract if he can put up a filin' fee and the first payment." The sheriff glanced toward the cowhands who rode with Frank. "That applies to you, Mr. Claymore. And even to your cowboys."

He waited for the full import to reach Frank, then added, "The first in line when the county clerk opens his office will be the first to buy. Ain't no law says a bunch of men couldn't start that line a couple of days early."

Frank's mind raced, but he had a moment for gratitude. "Ed, if there's ever anything you want . . ."

The sheriff shook his head. "All I want is a peaceful county. Ain't been a bad killin' here since Billy Valentine."

To avoid a hopeless crush inside the courthouse halls, the county clerk declared that he would accept land applications at 7:30 on a Saturday morning, at a window opening out upon the courthouse square. The procedure was borrowed from a couple of counties that had already been through this agony and had found the crowd more manageable out of doors. There, at least, nobody bled on the floor.

About noon on Thursday some fifty horsemen rode into town from the north, followed by two chuck wagons and two extra wagons carrying their bedrolls. Frank Claymore, Homer Whitcomb and Mark Akins headed the procession. They bestirred the town's dogs into a wild fit of barking and attracted several dozen curious children, who stared at the invading army until frightened mothers rushed them indoors and out of danger. Conventional wisdom held that cowboys were a heathen lot seldom to be trusted, and never when they came in bunches.

Frank looked back to be sure they had lost no riders at the Last Chance Saloon, which posted the town's north boundary. He had with him every man who worked for him and for Mark, and a few extras recruited on short notice.

Behind Homer rode all the Whitcomb sons, headed by James, the eldest, as savvy a bunch of hands as Frank had ever been privileged to work with. He only wished they weren't so damned eager to try new notions. James had been badgering him with a theory that if they ran fewer cattle they would have healthier cows and a bigger calf crop, as well as calves that weighed more by weaning time. Frank thought James's education had been sadly neglectful in arithmetic.

Frank reined up at a vacant lot he had quietly bought through an intermediary so George Valentine could not legally prevent the chuck wagons from camping in town. The lot faced the courthouse square. The cowboys rode on to a livery barn and unsaddled their horses while the wagon cooks methodically set up camp just as if this were a normal cow works. From the corrals the cowboys marched directly through the courtyard gate and formed a line in front of the county clerk's window. By the time townspeople began to discern their intent, the Claymore men held a strong claim on the courthouse square.

Sheriff Ed Phelps strode down to the two chuck wagons where Frank Claymore had seated himself triumphantly upon a bedroll, a cup of coffee in his gnarled hands. Frank nodded toward the nearest chuck box. "You'll find cups in the drawer."

The sheriff poured coffee from a blackened pot and faced Frank with a bemused smile.

Frank asked, "We doin' anything illegal?"

"Not so long as the owner of this lot doesn't object."

"I'm him, and I don't. Figured the men could come and eat in relays, just like when they're workin' a herd. The others can hold their places. Is that legal?"

"No law I know of says how a waitin' line has to operate. The law just says the clerk has to take the applications in the order that they show up at his window. Whoever's strong enough to hold a place, it's his." He frowned at the cowboys who were walking in to eat. "I don't want any guns on that square except mine, Mr. Claymore. If any of your men are armed, I want them to bring their pistols and put them in the wagons."

Frank nodded. "Most of them don't even own a gun; that day's long gone. It's one change I don't mourn over."

The sheriff seemed satisfied. "Thanks for the coffee, Mr. Claymore." He started to leave but stopped. "Looks like you've got some more company."

George Valentine came around the corner in a buggy and hauled his trotting team to a stop. Frank took satisfaction from the distress on George's round face. Rusty Farraday sat beside George, but Frank gave him only a cursory glance, as much as he thought the man was worth. Farraday had never recovered financially from the loss of his saloon. He had become George's errand runner, nothing more. He slept in a shed behind one of George's stores and put away prodigious amounts of whiskey, which left its mark in florid cheeks, in eyes sometimes unable to focus.

George did not dismount from the buggy. He declared, "You can't do this, Frank."

Calmly Frank said, "Ask the sheriff."

The sheriff was solemn. "The law just says first come, first served. It doesn't say how early the first ones can be here."

George's face colored helplessly. "Who gave you permission to camp these wagons here, Frank? This is private property."

Frank nodded. "I know. I bought it."

George looked again at the sheriff, as if for help. The sheriff said, "All I can do is keep the peace."

George declared, "That may be hard, when people find out what Frank Claymore is tryin' to do here."

"Not tryin'," Frank said with gravel in his voice. *"Doin'!"*

George said, "The law clearly states that these lands are to go to bona-fide buyers. Every man over there is one of your hands, Frank."

"Not all of them. Some are Mark Akins's boys. And some are old friends who don't work for either one of us, just men who want a piece of land they can call their own."

"Land they can sell to *you*," George argued. "You've made an agreement with these men to sell that land to you when they have clear title. That violates the intent of the law."

Frank said, "Have any of these men told you so?"

"I don't have to talk to them. I know."

"You think. Thinkin' and knowin' are as different as Adam and Eve."

George climbed down heavily. Frank stiffened, wondering if he meant to fight. At their age, it would be a ridiculous sight. George handed the reins to Farraday. "Go put the buggy away, Rusty. I'll talk to the judge."

Frank watched with concern as George hurried up the hard-packed pathway toward the courthouse doors. The sheriff said, "I already talked to the judge. He's inclined against you, but he says there's not a thing George can do." He narrowed his eyes in warning. "Not a thing *legal*."

The town's hostility quickly became apparent as word spread. Townspeople clustered angrily across the street, augmented by farmers in from the country as afternoon wore into evening. Frank stayed close to the men, as did Homer and Mark, urging them to acknowledge no insult, answer no challenge. It was a struggle for some, particularly the younger hands, to endure taunts from lesser men. Cowboy nature was to regard all others as lesser men, for no man stood as tall as a man in the saddle.

Frank said firmly, "It don't matter what they call you today. Come Saturday they can call you landowners."

By nightfall several young strangers had stationed themselves at the end of the line. Frank eyed them closely but saw in them no signs of belligerence. They talked in accents peculiar to Frank's ears. Homer's son James said they were farmers from some German settlement down in the hill country, and they hoped there might still be some tracts left when all the cowboys had gotten theirs. They seemed ill prepared for taking a stand in line this early. None had even a bedroll. When James saw they were going without supper, fearful of losing their places, he told them to go to one of the chuck wagons and see if there wasn't something left.

"Your places'll still be here when you get back," he promised. "Just don't you try movin' any farther up."

Frank grumbled. "Homer, sometimes I wonder about your boys and their upbringin'. It ain't enough them people are farmers. They're foreigners, too."

Homer replied, "We was all foreigners once, except old Red Shield and his folks."

The line lengthened considerably during Friday. Some comers quarreled and fought each other for places. Frank told his men to take no part so long as their own positions were not challenged. The sheriff broke up a couple of fights, but the combatants went at it again the moment he left. He gave up after a while, setting his deputy Willis to keep watch from the courthouse steps.

Disgustedly he said, "If there's a killin', come and tell me. Otherwise I don't want to know about it."

By Friday night Frank and Homer walked around the courthouse square and counted fully two hundred men. None was armed; the sheriff had seen to that. Nevertheless Frank sensed an ugly mood. The crowd was black powder waiting for a spark.

Homer suggested, "I think we better tell our boys to drift over to the wagons for a cup of coffee and fetch back a big chunk of firewood apiece."

Frank cautioned, "I don't want to do anything that won't set right with the sheriff."

"What's wrong with everybody havin' a little firewood?" Homer asked innocently. "It might get cold tonight."

As the hours went on, Frank noted that Homer's sons seemed to have made friends with the German-speaking strangers who had come early and stood just behind the cowboys in line. Frank watched with some concern. "I was always careful who *I* made friends with."

Homer smiled. "One reason you never had very many. Times like this, a man needs all the friends he can get."

The men spread their bedrolls where they held their places in line. Frank cautioned them to sleep in their clothes. "If there's trouble," he warned, "it won't wait for you to put your boots on."

Frank slept in his, too. Rather, he lay there; he did not sleep. He wished he were at home in his own bed, with Letty. It had been years since a bedroll on the hard ground had given him rest. Aching from shoulders to knees, he kept his eyes open most of the night, ready for trouble. At daylight it had not come, and he was weary from the waiting. The cooks were at work. Frank saw to it that only a few men went to the wagons at one time, bringing back their filled plates so they would be gone but a few minutes.

A little after seven the county clerk appeared at the gate, but he stopped there, eyeing the awakened crowd of men with more than a little dread. He turned back after a minute, and when he reappeared, the sheriff and deputy Willis strode on either side of him. As he unlocked the courthouse door, twenty or thirty shouting men rushed him from far back in line. The clerk hurried inside, Willis just behind him, and slammed the door shut. The sheriff stood with his arms spread, blocking the door. "You men stop!" he shouted. "Nobody goes in the courthouse."

For a moment it appeared they were going to overrun him. Homer said, "We may have to go help him, Frank."

"We'll hold our places," Frank said firmly. "He's paid for the job he does."

The sheriff held his pistol at arm's length, pointed at no one but ready for instant use. "Nobody goes through this door unless I carry him in there dead!"

The men milled, the crowd growing quickly. Behind them Frank saw George Valentine talking, motioning excitedly. Some of the men in the group began looking back in the direction of the clerk's window, and the Claymore cowhands.

Frank said, "Boys, I believe you're fixin' to need Homer's firewood."

A roar went up from the knot of men, and the rush began with a swiftness that took Frank's breath. They came running shoulder to shoulder in a flying wedge that struck the line of cowboys and momentarily knocked them reeling. The line stiffened, and the lengths of firewood began to swing. Men stumbled backward in a daze. Frank saw one of Homer's sons go down, and he stepped in with his cane, hooking its curved end around the attacker's throat. While Frank had the man choking for breath, Homer's boy came up with his fist. Frank quickly recovered his cane. He saw somebody shove Homer, who stumbled and fell heavily. "Homer," Frank shouted, "you get out of there. You're too old for this foolishness."

Homer sat up and struggled for the breath that had been knocked out of him. He did not otherwise seem hurt. Frank could not remember that he had ever seen anything hurt Homer much; he had been charmed all his life.

Men shouted and cursed, swinging fists and clubs and chunks of firewood. The cowboy line surged forward, fell back, then moved forward again. After a few minutes it was clear they would hold the field. Homer's sons and the young farmers they had befriended stood back to back, defending each other from those attackers who still had the strength for one more rush. Several men were down on bellies or backs, others on hands and knees. When one appeared about to rise and fight again, Frank would strike him smartly with his cane.

George Valentine stood on the outer fringes of the fight, shouting encouragement to the attackers. "Don't quit now!" he was yelling. "Don't let them steal your land and sell it to a rich man!"

Rusty Farraday had entered the fight very early, had taken a rap with a piece of wood and had retired to the fringes with his hands against his head. The spirit was still there, as in the old days, but the flesh had gone to fat and whiskey.

The fight did not end with any decisive retreat. It died a slow and lingering death, two men fighting here, two there, the rest drawing back in exhaustion and watching almost dispassionately, many through eyes blued and swelling. Faces bled. Clothes were torn and ribboned, shirts hanging by little more than the sleeves. Frank did not remember that he had seen so much blood since the battle on Dove Creek. The difference was that here no shot had been fired. No one was dead, though a few probably wished they were.

George Valentine stood alone, shoulders slumped, eyes lost somewhere between rage and defeat.

Frank heard a clatter as the clerk opened the office window and propped it with a long stick. "Who's first?" the official asked, trying not to show his anxiety.

"I am," Frank said sternly, walking to the head of the line, a well-used cane easing his way. He pushed his application papers through the window, filled out with a request to buy the two sections upon which stood the medicine hill.

The wheels of bureaucracy turned slowly, and a goodly part of the morning was gone before the final cowboy reached the window, applying for a parcel he would later sell to Frank Claymore and partners at a profit that would repay him well for bruises and contusions suffered today. The young farmers who had fought beside the Whitcombs finally had their turn at the window. Reluctantly, but acknowledging his debts, Frank advised them on the parcels to ask for, good lands that would not interfere with the contiguity of the blocks he and the cowboys had put together. James Whitcomb was already talking to them about the possibility of buying any hay they might raise.

When it was all done, George Valentine remained in the courthouse yard, dejectedly watching. Frank was surprised that he felt no triumph over George. Viewed in even the best light, Frank had lost a sizable part of the valley. He started to walk away, but he felt the sting of George's gaze. He moved toward him, expecting George to turn his back.

George stayed. He said, "I thought I had you this time, Frank. I should've known better. In the end, you've always won."

"No, George. My boys whipped yours, but I'm losin' a lot more of my valley. Even that day when me and you fought at Davis, you already had Rachal before the first blow was struck. *You've* always won, George."

George's eyes seemed less severe. "Maybe we've both lost. We ain't either of us had things the way we wanted. With me, Frank Claymore always stood in the way."

"And with me, there was George Valentine. We could've had a lot if we'd stood together instead of squarin' off." Regretfully Frank said, "Now I reckon it's forty years too late." He looked behind him at the cowboys, many of them battered and bloody, lucky to be on their feet. "Time was when we fought our own battles instead of settin' somebody else out there to fight them for us. Forty years too late for that too, I suppose. If we hadn't both wanted the same woman . . ."

George frowned. "How long's it been since you seen Rachal?"

Frank's eyes narrowed. Surely George wasn't still jealous. "Not since Billy was a baby in her arms, and that's the truth."

"Maybe it's time you seen her, Frank. Maybe it's time we put this fight behind us and accept ourselves for a pair of worn-out old mossyhorns."

Frank's pulse quickened. To see Rachal, even after all this time . . . Despite the closeness he had finally achieved with Letty, the thought of Rachal still stirred warmth from old embers that had never completely gone cold.

Rusty Farraday limped up behind George, his head bandaged. He looked incredulous as George said, "Come over to the house tonight, Frank. I think it's time we put an end to this."

Frank was as incredulous as Farraday. To end the feud after all these years . . . it seemed an impossible wish. But George looked weary of it, and Frank knew he was. "Tell Rachal I'll be there."

He quickly saw that not everyone in town was willing to accept the morning's events as gracefully as George. Hostility crackled like electricity in a spring thunderstorm. The sheriff came to the lot where Frank's wagons stood and expressed relief when he saw the cooks breaking camp.

"The boys're leavin' town," Frank told him. "They finished what they come to do."

"I'm glad. There's a war fever here. Somebody could get killed if they stayed around."

"Rest easy, Ed. There won't be no more trouble."

Homer was pleased when Frank told him George was ready to patch things up. But he frowned over Frank's eagerness to see Rachal. Homer said, "You're expectin' her to be like she was forty years ago. She ain't, Frank."

"I reckon I've got a few extra lines in my face, and my hair's gone gray, but otherwise *I* ain't changed."

"Letty'll be concerned if you don't come home. Might be better if you wait. Let's bring in Letty and Naomi to go with you when you see Rachal and George. Women are natural peacemakers."

"This goes way back before Letty's time. It ain't her place to have to patch it up."

Homer persisted. "There's a lot of people in town ain't feelin' kindly toward you. Some of us ought to stay close."

"You go on home," Frank said firmly. "Ain't a man in this town has got the nerve to raise a hand against me."

Frank had never spent a night in George's town until he brought in the chuck wagons. He took a room in the hotel so he could rest awhile, bathe and shave. He didn't want Rachal to see him looking as if he had slept in his clothes, which, of course, he had.

It was only as an afterthought that he shoved a pistol into the high top of his right boot. He had tried to put aside

Homer's warning about local hostility; Homer had always had an active imagination. But Frank realized that as an old man moving slowly on a cane, he might be a tempting target for some damned fool. One look into the muzzle of Frank's six-shooter would be an educational experience for any such idiot. Samuel Colt had equalized big man and small, young man and old.

He took supper alone in the hotel's dining room. Other patrons seated themselves as far away as possible and showed him their backs. The hell with them, he thought, and went on with his supper. The pistol was uncomfortable in his boot, but the knowledge that he had it was reassuring.

He limped out onto the gallery and paused in the yellow light of lanterns hanging from the eaves on either side of the front steps. His mouth dropped open as he saw Homer Whitcomb and his oldest son James sitting together on a bench. "I thought you-all went home," he said.

Homer grunted. "Our horses was tired."

Frank flared, realizing they had little confidence in his ability to defend himself. The moment passed. "You ought to've come in and eat with me, long's you were here anyway."

Homer said, "We et down at old Dutch-oven's. He don't frown on cowpunchers like them hotel people do." He stood up. "We'll walk with you. I need a little air after old Dutch-oven's steak and biscuits."

If Homer had asked, Frank would have turned him down. That, he reasoned, was why Homer did not ask. James, who had grown into a taller, sturdier man than his father, walked in silence at Frank's side. He had developed into a fine cowman but not a talker. Homer had never given him the opportunity. The people they met on the street said nothing, but many gave Frank a sullen stare. He did not tell Homer so, but he was glad the Whitcombs had stayed.

In a few minutes they reached the block on which the Valentine house stood, still the tallest structure in town other than the courthouse. Frank was surprised to find it dark. He could not see a lamp burning anywhere.

"I'm obliged for the escort," he said, "but from here on I go by myself."

James said, "I think we ought to stay with you."

Sternly Frank replied, "This is for me and George to work out, and Rachal. I want you-all to go back now."

Reluctantly Homer said, "We'll be down at the wagon yard if you want us. We taken a cot apiece."

Frank moved on, his heartbeat quickening. It bothered him that he saw no lights in the house, until he recognized the red glow of a cigar. He decided they were waiting for him on the porch. He could make out the dim form of a man behind the glow and knew it would be George. Rachal must be sitting there too, but Frank could not see her in the darkness. His breath came short, and he worried a little that he would not know what to say to her after such a long time.

"George?" he said quietly. "Rachal?"

George's voice answered, and Frank could see the dark form rise from a chair. "I'm here, Frank. I waited for you on the porch because there's been a change."

"A change? What change? Where's Rachal?" The beginnings of alarm brought his heart up high in his chest. For the first time the thought struck him that this might be an ambush. That Farraday! Where was that damned Farraday?

George said, "I meant for us to talk, Frank. Truly I did. But we'll have to put it off awhile."

"Where's Rachal?" Frank demanded. "I come here to talk to Rachal!"

"Tonight ain't the time, Frank. I'm sorry I misled you. Good night." George moved to the door and started into the darkness of the hall.

Frank followed, cane thumping solidly on the wooden steps. "You come back here, George. I ain't done talkin' to you!"

He was on the top step when he saw the flash and heard

the shot explode from the hallway, so loud that his eardrums were pierced by pain. Old instincts instantly came alive. He reached down into his boot and brought up the pistol with both hands. He aimed at the form in the hallway and squeezed the trigger. The flashes were blinding, and violent recoil threatened to hurl the pistol back over his shoulder.

Through the roaring that echoed in his ears he heard George's cry, and a woman's scream. He saw the dark form of George Valentine slump against the wall, then slide to the floor.

"George!" Frank shouted in dismay. "What did you do this for? George?"

He dropped the pistol and hobbled into the hallway. George lay on the floor. Frank put a hand on him, feeling for life, and knew George was beyond real pain. Frank's eyes burned, not entirely from the sulfurous smoke that filled the hallway.

"George!" he cried. "I didn't come here to do this. George!"

He wept over the body, but George would never hear him.

Boots pounded on the porch steps, and men rushed into the hall. Somebody struck a match, and somebody cursed. "It's Frank Claymore. He's murdered George Valentine!"

Frank had difficulty finding his voice. "I didn't murder him," he declared brokenly. "He shot at me first."

Someone lighted a lamp. Frank looked around quickly. "Rachal!" he cried. "Rachal, where are you?"

The sheriff was there in a minute. So were Homer and James. Frank pleaded, "I didn't want to kill him. I come here in friendship. But he taken a shot at me."

The sheriff searched George's body, alarm building in his eyes. He asked the growing crowd, "Did anybody pick up a gun?"

No one had, except the pistol Frank had dropped. At least no one admitted it. Frank saw Rusty Farraday standing there, looking bewildered. Instantly he was convinced: Farraday had George's pistol.

The sheriff asked grimly, "How could he shoot at you, Mr. Claymore, if he didn't have a gun?"

"He had a gun. Somebody picked it up. Search Rusty Farraday."

He saw disbelief in the eyes around him, even the sheriff's. From up the stairway, beyond the narrow reach of the lamplight, came the hysterical wailing of a woman.

Rachal, he thought before he lapsed into despair. *Rachal, what have we done to you?*

12

The clock struck in the courthouse cupola, drawing Claymore's attention from the Indians' departing wagon. He stood with Homer and the sheriff and the deputy Willis, waiting until most of the crowd had gone. He knew he would still have to face some of them in the hotel lobby. The town's animosity gnawed at him like a thorn festering beneath his skin.

Homer walked beside him across the street and up the broad steps to the hotel gallery. Willis followed, one pace behind. Frank was tempted to kick at him, as he had seen a horse kick at a dog venturing too near its heels. He knew he would probably fall. The last thing he needed was to stir that old arrowhead to anger, or fracture his bad hip.

It jarred him to see Tobe standing on the gallery, badly out of place. For a moment Claymore was disoriented. "What're you doin' here, Tobe?"

"I brung Mrs. Claymore," the old black man said. He held the screen door open to Frank.

A chubby woman moved past him, her arms outstretched for Homer. Homer declared happily, "Mother, I'm glad you got here."

Letty Claymore pushed herself up from a heavy horsehair chair. She took a step toward Frank, arms upraised. Frank felt a glad warmth and wanted to tell Letty he was happy to see her, but such words had never come easily. He put his arm around her and let that say it all.

Letty told him, "I held out as long as I could." She looked into his face with worried eyes. "It's not going well, is it?"

"I ain't had a friend in that courtroom except Homer."

Letty seems tired, he thought. *And why not? Living with an ungrateful old reprobate like me for thirty years would've killed any other woman.* An unpleasant afterthought came. *Maybe she'll be better off without me. Maybe Rachal is better off without George. Maybe both of us old warriors outlived our day.*

Letty said, "There'll be friendlier faces in the courtroom tomorrow. Naomi and I have been working on that." She turned Frank half around to see a thin, tall figure, one sleeve of his coat neatly folded and pinned near the shoulder. The hair was white and the face etched like a plowed field, but the eyes were as piercing as when Frank had first seen them forty years ago.

He declared, "Alex McKellar!"

The old Ranger's face was grim, but his grip was so strong that Frank's arthritis sent a sharp pain up his arm. "Frank Claymore," McKellar said, "I always seem to meet you under the worst of circumstances."

"That's the kind I always seem to get into," Frank replied.

McKellar's eyes probed like the arrow point that occasionally still stirred in Frank's stomach. "Did you kill George Valentine, as they charge?"

"Not as they charge. In spite of what they claim, he shot at me first."

McKellar nodded in satisfaction. "You have never lied to me, Frank. I'll tell them that, when I am on the stand."

The prosecuting attorney and Frank's defense attorney entered the lobby together, a companionship that did not improve Frank's gloomy disposition. Elihu Mallard challenged McKellar as if he were some intruder. "And may I ask who you are, sir, that you are such an expert on the behavior of Frank Claymore?"

McKellar drew himself up to his full six feet three or four, his eyes suddenly fierce. Frost clung to every word.

"Sir, I am Captain Alexander McKellar."

Recognition of the name left the prosecutor stammering. Anderson Avery strode forward, hand outstretched. McKellar drew back in suspicion until Avery introduced himself. Avery declared, "Mrs. Claymore told me she would persuade you to appear as a character witness, but I feared it would not come to pass. I am gratified, sir."

Frank studied Letty with wonder. He was unaware that she had even met Anderson, much less discussed the conduct of the case with him. He knew he should not be surprised. She was acquainted with every politician and jackleg lawyer from Dallas and Austin west.

McKellar seemed only to tolerate Anderson, nothing more. Frank considered that a mark of good judgment; he had reluctantly decided Anderson's only real interest in this case was his fee, much of it already paid in advance. McKellar sighed in relief when the two attorneys were gone. Hat in his hand, he bowed slightly. "If you will pardon me, Letitia, and Mrs. Whitcomb, I shall go and rest awhile before supper. The trip has been a long one."

Letty kissed the old Ranger on his dried-leather cheek. "You'll never know how grateful I am that you came."

"I could do no less for the daughter of Thomas Zachary." He glanced at Frank. "Or the man who saved his life."

McKellar climbed the stairs slowly and carefully, but pride would not permit his using a cane, Frank thought. He would look the Ranger until the day he died.

Homer had his arm around Naomi's thick waist. "They serve a pretty good supper in yonder," he said, nodding toward the dining room. "You'll eat till you bust your buttons."

Mother Whitcomb shook her head. "They've got a man in charge. It won't be any better than Dutch-oven Devers's."

The dining room atmosphere was far more pleasant than it had been during earlier meals. Old friends, some Frank had not seen in years, kept walking up to his table to shake his hand. One would thank Letty for asking him to come. The next would thank Naomi. The women offered no explanation. When Frank looked at Homer, Homer said only, "The girls've been busy."

Frank had never been one to let sunrise catch him in bed, but he was awakened earlier than usual by noises in the hotel, people arising in other rooms, slamming doors, stamping down the stairs. He could tell by challenging voices that the dining room had not opened as early as somebody thought it should. Grunting, daring his arthritis, he rose stiffly and began to dress in the dark. In the other bed Letty looked at an alarm clock and told him it was too early.

"Sounds to me like I'm the last one up," he said. "I'll go down and see if they've learned to make decent coffee yet."

He found Alex McKellar in the dining room. Mark Akins was there with two of his brothers and several of their sons, whose faces all seemed to bear the strong stamp of their old granddaddy, Bige Akins. If they had his character as well, Frank thought, there was hope for Texas yet.

He found men who had worked for him ten and twenty years ago, men to whom he had sold their first cattle on credit, men to whom he had lent money to pay down on land. Handshaking let his breakfast go cold, and he left most of it uneaten. Many of the old acquaintances left the hotel, heading for the courthouse early to assure themselves of seats. Anderson Avery came down, looking pleased. The judge arrived, taking his customary seat in a far corner, in splendid judicial isolation. He had finished his breakfast and was about to leave the room when the prosecuting attorney showed up. The judge tugged at a heavy gold chain that crossed his broad vest and peered critically at his watch. He warned the prosecutor, "I hope you are not particularly hungry, Counselor. Court convenes in ten minutes."

The deputy Willis had sat near the door, nervously tapping his foot as he watched Frank. The judge's words were what he had waited for. He came to Frank's table and said with grand authority, "You'd better get a-movin'. You heard the judge."

Frank's face heated. Damned pup shouldn't try to shame him in front of the womenfolks. While he was trying to think of an appropriate answer, Naomi blistered the deputy with a look. She said, "Willis, when you were a little boy, I thought you were the snottiest-nosed brat I'd ever met. It's a comfort to know that time doesn't change *everything*."

Reddening, Willis said he would wait outside. Frank pushed to his feet and took Naomi's hand. "Mrs. Whitcomb, I'm goin' to tell you somethin' I never told you before; I was always afraid it would go to your head. The day Homer found you was one of the best days of my life."

Caught off guard, she tried to keep from smiling but could not. "Letty, I've known Frank Claymore for close to forty years, and this is the first compliment he ever paid me."

Frank said, "I ain't goin' to make it a habit. Come on, Homer. Willis is liable to throw a shoe."

The courthouse hallway was crowded with frustrated townspeople, milling in angry confusion, protesting to Sheriff Ed Phelps that they were unable to find seats in the courtroom. Phelps kept his impatience under admirable restraint and explained that seating was on a first-come, first-served basis. Those who had come too late had just as well go home. He spied Frank and Homer, the women just behind them. "Make room for the defendant," he ordered. "Clear the way there!"

Fixin' to lose himself the next election, Frank thought.

Homer took the lead. Willis brought up the rear, staying back a little from Naomi. Frank expected the usual courtroom animosity and tried not to look at the people. But when they began speaking to him he realized the room was packed with his friends. Even most of the cowboys from the ranch were there. Forgetting for a moment his predicament, he demanded of Homer what the men were doing in town instead of being out on the ranch where they belonged, doing honest work for their wages. The moment passed, and he took comfort in their support.

The jury filed into its box. Some of its members nervously studied the crowd.

Prosecutor Mallard was unfamiliar with local faces, but he seemed to sense that these were different. He conferred quickly with the sheriff and frowned as his fears were confirmed.

A hush fell over the courtroom when the towering figure of Alex McKellar entered. The people turned to stare at this man whose name was known all over Texas. Even Judge Whitmore Holmes stepped down from the bench to shake his hand while the prosecutor watched uneasily. "It is indeed an honor, sir, to have such a respected gentleman be a guest in my courtroom," the judge said.

McKellar responded with dignity, "I am not simply a guest, Your Honor. I have come to testify to the good character of my old friend Frank Claymore."

The judge blinked in surprise and cleared his throat. "Of course, sir, of course. Your presence here honors us all. And should you for any reason feel the need to use my chambers, please know that they are open to you without your having to ask."

Court was called to order. Rusty Farraday hobbled to the witness chair. The judge said, "Mr. Farraday, you were sworn yesterday, so you may consider yourself still sworn." Seating himself, Farraday eyed the crowd suspiciously, discomfited by the absence of his friends.

"Now, Mr. Farraday," the prosecutor said, "you have described to us the sequence of events on the day of the land filing here. As I recall your testimony, you were somewhat injured during the unpleasantness."

A ripple of laughter ran through the Claymore cowboys. The judge rapped for silence.

"Well, sir," Farraday replied, "I got hit up beside the head with a chunk of firewood about this long." He held his hands two feet apart. "Right yonder sits the man who done it." He pointed into the audience, at one of Claymore's men. "I was studyin' on filin' charges, but it didn't seem important after Frank Claymore murdered George Valentine."

Anderson Avery objected, and the judge warned the witness not to voice personal opinions. "Well, I was studyin' on it," Farraday countered.

Elihu Mallard paced the floor, taking a sidelong look at the crowd. Yesterday Farraday's declaration would have brought a strong voicing of approval from the audience. Today it had been met with coldness. "Now, Mr. Farraday, I am sure everyone in the jury knows what happened insofar as the rush for filing is concerned, but I would like you to tell it in your own words, for the record. What happened after you were struck and put out of the struggle?"

"Well, sir, Claymore's bunch stole the head of the line, and they kept it."

Avery objected to the word *stole*. The judge said, "You are expressing your personal opinion again, Mr. Farraday. I must caution you about that."

"Stole—taken—whatever you want to call it, they got off with most of the good land. You watch, that Frank Claymore'll have all of it unless we stick him for what he done to George."

Avery stood up quickly to make a lengthy speech, and the judge also delivered one, but the points were lost on Farraday. He shrugged. "Mr. Mallard just asked me to tell you what happened, and I told you."

The prosecutor said, "It was after the Claymore men had finished filing that you saw George Valentine and Frank Claymore approach each other, was it not?" Farraday nodded. Mallard continued, "Now, will you please tell the court what transpired at that point?"

"Well, sir, George said he was gettin' too old and too tired to keep fightin' anymore. He thought it was about time him and Claymore smoked the peace pipe. Claymore said the notion suited him all right. George told him, he said, 'Come to the house tonight and we'll talk it over.' Claymore said he would." Farraday's voice went bitter. "Everybody knows the rest of it. He went over that night with a gun. He shot and killed George Valentine like me or you would kill a dog."

Avery started to object but turned up his hands and sat down again. Frank leaned in to him and demanded, "I know that even you don't believe me, but you've got to ask him about that gun. I'd swear at the pearly gates that it was Rusty Farraday picked up George's gun and made off with it."

Avery nodded but motioned Frank for silence. Frank slumped, his little bit of breakfast gone sour.

The prosecutor said, "Now, Mr. Farraday, when was the next time you saw Mr. Valentine and Mr. Claymore together?"

"It was after I heard the shootin'. I was in my room out back of the store. I went a-runnin' to see, and there was George layin' on the floor, takin' his last breath, and Frank Claymore leanin' over him."

"As you know, the defendant has stoutly maintained that George Valentine fired upon him. Did you see a gun anywhere that night?"

"Just Claymore's, where he'd dropped it. I started to pick it up, but the barrel was hot. Somebody else got it."

"You are absolutely sure you did not find a gun of any kind on or about the person of George Valentine?"

"No, sir, not a sign of one. Frank Claymore just flat lied about that." His face was flushed, and he had the look of a man who had drunk his way through a hard night, building his courage for this day. Nevertheless, he managed to look Frank Claymore in the eyes. "I told George I thought it was a bad idea. I told him I didn't trust Frank Claymore. But George said he was tired of the fightin' and wanted to see an end to it."

The prosecutor said, "I believe the state has finished its questioning of this witness, Your Honor."

Farraday looked immensely relieved and started to step down. The judge struck his gavel sharply. "Not yet, Mr. Farraday. Counselor Avery may have some questions of you."

Avery rose and approached Farraday, carrying a handful of notes he had penciled. "Thank you, Your Honor. It happens that I do." He paced a moment, passing in front of the fidgeting Farraday twice before whirling the third time and pinning him with his eyes. "You said Mr. Valentine told you he had wearied of the fighting and wished to end it. Did he happen to tell you how he planned to end it?"

Farraday began flexing his fingers, his face turning redder under the pressure. "I reckon he just figured on shakin' hands."

"You reckon! He didn't tell you?"

"No, sir. I'm just a hired man."

"Then how do you know he did not intend to end it by shooting Frank Claymore when he showed up at the house?"

The prosecuting attorney objected, and the judge agreed. Avery altered the question slightly. "Did you hear him say he intended to shake hands and call for peace?"

Farraday looked to Mallard for guidance. "No, sir, he didn't. I just figured . . ."

"So, for all you know, he may very well have intended to lure Frank Claymore there and kill him."

"How, when he didn't have no gun?"

"In the confusion, could not someone have picked up the gun? Someone who felt a hostility toward Frank Claymore and wanted to see him prosecuted?"

"No, sir, there wouldn't nobody've done that."

"You have told this court of your own long antagonism toward the defendant. Might you not have picked up the gun that night and hidden it away?"

A murmur of speculation ran through the partisan crowd. The prosecutor protested, "Counselor has no evidence . . ."

The judge waved Mallard to silence.

Avery pressed. "What if I told you, Mr. Farraday, that

someone *saw* you pick up the gun and secrete it on your person, so that you might later dispose of it in privacy?"

Farraday's face went scarlet. "I'd say somebody was a goddamned liar! I never picked up no gun. Even if I had, it was so dark in there that nobody could've seen me do it."

Avery paused a moment. "Dark, was it?"

"Till they lit a lamp, it was like the inside of a vault."

"Therefore, Mr. Farraday, if someone else picked up that gun, you could not very well have seen him, could you?"

Farraday swallowed, knowing he had been boxed. "It didn't happen. I know it didn't happen."

"When the room was finally lighted, Mr. Farraday, how many men would you say were there besides yourself, the victim and the defendant?"

Farraday considered. "I don't know. Seven or eight."

"Were any of them friends of the defendant?"

Farraday looked at Homer. "Homer Whitcomb and one of his boys."

"The rest were not friends, then. Were any of them enemies of the defendant?"

Farraday flexed his fingers again, pulling at them as he might milk a cow. "Well, some sure didn't feel none too kindly, not after gettin' whipped out of the line that day."

"Would you not say, then, that some of those men had more than adequate motive for wishing to hide George Valentine's gun and place Mr. Claymore in the position in which we find him today?"

Prosecutor Mallard contended bitterly that this was an effort to force the witness into a supposition, an offense to which learned counsel himself had objected only a short time before.

"Well taken," Anderson said, "and I retract the question. Would you say then, Mr. Farraday, that these men did not have sufficient motive for wishing to see Mr. Claymore in jeopardy?"

The judge pointed his gavel at Anderson. "Counselor, I hope you do not believe you are fooling this court. You are attempting to bait this witness into a statement against his will. It is not his place to be making suppositions here. Please confine your questions to facts."

Avery glanced at the jury. Some of its members were whispering to each other. Frank could not decide if that was a good sign or bad.

Avery turned back to Farraday, staring at him until the man dropped his gaze to the floor. "Mr. Farraday, you testified that you distrusted the defendant and feared for the safety of Mr. Valentine. Is that not correct?"

Farraday nodded. "That's the way I felt."

"In view of your anxiety, then, is it not strange that you did not remain close by to help protect your old friend against this man of whose motives you were so fearful? Is it not strange that you remained in your room and left him to his fate?"

Farraday, perspiring heavily, began to tug at his collar. "It was because of that woman."

Avery's jaw dropped. He was clearly surprised. "What woman?"

"Her—Rachal—George's wife. I never liked to be within a mile of her when she was throwin' one of her conniption fits. And she sure throwed one that day."

Frank tensed as Avery threw a quizzical glance at him. Avery turned quickly back to Farraday. "You mean you feared a woman's tantrum more than you feared what Frank Claymore might do?"

Farraday declared defensively, "You-all never knowed her. She always stayed in the house and never had no truck with the people of this town. But *I* know her, and George knowed her. When she taken one of her screamin' fits, there wasn't nobody wanted to stay around her. Not even her young'uns. She's crazy, that Rachal."

Frank pushed angrily to his feet. "Farraday, you've got no call to say such a thing about that poor woman. She's suffered enough."

Avery motioned urgently for Frank to sit down. He turned

back to Farraday. "You say she was given to tantrums. What kind of tantrums?"

"Screamin' ones. Words I never heard come from no other woman—no *decent* woman, I mean. She'd carry on how the whole world was whisperin' evil about her. Times, when I hadn't said a word, she'd cuss me for things she imagined I'd told somebody. She'd call me a no-account whiskey peddler and say I had no right to judge her for one mistake. When I'd tell her I didn't judge her, she'd get worse. Throw things, sometimes.

"It was Billy Valentine done it to her. She taken it in her head that everybody still gossiped about Billy. They knowed he wasn't George's son, even though George give his name to him and done the best he could to raise that boy as good as he raised his own." Farraday's eyes fastened on Claymore, accusing him. "Billy was your son, Claymore, but you never give George no credit for raisin' him. You never knowed how much he loved that boy, how many times he stood up for him and stopped Rachal from takin' the whip to him—you never knowed how George grieved when Billy died . . ."

Frank's stomach drew into a knot. He did not want to believe. He asked huskily, "Rachal—she whipped Billy?"

"When George wasn't lookin' . . . every time she got the chance. That's why George kept Billy with him so much. Only mother I ever seen that hated her own child. Said he was the devil's son, not hers. Said he had brought nothin' but shame on her since before he was even born. When Alex McKellar yonder brought him home to bury, you'd've thought she'd shed a tear for him. All she done was look at him and say, 'Well, the devil has finally got him back.' She went upstairs and didn't even come down for the funeral. It was George done the buryin', and the cryin'. He done it for the both of them."

Frank trembled, wanting to reject but somehow realizing it must be true. He remembered the whip scars on Billy's back, the scars he had blamed on George.

He remembered so many things he had blamed on George . . . He sat paralyzed, his stomach cold.

Prosecutor Mallard had stood in shocked silence. Now he objected. "Your Honor, I have listened to all this testimony, and I must confess that I have tried in vain to see how it is germane to the case at hand. We are not trying Rachal Valentine for her temper, or for being a poor mother. We are trying Frank Claymore for the murder of the founder of this community, a good man and true."

Frank did not look up, but he was conscious of Letty conferring earnestly with Anderson Avery. He was aware when she and Naomi left the courtroom with Sheriff Ed Phelps. Homer put a hand on Frank's shoulder, intending to comfort. But there was no comfort for Frank.

My God, George, he cried silently. *What did I do?*

Avery said, "Your Honor, I believe I will satisfy you in due course that all this is germane."

The judge frowned, making no reply, and Avery did not wait. "Mr. Farraday, you said Mrs. Valentine threw one of her tantrums the day of the shooting. Can you tell us what brought this display about?"

Farraday grimaced. "It was when George went home and told her Frank Claymore and his men had won the land race. She went to ravin' and beatin' on George with her fists and callin' him a damned fool. She throwed a vase at him and cussed Frank Claymore for bein' the man who put the shame on her. She swore she'd rather see Claymore dead than have him set foot in her house." Farraday's eyes went to Frank. "You always thought George Valentine hated you, Claymore, and I reckon he did, in his way. But Rachal Valentine hated you a whole lot worse."

Frank closed his eyes, but he could not turn away Farraday's words. He tried to shut out the buzz of speculative conversation in the courtroom but could not. Avery whispered in his ear, "I must confess, Mr. Claymore, I never believed you about that second gun. Now suddenly I find myself wondering. Could it be that it was not Farraday who hid it, but Rachal Valentine?"

Sternly Frank shook his head. "Rachal wouldn't've done that to me. She *wouldn't!*"

"She was there. You told me you heard her scream."

"I never seen her. I tell you, Rachal would never do such a thing to me."

Judge Holmes asked, "Does the defense have any further questions for this witness?"

Avery replied, "No, Your Honor, not at this time."

Holmes tapped the gavel lightly to quiet the crowd. "Mr. Farraday, you may step down, but do not go away. Does the prosecution have any more witnesses?"

Mallard replied, "No, Your Honor. The prosecution rests."

Avery walked up to the bench and spoke quietly to the judge. Holmes nodded after a moment, then declared, "This court will take a short recess."

Frank turned to Homer, fighting down the anguish that threatened to engulf him. "Could I have been wrong about George all these years, and Rachal?"

Homer looked away. "I've told you a hundred times, Frank. You know all there is about cattle and horses, but you don't know a damned thing about people."

Frank turned to search for Letty. Homer said, "Her and Naomi and the sheriff went up to the Valentine house to talk to Rachal."

"There ain't no reason . . ." He stopped.

Homer said, "There's a lot Letty don't know about cattle and horses, but there ain't much she don't know about people."

Frank slumped with his head in his hands. Memory carried him back to a long-ago time when three hopeful young men had driven a cattle herd west from the Colorado River to the Clear Fork, three strong young men shoulder to shoulder, challenging the world.

My God, George. What did we do to one another?

Very few people left their seats, afraid they might not get them back. Frank became conscious of movement and opened his eyes. Judge Holmes came out of his chambers and mounted the bench. He pounded the gavel and called the court to order. He waited until the crowd quieted. "Counselor, is the defense ready with its first witness?"

Avery said, "We are, Your Honor. The defense calls Mrs. Rachal Valentine."

Frank turned cautiously, the arthritis paining him. At the back of the room, Letty and Naomi stood beside the door. Sheriff Phelps moved slowly up the aisle, giving the support of his arm to a thin woman dressed in black. Her face was hidden by a veil. Frank's heartbeat quickened as he watched the halting steps that brought her nearer and nearer to the place where he sat. He looked in vain for something about her that he could recognize. He pushed shakily to his feet as she came up even with his chair.

"Rachal? Is that really you?"

She stopped and faced him. Slowly she raised the veil.

Frank felt as if he had been kicked in the stomach. The face he saw was not the face of Rachal—not the Rachal he remembered. This was an old woman, her face lined with the bitterness and burdens of the years. The only feature he thought he might have recognized was her eyes, and those only a moment, for they hardened as she stared at him. Her mouth curved downward at the corners, and she tilted her head back in hostility.

"Rachal?" he said again, almost pleading.

She turned away without answering. The sheriff held to her arm until she stepped up onto the low platform and seated herself in the witness chair. He stood then beside her, his face grim.

The bailiff hesitantly administered the oath, trying not to advertise his curiosity by staring into her face. He was seeing her for the first time though she had lived in this town for years. Her reply was so quiet Frank could not hear it.

He looked at her, his heart beating so rapidly he was half afraid it might fail him and let him die right here in the courtroom. His mind raced with memories of the girl at old Fort Davis, with the images he had carried so long. In none could he find the bitter old woman who sat there giving him a stare that could kill.

Avery began his questioning casually, establishing that she was indeed Rachal Valentine, widow of the late George Valentine. He asked her to think back upon the events of the fatal day. Frank half expected to see her weep, but she did not. She answered in clipped tones and did not take her eyes from Frank.

Avery said, "Mr. Farraday has testified that you opposed your husband's invitation to Frank Claymore that he come to your house and discuss an armistice to their old feud. Would you tell us why?"

Her voice hardened. "Because Frank Claymore has always fouled whatever he touched. Because he put a shame on me years ago that I never could cleanse. Because Frank Claymore is an agent of the devil."

"And you were opposed to an entreaty for peace?"

"George Valentine was a weak man. He'd talked about peace before, but I always set him right. I told him we'd never rest till we ruined Frank Claymore for once and for all, till Frank Claymore was a broken man cryin' for mercy. A piece at a time, we taken his precious valley away from him, but I had to keep drivin' George, or he'd've let up. I begged him to send for more help the day of the filin'. He stumbled around instead and let Frank beat him. Then he invited Frank to my house—*my* house—to talk about peace.

"I told him *I* would never have peace till I saw Frank Claymore broken and dead. And now I will, because he's done murder and been caught at it." Her eyes seemed afire. "At last, Frank Claymore, I'll see you die, like I died forty years ago!"

The courtroom was in a total hush.

Avery said, "Mrs. Valentine, did you not convince your

husband then that the only course was to shoot Frank Claymore? And when he tried and failed, and Frank Claymore shot him in self-defense, did you not pick up the gun your husband had used and hide it away?"

Rachal trembled, but not from weakness or fear. Hers was like the trembling of a spring under tension. She declared, "My husband did not fire at Frank Claymore."

"My client swears that he did. My client says he fired back to save his own life. You know your husband did indeed shoot at him, don't you? *You* are the one who grabbed up his pistol and took it away!"

"No!" Rachal almost screamed. "George didn't have the guts to shoot at him. *I* did."

Avery stiffened.

Frank caught a breath and held it, his face afire.

Avery managed, *"You* did? You shot at Frank Claymore?"

"I had to. George wouldn't. I told George I'd see Frank dead before I'd have him in my house. George sat out on the porch and waited for him, to tell him their talk had to wait. But Frank wasn't satisfied with that, no sir. When George came back into the house, Frank started after him. Frank Claymore in my house. I was standin' there in the hall, ready for him. I shot at him and missed. He thought George had done it, and he shot George.

"So you see, George was unarmed, and Frank Claymore shot him down. That's murder, isn't it?" Met by silence, she turned desperately upon the judge. "You're goin' to hang him for it, aren't you?"

The judge could only stare at her. She turned to the jury and pointed at Frank. "There's the man who's stood in your way all these years. All you've got to do is say the word, and they'll take him out and hang him, like he ought to've been hung forty years ago." Most of the jurors looked away from her burning gaze. She shifted her attention desperately to the special prosecutor. "It's up to you to make them hang him. That's what you're paid for, isn't it? *Isn't it?"*

Tears ran down her cheeks as she stood up, purse in her

hand, and looked at Frank. "Damn you, Frank Claymore, you're not goin' to win this one too. I swore to God I'd see that you never win again."

She reached into the purse and brought forth a pistol. Dropping the purse, she raised the weapon in both hands and leveled it on Frank.

The crowd gasped. People began rushing and shoving to be out of the line of fire.

Frank could only stare wide-eyed into the muzzle. He felt as if he were frozen in place. He made no effort to evade.

Ed Phelps moved quickly as Rachal cocked the hammer. He shoved his hand over the weapon and pushed downward. She jerked the trigger, but the pistol did not fire. Phelps wrested it from her fingers and pointed it at the floor. Blood ran from the fleshy part of his hand between thumb and forefinger, which had taken the hammer's bite.

"Damn you, Frank Claymore," Rachal seethed. "God damn you to hell!"

He already did, Frank wanted to tell her. *He done it forty years ago.* The misery lay heavily upon him.

Phelps spoke quietly. The deputy Willis took Rachal's arm and escorted her through the door into the judge's chambers. Prosecutor Mallard trailed after them.

Anderson Avery wiped a handkerchief over his face and turned to Judge Whitmore Holmes, who sagged in his big chair, his face pale. "Your Honor, the defense had a great many character witnesses to call, but under the circumstances I deem that an unnecessary use of the court's time. The defense respectfully requests that charges against Frank Claymore be dismissed."

Ed Phelps took Frank and Letty into his office and discreetly found business elsewhere to occupy him. Frank slumped on a hard chair and stared at the floor. Worriedly he murmured, "They've had Rachal in the judge's chambers a long time. What do you reckon they'll do with her?"

Letty took his hands. "What *could* they do, put her in jail? She's been in a jail of her own making all these years. She seldom left that house. I doubt she'll ever leave it again."

"All those years," Frank said in misery, "I never once had any notion that Rachal hated me." He looked up into Letty's face, then leaned his head heavily against her shoulder. All his life he had been unable to tell anyone he was sorry. He found himself telling Letty now. "I wasted the best years of our lives, wishin' after her . . . years we'll never get back."

Her hands were gentle in their grip. She said, "But we've had some good years, too. And we still have a lot of years left."

His arthritis gave him a twinge. "Damned unlikely." He wished he had somehow learned to say straight out what he felt for Letty. He could not do it, even now.

He did not have to. She leaned to him and gently kissed him. "Just take me home," she said.

The four of them rode in the buggy—Frank and Letty, Homer and Naomi. As if a great weight had been lifted from him, Homer had begun talking when they left the courthouse. He was still talking, and the subject had never changed.

Naomi finally demanded, "Homer Whitcomb, can't you talk about somethin' besides cattle and horses?"

Homer shook his head. "That's all there is."

Frank turned and looked at the long line of cowboys trailing behind them, out of the buggy's dust. James Whitcomb rode in front, his younger brothers just behind him. Frank gave them a long study, and he approved what he saw. It would be their ranch one day, probably sooner than he wanted to acknowledge. It would be their valley. They would know how to bring it back to the beauty he and Homer and Letty and Naomi had seen in it, a long time ago.

Ahead, Medicine Hill stood tall against the afternoon sky, its long shadow reaching far toward the creek that kept life astir in this valley. It drew Frank's gaze, as it always had. Of all the landmarks in the valley, this was the only one unchanged, the only one that looked today just as it had when he and Homer and Beaver Red first pushed their horses across that great breadth of dry prairie and he had climbed to its top to look out upon a land that had remained much the same for perhaps ten thousand years.

He became aware of an old wagon near the rocks, moving out slowly to intercept the buggy. He saw, after a time, that Red Shield's son sat alone on the wagon seat. Josiah drew his team to a stop and waited afoot beside the trail. The buggy halted. Josiah reached up his hand toward Frank.

"Your trouble is over?" he asked.

"It's over," Frank said.

"My father knew it would be so. He told me."

Frank looked toward the rocks. "Did you leave him up there all by himself?"

Josiah nodded, a heavy sadness in his eyes. "He is there, but not by himself. He is with his spirits."

It took a moment for Frank to realize what Josiah meant. Forty years suddenly fell away. Frank gazed at Medicine Hill and saw through the eyes of memory a proud young warrior dogging him all the way to the edge of the creek, each man ready in an instant to kill the other. Grief pinched his throat.

He had been forced to put too much of the past behind him today. It was more than he knew how to handle. He took Letty's hand for strength.

A fresh wind moved along the valley and brought him the sweet scent of new grass, as it had done the day he had spilled his first herd down the eastern rim. From far to the north he heard a distant roll of spring thunder.

A new season was beginning.

"Let's go home," he said.

EYES
OF THE
HAWK

1

No one wants you to tamper with a legend, especially by telling the truth. Over the years I have often been asked what I know of the Texas legend of Stonehill town, and of the man the Mexicans came to call the Hawk, the man who killed that town in vengeance.

I have found it convenient to live with the legend, for that is what people want to hear. The legend is mostly true, as far as it goes. But recently, feeling the growing weight of my years and knowing I may soon be learning the answers to other great mysteries, I have felt some need to set down the rest of the story as I know it. The truth will do no great injury to the legend, for the legend has a life of its own and will outlive both the truth and the teller.

Though I have lived out my graying years near what little remains of old Stonehill town, I do not often go there. Walking in the grass where her streets used to be, I can hear the wind whisper secrets through the sagging buildings that time has not yet crushed, and I imagine I hear ghosts of the years long gone rustling through her ruins. A chill comes upon me yet when I stand at the spot where he sat on his horse, looking down upon a boy who lay there in silence. I can see him shaking his fist in a black anger and shouting to all who could hear him that he would kill Stonehill town as mercilessly as it had murdered his son.

I prefer to remember Stonehill as I first saw it, the great freight wagons and the lumbering Mexican oxcarts challenging one another for space in the narrow streets, the busy clamor of a vital people searching for glory and riches that existed only in their dreams. They lived in hardship and squalor, and sometimes they died in a hostile wilderness, alone and afraid. But the leaders of the country told them this was necessary to the fulfillment of their manifest destiny. They accepted it, most of them, and never turned back. Good men, bad men, and those in between, they differed in many ways. But in one respect they were mostly much alike. They were people of ambition and nerve, and hunger.

I well remember my first meeting with Thomas Canfield in the old port town of Indianola. You won't find the place on a map; it was destroyed in later years by one of those killer hurricanes that occasionally roars in from the Gulf of Mexico to erase all trace of man and his works.

It was only a small town with perhaps one or two permanent stone buildings when I landed there off of the merchant vessel *James Callahan* in the winter of 1854–55. I was the youngest of several sons on a small cotton farm along the Mississippi delta in Louisiana. My parents were too poor to have slaves, so they had children instead. My limited schooling gave me enough skill with ciphers to understand that my share of the family holdings would not long shield me from starvation once I left the protective roof. At seventeen I put all my personal belongings upon my back, hired as a crewman on a boat hauling a load of cotton, and shortly found myself exploring the wonders of New Orleans. I found much there to interest and no little to tempt a boy whose pockets are empty, as mine soon were. I further discovered that few people would hire even a strong and willing white boy for wages when they had slaves to do the heavy lifting without pay. I also found people in general agreement that Texas was a wondrous land where money lay in the streets, just waiting for someone to pick it up. At first opportunity I hired as a laborer on the *James Callahan,* which was hauling manufactured goods to Texas and would be bringing cotton back.

It did not take me long to decide that a seaman's life was not cut to my frame, for I spent more time at the rail than at my work. The captain probably would have fired me had we not already passed over the bar and were well out to sea. Once the sickness passed, he saw to it that I made up for the lost time. It was, all in all, a miserable passage. We ran into one major winter storm that brought me fear of a type I had never known; I was certain I would soon drown in that cold, terrible water. But I was not so lucky, for all I did was become deathly ill from an attack of the grippe, brought on by working on deck soaked to the skin. I wished mightily that I could die and end the misery. But my protecting angel had remained in New Orleans.

Even at the beginning I had intended to remain a sailor only long enough to reach Texas, and my experiences on shipboard only served to deepen my resolve in this direction. I felt duty-bound to remain with the crew long enough to see the cargo unloaded, but I felt no such duty toward seeing the waiting cotton bales carried aboard. I took my pay from the captain's reluctant hands and quickly found how meager it was when I tried to convert it into the necessities of life ashore. It took much less time to spend than to earn.

Indianola offered no employment to such as I, and no money was lying in the streets. If there had ever been, the constant stream of humanity passing through had picked it up and made off with it long before I had my chance. I decided the fortune, if there was one, must lie somewhere inland.

I ate little and slept beneath a wharf while awaiting my chance. Even for a boy whose main concern was a hungry belly, there was much to marvel over. It was my first time to see the big Mexican oxcarts, their wooden wheels as high as a man's shoulder. The axles were crude and squealed in pain when not well greased, so that the carts' coming was known before they broke into view. The Mexicans themselves were a curiosity to me—little men, most of them, rattling away in a foreign tongue that made no sense in my ear. I had heard Cajun French, but I could find no similarity between that and the quick-fire Spanish these people spoke. I was fascinated by their wide *sombreros,* by the great jingling spurs worn by the horsemen.

I had heard, of course, about the two wars the Texans had fought against Mexico, and I had assumed those were long since over. They were not, except in name. The Texas freight wagons came lumbering into town, many hauling bales of cotton and general farm produce to be shipped back to the other states for money. I sensed the enmity which flared between these people and the little men of the brown-leather skin. Around the wharf I heard casual talk about a "cart war," a rivalry between the Mexican cartmen and the *gringo* wagoners over the freight business between the ports and inland markets such as San Antonio. I heard it said that many men had died or disappeared on those long, dusty trails that wound through the brush country, men of both persuasions.

On my second day I saw a Mexican and a Texan meet with knives in hand after a wagon and a cart hung wheels on an Indianola street. Nobody in the crowd moved to stop the fight until it became clear the Mexican was about to win. Then a broad-shouldered Texan with red beard and long rusty-colored hair swung a singletree and clubbed the Mexican to the ground. I was satisfied the cart driver was dead, but friends carried him away. Later I saw the little man sitting up beside a campfire, his head swathed in dirty bandages. I decided they were a hardy lot, these Texas people, whether light-skinned or dark.

On inquiry I found that the red-bearded man was named Branch Isom. He bossed a string of wagons that was loading goods I had helped carry off of the *James Callahan.* It was said he would be taking them to San Antonio by way of Stonehill. I had never heard of Stonehill, and San Antonio sounded considerably more romantic. Perhaps it was there that money lay in the streets. I went to his camp and found him sitting on a bedroll, leaning his back against the huge rear wheel of a freight wagon. He held a cup of coffee in one hand and an open whisky bottle in the other, taking a sip of each in its own turn. A coldness in his eyes made me hesitate in my last steps.

I said, "Mr. Isom, I am Reed Sawyer."

No change came in his eyes. He studied me in cold silence, then asked, "Is there any reason that should be of interest to me?"

"I would like a job with your wagons to San Antonio."

He scowled. "I suppose you'd expect to be paid for it."

"Only what is customary. I was paid fifty cents a day, meals and a bunk on the ship. With your wagons there would be only the meals."

His voice was as cold as his eyes. "You don't look healthy to me. You've probably got some disease you'd spread to everybody in the crew."

"I had the grippe on board. I am over that now. I am strong. I can do my share of the work."

He laughed, but it was not the kind of warm, friendly laugh you like to hear. "There are people in this port who would pay *me* to take them along, and they'd work for nothing. Why should I pay *you*? Get away from here, boy, before I sic my dogs on you."

I saw the dogs, big ugly gray brutes of uncertain ancestry. They looked as if they would chew a man's legs off on command. A chill ran up my back. I turned without saying more and walked away from Isom's camp. The smell of the coffee and the cooking food went with me, for I had not eaten all day. I bought a fish from a man on the beach, roasted it over an open fire, then slept in my accustomed damp place beneath the wharf.

It was the next morning that the Polanders arrived. They came up the trail from Galveston. I learned later that they had been with a larger group of mixed Europeans who had landed there but had been delayed in Galveston by fever, so that the main body went ahead without them. Now, after having buried one or two of their party they had come on, bound for a settlement already laid out for them many days' journey inland.

They seemed as strange to me in their own way as the Mexicans. Having had little time for the study of geography, I had only the vaguest knowledge of the various European countries' names, much less their locations. For all I knew, Poland was a part of Africa. Mostly I looked at the women, particularly the young ones. At seventeen, I found it particularly interesting that they wore the shortest skirts I had seen except in the drinking halls of New Orleans. The skirts ended above the ankles, a scandalous sight. The better people of Indianola were quick to decide that these were loose women, for only that sort would flaunt themselves so. Some of the immigrant women wore wooden shoes, and most had black felt hats with wide brims.

People were laughing and pointing, but somehow I was stirred to pity, not laughter. These immigrants looked as hungry and poor as I was myself. At least I had the advantage of being able to speak with the people around me. These Polanders talked in a tongue that no one in Indianola seemed able to understand. They tried making signs but had scant success even with that. I could only imagine how they had made themselves understood well enough in Galveston that they hired Mexican cartmen to haul their belongings. In four big two-wheeled carts were piled trunks and a few featherbeds and some wooden farm implements they had brought from the old country.

Branch Isom came along to watch the show, he and some of his wagon men. It was obvious he had little regard for the foreigners. He had even less when he saw they were using Mexican cartmen. "Birds of a feather," he grumbled. "Dumb heathens, there's not one of them that understands English."

A man at his side said, "I wonder if they understand *dog*."

Those ugly gray curs had followed. The man sicced

them onto the oxen that pulled the lead cart. Trapped in crude and heavy wooden yokes, the poor brutes kicked at the dogs and then tried to run. They only succeeded in dragging the cart into a ditch. It tipped over, spilling trunks and wooden plows and bedding onto the ground. The strange-looking foreigners went running after, trying to spare their goods further damage. They chunked rocks at the dogs and whipped them with sticks until the pair gave up and retreated to their master.

It was then that Thomas Canfield rode up. He seemed to appear from nowhere, sitting on a long-legged, beautifully built sorrel horse in the middle of the street. He was a tall man, not blocky and stout like Isom but well built just the same. He was then only in his early twenties but already mature in features, his bearing proud. He was clearly a man sure where he was going and unwilling to waste time along the way.

He said sternly, "Isom, do you want to talk some business, or had you rather bedevil a bunch of poor foreigners who have already had hell enough?"

Isom turned. His manner showed that this man on horseback was one he respected, though I also got the idea he did not particularly like him. "Hello, Canfield. What business could I possibly have with you?"

"That depends on how willing you are to talk price. Some goods came for me on that last ship out of New Orleans. I want them hauled to Stonehill."

The dogs stood by Isom's legs, their tongues hanging out. They still looked toward the ditched cart, considering the peril of renewed assault. One of them decided to try and started back toward the cart. Isom said sharply, "Here, dogs! Stay here." They obeyed. Isom had a voice that commanded obedience of man or beast. "What kind of goods?" he asked.

Canfield said, "Farm implements."

The foreigners did not understand the talk. It came to me later, when I took time to think about it, that they thought Thomas Canfield had come to their rescue and had ordered Isom to halt the harassment. One of the young women—just a girl, really—looked at Canfield with open admiration. In a minute Canfield caught the look, and he stared back at the girl.

Isom said, "Farm implements are heavy. I'll have to look at the load before we can figure."

Canfield didn't hear him; he was distracted by the girl. So was I. It was her ankles which got my attention at first. Growing up, I had had to take it on faith that girls even had ankles. But she had a pleasant face, too, and soft brown eyes that reminded me of a doe. Her full attention was devoted to Canfield, and his to her.

Isom repeated himself. Canfield nodded. They started together toward the wharf, Canfield still riding that big sorrel, Isom walking with the dogs behind him.

None of the American people helped the foreigners get the cart out of the ditch. Most simply went on about their business. In a few minutes some Mexican cartmen came along, and the Mexicans who were with the Polanders called on them for help. They had to finish unloading the heavy goods out of the cart. In a bit they manuevered the oxen up and got the big wooden wheels back on flat ground. Then all of the Polanders, women as well as the men, set in to loading their goods back into place. I stayed out of it at first because I didn't figure it was any of my business, but then I started thinking that if I helped I might be invited to share a meal with somebody. I didn't know what kind of food Mexicans or Polanders ate, but anything was better than fish roasted on a stick over an open fire, which was all I had had for three days. I pitched in and helped lift the heavy trunks and the wooden plows. Not until later did I realize I wouldn't recognize an invitation to supper if they gave me one. I never knew there were so many strange languages in one place.

One thing most people don't realize is that Texas was a mixed lot of humanity in those days. There seems to be a mistaken impression that early Texas had just two kinds of people: leftover Mexicans and Bible-reading, whisky-drinking, rifle-shooting, English-speaking immigrants from Tennessee. In truth, it wasn't like that at all. Texas drew people from all over the world because it was so big, and it had so much land to offer. It was considered a place for starting anew, no matter what fate had dealt to each person before. All kinds of people moved to Texas. Wherever you went, you found settlements of Germans, Swedes, Irish, French, Czechs. It was a Babel without a tower. It was a melting pot that never quite melted.

I didn't find a soul in the party that I could talk with, so I stood off to one side, looking hungry and waiting to see what might happen. In a little while Thomas Canfield rode back from the wharf with a grim look on his face. I assumed Isom had asked him more than he had expected to haul his goods. Canfield headed directly up to the Polanders and spoke to the Mexican cartmen who had come along and helped reload the cart. I could tell he was struggling with the language. In later years he could talk Spanish like a native. But even when I first saw him, he was able to understand and make himself understood.

In a little he was accompanied back toward the wharf by a couple of Mexicans. Branch Isom stood in front of a dramshop watching, his face clouded and angry. When Canfield returned he was followed by two smiling Mexican freighters. Isom turned and went into the dramshop, slamming the door against the wintry chill blowing in off the water.

Canfield rode by the Polanders, tipped his low-crowned hat and said, "Good morning." The voice was slow and Southern. The people didn't know what he said, but he spoke in a kindly way, so they smiled. Especially the girl.

I decided if he was feeling so good, it was time for me to present myself and hope for better than I had received at the hands of Branch Isom. I said, "Mister, could I talk to you?"

He glanced at me in surprise. I realized he thought I was one of the Polanders. "You speak English?" he asked.

"That's *all* I talk," I told him. "These aren't my people."

"I didn't mean to offend you. They look like a decent sort. It isn't their fault they were born somewhere else."

In those days nearly everybody in Texas except the Mexicans had been born somewhere else, but most of them not quite so far away as the Polanders.

I said, "I take it you're going inland. I was wondering if I could travel with you? I'll work at anything."

He looked me over carefully. "You have kin that you're going to?"

"I've got nobody here. I'm looking for work to do, and a place to go to away from this coast. This is a feverish country, and poor."

"Anyplace is a poor country when you've got no money. I judge you have none?"

"Very little," I admitted. "But I have a good back and willing hands."

He wanted to know where my gun was, and I told him I owned none. I couldn't tell whether that pleased him or worried him. It was a little of both, I think.

"Well," he said finally, "I can't guarantee that you'll find any work where I'm going, but you're welcome to come with me. I don't suppose you have a horse?"

I barely owned a pair of shoes.

As he rode up the street, I followed him afoot. Branch Isom stepped out of the dramshop with a bottle in his hand. His face was half as red as his hair and his beard. "Hold up, Canfield," he said.

Thomas Canfield pulled the sorrel to a stop. His manner was that of a man doing something because he chose to, not because he had been ordered to. "I don't believe we have any business, Isom."

"Yes, we do. You've hired those Mexican cartmen."

"They bid the haul for half what you asked me."

"They're Mexicans. I'm white."

"My freight has no eyes to tell the difference. But my wallet knows when I take only half as much out of it."

"You can't expect a white man to work that cheap."

I was tempted to remind Isom that he had expected me not only to work for nothing but to pay for the privilege. I held my tongue, confident that Thomas Canfield could maintain his side of the conversation. Canfield said, "The deal has been made. Next time you want to do business with me, Isom, don't try to get rich all at one time."

Isom took the advice as a challenge. "If you shipped with me, I'd guarantee protection for your goods. You ship with those Mexicans at your own risk."

"That sounds like a threat."

"No threat. I am only pointing out to you that there has been trouble on the trails: Mexican cart trains have been burned, and the shippers took a loss."

"White men's wagons have been burned too."

"Not mine. And mine are not going to be."

"Neither are my goods, Isom." His voice dropped a little, so that I strained to hear him. "I'll kill the man who tries."

He and Isom stared at each other with a look that was near hatred. Without anybody framing it in words, a challenge had been flung, and answered. Isom shrugged. "You're twenty-one."

Canfield nodded. "And a few years more."

Isom went back into the dramshop, the bottle in his hand. Canfield stared after him a moment, then turned to me as I walked up even with his horse. "You heard all that, Reed Sawyer?"

I told him I had. He said, "You may want to reconsider going with me."

"He didn't say he was going to do anything."

"Yes, he did. You were only listening to his words."

"I still want to go," I said. "I've been in this town long enough."

"Do you know how to use a gun?"

In truth, my poor marksmanship had been a source of shame to my father, for to most farm boys in Louisiana handling a rifle was second nature; it was a boy's job to keep meat in the house. I did not admit to my shortcoming. I said, "I grew up with a rifle in my hand."

"Then I'll provide you one."

I followed him to his camp, such as it was. He had staked a packhorse on grass at the edge of the little town. In camp waited a Mexican man several years older than Canfield. "Meet Amadeo Fernandez," Canfield said to me. I shook hands with the Mexican and said I was pleased to know him. He answered in Spanish. He smiled, so I knew at least that he was not cursing me. That was the only way I could have known the difference.

I made some comment to the effect that if I had known few people in Texas spoke English I might have chosen to go elsewhere. It was the first time I saw Canfield smile. Smiling was not a thing he did often, then or later in his life. He said, "The truth is the truth no matter what language it is spoken in. And a lie is a lie."

In the pack, spread out on the ground, was some flour for bread, some coffee beans, grease, and smoked pork. I hungered for the pork, but to my chagrin Canfield did not touch it. He said, "I had Amadeo buy us some fish. It has been a long time since I have had fresh saltwater fish."

Having contributed nothing toward the meal, I could ill afford to be critical. But I ate rather more of the bread than of the fish.

I felt it was not politic to ask questions about his business. He volunteered a little information, however, as we ate. He said he owned land north and east of Stonehill. He was farming part of it, raising cattle on the rest. His parents had moved to that region soon after the Mexican War and had broken out one of the first fields. Thomas was a good farmer, but his preference lay in other directions. He had gone west into Indian country with a party of horse hunters, capturing wild mustangs to bring back to the settlements for sale and trade. With his share of the profits he had bought the first land of his own. Later he went back into the Comanche hunting grounds with hired Mexicans and took more wild horses. This time the profit was his. He added more land to his holdings.

"All kinds of people are coming into this country," he said. "You saw those Polanders. A San Antonio priest bought property for them to break out and work, over past Stonehill. Some of them haven't brought any equipment. There's no one to buy it from where they're going, no one but me. I've been ordering farm implements shipped from New Orleans and reselling them to new farmers. Whatever I can make, I'll put into more land."

I ventured, "You must be a big man up there."

"Not yet. But I will be."

By next morning the Mexican cartmen had enough freight to fill out their loads. One of those big carts, drawn by two yokes of oxen, could haul up to five thousand pounds. The four Mexicans who had been carrying goods for the Polanders joined at the end of the line. Canfield talked worriedly in Spanish to Amadeo Fernandez. Together they rode back to where the foreigners waited. I followed at a respectful distance and listened to the arguments. I knew none of the language but surmised from the hand motions that the Polanders and their Mexican freighters intended to go along. Canfield was trying to tell them this cart train carried special danger, but he did not convince the four Mexicans. The Polanders listened in worried silence, understanding neither English nor Spanish. Finally a man came out of a warehouse and began speaking to them in still another language, which I learned was German. A couple of the Polanders understood that fairly well. So Spanish was translated into English through Canfield, then into German and finally, for the good of all the group, into the Silesian dialect spoken by the Polanders.

I could only imagine how much was lost or distorted through all the translations.

I began to think I should give Texas just a little more of my time, and if conditions did not improve I would move on to a more promising locale where everyone spoke my language.

At the time I thought the immigrants simply did not understand the seriousness of the situation. Later I learned they had already been through so much hell that the prospect of a little more caused no terror for them.

Canfield was looking at the girl. Talking to her was hopeless, but he tried. "I wish I could make you understand. You ought not to be on this trip."

She only smiled. It was not for the women to make the decisions anyway, not in those times or among the European immigrants. Canfield had no authority over the cart train; he was simply a shipper. But he would see his goods protected. I was to learn that when he felt something belonged to him, whether people or land or cattle, he would fly into the face of the devil to protect it.

Branch Isom and his wagons were still in Indianola when the cart train pulled out onto the well-beaten road. The wagoners had not yet gotten a full load, but a merchant vessel had docked late the night before and they would probably receive enough freight from it to finish out.

Isom stood in front of the dramshop with three of his teamsters as the last of the Mexican cartmen goaded his oxen into movement with the Polanders' goods. I was still afoot, of course, but so were the other people. Even the cart drivers walked most of the time. Thomas Canfield and Fernandez were on horseback, the Mexican leading the pack-horse.

I looked back at Isom and said to Canfield, "At least they will be well behind us."

Canfield shook his head. "They have mule teams, not oxen. They will catch up."

It took most of that first day to get up out of the low-lying, swampy coastal lands and onto higher, drier ground. Though it was winter, the sun was strong and the air muggy. I found myself sweating, and I feared lapsing back into the fever that had plagued me on the ship. But as we worked our way up into a drier elevation I began to feel better and take more interest in the life I saw around me. We were passing through a country already partially settled, much of the better land broken for cultivation. This was the fallow time for most of it. The farmers we saw were mostly breaking out new land to go into crops the following spring. Though the great high-wheeled carts were still a curiosity to me, I noted that the people we passed paid little or no attention to them. But the Polanders were another matter. People stared and whispered as the strange procession of immigrants passed. I knew most people were fascinated as I had been by their clothes, particularly those of the women. A boy of ten or twelve, riding bareback on a shaggy mule in the direction opposite our line of travel, watched with open mouth as the Polanders passed. He turned the mule around and whipped it into a lope back the way he had come. A mile or so down the road we passed a couple of crude farmhouses built of logs. At least a dozen people stood in front, the boy among them. They looked at the immigrants as if they had been a circus parade.

I was bringing up the rear afoot. Canfield and Fernandez had ridden up front somewhere. A couple of the farmers edged closer and closer and looked me over carefully. Finally deciding I was of another breed than the Polanders, they fell in beside me.

"What kind of queer varmints are those?" the older one asked me.

I told him I understood they were Polanders but added that I didn't rightly know what a Polander was. All I knew for certain was that they had come from the other side of the big water.

"What are they good for?" he wanted to know.

I told him I supposed they were farmers inasmuch as I had seen some wooden plows. But I hadn't been able to talk to them, so I didn't really know.

"Foreigners," he said with a snort. "Every time we look up there's another kind of foreigners passing by. Germans, Frenchies, Sweders—God knows what all. We no sooner taken this land away from those Indians and Mexicans than all these foreigners start coming in. You watch, they'll be taking it away from us one of these days."

From what I had heard Texas still had more than enough land for everybody, but I judged he didn't care to hear that.

Through the day we passed other freight outfits coming from the interior, headed down to Indianola and Galveston. When they were Mexican oxcart trains there was a great deal of laughing and yelling between their men and ours. When they were American wagons, the hatred that passed from one side to the other was so thick and heavy you could almost reach out and touch it. I had never realized how long it took to get over a war, even after the battles had stopped.

Canfield said the hatred had come first, before the wars, and it would last a long time yet because people on both sides kept studying on the differences between themselves. They didn't pay much attention to the ways they were alike. Each one was convinced the other was inferior. They all talked to the same God, but they saw Him differently and were sure He was on their side alone.

All the Mexicans I had seen up to then were the ones on this train and a few in Indianola. To me they were still as strange as the Polanders. The difference in languages stood like a stone wall between us. I asked Canfield how he got along with them to the extent that he even rode with one, that he let them freight his goods for him when white men were available to do it.

"I learned a lot from Amadeo," he said. "He worked for my father, and now he works for me. Sure, some Mexicans will lie to you. So will Branch Isom. Some of them will cheat you. So will Branch Isom. Some of them will even kill you if there's a profit in it. So will Branch Isom. So where's the big difference?"

Late that evening the Mexicans reached a place they wanted to camp. They found another cart train there ahead of them, coming down toward the coast. Both trains camped together to double their defense. I could tell there was a considerable amount of excited talk between the Mexicans of the two outfits, but of course I couldn't understand a word of it. As we fixed ourselves a little supper out of the goods in Canfield's pack he told me there was talk of a cart train being raided a couple of days' journey ahead. The attack had been driven off, but there had been some loss of life and a couple of carts burned.

Attempted robbery was the reason which went down in official records, but the cartmen knew robbery was no issue. This was part of a sustained warfare between Mexican and American freighters for supremacy on the trail. Many San Antonio merchants favored the Mexicans because they charged less for making the haul. The Mexicans had less investment in equipment and were willing to live by lower standards. Americans needed more money because of their higher investments and their higher expectations. The issues were simple. Only the solution was difficult. Canfield said he expected the outcome would be decided more on the basis of force than of equity.

In the long run, he added, most conflicts are.

We were under no obligation to help the cartmen stand guard, and it was clear that those of the coastbound train did not trust Canfield or me. One of the first Mexican words I learned to recognize was *gringo,* spoken like a curse. But Canfield and I each took a turn anyway, with Amadeo filling out the last part of the night. Nothing happened except a fight between Canfield's horse and one of the others. The sorrel quickly established dominance.

We were on the trail soon after sunup, the great carts creaking and squealing. A couple of the Polanders seemed to have trouble getting started. A woman of middle age was supported by younger women until a teamster made motions for her to be placed in a cart, where she could ride. I gathered that she had survived the fever—a common complaint along the coast—and she had not yet regained her strength. Canfield rode to the cart and helped lift the woman into it. He received a smile from the pretty girl for his efforts. I suspected that had been his object in the first place.

One of the cartmen had a lean brown dog. As the day wore on, the dog spent most of its time with the Polanders, who talked to him in their strange language and patted him on the head. He wagged his tail and seemed to understand them perfectly well.

I brought up the rear, carrying a long-barreled muzzle-loading rifle Canfield had lent me. Toward noon I began hearing a racket behind us and saw a wagon train gradually catching up. A horseman rode well out in front of it. As he neared I recognized Branch Isom's red beard, and the two bad dogs trailing along on either side of him. We pulled off the trail for nooning, and Isom brought his wagons past. He looked us over with hard eyes and said nothing. Not a word was spoken by anyone on either his train or ours. The only communication was between Isom's two dogs and the brown one which belonged to our train. They had a snarling match that led to a moment of tooth-snapping conflict. Isom rode back and popped a whip over the dogs' heads. His two pulled out of the fight and followed him, though they looked back and continued the quarrel so long as they were within range.

One of the cartmen patted the brown dog and spoke approvingly for his bravery in battle. He would have lost if the fight had been allowed to go on much longer, but it would have been to superior numbers, not to superior gallantry. The pretty immigrant girl got something out of a cart and smeared it on the dog's wounds, talking softly in words the dog seemed to understand even though I did not.

While we rested, one of the immigrant men came to me and began talking. He pointed to my rifle and made motions I could not decipher until finally he mimed the act of

EYES OF THE HAWK

pulling a bow-string. I realized he was asking if there was
a chance we might encounter Indians. I didn't know.

Canfield said, "No Indians. They're a long way west."
Evidently his meaning was understood, for the Polander
seemed relieved.

I said, "These people are in for a lot of trouble if they've got
to go through this every time they want to talk to anybody."

Canfield said, "They'll get with their own and stay with
their own. There'll be a few who will learn enough English
to get by, and those will take care of the rest. I've sold
plows to some Germans, and that's the way they've done it.
These immigrants don't scatter amongst us much; they stay
close together and lean on one another. They'll make it."

Watching these people, the language difference a bar-
rier between us, I could only guess at what they had left
behind them, what they had been through to get here.
Later, when the barriers began to break down, I would
learn that the Polanders were something like the Israelites
of the Bible, made slaves in their own country and finally
driven out. They had been conquered and divided up by
the Prussians and others and their lands had been taken
away from them until they faced the proposition of leaving
or starving. There had been a few Polanders in Texas at the
time of the revolution from Mexico, and some had been
executed on Santa Anna's orders after the fight at Goliad.
A few were with Sam Houston when he won the battle of
San Jacinto. These wrote letters home, and so over the
next few years they kept drawing in friends and family
until they had several small communities spread across
the country. The stories about money lying in the streets
had probably reached Silesia too, just as they had reached
Louisiana.

I doubted they were any more disappointed than I was to
find out how little money existed in Texas, and none of it
lying in the streets. They had chosen a hard time to come.
Actually, it was always hard times in Texas. The rich you

could count on one hand. The poor you found in multitudes.

Late in the day the Mexicans began stepping out on the trail and looking forward. The *capitán* rode back and visited with Amadeo, then the two spurred their horses and rode far out ahead, beyond sight. A while before dark they were back, disappointed. Canfield said they had hoped to meet another cart train coming down the trail so they could camp together for mutual protection, but they had found none. Now they could not put off camping any longer; it would soon be night.

The Polanders would probably have helped with guard duty if they had been asked, but no one knew how to ask them. So far as we could tell, they had not a single weapon with them. They had not been accustomed to owning or using them in the old country; the Prussians would not have allowed it. We two *gringos* and the Mexicans divided the guard duty between us. I had not thought about it until Canfield mentioned it, for I was not used to having to consider such things, but the *capitán* had camped the train in a broad, open area. If the moon was again bright and cold as the night before, we would have good visibility.

Because I could talk to no one else, I took Canfield as my example and copied whatever he did. He was concerned but not really fearful. I could not say the same for myself. I had never held a gun in my hands for possible use against another human. I asked, "Do you have to do this all the time?" It crossed my mind that I was still only two days' walk from the coast.

Canfield said, "When I was a boy we saw a few Indians, but they've all been pushed west. Once we're home nobody will bother us. But the trail is always a place to be watchful. Especially as long as this cart war goes on."

It seemed to me it would have been the better part of valor to have shipped his goods with Isom or some other wagon man no matter what the rate had been. I said as much.

Canfield told me sternly, "In this country you must never show a feather. Give up to them once and you're beaten." Through the years to come I was to learn just how deeply he believed that. Once challenged, cost was no factor to him. He never showed a feather.

The night chill closed upon us as soon as the sun dropped out of sight. When the people spread their blankets to sleep, one of the immigrants threw fresh wood upon their campfire. Canfield quickly dragged it back out of the flames. He tried to explain that for safety's sake it was better to keep a dark camp. I don't think he quite conveyed the message, but he had such a commanding way about him that no one presented any challenge.

I took the first watch. I doubted I could have slept anyway. Thomas Canfield seemed able to command himself even in the matter of sleeping, for within a few minutes after he rolled up in his blankets he was gone. It took Amadeo Fernandez a bit longer. I sat hunched with my coat on and my blanket wrapped around my shoulders, my bare hands stiff and cold on the steel barrel of the rifle. There was no danger of my falling asleep on duty. I was chilled to the bone.

I had no way of telling time and had not learned to follow the stars. I listened for the Mexicans who stood watch farther up the line of carts. When at last I heard them changing guard, I got up, trembling from the cold, and carefully awakened Canfield. He wasted no time yawning. He seemed to know where he was and what he had to do from the moment he opened his eyes. He got up and went about it in a quiet, businesslike manner. I lay down on the spot he had vacated, hoping he had warmed the ground. He had not. I shivered a long time before I dropped off to sleep.

When I awakened it was suddenly and to the sound of shots. I flung the blanket away and fumbled in panic for the rifle. I saw flashes of fire and vague movements out in the night. I heard men shouting and horses running. I had never realized how quickly a man could fire and then re-charge a muzzle-loading rifle until I saw Thomas Canfield do it.

My heart pounded and skipped. I shouted, "What do I shoot at?"

He replied, "Anything that moves out there. We've got no friends past the cart line."

Some riders carried torches. Though they held them high, the flickering light showed the horses a little. Some-where up the line I heard a man scream, and I saw a torch thrown into one of the carts. Behind me the immigrant women were crying, huddling together.

From out of the night a shape lunged at me, and I raised my rifle. It was close range, but I missed. Canfield was busy reloading. The horseman spurred into me, knocking me down and making me lose my hold on the rifle. The rider hurled a blazing torch into the nearest cart, one which held immigrant goods. A Polander jumped onto the cart and grabbed the torch, flinging it back into the horseman's face as the man fired a pistol. The horse squealed in panic at the blaze and whirled around while the man cursed. Canfield finished loading his rifle, brought it to his shoul-der and fired. The man was driven back in his saddle. The horse broke into a run. The rider slid over its rump and landed roughly on the ground. Instantly Canfield was kneeling over him, a long hunting knife in his hand, the point pressing against the man's throat.

"You move," he said, "and I'll kill you."

The man groaned. The rifle ball had taken him hard.

Canfield glared at me as he reloaded his rifle. "I thought you said you could shoot."

I had no answer for that and did not try one.

"Watch him, then," Canfield said tersely and turned his attention back to the men out there in the moonlight. He called a time or two for Amadeo. Both of us had lost sight of the Mexican.

The shooting died. The raiders pulled back, for they had flung their torches and had found the defense too strong. Down the line, one cart blazed. Despairing of putting out the fire, several Mexicans grabbed the tongue and pulled the vehicle away from the others to prevent its fire from spreading. Canfield said with concern, "I'm going to see if that's one of the carts carrying my goods."

The wounded raider kept groaning. I did not know what to do about him, so I did nothing except watch.

One of the Polanders touched my shoulder and pointed to the other side of the carts. He said something I did not understand except that the word "Mexican" somehow came out of it. I handed another Polander my rifle and pointed to the wounded man, hoping he understood that I meant for him to stand guard. He took the weapon nervously. Following the older man's repeated beckoning, I found two of the immigrant women kneeling over a fallen Amadeo. They spoke softly, trying to comfort him. He probably did not hear them. As little experience as I had had with that sort of thing, I sensed he was dying. I touched him and felt the stickiness of warm blood and came near being sick. I brought my hand quickly away, as if I had stuck it into fire. In the excitement I had forgotten about the cold, but suddenly it came back to me, and I was trembling all over.

Canfield called me. I responded with what voice I could muster. He came around the cart, knelt quickly and called Amadeo's name. The Mexican's breathing was spaced in ragged patches, and in a few moments it stopped. Canfield talked softly in Spanish, gently shaking the man as if he thought he could force breath back into the body. Finally he pushed to his feet and walked back to where the wounded raider lay. Canfield towered over him with fury in his face.

The man pleaded, "Help me."

Canfield looked at me. "Go relight one of those torches at that cart fire and bring it here so I can see."

I did. He held the torch over the man's face. "I know you," he said accusingly. "I've seen you in Stonehill. You're with Isom's train, aren't you?"

The man cried, "I'm bleeding to death. Help me."

"Tell me first," Canfield insisted. "It was Isom who led this raid, wasn't it?"

One of the Mexican cartmen dropped to one knee to tear the clothing away from the wound deep in the raider's shoulder. Canfield pushed the man to one side. He said something in Spanish, then said for my benefit and the prisoner's, "We'll treat you when you've told me what I want to know. Till then, nobody touches you."

"I'll die," the man cried weakly.

"Then die," Canfield said. His voice was as cold as the night. "It's up to you."

He stood over the man, a terrible look on his face. I saw a ferocity I had never seen anywhere before. Slowly the Mexicans began gathering around. They talked quietly among themselves, and I heard a word that I later learned described the look they saw in his eyes: *gavilán.* The hawk.

At that moment I think Thomas Canfield might have killed anyone who had stepped in to thwart what he was doing. I suddenly found that I was a little afraid of him, a feeling I never quite lost. There was a look about him then—and I saw it again at times through the years—that turned my blood cold.

It was, for a little while, a contest of wills between Canfield and the wounded *gringo.* Finally, as it would always be, it was the other man who gave up first. He lifted his hand a little way, pleadingly, and whispered, "I'll tell. Help me."

"Tell first," Canfield said.

The man tried, but he had waited too long. The strength was gone from him, and his voice. His lips moved, but no discernible words came. Canfield knelt and grabbed the man's collar. He shook him. "Louder! Tell me! Was it Isom?"

He had won the contest, but the victory cost him a price he had not intended to pay. The man died without telling him what he wanted to know. Canfield stood over the dead raider and cursed him for taking the life of a better man.

2

Dawn came and we buried the dead, but not together. Canfield would not have that. It was a custom of the time that Americans and Mexicans not be buried side by side, but this was not Canfield's reason. He said bitterly that Amadeo Fernandez was a God-fearing man too good to keep company with an outlaw throughout eternity. We buried them on opposite sides of the trail. Canfield quoted Scripture by memory. The Mexicans worried that Amadeo needed the services of a priest to keep him safe from the devil, but many a good man had been buried along this road without the benefit of clergy. The immigrants bowed their heads and offered up a prayer. I did not know if it was for Amadeo or for their own deliverance. None of them had been hurt during the shooting, and their possessions were but little damaged.

The dead *gringo* had carried little worth salvaging except for a knife and pistol, unused, and his rifle. Canfield gave me these in recognition of the fact that I owned no weapons and that henceforth I might have need for them as a result of having been in the cartmen's company. A little silver was found in the man's pockets. Canfield took this for Amadeo's widow.

I tried the accuracy of the rifle by resting its barrel in the fork of a tree and aiming at a dried cowchip forty yards away. The bullet kicked up dust short of the chip. I was satisfied that the rifle was more accurate than the man who fired it. Canfield seemed to agree, though he did not say so.

The pistol was one of the cap-and-ball style of the time, heavy as a sack of lead bars. It took a while to accustom myself to wearing it, for I developed a strong list in its direction.

The outlaw's horse had gotten away, but I probably would not have had more than temporary possession had we managed to capture it. There was always somebody around to claim a horse if there seemed any doubt about its true ownership.

I was set to walk, but Canfield pointed his chin toward Amadeo's horse. "You'd just as well ride. I don't care to lead him."

The stirrups were longer than was comfortable, but I put up with the inconvenience because refitting them would take time. I had no wish to be left alone now, even for a little while. I felt nervous about riding a dead man's saddle. I asked, "Did he have a family?"

Canfield was grim. "A wife and two boys."

"What happens to them now?"

"They'll stay on my place as long as I have one, and as long as they want to." His jaw ridged. I could see vengeance in his eyes, but there was frustration too. Though he was convinced Branch Isom had been at the foot of this, he had no legal recourse. One thing I learned about Thomas Canfield as time went by was that he had two characteristics in abundance: determination and a long memory. He had also a third: an inability to forgive. Somewhere, sometime, his chance would come. He was always ready. Meantime, he could wait.

A change came over the people on the cart train. Quietly, without anyone saying anything or making a show of it, leadership shifted to Canfield. The Mexicans showed him respect rather than general indifference. The *capitán* came to ask Canfield's opinion before he stopped for nooning or to make camp. The immigrants gave way each time he rode back to the rear of the train. They were fascinated, yet they feared him.

The Mexicans had a name for him now, though they did not use it in his hearing. They called him the Hawk.

I had seen larger towns than Stonehill but none more alive for its size. Its streets were crowded by great tarpaulin-covered freight wagons drawn by as many as sixteen mules or horses; by the creaking Mexican carts with their many spans of muscled oxen. Between the wagons, often seeming in some jeopardy of being crushed by the huge wheels, walked or ran people of all descriptions, a variety I thought would rival New Orleans. They all seemed to have someplace to go or something important to do.

Here, Canfield told me, two busy trails came together, one from Galveston and Indianola on the coast, the other from Mexico and the Rio Grande, joining here for the journey on to San Antonio, and north and west. This town was still new enough that the unpainted lumber had not yet darkened on some of its buildings. The courthouse, a simple two-story affair built like a square wooden box, stood in the center of the activity and told one and all that this was the seat of a newly organized county which destiny had marked for greatness.

It seemed to me that an inordinate percentage of the business houses were dramshops of some kind. The word "saloon" had not come into common usage as it would later on.

Canfield said, "One can become poor dealing in the necessities of life, but only a bad choice of location can make a pauper of a whisky merchant. For that purpose, there is not a bad location in Stonehill."

A newly painted sign over the door of a general store and post office declared: "Stonehill, the Jewel of Texas— Brightest Point in the Lone Star."

"A pesthole," Canfield countered.

I was too impressed by the busy, bustling aspect of the

town to accept that judgment at face value. I said, "It must have a place."

"It does. If it were in my power, that is where I would send it."

I was in no position to argue the point, for he had been here before the town. I said, "I'll wager I can find employment."

"Perhaps. But you came in with a Mexican cart train, and that will go against you. A lot of local money is tied up in freight wagons and the wagoner trade."

Once he had broached this matter I began to pay attention to the people who watched us. I saw hostility in some faces, now that I began looking for it. The experience shook me. I had never had reason to encounter hostility back home. On the delta I had only friends. In Texas barely a week, I already had enemies. I was unprepared for so much progress.

As we passed a dramshop a young man strode out to meet us. Perhaps the word "strode" is too bold, for he weaved a bit. He had a broad and easy smile, and he waved at Thomas Canfield. "Hello, big brother," he shouted.

Thomas' eyes crackled. His voice was sharp. "Kirby! What are you doing in town?"

"I came to help you unload your goods."

"You were needed more at home."

Kirby Canfield had not shaved in days, but his beard was still soft and boyish. So was his manner. Thomas' harsh rebuke seemed not to touch him at all. He kept his grin.

"You're late," he said. "I thought you would be here yesterday."

"I suppose," Thomas said severely, "that you came the day before that, just to be sure?"

"I try to do my part."

"And so you've been drinking and gambling in this town for two days?"

"Not gambling," Kirby Canfield smiled. "You only gamble when you lose." He stuck his hands into his pockets and jingled a collection of coins. "You have your talents, brother, but you've never seen fit to acknowledge mine."

Thomas gave him no ground. "Since you came to work, I'll see that you do."

"Give me a stirrup," Kirby said, "and I'll swing up behind you."

"You'll walk, and burn the whisky out of your blood."

We had kept moving all this time. Thomas rode up beside the Mexican teamster on his lead cart and pointed leftward at the next corner. His two carts pulled out of the train. The other carts lumbered along, filling the gap we had left.

The immigrants at the rear of the train attracted considerable attention from the townspeople. As they came up even with us the patriarch of the group nodded gravely and acknowledged Thomas Canfield, thanking him with a gesture and a few strange words. Thomas nodded back, but his eyes searched through the immigrants until they found the girl. I saw a long, silent look pass between them. Thomas turned his head and watched a minute or two after they had gone past us.

"Good luck," he said, too quietly for her or the others to have heard if they had been able to understand him.

We proceeded down the heavily rutted street to a small frame storage building set apart from the principal business district. It was not properly a store, for Thomas kept no store hours. I found when I got to know him better that such a thing was against his nature. This was simply a spartan little warehouse where he could meet a prospective implement customer at their mutual convenience for an exchange of goods and coin of the realm. He went there only on arrangement and stayed only so long as was necessary. Most Stonehill business was strictly for cash. Credit was hard for the borrower to find and for the lender to enforce, because this was a horseback society, always moving.

I helped unload the carts, but Thomas saw to it that his

brother did the heaviest lifting. I had not entirely recovered
from the effects of the sea trip and was soon tired. Nor was
I an employee of Thomas Canfield; my only obligation was
gratitude. During the last part of the unloading process I
sat on a rough bench with Thomas while Kirby and the
Mexicans finished the work. Kirby sweated so much that
he appeared to have been caught in a rainshower. Thomas
showed him no sympathy, though Kirby expressed a certain good-natured sympathy for himself.

A carriage approached, drawn by a pair of matched
bays. On the seat hunched a thin man of middle age,
dressed rather well by the standards of the time and place,
though he would have been considered threadbare in the
better delta towns. Beside him sat a young woman who
quickly took my attention. About my age, she was brown-
eyed and brown-haired and had a smile like sunshine. That
smile was for Thomas Canfield, however, not for me.

Thomas stood up as the carriage came to a stop. In his
eyes was a respect I had not seen him give to anyone else in
the few days I had known him. "Good morning, Laura.
Good morning, Mr. Hines."

I remembered seeing the Hines name on the general
store and post office back on the main street. "Good morning, Thomas," the man answered. He touched the brim of a
dusty Eastern hat. He returned Thomas' respect in kind. "I
see you have brought in another shipment. If ever I were to
give thought to selling farm implements, you would probably undersell me." No malice or resentment was detect-
able in his voice.

Thomas came dangerously near smiling. "I would if I
could, sir."

"That is as it should be. A bit of competition helps hold
greed in check and keep us honest."

The girl had never taken her eyes from Thomas. I had
just as well not been standing there for all she saw of me. I
wished she were more observant. She said, "I hope you
will come some day for Sunday dinner, Thomas."

"I hardly know when Sunday comes," he replied. I could tell that he liked her, but I did not see the same look in his eyes that he had given the Polander girl.

She said, "I'll have to send you a calendar."

"That would be nice," he said. By the tone of his voice, though, I knew he would not be waiting in suspense.

Hines said to Thomas, "My best regards to your good mother." He fingered his gray-tinged muttonchop whiskers as he briefly appraised first Kirby and then me, showing us no ill will, at least. He flipped the reins and set the team moving. Laura Hines turned and looked back over her shoulder, but only at Thomas, not at the rest of us.

Thomas stared after them. "Even Sodom and Gomorrah had a few good people. Linden Hines started this town. He's like a father with a wild son he can't control." He glanced at Kirby. "Or a man with a brother."

He paid the cartmen in silver. There was considerable bowing and beaming and wishing of happy times. At least, that seemed the gist of the talk. The only Spanish I had learned was a few words of profanity that had seemed effective upon the oxen.

Once the Mexicans had taken their leave, I decided it was time I did the same. Unless I found a source of income shortly, I would have to learn to live without eating. I told Kirby Canfield it had been a pleasure to make his acquaintance. I shook Thomas Canfield's hand and thanked him for his courtesies.

He frowned. "I've already told you to expect nothing from this town."

I assured him I intended to stay only long enough to replenish my thin purse, then proceed to San Antonio or farther into the interior. He thanked me for my help in fighting the raiders, though I had only fired some wild shots. I hoisted my little roll of blankets across my shoulder on a short rope and picked up the rifle Thomas had said I was entitled to. I started up the street, looking hopefully at each business house, trying to decide which might offer employment befitting the talents of a delta farm boy. This place was a long way from the cotton fields, both in miles and in character.

I tried six or seven places and met the same cold response at every one. Some mentioned that they had seen me in bad company. Others implied it or showed it with their eyes. I still had a little money but resolved to preserve it at all costs. I found a small place which advertised itself as a restaurant and volunteered to chop wood in return for a meal. The proprietor expressed some reservations about my strength for the work but said as an act of kindness he would feed me. All I had to do in return was to chop about half a cord of mesquite wood piled in the back. I accepted with proper gratitude. I was inclined to eat first and work afterward, but he expressed the opinion that a laborer performed best on an empty stomach.

It might have been cheaper for him had he allowed me to eat first. By the time I had chopped the wood I had a ruinous appetite. With no shame whatever, I filled my plate to its edges and sat down to the task. I was well into my second helping when a rough-looking teamster came in. Almost immediately his attention went to my rifle, leaning in the corner. He whispered to the proprietor, who had been morosely studying my progress with his foodstuffs.

The proprietor did not give me a chance to fill my plate a third time. He picked it up as I finished the last bite, and he stood waiting for my coffee cup. I complimented him on his skill in the kitchen, picked up my rifle and bedroll and went outside.

There I was confronted by the teamster who had been in the restaurant. With him were Branch Isom and ten or a dozen more. Had I known more about the character of Stonehill I would have brought up the rifle to a strong defensive posture then and there. It would have been all bluff, however. The rifle was not loaded.

Isom's eyes were narrowed and cold. "You're the boy that wanted to be paid to come up from Indianola."

I bristled a little. "And you are the gentleman who offered to let me pay for the privilege of working."

Isom's gaze fell to the rifle. "Where did you get that?"

I realized he knew very well. I said, "Some raiders attacked the cart train I was with. One of them left it there."

I doubted that these men knew for certain that the raider had been killed. Looking from one hostile face to another I decided my life would not be worth a secondhand chew of tobacco if I told them.

Isom said, "I believe you stole it."

"I picked it up on the field of battle." I had read somewhere about the spoils of war belonging to the victors, but this did not seem an appropriate time to go into history.

A teamster said, "It's Fitz's rifle, all right. Got his initials carved on the stock."

Isom took a step toward me and stopped. I could see little of his eyes because of the heavy red brows. "What happened to the man who carried it?"

I suspected they had guessed but were not quite certain. It was not my place to bear ill tidings to strangers. I said, "You should know better than I do. You were with him."

I did not see Isom's fist coming, but a sledgehammer could not have struck me harder. I staggered backward with lights flashing in my eyes. He hit me again and I landed on my back, on top of my rolled-up blankets. The rifle fell. I acted by instinct, though not very well. I got to my feet, took a couple of hard swings at him and missed, then was knocked down again for my trouble. I scrambled at him from hands and knees and managed to get both arms around his legs, tripping him. We rolled in the dirt. I hit him three or four times, but never as hard as he hit me. From the first it was clear I was going to lose.

Toward the end I was seeing through a painful blur. Thomas and Kirby Canfield had walked up. Kirby seemed about to come to my aid, but Thomas held him back. It was my fight.

It came to me later, when I knew him better, that Thomas

Canfield was not a crusader. He did not go rushing about looking for other people's fights. He would have taken no part in the Mexicans' fight against the raiders had he not had a shipment of freight on their carts. He took no part in my fight. Had it been over something or someone who belonged to him, he would have.

At last I was lying beaten, hardly able to move. Branch Isom had his knee on my chest. "Now, boy, you tell me what happened to Fitz."

Thomas Canfield said evenly, "Let him up, Isom."

Isom glanced at him with uncertainty. "This is not your affair."

"I believe it is. *I* killed your man Fitz."

Isom pushed to his feet. "He wasn't my man, Canfield. He quit me on the trail."

Canfield's voice was as cold as January. "Only after I shot him. He was your man, Isom. You led him, and you killed a man of mine who was worth more than a dozen of you and the scoundrels who hang around you in this scabby town."

It came to me suddenly that they were about to try to kill one another, and I was lying on the ground between them. But I could not move. I lay there trembling, not able even to breathe.

Isom said, "You're wrong, Canfield."

Canfield's voice dropped lower. "You're a liar."

Fury flashed in Isom's eyes, and his hand went to the pistol. As I watched, he drew it from the holster, then stopped, the muzzle pointed more or less at me. The fury in his eyes melted to something else, to uncertainty, to fear.

I turned my head toward Canfield and saw that his pistol was up and aimed straight at Isom. His finger was tight on the trigger. In his eyes was a cold hatred far removed from the quick fury that had drained from Isom's. I could see his finger turning white. I lay paralyzed with fear of my own, knowing that if he fired, Isom's last convulsive act might be to kill me.

Isom tried to bring up the muzzle of his pistol but could not. He seemed frozen, staring into the face of death. After what seemed an age, he let his pistol slip back into its holster.

Weakly he said, "I see no reason to kill you, Canfield."

For another heartbeat, Canfield seemed still determined to fire, but the moment had slipped away from him. Isom's hand lifted clear, showing he was no longer a threat.

If Canfield had intended to shoot him, he had waited too long. For a moment he had had all the excuse he needed. No one could have blamed him. Now that moment was gone.

Isom swallowed. His eyes cut away from Canfield, betraying his fear. From where I lay, I could see his legs tremble even if others could not.

Canfield lowered his pistol reluctantly. Regret was in his eyes, regret that he had not followed through when the moment was right. I could not know, then, how he would grieve in later years over that missed opportunity.

Isom backed slowly away, trying to recover the lost bravado, to deny he had shown the feather. He reached for strength but never quite found it. His shaky voice gave him away. "You watch what you say about me, Canfield. I won't stand still for your slander."

Canfield said nothing. There was no need, for he had made his point and had shown himself the stronger man.

Isom watched narrowly until the rancher's pistol finally returned to its holster. Only then did Isom turn away, walking unsteadily into the nearest dramshop. Some of the dozen or so men followed him. Others simply pulled back to some distance and kept watching. Isom's defeat had been their own, for now at least. The sense of humiliation clung to them.

Kirby Canfield was the first to speak. The tension drained away, and he laughed uneasily. "You beat him, big brother, in front of everybody. That should be the last trouble we'll ever have from Branch Isom."

Thomas' rejoinder was severe. "If you believe that, then you're a fool. He'll have to get back at us now or leave here for good." He turned to me, catching me under the arms and helping me to wobbly feet. "You put up a good fight, Sawyer, for a boy in your condition. I should have stopped it sooner. In a way it was my fight, not yours."

The two Canfields helped me away. It would have been easy for the remaining Isom crowd to have shot any or all of us in the back, for the Canfields did not deign to look behind them, and I could not. After a little while they sat me down on the edge of a wooden porch at the Hines store. "Go fetch the wagon here," Thomas ordered.

When Kirby went to obey, Thomas said to me, "I told you you'd find no friends in this town."

Weakly I acknowledged his perception.

He went on, "I can't pay you much because I have little cash money. But there's room for you at our place if you want to work and are in no hurry to run up a fortune."

I told him I would consider staying at least awhile. It was becoming plain to me that I should learn a lot more about this country before setting myself loose upon it, alone. In truth, I felt as if I were crawling beneath a sheltering arm.

I rested the first couple of days in and about the old double cabin and gorged myself upon the simple but good cooking done by Thomas Canfield's mother. She was a small, spare woman bent at the shoulders by a life of hard work. She said a thing or two that indicated Mr. Canfield—Thomas' father—had been dead several years. She said nothing about how he had come to die, and I did not ask. I was gradually coming around to the notion that when Texas people wanted to talk to you about something, *they* would introduce the subject.

After those first days of shameful indolence I went to work clearing mesquite and other brush from a flat, deep-soil pasture Thomas was preparing to break for the plow.

He was resolved to increase his cultivated acreage in the coming spring. It soon became apparent to me why he had so little money. Every bit of cash which came his way— above what went for immediate necessities—was converted almost immediately into land, wherever he could find any for sale within riding distance of the home place. His properties were scattered like the squares on a checkerboard, and he was constantly striving to solidify them.

He gave me the first of many lectures I was to hear from him about the importance of owning land. I suspected he had inherited the hunger from his father, who had taken up the original ground in the Canfield name.

"Land is where the real wealth lies. Businesses come and go. Towns grow and then die. But the land is constant. Whenever you have the chance, Sawyer, grab onto the land and hold it. Everything else is just rainbow."

Over the next month or so he sold most of the implements stored in Stonehill and ordered more out of New Orleans. The profit went to buy a parcel of unbroken rangeland from absentee survivors of a San Jacinto battle veteran who had received the property as a reward from the Republic of Texas, before statehood, but had never lived on or worked it.

All winter he talked of making up another expedition into the Indian country farther west, so he could bring in another stock of mustang ponies to break and sell. The wild horses, subsisting on winter range, would be at their weakest and could not so easily outrun those helped along with grain. But we remained so busy that spring planting time caught us, and we could not go.

Some people like Thomas Canfield seem born to lead, to accumulate and build. Others, like Kirby, seem content enough to follow and to work for someone else. Kirby lacked his brother's passion for acquisition. He tended toward observation of the lilies in the field, toward savoring the full flavor of each day which came to him. He seldom deferred today's pleasures in the hope of accumulating in-

terest for a greater payment at some vague future time. He
worked hard and carried his share of the load, for to do less
was considered a poor show of one's manhood in those
days. But in the evenings when Thomas busied himself
with ledgers and survey records and maps, when Mrs.
Canfield spun yarn on an old wheel so they wouldn't have
to buy cloth, Kirby was likely to be playing an old fiddle or
proving the dexterity of his fingers with a deck of cards. He
even taught me how to play.

Back home it had been given to me as holy writ that
cards were a device invented by the devil to aid him in
stealing men's souls. Kirby never took advantage of me by
playing for money. We played only for pleasure. Still, the
old preachments plagued me every time my fingers closed
upon the cards.

Kirby would laugh. "Anything is made a bit more pleasant for being just a little wicked."

Occasionally he liked to slip away to Stonehill. Al-
though he was a grown man and Thomas had no authority
to prevent him, Kirby usually waited until Thomas was
away from home for a day or two. He tried to get me to go
with him, but I declined the first couple of times. I had
vivid recollections of my rough experience in that town.
Finally, however, I succumbed to temptation, for the town
with its bustle and great activity was always an object of
curiosity. Most of the people who had frowned before had
forgotten my past associations. They seemed to remember
only that I was connected with the Canfields. This threw a
thin protective cloak over me.

I found that Thomas Canfield was not the only ambitious person in the Stonehill region. Branch Isom, the
freighter, had bought out a dramshop and operated it in addition to his line of wagons. He had built an extension onto
the back and set it up with gaming tables. These drew Kirby
Canfield as a bin of oats draws a frisky young horse. He
tried his luck there and more often than not found it good.
I was glad I had never played him for money.

Had he chosen to do so, I think he might have sustained himself by his proficiency with cards. But when I suggested the possibility, he said, "I play for diversion. If I ever depended on it for a living it would be pleasant no longer."

On our way home we rode by the little fenced cemetery on the slope above the ranch headquarters. Kirby dismounted and took off his hat while he stared at a headstone. "Papa was the only one who understood about me," he said, the fun suddenly gone from him. "I think he had a little of that streak in him too. If he hadn't, he might still be alive."

It was the first good chance I had had to ask, "What happened to him?"

"When things got too thick around here for him, he would occasionally ride over to Stonehill for a few drinks. It was a harmless thing, or should have been; he never did it very often. One night he just happened to get caught in the middle when a couple of teamsters started shooting at one another. Papa was the first man killed."

"The teamsters . . . did they die too?"

Kirby nodded. "One of them went down in the fight."

"And the other one?"

Kirby looked away. "Thomas found him."

We were struggling with our work oxen, breaking the hard ground for spring planting, the day the San Antonio priest came to us. His face was grave. He spoke good English, though his accent was heavy and I had to listen with care to understand him. He nodded to Kirby and me, but he seemed to sense on sight that Thomas was the man in charge.

"Are you aware," he asked Thomas, "of the desperate situation in New Silesia?"

I knew that was the name of the village the immigrants had built for themselves. Though it lay only about ten miles north, my work had never taken me there.

Thomas said, "I didn't know there *was* a situation."

"If you care for your fellow man," the priest told him, "you should go and see for yourself. Surely you can do something to help those poor people in their misery."

Thomas' face clouded. "Have you been to other places around here for help?"

"I just came from Stonehill. I find the town well named. The merchant Hines has pledged some help, but most of the others say let those people go back where they came from."

Thomas frowned. "Perhaps they should."

"They cannot. Nothing is left for them in the old country. They have not the means to move ten miles. They must stay."

I had seen slaves living in little more than chicken coops on some delta farms where owners took insufficient care of their property. But at their worst most of them fared better than the people we found as we rode into the immigrant village. The newest arrivals had come in the dead of winter and for shelter had been able to do little more than dig into the cold ground, covering the holes with a matting of thatched grass for a roof to try to see them through to spring. Some who had been there longer had built picket houses, copied after the style of Mexican *jacales,* but these with their mud chinking and brush roofs had been poor shelter against the elements.

Ragged children bunched before the miserable hovels, watching with wide and hungry eyes as we passed. It occurred to me that there were few dogs. Children without dogs were like coffee without sugar, or meat without salt. These families had nothing to feed to a dog. Adults crossed themselves as the priest passed them. Both men and women still wore the same odd clothing I had seen among the immigrants who had accompanied us from Indianola to Stonehill.

It was as if I had been picked up suddenly and transported to some strange land beyond the seas. I found it little wonder that people in Stonehill had nothing complimentary to say about this alien settlement. What we do not understand, we reject.

Thomas Canfield's face became like stone, grim and brooding. He looked carefully at each person he saw on the street. At length he asked the priest, "Where are the ones who came in last?"

"You have seen most of them. A few are out breaking their fields."

"There was one family . . . I don't know their names. They had a girl, sixteen or seventeen."

The priest considered. "The Brozeks, perhaps. They have a girl named Maria."

"Show me."

We rode almost to the end of the village. Thomas saw the girl before the rest of us did, and he straightened. She was sweeping the bare ground clean in front of a crude dugout, using a rough broom fashioned out of dried weeds tied to a mesquite branch. It seemed a futile thing to be sweeping bare ground, but it was at least an effort at cleanliness. It was an act of defiance.

Her eyes went right to Thomas and held there. The two stared at each other a minute, and Thomas took off his hat. "Hello" was all he said. She responded in words I did not know, in a voice almost too soft to hear. It struck me that she was thinner than on the trip from Indianola, and even then she had been barely large enough to cast a decent shadow.

Thomas said to the priest, "Tell her we are going to help. We don't have much except cattle, but we'll bring some of those. They'll have milk and meat."

The priest translated. The girl never took her eyes from Thomas more than a moment. She said something which the priest told us was simply "thank you."

As we rode away, Thomas turned in the saddle and looked back.

We gathered some of his cattle, which he had scattered

widely on the land he owned and upon unused land which lay between his tracts. He picked some recently calved cows which had udders swollen with milk. "They are wild, and they'll have to be tied, but they'll give milk for the children," he said. He picked some fleshy long-aged calves and yearlings, though after a hard winter none were really fat. It was a sacrifice of some dimensions, but he did not grieve over it. We drove about twenty beeves and as many cows into the stricken village.

There we found Linden Hines and his daughter Laura distributing flour and coffee, and some woolen bolt goods out of his mercantile store. Thomas tipped his hat to Laura, whose face glowed at the sight of him. Gravely he shook hands with Hines. "It's good to see you, sir. I knew you would be the only man in Stonehill with enough Christian charity to bring anything here."

Hines shook his gray head. "This isn't all mine. Branch Isom wouldn't want it talked about, but he contributed part of it."

Thomas blinked. He seemed somehow angered, somehow affronted. "Isom? What can he ever expect to get out of *this* place?"

The priest walked from the small crude building which passed for a church. He smiled as he came and thanked Thomas for being a man of his word. "You may have saved some poor children from dying, and others from becoming orphans."

Thomas looked for a place to pen the cattle. A couple of the Polander men hurried ahead of us, pointing and talking in their language until they reached a rough enclosure built of mesquite. They let down the crooked bars that served as a gate and helped haze the cattle in.

Most of the village people had gathered, all trying to talk to us at once. Laura Hines had followed along and stood at the edge of the crowd, saying nothing but watching Thomas with admiration. To me the talk was a babble, though the priest did not have to translate the gratitude, the smiles on haggard faces. He went through a ceremony which I surmised was some form of blessing on the gift of cattle.

The girl Maria was there with some younger brothers and sisters and her parents. I remembered them from the trip. She smiled at Thomas, and he smiled back.

I glanced at Laura Hines. She looked puzzled, her smile gone.

Thomas beckoned the priest. "Father, I want you to talk to this girl for me, please. Tell her that if it is all right with her, and with her father, I'd like to come here and call on her."

The priest showed misgivings. Clearly he thought Thomas was asking a price for the cattle. "These are a moral people," he said.

"If I had not thought so I would not have helped them. There are already more than enough of the other sort in this country."

"But you cannot even talk to her."

"We'll talk. You just ask her."

The priest spoke. The girl turned excitedly to her parents. I could see the question in the eyes of the older couple as they stared at Thomas. Perhaps they remembered the coldness they had seen in him as he waited for the wounded raider to talk or to die. But that had to be weighed against his sacrifice in bringing cattle here to feed the hungry. If this was the judgment they were making, the cattle won.

I suppose girls where she came from were trained to be reserved, and she tried. But her eyes, brown and big and pretty, sparkled with delight.

Thomas said to the priest, "I lose track of time when I am busy. What day is this?"

"Friday."

Thomas nodded. "Tell her I will be here Sunday."

I looked around for Laura Hines, but she was gone.

3

He was there that Sunday and almost every other for a long time. His one suit was tight on him because it had been made several years earlier, before hard work and maturity had muscled him. But few people there in those days kept up with styles. A tight suit or a threadbare one was better than no suit at all. Many people had none at all.

Thomas did not allow romance to spoil his penchant for hard work or for business. He did not *send* Kirby and me out to work, he *led* us, and usually he did more than either of us. Even with all his other responsibilities he managed to sell some farming implements, to keep the cash turning. Sometimes he willingly allowed profit opportunities to escape him, however. He distributed a number of plows and other tools among the Silesians with the understanding that they would pay when they were able. I was convinced he would never realize a dollar and would have to mark these in his blue-backed ledger as a gift, along with the cattle. I did not know at the time how dedicated these immigrants were both to hard work and to their own good word.

When the planting was done and the new calves branded and worked, we had a while when the home duties could be allowed to slacken. True, the fields would need to be cultivated to keep the emerging crops free of weeds, but Amadeo Fernandez's widow and two sons still lived on the place. The boys were big enough that together they did a man's work. Thomas said we could leave the cropland to them for a while. It was time to ride west and gather mustangs.

The thought set my heart to pounding. It had seemed adventuresome, far out in the future. But suddenly confronted with the fact of going, I realized with a chill that we would be venturing into Indian country. Kirby assured me with card-player confidence that the chances were two to one we would never see an Indian. I found myself looking with trepidation at the third chance.

Thomas told Kirby he was to stay to look after their mother and supervise the place. Kirby's face flushed with a touch of anger, but he said nothing. The Fernandez boys begged to go, but Thomas told them gently that they might do so the next time.

Mrs. Canfield cooked us a good breakfast before daylight of a Sunday morning, and we set out at daylight, each riding a good horse and leading another. We rode by New Silesia, for Maria would be expecting Thomas. She did not expect him so early, however, and he had to wait restlessly for her to come out of mass at the little church. I had not seen her since the day we had delivered the cattle. She had fleshed out a little, with color in her cheeks and a warm smile in her eyes. The smile was not for me, of course.

She had learned some random words of English. Thomas even spoke some words of Polish. At least I assumed that was what they were, because they did not have the sound of Spanish. It occurred to me, though I was inexperienced in that field, that romance can be an educational endeavor.

I tried to find something else to occupy my interest and give the couple privacy, but Thomas called me back before I strayed far. It does not take long to see all one wants of poverty.

In the limited vocabulary they had established between them, Thomas had made Maria understand he was going away for a while. She was tearful, but it was the way of her people that the man made the decisions and the woman quietly agreed; at least that was the way they made it appear.

When we left, Thomas kept looking back so long as the village was in sight. The girl stood there by herself, watching as long as there was anything to see.

We rode by a Mexican settlement somewhat farther west and picked up three Mexicans Thomas had known for years. They were good, dependable hands, he said, though given to extortion when it came to wages. They wanted fifty cents a day. He got them to agree to forty, and to furnish two horses apiece for the work.

Only two of them actually rode away with us. The third disappeared into the brush. Thomas seemed to have no concern, so I decided not to worry about it. That night, when we camped, that Mexican came into camp with a fourth man, a tall, bewhiskered countryman with one eye gone and the other fierce as a panther's. He shook hands with Thomas, stared at me with silent suspicion, ate a little supper and disappeared back into the brush.

Thomas let me simmer on my unasked questions awhile before he told me, "That's Bustamante. The law is interested in his whereabouts."

I did not doubt that. "What for?"

"Murder."

"And you'd take him with us?"

"He's one of the best mustang runners you'll ever see. Out yonder, there is no law."

That was a point which worried me.

Whatever preconceived notions I had had about adventure quickly faded in the bright sunlight of reality. Catching mustangs was mostly hard work and very little adventure. Thomas at one point remarked that the Indians did not often bother with the mustangs except to shoot them for meat. It was much easier to take broken horses from the settlements than to catch and break mustangs for themselves. After a few days I could see why.

A set of traps and corrals Thomas had built on previous excursions was still standing but in need of repair to be able to hold wild horses. The task involved more digging,

lifting and cutting than riding. An Indian battle would
have seemed a welcome relief from all that manual labor.
Once we finished repairing and extending the corrals, we
started hunting mustangs. My first reaction upon the initial
sighting was disappointment. They were small animals,
ungainly in appearance, their manes long and shaggy,
their tails bristling with burrs and almost dragging the
ground. But they were deceptively swift of movement, elu-
sive as jackrabbits. The chase had its moments of thrill and
hard spurring as we brought the wily horses down to the
wings and traps, but those moments were quickly over and
gone. Then the hard work started again.

I did not sleep much the first couple of nights, worrying
about Indians murdering us in our blankets. I did not like
Bustamante's looks either. I was glad we had no money with
us, for I was convinced he would have murdered us all for
a dollar and a half. At times, the look in his single eye
hinted he might even do it for nothing more than the pleasure. I quit worrying about the Indians before I quit worrying about Bustamante. I became convinced that if any
Comanches had come upon us and had seen what we were
doing, they would have left us alone. Thomas had said
Indians did not bother the insane.

Once we had caught a band of horses, Thomas would
pick out those he thought might have market value in the
settlements. We let the others go. For seed, he said. We then
set in to rough-break the good ones so we could take them
home without undue trouble. This involved, more than
anything, teaching them respect for rope and halter. It
was with the *reata,* a leather rope, that Bustamante showed
his greatest skill; I marveled at how he could judge distance
so well with one eye. He would catch a horse by its forefeet
and trip it, let it up and trip it again until it became educated to the power of the rope. After the horses had been
through enough of this bruising exercise, we placed make-
shift hackamores on them, tied them firmly to posts or trees,
and scared them into running against the end of the tie

rope, jerking them back or jerking them down until the hackamores had rubbed their heads raw. It seemed brutal, but it was a traditional Mexican system for teaching them that the rope was master, always to be obeyed.

We even rode some of them, or attempted to. The Mexicans were good at this, especially the fearless Bustamante, but I invariably hit the ground faster than I had left it. Thomas commented that I could ride little better than I could shoot and suggested that I quit trying. He did not want to take me home with a broken leg and lose my services altogether. I conceded the wisdom of his advice.

Exhaustion made me sleep well at night, but I remained watchful during the day. An Indian could not have gotten closer than a quarter mile without my seeing him. I gradually put aside most of my dread of the dark Bustamante, too, though I contrived whenever possible to keep Thomas between him and me. When we finally haltered our catch and tied each animal to a long lead rope for the trip home, I felt an odd mixture of both relief and regret that we had not seen a single Comanche. I thought how disappointing it would someday be to my grandchildren—if I ever had any. I decided I would do like most other garrulous old liars and make up a story to please them.

The Mexicans left us for their own homes. Bustamante disappeared into the brush as quietly as he had first come.

I expected Thomas to go first by New Silesia to see Maria, but he fooled me. He rode by the fields to see if they had been properly cultivated during our lengthy absence. He expressed pleasure in the hoe work done by the Fernandez boys, Juan and Marco. That pleasure faded when he found out Kirby was in Stonehill and had been for three days.

The little Mrs. Canfield rocked restlessly and knitted on some kind of black shawl on the breezy dog run of the double cabin. She said, "I tried to tell him he'd better stay away from town. Been a right smart of trouble."

Thomas stiffened. "What kind of trouble?"

"Fights between the wagon people and the cart people. Been some men killed on the trail and one or two in town. Government's got soldiers patrolling the trails now, guarding carts and wagons. A patrol was by here just yesterday, trailing some raiders who got away. They had burned up a good part of a cart train headed for San Antonio."

Thomas said, "That doesn't concern us."

"Might concern *you*," the old woman said, laying the knitting in her lap. "Didn't you send orders to Indianola for implements to be sent to Stonehill on Francisco Arroyo's carts?"

Thomas blinked in sudden concern. "I did."

"We heard Francisco got hit two days short of Stonehill. Lost three men and four carts. That's how come Kirby went to town, to find out how much of a loss you taken."

Thomas Canfield seldom wasted anything, including profanity. He employed a few choice words suited to the occasion and started toward town. He shouted back at me to take care of our mustangs.

Next morning I was in a corral with the horses we had captured when I saw two men coming in something of a hurry. I thought at first they were Thomas and Kirby, but they were strangers, or almost so. I had seen both in the Isom dramshop when I had been there with Kirby. They were rough fellows, the kind you do not normally associate with hard labor and honest endeavor. They stopped to water their horses, and they eyed our mustangs as if contemplating a trade. It occurred to me that they could make any trade they might decide upon, for my rifle was at the house. But they seemed to agree after some consultation that the horses they rode were more dependable than the wild ones in our corral. They proceeded in a northeasterly direction at a strong trot that could carry a man many a league between sunup and sundown.

Perhaps an hour later a number of horsemen approached from the same direction where I had first espied the two.

This time, for precaution, I hurried down to the cabin and fetched my rifle.

They were blue-uniformed government troops, with Thomas and Kirby riding at the lead. They came directly to the place where I stood, halfway between the log house and the pens. Thomas did the talking, what little was done.

"We are following two men."

I pointed out where they had gone.

An officer said, "We can take the trail from here, Mr. Canfield. You have been of more than enough service to us."

"I'll stay with you until the job is done," Thomas said sternly. His sharp eyes were on Kirby. "You'll stay here."

Kirby did not argue. His beard was four or five days long, and his eyes showed he had traveled in considerable discomfort. Kirby was ordinarily a jovial sort, but he watched darkly as Thomas led the soldiers northeastward.

He complained, "Thomas doesn't give me credit for anything."

I had no inclination to insert myself into an argument between the brothers, so I did not ask him what his trouble was. He told me anyway. "Thomas lost a good part of his shipment. I hung around town, drinking a lot less than I made out. I figured sooner or later I would hear something, and I did. If it hadn't been for me they wouldn't have known who to go after."

"Then those two raided the cart train?"

"They were in the bunch. A couple more put up a fight in town. The troopers blew their lights out for good."

Long shadows fell behind the soldiers and their mounts as they returned shortly before sundown. They led two very tired horses. Across the saddles, two men were tied belly down on the last horseback trip they would ever make.

Thomas watched somberly as the soldiers watered their weary animals. He said to the officer, "You and your men are more than welcome to camp anywhere that suits you.

We'll slaughter a fresh beef for you. You've done a hard day's work."

The lieutenant's shoulders were sagging. "I'd appreciate it, Mr. Canfield. There will be bad feelings in town. I had rather we face it in the daylight, when we can see everybody."

The two bodies were laid out in a shed. Thomas looked at them with no more compassion than if they had been wolves caught chasing calves. A fierceness was in his eyes.

In the morning he lent the soldiers a wagon, for the bodies had stiffened. The officer suggested that it might be just as well to bury them then and there. Thomas said coldly, "Let Stonehill bury its own. This place is for ours."

He had lost about half of his shipment. Losing those implements meant losing land he might have bought with the profits. By the time he forgave these men, if he ever did, the headboards on their graves would probably have rotted away.

Kirby suggested, "I'll follow the soldiers into Stonehill and see what happens."

Thomas' eyes were grim. "No. We'll all stay out of Stonehill. A town which caters to people like that can do without our patronage."

Kirby argued, "We have to have supplies of one kind and another. Stonehill's the only place to buy them."

Thomas nodded. "It doesn't have to be that way. New Silesia is no farther than Stonehill."

"It doesn't even have a store."

"It can have one. There are enough farmers and cattle people in the vicinity to make a store work if someone will finance it. I can get credit in San Antonio. I'll finance it."

That took me by surprise. I remembered his many lectures about the permanence of the land, about the vagaries of towns and retail business. But I realized the store in New Silesia would not be undertaken as a business venture; it was an instrument of revenge.

He rode to New Silesia that afternoon, telling me he

might not be back for a few days; he was going from there to San Antonio. He left orders for Kirby and me to keep working with the mustangs, gentling them for sale. It was a week before we saw him again.

The old storekeeper, Linden Hines, was there before Thomas returned. His daughter Laura was driving. I helped her down from the carriage, warming to the quick smile she gave me and the momentary chance to hold her hand. Her father said nothing beyond the fact that he wanted to talk to Thomas, but we could see in his pale eyes that he was troubled. He sat on the dog run, gossiping idly with Thomas' mother, who seemed joyed by the company. They talked of the hardships and the spiritual rewards of earlier times, but his gaze was always to the north, watching for Thomas. I tried to engage Laura in conversation, but her mind was not on me. She was helping her father watch.

When Thomas finally appeared, it was hard to tell whether the old man was cheered or depressed. In an odd way, he seemed both. There was no question, however, about Laura's reaction.

Thomas howdied and shook with Laura and her father. They talked in general circles before the gray-haired storekeeper came down to cases. "I heard you're going to open a store in New Silesia."

Thomas blinked in surprise. "News travels fast."

"I have friends in San Antonio." Hines frowned, looking off across the prairie. "It will hurt my store, of course. I had always regarded us as friends, Thomas."

Thomas studied him in regret. "This is not done with any malice toward you, Mr. Hines. We are friends. But we Canfields have no other friends in Stonehill. I would not grieve if I knew I would never have to set foot in that town again."

The old man nodded. "Then this is done against Stonehill, and not against me?"

"I have never had any wish to hurt you. Or Laura." He

glanced at the girl. There was nothing in his eyes to match what I saw in hers.

The old man asked, "What do you know of the store business, beyond selling farm implements?"

"Nothing." An idea seemed to strike Thomas, and he appeared in some danger of smiling. "I could use a partner who *does* know the business."

"Me?" The old man seemed intrigued by the notion for a moment. But he shook his head. "It would be disloyal to Stonehill. That town is like my own child."

"My parents had two children," Thomas pointed out.

"I could not divide my loyalties. I gave the first breath of life to that town. It has grown away from me, like an unruly son sowing wild oats, but it will outlast that. The wildness will pass."

"I doubt that, sir. There is a malady in it that has rooted too deep. It will never be yours again."

The storekeeper mused, looking at Thomas' mother. "Do you believe you or Kirby could ever do anything so bad that your mother could never forgive you, could never take you back and love you?" He shook his head. "Stonehill is my town."

"It will break your heart, Mr. Hines. Or kill you."

"Not Stonehill. It is my child." He dismissed further argument with a small wave of his hand. "You'll not want to spend your own time running your store, Thomas. I have a young man named Smithers; you've surely met him. There is not always enough for him to do in my place, and I have dreaded having to let him go."

"I would be pleased to have him."

So it was that Thomas Canfield branched out into yet another enterprise. For the next few weeks he spent the larger part of his time in New Silesia, supervising carpenters who put up a frame store building for him. Not all of his time was spent on business, evidently, for when the carpenters had finished the job in town he brought them to the ranch. He set them to building a new house. Thomas was not in the habit of volunteering much information, but in this case it was not necessary. We all knew who the house was for.

Kirby and I kept busy cultivating the crops or peddling mustangs to prospective buyers sent or brought by Thomas. When we had sold what he wanted to sell, Thomas surprised Kirby and me by giving us a bonus. I was not sure what to do with mine.

"Land, Mr. Sawyer," Thomas advised. "Whatever you save, put it into land."

I did. I bought a small piece of unimproved rangeland to the west of New Silesia, paying part in cash—all the cash I had—and signing a note for the rest. Because I had no cattle to turn loose on it, Thomas leased it from me and paid me enough that I was able to make payments to the San Antonio bank which carried the paper.

The night after becoming a landowner, I sewed a new patch atop an old patch on my britches and pondered the glories of wealth in land.

Mrs. Canfield had never met Maria. One Sunday morning Thomas took a wagon to New Silesia and brought Maria back to show her how well the carpenters were doing. He made official what we had known for a long time, that he and Maria would marry when the house was finished. I had worried over what Mrs. Canfield would think of Maria in view of the fact that they could not talk much to each other. The two women fell into each other's arms, and my worry evaporated like spilled water in the summer sun. I was amazed by how much English Maria had learned since the last time I had seen her.

Though we had much work to do, Kirby became restless. We played cards some nights, for matches rather than for money, and he usually won though his heart was not in the game. In his hands a card seemed to turn magically into whatever he wanted it to be. I was little challenge. He tried to teach the Fernandez boys, but they were too young and no challenge at all. He would even have played against

Mrs. Canfield, if she would have stood for it, but like my own parents she remained convinced that playing cards were the antithesis of holy Scripture. Whenever she found a deck of cards they went into the blazing cookstove. Fire, she declared, was the proper element for Satan and his instruments.

The wedding was performed in the little church in New Silesia. Most of the Polander people were there. Not all of them could get into the church, but those who couldn't stood outside and listened through the open windows. I was inside but had just as well have been outside for all I understood of the service. The only part I was sure of was when the priest said Thomas and Maria were man and wife.

The only people who came over from Stonehill were Linden Hines and his daughter Laura. She tried hard to keep smiling, but this was more like a funeral to her than an occasion of joy. Kirby stood beside her and held her arm, which I wanted to do but lacked the nerve. That didn't help her.

A broad grin was spread across Thomas' face as he walked out of the church with his new bride on his arm. I had never seen that look on him before, and I never saw it again.

Times had improved some for the Polanders. A wedding was a festive occasion, celebrated by everybody in town, with more food than an army could eat, and more than a little of spirituous liquors, these mostly furnished by Thomas, who ordinarily would not have approved much more than his mother would. A big dance was set for the wedding night. I looked forward to it because I thought finally I would have a suitable opportunity to put my arms around Laura Hines. But when the music started and I looked around for her, she was gone.

Thomas never did anything haphazardly. He even timed the wedding so he would not miss anything important at home while he took Maria for her first trip to San Antonio.

The crops were fairly well laid by, and it was too early to brand the new calves; screwworms would have eaten them alive. It should have been the best possible time to have taken a long trip. It would have been, except for Kirby.

I figured out very soon that he had been waiting for Thomas to get so far out of reach that Kirby could do whatever he wanted. He stayed just long enough to wave the newlywed couple on their way, then saddled his horse.

"You take Mother home, Reed," he told me. "I'm going to go find some card players who can keep me from going to sleep in the middle of a game."

I tried to argue him out of it. I told him Thomas wouldn't like it, a point I probably should have kept to myself. It seemed only to urge him on. He didn't say he was going to Stonehill, but that was obvious. He rode off in Stonehill's direction, new suit and fresh shave and all, while I walked along after him, futilely throwing out every argument I could think of. He spurred into an easy lope and left me talking to myself.

His mother wanted to know where he was going. I evaded any direct answer, but she knew anyway; I could tell by the set of her jaw. As we rode along in the wagon together I saw tears come into her eyes. She said, "I used to look forward to the day when my sons were grown, so I would never have to worry about them anymore."

That night I sat down by lamplight and wrote a letter to my own mother in Louisiana, the first one in many months.

I thought Kirby might come back that night, but he was not there for breakfast. Mrs. Canfield said nothing, not about Kirby or anything else. She was normally a fair to middling talker, and I expected her to relive the whole wedding over the breakfast table, but the only time she spoke was to ask me if I wanted more coffee. I didn't; I wanted to get out of that cabin as quickly as I could.

I rode among the cattle all day, looking for screwworm cases. Marco, the older of the Fernandez boys, was with me so we could rope and throw cattle as a team and doctor them where we found them. Juan, the younger, remained in the fields, hoeing out the careless weeds. When I rode up to the shed late in the afternoon, I saw that Kirby's saddle was still not on its rack.

Mrs. Canfield met me at the door, her face uneasy. "Reed, I hate to ask you to ride into Stonehill alone, but I wish you'd go see if you can fetch Kirby home. The devil has many allies in that place."

I ate a hurried supper, then saddled a fresh horse, a young bay named Stepper that Thomas had kept out of that set of mustangs. Almost as an afterthought I shoved a big pistol into my boottop. It was a useless gesture; I probably would never have pulled it. But it gave me a feeling of some security, rubbing a blister on my leg.

Just before dark I began to make out a movement on the town road ahead of me. It was a carriage of some kind, flanked by a couple of riders. For no good reason I could think of, my uneasiness increased. I put the bay mustang into a long trot, which it resisted, almost pitching me.

Linden Hines and his daughter Laura were in the carriage, a couple of Mexicans riding horseback beside them. A wagon followed fifty yards or so behind.

One look at the Hineses' solemn faces told me my uneasiness had been fully justified. Laura began to weep. Her father said evenly, "We are bringing Kirby Canfield home."

I looked back at the wagon, the heart dropping out of me.

The old man's voice went lower. "He was shot down in a gaming place in Stonehill."

I took a grip on the big horn of the Mexican saddle I rode. When the shock had passed a little I asked him who did it.

"A tough named Johnroe. I am told there was some disagreement over cards."

I knew before I asked him. "The gaming place . . . was it Branch Isom's?"

He nodded, seeming a little surprised at my guess. "But Isom had nothing to do with it," he said. "In fact, he was in my store when we heard the shots. Laura can tell you. She was there."

The girl nodded, but she did not look at me.

Convenient, I thought. How could Isom better take out his revenge on Thomas Canfield—a man he was afraid of—than to have someone kill his brother, with Branch Isom himself in the clear?

I had gone out into Indian country and helped hunt mustangs, but I knew this thing was beyond my courage. "You-all going to tell Kirby's mother?"

Hines nodded sorrowfully. "All the way from town I have been trying to decide what to say. The Canfields have been among the best friends I ever had. But my town has cost them dearly."

Laura Hines looked up. "I'll tell her."

I think Mrs. Canfield sensed it before we quite got there. She stood in the dog run, watching the carriage and the wagon. The fact that I was with them told her Kirby was too. Without a word, she just looked at us, and died a little. She never shed a tear, at least where I could see it. Whatever crying she did, she held until Laura had gone into the cabin with her.

Laura came back outside, looking for me. She had been crying, whether Mrs. Canfield had nor not. "Reed, you'll have to go to San Antonio. Thomas has to know."

The trail to San Antonio was an old one, cut by wagons and carts past any counting. I had no trouble staying with it through the long, dark night. My horse gave out toward daylight. I stopped at a stagecoach stand and talked the people into lending me a fresh one. They weren't going to do it until I mentioned Thomas Canfield. They seemed more than willing then, and genuinely distressed when I explained my mission.

Thomas and Maria had a room in the Menger Hotel, Mrs. Canfield had told Laura. Though I had never been in San Antonio, it was no trouble to find the place. As was the custom in old Mexican towns, all roads led to the center like a wagon spoke leads to the hub. The Menger stood with a squared-off German elegance next to the ruins of the Alamo. Commerce moved up and down that street as if nothing had ever happened there. Hardly anybody seemed to look at that shell-marked old mission except me, and for a minute or two I could look at nothing else, remembering the stories I had heard of the good men who had died fighting there. It seemed somehow sacrilegious that the U.S. Army was using the blood-bought building for a quartermaster depot. But I turned away from the Alamo, for that trouble had been more than twenty years in the past, and my problem was *now*. I made my way around several spans of Mexican burros that struggled to pull a wagonload of heavy freight, and I tied the borrowed horse at the rail in front of the hotel. I dusted myself the best I could with my hat, for the Menger was a place that bespoke gentility. I entered the little lobby, pausing to look up in awe at the balconies that towered high above the ground floor. Even New Orleans could have nothing better or taller than this.

The man at the desk betrayed a touch of German accent when he asked what service he could render me. I told him I had to see Thomas Canfield.

"Mr. Canfield and his lady, they went upon the city out."

"I have to see him," I said. "I have a death message for him."

That got the clerk's full attention, but it did not help me find Thomas. "I wish to help, sir," he apologized, "but I know not where to tell you to seek. Best perhaps you sit here and wait."

The smell of food from the kitchen reminded me I had not eaten. It was coming on noon, but I went into the dining room and asked for breakfast. I sat so I could watch the front door. I put away some ham and three or four eggs, then went back into the lobby and took a soft chair where I could see who came and went. My intentions were good, but the flesh was weak after a night's ride. I drifted off to sleep within minutes after I sat down.

A strong hand shook my shoulder and startled me awake. "Reed Sawyer! What is wrong at home?"

It took me a moment to realize where I was. I stared up into the worried eyes of Thomas Canfield, and beyond him, Maria. There was no easy way to tell him. "Kirby was shot in Stonehill. He's dead."

Maria choked off a cry. Thomas made no sound. I don't think he even blinked. His eyes went fierce, like the night he watched the raider die. "Was it Branch Isom?" he demanded.

"No," I told him quickly, trying to head off that line of thought because I feared he would ride straight to Stonehill and kill Isom, or try. "Mr. Hines said Isom wasn't there. It was somebody named Johnroe."

Thomas seemed to stare right through me. "I know Johnroe. His hand moves as Isom directs it. I suppose the law has done nothing."

"I don't know. I came straight to you." But I knew within reason, just as Thomas did. The law had done nothing and would not.

Thomas gritted, "Something *will* be done." He turned to Maria, softening a little. He gently rubbed away a tear that ran down her cheek. "I am sorry, little girl. We have to go."

She put her head against his chest. "I am sorry also."

Thomas looked back at me. "Is anyone with my mother?"

"Laura Hines. She and her father brought Kirby home."

He nodded. "Laura. Whenever help is needed, she's always there."

It was almost on my tongue to ask him if he did not know why. I caught myself.

It was a fast but silent trip, and I slept a good part of it. Thomas wore out several teams, changing them along the way with people he knew, like those at the stage stop. I don't believe he spoke twenty words beyond what was necessary. Maria sat beside him, but as he had always been and always would be in times of stress, Thomas seemed somehow completely alone, drawn up within himself like some brooding, secret spirit out of another time and another life. That Maria accepted this without protest was a source of wonder to me, but I supposed all things here seemed mysterious to her compared to that far-off country she had come from.

Thomas' determined pace brought us to the Canfield place in the early hours of the night, the last set of horses dripping sweat. He pulled up in front of the double cabin. Linden Hines arose from a rocking chair on the dog run and walked out to meet us. He gave Maria a hand down from the carriage.

Thomas demanded, "How is my mother?"

"Laura finally got her to bed. It has been a long day."

Thomas put a hand on the old storekeeper's shoulder. "For all of us." We quietly went inside, where Laura arose from her chair beside Mrs. Canfield's bed. She tiptoed to us, putting a finger on her lips, but it did no good. Mrs. Canfield called, "Is that you, Thomas?"

"I'm here," he told her.

The rest of us went back outside, leaving them alone. Maria stood uncertainly in the doorway, trying to decide if she belonged in there with her husband, finally coming out with us. She and Laura stood on the dog run, looking at one another. It was an awkward moment for me, knowing how both women felt about that man beyond the door, knowing both had cause to hate each other. But Maria reached out and touched Laura's hand.

"You do good thing, Laura. You are good friend."

Laura's voice broke. "I have always been a friend to the Canfields, all the Canfields. You're a Canfield now."

"Always, you be *my* friend."

If I had any doubts, the funeral at the ranch showed me how many friends the Canfields really had. Ranchers and farmers from a wide area came out, along with a goodly part of the Polander community, many of them afoot. I saw few people from Stonehill, other than Linden and Laura

Hines, and quite a few of the Mexican oxcart freighters the Canfields had done business with. It struck me as never before how many of the Mexican people were friends of Thomas Canfield. The mustang hunters were there, except Bustamante, and many others I could not remember seeing before. It came to me that the Canfield family had settled here when most of the other people *were* Mexicans. Somehow they had avoided the enmity that beset so many later settlers.

One official representative of Stonehill *was* on hand. The county sheriff and one of his deputies stood at the edge of the crowd, saying nothing but watching everybody, most of all watching Thomas. Thomas was aware of them, but he made no move in their direction or they in his until the services were over, the coffin had been lowered and earth was being shoveled into the grave. Maria was saying something about it was wrong to bury people here; this was not consecrated ground. But Thomas seemed not to hear her. He stood with his mother and Maria, solemnly accepting the condolences of the visitors as they filed by. When all were finished and most had started home, I noticed that many of the Mexicans were staying, huddling to one side. It came to me that every one of them was armed.

Instinctively I knew they were waiting for a signal from Thomas. To them this was another incident in the cart war. True, it had happened to a *gringo,* but the *gringo* had been their friend. Indirectly, in their view, he had died for them.

The sheriff sensed it too. His face was taut; he dreaded having to talk with Thomas. But he could delay it no longer. With hat in hand he spoke his condolences to Mrs. Canfield, then to Thomas. He jerked his head sideways. "Thomas, I wish you'd step out here a ways. We got some talking to do."

Thomas looked at his wife. "Maria, would you please take Mother back to the house?"

Both women looked apprehensively at Thomas, but he assured them there was no trouble. They started reluctantly,

Laura Hines moving in supportively to take Mrs. Canfield's right arm. Thomas watched them go, then turned to the sheriff and the deputy.

"My brother was killed the day before yesterday, Sheriff. What has been done?"

"I've investigated the incident thoroughly. I've talked to all the witnesses."

"Do you have Johnroe in jail?"

"No, the gentleman left the county immediately after the shooting."

"Then you should be after him."

"There is no case against him. All the witnesses told me your brother accused him of cheating at cards, then drew a pistol. They told me Johnroe fired in self-defense."

"Did my brother fire at him?"

The sheriff hesitated. "There was only one shot. Your brother had been drinking. He was slow."

"Not that slow. Your witnesses lie, Sheriff. You know that."

"I do *not* know that."

"You know the whole thing was deliberately planned. You know Branch Isom was behind it."

"Mr. Isom was not even present. Your friend Linden Hines will tell you that, if he hasn't already."

"He told me. Isom used him. He knows it, and I know it, and you know it."

"Mr. Isom is as upset over this as any of us. He wants no trouble, and I want no trouble."

"If you don't do something about Johnroe, I will."

"You'll not find him in Stonehill. I don't want you coming there looking for him, and perhaps getting someone else killed in the process. I don't want trouble with you"—he looked past Thomas at the cluster of waiting Mexicans—"and I don't want trouble with your friends."

"Do I have your word that Johnroe is not in Stonehill?"

"You have. And if he ever shows up there again I'll arrest him. For his own safekeeping."

Thomas had that look in his eyes. "Then you had better find him before I do."

The sheriff blustered, but he could not hold his ground against that hard stare. When he looked down, Thomas turned his back on him. The sheriff appeared to have something more to say but saw the futility of it. He nodded at his deputy, and they mounted their horses. Thomas did not look in the men's direction, but he was listening to the fading sound of the hoofs. After a bit he walked slowly toward the Mexicans. He addressed them in Spanish. I had learned enough to follow a little of it. He thanked them for their sympathy. Past that, the conversation turned from difficult to impossible for me. I heard the name "Johnroe" two or three times, and "Bustamante" once. At first I thought Thomas might be planning to lead them into Stonehill and take the town apart; he was capable of it. But presently the Mexicans dispersed, riding off in the several directions from which they had come.

Life on the ranch settled down to something of routine again, somewhat quieter and grimmer. Thomas was living in his new house with Maria, so I saw less of him than before. When I did see him, he had little to say beyond whatever was necessary to the work at hand. His face had seldom been host to a smile even before Kirby's death. He probably smiled when he and Maria were alone in that house, but I never saw it. His eyes had a steely look that indicated his mind was elsewhere. We took care of the fields and worked the cattle and did what we could to doctor the screwworm cases, but all the time in his mind he was killing Johnroe.

As winter came on, Maria showed signs of gaining weight. She had been so thin that I thought the weight became her. It took a while for me to realize there was more to it than just having food enough. Thomas was busier than ever, partly because of the store in New Silesia. At first he took Maria with him when he had to make a trip to San Antonio, but as she became heavier and nearer to her term, she stayed at home. After supper, when he was away, she would come down to the old cabin and sit in a rocking chair beside Mrs. Canfield on the dog run, the two women waiting together for Thomas to come home. Nights when he didn't, Mrs. Canfield would go up to the new house and sleep where she could be near Maria. A couple of times she sent for Mrs. Fernandez with considerable agitation, but nothing happened.

After the second time, Thomas decided to defer all other business trips until the baby was safely "on the ground." He would ride out during the day, but always he was home before dark. Nobody told me anything, but I sensed that the time of delivery was at hand.

The mesquites were putting on their first new leaves, pale green and so thin they seemed transparent. The nights were still cool, but the days were warming enough that it would not be long until time to put corn and cotton into the ground. Maria was so heavy I wondered if she might not be going beyond her normal term.

One morning before daylight I went out to rustle horses and saw a blanket-wrapped form on the ground, near a mesquite-pole corral. As I approached the blanket was suddenly flung aside, and I was looking into the muzzle of a huge pistol. My heart leaped as I recognized the evil eye staring at me over the barrel.

Bustamante.

He recognized me and lowered the pistol. *"El patrón,"* he said. He had come to see Thomas.

I indicated that Thomas was up at the new house, but Bustamante insisted that I bring him down to the corrals.

Thomas came irritably to the door when I knocked, asking me if I didn't know Maria needed her sleep. But his attitude changed to excitement when I told him Bustamante was waiting. He disappeared for only a moment, coming back fully dressed, pulling the long ears of his left boot. He strode briskly ahead of me. I did not see Bustamante until the tall Mexican stepped out from the shadow of a fence. The sight of him was like ice pressed against my chest.

Thomas motioned for me to stop, not to come any closer. I watched them from twenty or thirty paces, catching the tone of an intense conversation but none of the words. At last Bustamante reached inside his shirt and brought forth a leather pouch, hanging around his neck on a string. Thomas loosened the puckerstring and looked into the pouch. He nodded in satisfaction and dropped the pouch on the ground. He brought a handful of coins from his pocket and placed them in Bustamante's outstretched hand.

The men silently shook. Bustamante mounted a long-legged black horse that bore Thomas' brand and loped away, disappearing quickly into the brush.

Thomas leaned down and recovered the pouch from the ground. When he turned I saw a smile, a cold one and mean. He seemed to have forgotten about me, for he was startled to see me standing there.

"Go on about your business, Reed," he said.

I caught up my horse and set out to bring in the mounts for the day's work. As I rode away I saw Thomas at some distance beyond the barn, a shovel in his hand. While I watched, he dug a hole and dropped the pouch into it.

A week later, word drifted down to us from San Antonio that the gambler Johnroe had been killed there. Four days after his arrival, a tall, ugly, one-eyed Mexican had suddenly confronted him on a sidewalk and plunged a knife into him to the hilt. While the man lay dying, the Mexican coldly cut off both of his ears, mounted a black horse and rode away.

Very mysterious, people said. It was probably over a gambling loss.

The news seemed to affect Thomas not at all. Maria had just presented him a son.

He named the boy Kirby.

4

Because we lived and worked a long way from the largest towns, we let the war slip up on us. We knew, of course, that sectional bitterness had built for years, but mostly we looked on it as a quarrel between the Southern people who owned slaves and the Northern people who wished they did but couldn't. Not many folks down in our part of South Texas had slaves, either; they were too poor for that kind of luxury. So long as the Yankees stayed out of our country and left us alone, we didn't do much except clench our fists a little when we read an occasional angry newspaper editorial. We went right back to our own personal concerns as to whether it would rain, and whether the corn was going to make, and what kind of calf crop would hit the ground. All else was talk, and talk was a surplus commodity without a market.

But war did come, and a lot of us let ourselves get swept up in the emotion of it. We did foolish things, like volunteer for the Texas companies that were joining the Confederate army.

Thomas seemed immune to that kind of emotion. His was reserved for whoever and whatever belonged to him. A war way off in Virginia was too far from his land to be of deep concern to him. He grieved over the thought of all the suffering, all the wreckage that came out of the first fighting, but he did not anger. He told me it was a long way from Texas, and he saw no reason it should ever affect us.

Even Thomas Canfield could be wrong.

Peace, of a sort, had settled over us. The cart war had ground itself to a standstill. The Texas Rangers and the federal troops—before the bigger war pulled them away—stomped hard on some participants. A few of the worst men on both sides found themselves invited to a quick, quiet hanging, which got everybody else's attention. Most people involved in the feud decided they did not hate each other enough to risk that kind of rough justice.

I half expected the Rangers to fall on Thomas for what had happened to Johnroe. Talk spread around Stonehill that he was somehow responsible. But the lawmen seemed to figure that the killing of Johnroe by some unknown Mexican probably saved them the trouble of a hanging, sooner or later. Or, perhaps they were simply afraid of Thomas. A lot of people were, by then.

I thought Branch Isom might find some way to continue the trouble at no danger to himself, but he did not. Though I took pains to stay out of Stonehill, I heard enough talk to keep up with what went on there. Some of the Mexicans said Isom had fetched himself a bride from San Antonio. He was building a house in Stonehill larger than the one Thomas had built on the ranch for Maria. I figured this was a show of rivalry, but I never mentioned it to Thomas. Nothing brought anger to his eyes like hearing the name of Branch Isom.

The anger came often enough to its own bidding; I did not like to be the one who drew it forth. I much preferred Thomas' company when he sat on the edge of his porch, watching his son take his first faltering steps in the yard, falling over an affectionate pup one of the Fernandez boys had brought to him. Thomas rarely laughed, even with the baby, but the deepening lines in his face would seem to ease, and he would look—for a little while—as young as he really was. He would sit in silence with Maria's loving arm around him and watch that little boy with a feeling akin to worship.

Thomas had stayed out of the cart war except when his

own property was involved, and he was determined to remain out of the Confederacy's war too. He said little about it, but he leaned toward the views of old Sam Houston, who tried desperately to keep Texas from seceding and, when it did anyway, retired to his home down in Huntsville to live out his days without ever endorsing the Confederacy.

I tried to see it Thomas' way, but too many things kept pulling at me. I received a letter from home telling me a couple of my brothers had marched out to fight for Jeff Davis. I saw quite a few younger men from around Stonehill and New Silesia do the same thing, laughing and hollering and promising to be home in six months. They could not all be wrong, no matter what Thomas said.

The Polanders avoided being caught up in the war much. They had been in the country too short a time to understand what the fighting was about—if any of us did—and most of them did not know much English. The army recruiters quickly decided they were too dumb to be of much use. The Confederates were so confident about whipping the Yankees in a hurry that they did not want to share the glory with a bunch of foreigners anyway. They saved that honor for the true Southern boys.

My conscience nagged me as more and more men went to war while I stayed home on the ranch. Finally I received a letter telling me one of my brothers had taken down with the fever and died on the way to the fighting. Though he had not reached the battle, my mother considered him a patriot, a martyr to his country. She said nothing about me picking up my brother's sword. I got that idea all by myself. When a cowboy named Bill Eskew announced that he was going to San Antonio to join the war, I decided to go with him.

Thomas took the news with a deep frown. "It's not our fight."

"It's mine," I told him. "I've lost a brother."

"You never could shoot straight. What use will you be?"

But he dropped the argument when he saw I had made

up my mind. He shook my hand and told me I would always have a place with him when I came back. Maria—by now beginning to push out in front again—kissed me on the cheek. The old lady Canfield hugged my neck and wet the side of my face with her tears. I tried not to look back as I rode away, but I couldn't help it. Until we passed over the hill, Bill and me, I spent most of my time twisted around in the saddle, trying to fix it all in my mind as if I might not ever see it again.

I almost didn't.

We halfway expected to be wined and dined and have a lot of fuss made over us in San Antonio, but the "new" had worn off by that time. They had already seen a lot of men march away, some west to invade New Mexico and Arizona, the rest east to join up with the main Confederate forces off in Virginia and such. Nobody paid much attention to us or bought us any drinks, and the officers didn't treat us as respectfully as the recruiters had led us to believe. They handled us a lot like we used to treat fresh-caught broncs in teaching them to respect the rope and follow directions. I was considerably disappointed with the war before I ever saw any of it.

I was even more disappointed when I *did* see it. I had seen blood spilled in Texas, but this was not the same. We didn't hear the bands play much. Bill Eskew got shot in the stomach the second battle we got into, and I had to watch him take two days in dying.

There is no point in going on with a lot of detail about my years in the army. Like Thomas had kept saying, it was a long way from Texas and had nothing to do with the Canfields. I got nicked a couple of times, but never anything serious until the last year of the war. A rifle ball struck me in the hip and knocked me off of my horse. When I came back to consciousness I found Yankee soldiers running around me afoot, going the way I had come from. They were too busy to stop either to finish me off or to patch my wound. First time I got the chance I dragged myself into some bushes on my belly and hid. I soaked up most of my coat trying to get the blood stopped. I lay there until almost dark before the Yankees passed me again going the other way, and some good Reb boys came along in pursuit.

My hip was a long time healing. They furloughed me home to Louisiana. That way I was a burden to my family instead of to the Confederacy, which already had more burden than it could carry. The war was over before the healing was. Hobbling around on crutches, not able to do any respectable work except patch harness and such, I watched the straggling remnants of a beaten army come limping home a few men at a time. I watched the grief of families who finally had to admit that some of their own had simply disappeared and would never come home. Another of my brothers was one of these. My mother went to her grave wondering what had become of him. None of us ever knew.

There came a time when I could ride a horse. It wasn't easy, not like before, and it never would be quite the same again, but I knew I could at least take care of myself and put up a showing of respectable work. I had been thinking of Texas for a long time. After the many years away, the delta was no longer my home. When my grieving old mother breathed her last and we put her under the deep black soil, nothing was left to hold me. I made my way downriver to New Orleans like before and found a freighter about to set sail for the Texas coast. The captain had seen more than enough of crippled, hungry ex-soldiers, but he decided I could earn a bunk helping the cook. I spent most of that voyage in a hot, steaming galley. But it was worth it all to see old Indianola materialize through the early-morning fog. The town had grown since I had seen it that other time, but I had no difficulty finding the place where I had slept beneath the wharf while awaiting passage inland.

The wharves were sagging beneath the weight of cotton bales consigned to hungry mills back East, and the ships were unloading machinery and other goods for which Texas had starved during the long war and the blockade that had strangled its ports. Nobody in Texas had much solid Union coin, but they bartered cotton and tobacco and corn.

As before, I was dependent upon the generosity of people I had never seen before. Like most Confederate soldiers I had been paid little, and that in a currency no longer worth the paper it was printed on. The ship's captain gave me a few dollars for my labor, barely enough to buy a few days' meals and lodging ashore. My heavy limp and the cane I leaned upon made me a poor candidate for employment in a place where many able-bodied men hunted desperately for work. But I owned a little land near New Silesia, and I had Thomas Canfield's old promise of a job.

As before, I began looking for a freight outfit that might take me inland. I saw a line of big, heavy freight wagons near a wharf and made my way hopefully in their direction. I walked up to a man who appeared to be in charge of loading and asked where his wagons were bound. He looked me over carefully before answering. He probably guessed my situation without being told; a lot of others like me were making their way to an old home or looking for a new one.

"San Antonio," he said.

"By way of Stonehill or New Silesia?" I asked hopefully.

He frowned. "I don't remember you from Stonehill, and you don't talk none like them damned Polanders."

"I've been gone a long time," I told him.

A heavy voice spoke behind me. "I heard you mention Stonehill."

I turned and almost fell. There, staring me in the face, was Branch Isom. He carried more weight than when I had last seen him, the red beard was gone, and the lines were cut deeper into that ruddy face. But there was no mistaking the man. My hand tightened instinctively on the cane, and my first thought was that I would have to fight in another minute.

Recognition came much slower to him. I had aged a lot, thinned a lot. But after a long moment he said, "You're Reed Sawyer."

I could only nod, waiting for the trouble to come. An angry thought flashed through my mind, that I had outlived the war only to come back here and, more than likely, end my days on the wharf at Indianola.

To my surprise he showed no enmity, no grudge over old battles. If anything, he betrayed a touch of regret. He said, "The war was not kind to you."

"Kinder than to some," I told him. "At least I'm here."

"And looking for a ride home?"

If he had forgotten our first meeting, I had not. My first treatment at his hands was something I would remember to my last day. I said, "You needn't bother about me. I'll find one." I started to turn away.

He touched my shoulder and stopped me. "We'll be rolling in a couple of hours. I'll be glad to have the company of an old friend."

"We never were friends, Branch Isom," I said.

"That was a long time ago. Things have changed. You're a soldier home from the war. I've tried to bury old enmities."

You've buried a lot of old enemies, too, I thought, but I had the judgment not to say it.

I had no wish to travel with Branch Isom, so I made a couple of excuses and worked my way down into the town, hoping I might find someone else going my way. Luck was not with me. In a couple of hours I saw the wagons moving out in a line and resigned myself to a long stay in the coast town. But a light carriage drawn by a couple of nicely matched bays came down the street. Branch Isom waved to me and pulled the horses to a stop. "Ready to travel, Sawyer?"

I had no more excuses. I had been prepared to argue that a long ride on a heavy freight wagon would probably jolt my knitting hip too much, but I could see he meant for me to ride in the carriage with him. I put old hatreds behind me in the stresses of the moment and joined the devil.

He put the bays out in front of the wagons so we would not have to eat the dust, then slowed them to a walk that would not outpace the train behind us. He wore a good suit, better than any I had seen during my short stay in Indianola. The carriage, though not new, was a symbol of some prosperity. Prosperity, I knew, had long been a stranger to most people in Texas. My first thought, a natural one in view of past history, was that he had stolen it. But again I had the judgment not to ask.

He did most of the talking. He inquired about my war experiences, and I told him in a sketchy way. I had a hundred questions I desperately wanted to ask him, but most were about the Canfields. I could not believe enough time had passed that they would be a welcome subject for him. Perhaps sensing my curiosity about his relative well-being, he volunteered to me that freighting had made him a lot of money during the war. The Union blockade had closed the Texas ports within the first months. Cotton, always one of Texas' most important money crops, had stacked up by the thousands of bales, shut out of its traditional markets. But Texan ingenuity had not allowed this condition to become permanent. Soon the bales were on their way to the Mexican border in long, dust-raising wagon trains. Carried across the border, they were sold to European buyers for gold coin or traded outright for munitions and other Confederate needs. Union ships had no authority to prevent the shipment of merchandise in and out of Mexican ports. The great wagon trains wore deep ruts into the trail to Brownsville and Matamoros. Not only had Branch Isom joined his wagons into this trade, but he had bought many more and expanded.

Isom told me, "We put a lot of cotton across that river and brought back a lot of guns and powder and equipment for you boys fighting the war. We did all we could, but I guess it wasn't enough."

ELMER KELTON

It appeared to me it had been enough for *him*. Indirectly he told me as much. "I always took my payment on the Mexican side, in gold. I never did trust that paper money. People who did, like old Linden Hines, they're broke now."

"Linden Hines, broke?" That news hit me hard. Stonehill had been his town; he had started it.

"Lost his store, the freight wagons that used to haul goods for him, everything. Had a barrelful of that Richmond money when the war was over. It's not fit for wallpaper."

That hurt. I had always had a good feeling about that old man. "What does he do now?"

"Lives in the past, mostly. His daughter keeps books for me. I try to find the old man some things to do. Isn't much he *can* do, though. His health broke toward the end of the war, when he saw he was going to lose everything."

Suspiciously I asked, "Who got it?"

"First one and then another. San Antonio banks, mostly. He borrowed to keep the wagon outfits supplied, trying to help with the war. They lent paper but wanted gold back. I finally bought his store from him, but the money went to satisfy the banks."

"It's not fair if he did it all to help his country."

"Nothing is fair in this life. A man takes care of himself. Like your friend Thomas Canfield. He pulled into his hole like a badger and didn't give anything away."

That gave me the chance to ask what I had wanted to.

"He's all right? His family's all right?" I had received a few letters from Thomas' mother, early. Mail had a hard time finding me later on.

Isom's voice hardened. "Sure he's all right. Anything he ever owned, he still owns. Land-poor, maybe, without a dollar of real money to his name, but he'd eat jackrabbits before he'd borrow a dollar on one foot of that land." Isom grunted. "He can keep his land as far as I'm concerned. Give me a going business anytime, like mine . . . the town, the freight line. That's where the money is."

"Last I heard, a long time ago, Thomas and Maria had a baby girl."

Isom nodded. "She'd be three now, or maybe four. She was born after my little boy came."

I don't know why I should have been surprised at the thought of Branch Isom having children. The meanest dog can sire a litter of pups. But the thought of him bouncing a child on his knee didn't fit the image I had always carried in my mind. It was even more of a surprise, then, that he set in to telling me all about his boy. His name was James, and he was four. He could ride horseback by himself, and he could name most of the horses and mules in half of Isom's many freight teams. Once started, Isom seemed unable to stop talking about him. Somewhere in the conversation he told me Mrs. Isom had never been able to have another child. I suppose that was why Isom seemed to put so much store in this one, because there would not be another.

I kept expecting, sooner or later, that old grudges would surface in Isom's conversation, that he would turn his anger against me on the trail where nobody but his own men would see or know. But he never did. It was as though the old differences had never existed. In the few words he spoke of Thomas, I knew the angers of the past had not died, but for me personally he betrayed no resentment. Perhaps he took my army service into account, or my crippled hip, and he wiped the slate clean. All the way to Stonehill I remained uneasy, expecting trouble. It never came.

The town looked little different. Some new houses had been built. The streets were moderately busy, mostly with freight wagons engaged in the gradual renewal of normal commerce. I noticed a fair number of Mexican carts, holding their own against the *gringo* freighters. Isom seemed not even to see them. He pulled the carriage to a halt at his open double gates and watched his freight wagons enter a huge corral, all but the last one in the line. He signaled for the driver to follow him. "That one," he said, "is for my wife. Things for the house, ordered all the way from England. Even a piano."

Coming into Stonehill had increased my uneasiness. It had seemed a forbidding town, especially since the death of Kirby Canfield. Even after the many years, I still had that feeling about it.

I said, "I'd better get down here. I'll find a way to get out to the ranch."

Isom nodded. "You know I can't take you. Thomas Canfield and I have not set eyes on one another in years. It is best we keep it that way. I'd be glad to lend you a horse."

I did not want to arrive at the Canfield ranch riding a horse that belonged to Branch Isom. I thanked him for his generosity and assured him I would find a way. He asked me to come up to his house and meet his wife and see his boy, James. I told him I would, another time. He pulled away and left me in the trailing dust, much relieved to see the last of him even though he had shown me nothing but friendliness since Indianola. Old suspicions die hard.

I had no idea, at first, what my next move should be. I was not sure who I might still know here. It was in my mind that I could seek out some of the Mexicans who had worked for or dealt with Thomas years ago, if any still lived in Stonehill. I started up the dusty street, one hand holding the carpetbag containing nearly everything I owned, the other holding the cane for support. I looked vainly for a familiar face.

Reading the signs, I learned that Branch Isom had his roots sunk deeply into this town. A dramshop bore the names "Smith & Isom" in small letters beneath the title "Texas Lady." A blacksmith shop and livery barn proclaimed "A. Dandridge & B. Isom." I came in a while to the big general store that had been built by Linden Hines. The sign declared,"General Mercantile. Branch Isom, Prop."

I felt a little as I supposed the Europeans must have felt when a usurper took the throne.

Laura Hines had remained on my mind during the long war years. I had more or less reconciled myself to the idea that there would never be anything between us except friendship, but I knew no other face that appealed to me quite so much, so I let hers be the player in many a fanciful daydream, some of a high order, some I would never have wanted her to know about. Futile or not, the dreams had been a means of lifting me out of intolerable reality and, perhaps, keeping me from losing my mind.

Isom had said she was keeping books for him. I stood in front of the store a minute, bracing up my courage, wondering how far I had let my dreams stray from truth. I had long suspected that I had made over her face to suit myself, so that the one in the dreams was probably at considerable variance with reality.

I made my way past barrels and boxes on the wooden porch and stood in the open double door, trying to accustom my eyes to the dim interior. I heard Laura before I saw her.

"Reed? Reed Sawyer?" She came out from behind a tall counter in the rear of the store. I could not see her clearly because it was dark in there, and my eyes were filling up, too. "It's me," I said.

She threw her arms around me, putting me off balance and almost causing me to fall. My hip shot through with pain, but I tried to hide it. She stood back a little to stare at me, her hands keeping a strong grip on my shoulders.

"We were afraid you were dead," she declared.

"I wrote."

"The mail service broke down, toward the last."

She made a good deal of fuss over me, which I enjoyed, but I sensed that it was friendship, nothing more. All those daydreams had served a purpose at the time, but they were dead now. I felt like crying.

She had changed a lot, or perhaps my creative memory had been at fault. She was mature, a woman well past twenty, face still pretty but eyes sad from the unhappiness she had seen. I realized we were both ten years older than when we had first met.

"You look wonderful," I said. That was true. She did, to me.

She brought herself to ask about my cane, about my thinness. I admitted that I looked as if I had barely escaped the grave, but I was sure I would get much better now that I was home.

"First thing you need is a good meal," she said. "I have the books in good shape. I'm going to take you home with me and cook you a real dinner."

I protested, but weakly. Nothing could have pleased me more.

She said, "It will do Papa good to see you. He hasn't seen much in a long time to make him smile."

I thought I knew what to expect, but seeing Linden Hines was like a blow to the stomach. He was an old man, a shell. He smiled at the sight of me, but the smile lived only a minute. He had given up the will and surrendered to infirmities that he normally might have stood off for many more years.

"I am glad you came back, Reed," he said. "So many didn't. It cost us so much . . ."

The casualties of the war had reached far beyond the battlefields.

I remembered that the old gentleman had been partial to a good toddy. While Laura was busy fixing dinner I thought I might cheer him a little. I said, "It has been a long, hard trip, and I think a drink would do me good. I would be obliged, sir, if you would go with me."

That faint smile returned. "I would be honored, sir."

Neither of us moved very fast, me burdened by my bad hip and my cane, he by his health. We went into the place called Lucky Lady, which Mr. Hines indicated was as good as any in town. Business seemed slack, but it was a time of day when most respectable people were working, if most people in Stonehill could be considered respectable. Thomas Canfield had always regarded the Hineses as something akin to Lot's family, two good people in a town of arch sinners.

We had our drinks, and I laid the coins on the bar. A voice came from the back of the room. "Keep your money, Sawyer. The drinks are on the house."

Branch Isom had entered the back door. I told him it was not necessary, but he protested that it was an occasion when a soldier came home, especially the friend of an old friend like Linden Hines. He went behind the bar, opened a door somewhere and fetched out a bottle. "This is the best I can buy, too good to sell across the bar." He poured our glasses full, and one for himself. He held up his glass in a toast: "To the soldiers of Texas, wherever they fought."

I looked closely at Mr. Hines, expecting him to betray resentment toward this man who now owned all that used to belong to him. But I saw no such emotion there. He nodded at the toast and downed the whisky and said something about its being good.

Isom said, "And now, gentlemen, I must leave you. I have pressing business all over town. Come in again, Sawyer. Mr. Hines, my compliments."

Hines thanked him for the whisky, which prompted me to do the same. I had been so surprised by Isom's generosity that I stood off balance. I could not escape a feeling that I was a calf being fattened for slaughter, though I could not imagine how.

I was not used to whisky and never held it well. It glowed like a comfortable fire in my stomach, though. Mr. Hines seemed ready to go home, so we started. He took the lead, picking his way among a group of teamsters who had just come in. They did not move aside for him. They would have, a few years earlier. My cane brought me no particular respect either. They were used to crippled ex-soldiers coming home.

From the porch down to the street was a fair distance,

and I was a little slow negotiating the three steps. Mr. Hines was ahead of me, looking back to be sure I didn't slip. I heard a rumbling and a loud shout and glanced up the street. A big freight wagon was bearing down on Mr. Hines.

"Look out!" I shouted to him and tried to hurry. I caught one foot on my cane and fell down the steps. I could hear the wagon driver cursing and shouting at his mules. Through the dust and the blur of movement I sensed that Mr. Hines had stepped back quickly enough to be in the clear.

"Why don't you watch what you're doing, old man?" the driver shouted back, once the danger was past. "Damned old relics, ought not to be allowed on the street without a guardian."

I got up angry enough to do battle, even in my condition. I shouted after the driver that an old pioneer like Linden Hines was due respect, but the words were lost in the air. Nobody cared what he had been in the past. They saw only what he was now, a worn-out old man existing on others' generosity. The generosity of Branch Isom.

My conscience began nagging me. I knew all my indignation had not been over the general lack of gratitude to Linden Hines. Some was for myself. My being a wounded soldier seemed to have little meaning either; few people exhibited any gratitude. I supposed it was because we had lost the war. I had just as well have stayed home.

Laura put more steak on the table than we could eat, even with the appetite I had saved up through a long lean time. Beef was cheap, she said, even free for those who had a horse and could go get it. The war had blocked most outside markets for years. So many men had gone into Confederate service that herds went untended, unbranded. Cattle had multiplied to a point that South Texas ranges were badly overstocked, the grass short. The unbranded ran wild and free for the taking, with no one to object.

Before the war, cattle had represented wealth. Now, if anything, they were a liability.

"Eat some more," she said. "You're doing some rancher a favor."

I made the sacrifice, to my later discomfort. My thoughts returned then to the Canfield ranch. If I dallied much longer I would be obliged to stay the night. That would be an imposition on the Hineses. Their house was small and had no real place for me. I began making my excuses to leave.

Laura said, "I'll take you out there. I'll get a wagon from the company barn."

I told her I did not want to be any more burden than I had already been. Also, I had let myself become more beholden to Branch Isom than I would ever have imagined in olden times. I felt uncomfortable, owing a debt to a man like that, and I told her so.

She frowned. "That's Thomas talking, not you. Branch Isom has many faults, but he's not a completely forsaken sinner."

I figured she felt obliged to loyalty because she worked for him, and he occasionally extended cheap courtesies to her father. It struck me as unfair that Isom had enriched himself from the long conflict while soldiers like myself had paid a hard price.

Laura would not accept my refusal. I said my good-byes to her father, then walked with her to the big barn where empty freight wagons stood in a neat line and dozens of horses and mules milled in dusty corrals, pulling hay from crude racks built of mesquite. I looked around uneasily for Branch Isom, hoping not to have to belittle myself by thanking him once again. The stablemen never questioned Laura's request for a light spring wagon. I could tell she carried weight around here. One of the men confided to me, out of her hearing, that she officiated at the monthly pay table. Bought loyalty was effective, if sometimes shallow.

We rode in silence much of the time. After several years of absence I was busy taking in the country, remembering. It was drier than when I had left it, the grass poor. I could see cattle in every direction, thick as fleas on a butcher's dog.

When Laura talked it was mostly about Stonehill, which seemed to have prospered more than the average Texas town during the war because of its importance on the freighting roads. I asked about New Silesia, well remembering how nearly it had come to starvation in the beginning. She said it had suffered some harassment early because so many of the people were opposed to the war. It had not grown much but had solidified its position. Unlike Stonehill, it had been largely self-sufficient. What the Polish immigrants could not raise or make for themselves, they managed to do without. For this reason they had not suffered unduly from the collapse of the Confederate currency; they had little of it in the first place. Laura said they had broken out more fields and strengthened their hold on the little they owned. Like Thomas Canfield, they drew their strength from the land and regarded it as the only thing solid in life. Money was but sterile paper or metal. The land was alive.

When I asked about Mrs. Canfield or Maria or the two children, Laura talked easily. When she spoke of Thomas she was slower and more thoughtful, and she did not look at me. Earlier I had been tempted to ask why she had not found another good man and married him. Before we reached the ranch, I knew without asking.

Approaching the headquarters, I could see little change. There were still four houses of varying size, the double cabin for the old Mrs. Canfield, another for the Fernandez family, a small one for single hired hands, and the big frame house Thomas had built on the slope for Maria. From a distance I could see it needed paint. That, in itself, told me much about financial circumstances.

Two men were in the round bronc-breaking corral, one riding a crow-hopping young horse, the other throwing a sack under its feet to try to make it pitch. I was astounded when Laura told me these were the Fernandez boys. In my mind they should still be as young as when I had left. Now they would pass—at a distance—for grown men. But this was a country that did not tolerate childhood very long. The boys quickly tied the bronc and scaled the fence, then ran to meet us, hollering at me all the way.

It was getting to be a grim joke, everybody saying first off that they had assumed I was dead. I told them I hated to be such a disappointment. They ran ahead of us up to the big house, shouting for the Canfields to come out. The old lady was the first onto the porch. She threw up her hands and came running to meet me. She had grayed more in the nearly four years I had been gone, and the lines had cut deeper into her face, but I thought she had fared far better than Linden Hines.

Maria came out then, her brown eyes shining and beautiful. Like Laura, she had matured into a fine-looking woman. Her face was still pretty and fleshed out better than I remembered it. Her waist was fuller, the result of bearing two children, but if anything that was an improvement. Before, she had looked as if a strong wind might carry her away.

A small girl, who had to be past three now, peered shyly out from behind her, keeping one hand full of her mother's skirt, pulling it out to cover all but one big brown eye, very curious.

The two women both hugged me at the same time, while the little girl ran and threw her arms around Laura's neck, then clung to her while she looked at me with both curiosity and a little fear. Youngsters like this, growing up far out in the country, were not used to strangers. I heard the girl saying, "Aunt Laura." I saw the gentle way Laura and Maria looked at each other, and it occurred to me how unusual a friendship theirs really was.

It was a while before I knew the little girl's name. The old lady called her child, and Maria called her something I never quite understood, then or later. It was in Polish. Eventually Laura spoke of her as Katrina when the girl led

her off into another room to show some doll clothes her
mother had sewed from scraps.

Maria's English had improved, though she still spoke
with an accent. She looked at me with pity. "We must make
for you much food. We must get you fat again." I never had
been given much to weight, but I realized I must look like
starvation now.

Not until near dark did Thomas come home. I saw
Maria's eyes light at the sound of the wagon. If I had ever
doubted that he had chosen well, that look dispelled all
question. The boy Kirby sat beside him on the wagon. The
original spring seat was gone, replaced by a flat board that
jolted the innards. The two had been shoveling stock salt
into troughs at some of the watering places. The boy's
rough clothing was crusted with it. He was six now, or near
it, and as shy of me as the girl had been. Thomas tied off
the reins and came up into the yard with a tired but happy
step. The boy remained a full pace behind him and eyed
me with dark suspicion. I had bounced him on my knee,
but he had been too small to remember that.

Thomas stared at me a long moment without a word. He
had aged more than the years alone would account for. He
was not original with his first words. "Reed, I thought they
had killed you," he said.

I didn't care what he said so long as there was welcome
in it. He gripped my arms in the Mexican style of *abrazo;*
much of his manner had come to him from the Mexicans.

I managed to say, "You told me I would always have a
home here." I wondered, for by the looks of things an extra
mouth might be a burden.

"I hope you never doubted that," he said.

"I probably won't be much help for a while."

He glanced at my cane but only shrugged. "You've already been a help, just coming back. Now I know things
have got to get better."

One of the Fernandez boys came up, and Thomas asked
him to take care of the team and wagon. He put his arm

around Maria, and they walked into the house. Laura watched them, then took the girl's hand and followed.

Only the boy and I were left. I asked, "How about it, Kirby?"

He just stood on the ground and stared in silent distrust.

I turned and went into the house alone, figuring he would open up to me after a while.

But he never did, not completely.

5

The first days on the ranch produced many satisfactions, but they also held frustrations. My hip punished me for my ambition in trying to ride horseback. I went three or four miles with the Fernandez boys, thinking the pain would stop sooner or later. Instead it became so bad I had to dismount and could not climb back into the saddle. I waited in humiliation while Marco returned to headquarters and brought a wagon to fetch me home.

"You're trying too hard," Thomas admonished. "Take your time."

I said, "I was brought up to work for what I get."

Thomas' face was sad. "You're not getting much here. I haven't the money to pay you anything."

"You feed me. You give me a place to lay my head down. I owe you for that."

I owed for much more. I was not simply a hired hand, and I was not treated as one. Maria and the old Mrs. Canfield competed with each other to see who could fix the best meals for me. The little girl, Katy—Thomas would never call her Katrina—toddled after me as if I were some good uncle, even if the boy never warmed to me.

"There is a lot of work you can do in a wagon," Thomas said. "You can carry salt. You can haul supplies from New Silesia." He tried to keep my mind and my hands occupied, to make me feel useful rather than a burden, even when I knew it was not true.

I would watch him ride his favorite horse, this spirited

mustang bay he called Stepper, which had never completely given up the fight and occasionally challenged Thomas' right to mastery. Thomas always won, but not without a contest. I envied him that ability and wondered how long it would be before I was a whole man again.

He asked me to go with him to San Antonio to buy goods for his struggling store in New Silesia. That store, since the collapse of Confederate currency, had become a financial tribulation to him. I sat in the lobby of a San Antonio bank and watched from a distance as Thomas humbled himself to a well-dressed Yankee banker, something I knew hurt him worse in its way than my wound had ever hurt me. He finally got most of what he had asked for, but the cost in pride was high. On the long trip home in the rough wagon, he was silent, withdrawn into a heavy shell.

When he finally spoke the suddenness of it startled me. He said, "You haven't seen your own place since you came home."

I had, one day when I was hauling salt. I had made several extra miles in an empty wagon to look upon the little piece of land I had bought with my saved wages before the war. It wasn't much, a fraction of Thomas' holdings, and it had not so much as a dugout on it for habitation. There was no point in my building one; it was too small a place to yield a living. But I felt a glow from the sense of ownership.

Thomas stopped the wagon on a knoll and gazed in silence. I could see cattle scattered across a wide, sunbaked flat and knew most of them were strays, not mine. The few cows I had owned before the war would be old mossyhorns now, the ones that might have survived.

Thomas said, "We kept up your brand for you while you were gone. We branded the increase every year."

I thanked him, though it seemed to me the work had been largely for nothing. Those cattle were worth no more than their hides and tallow would fetch, which wasn't much. And the land wasn't worth the lumber it would take to build a good house on it.

He seemed to sense what I was thinking. "Hold on to it, Reed. It will be worth a fortune to you someday. Land is the only thing that is real."

"Gold is real," I said. "This whole thing, today, wouldn't bring enough gold to plate a watch."

"Gold doesn't grow food. It doesn't keep the rain off of your head."

I spoke rashly, and immediately wished I had kept my mouth shut. "It seems to be doing very well for Branch Isom."

He shook from the impact of the name. "It will betray him someday. Through the war, when others were working for patriotism, he worked for gold. Now he puts it all back into Stonehill. He has no feeling for land; all it means to him is the roads to carry his freight wagons. That town will blow away someday, like tumbleweeds. The freight business will die with it. All his gold will be gone, and his sins will be visited on him like a plague. He will sit there with ruin all about him, but we'll have our land, Reed. The land will always be here."

We circled back by New Silesia, where he spent some time in the store with the manager Smithers, going over the ledgers. The store was like a stone weight around their necks; they had extended credit to too many people unlikely ever to pay.

While they talked about their business problems I looked over the little immigrant town. Thomas felt strong ties to it, mostly because of Maria and her people, but I was never at home there. I never had learned the language, not even enough to ask for coffee. The customs remained strange to me. Many of the Polanders had put up solid if unfancy houses—mostly of stone—in the years I had been away. I could not quite accept their way of building house and barn together, their milk stock staying in one end while the people lived in the other. I understood this was the way of the old country, but I never felt that friendly toward a cow.

Thomas was not much at going to church. Maria was faithful about it. Every Sunday she put the two children in a wagon and drove over to New Silesia. Sometimes Thomas went with her but found other things to do while she and her family and the children attended mass in the Catholic church. Other times he sent one of the Fernandez boys to make sure she had no trouble along the way. There were still people in the country who enjoyed harassing the Polanders. A couple of times, I went. The church service was alien to me, like most other things in the town. New Silesia seemed like something that had been lifted up from Europe and set down in Texas with few modifications.

We heard about the fever when it first moved up from the coast with one of Branch Isom's freighting outfits and struck in Stonehill. A Mexican wrangler told us several people in town had come down with it. Branch Isom sent his wife and young son to San Antonio to avoid their being exposed. There had been other epidemics, and none had ever touched the Canfield ranch. I remembered several times before the war that sickness had traveled inland with the freighting crews or immigrants. It would always run its course in a little while. Here and there somebody died of the fever, but people died of many other things too. Folks talk about the dangers we used to face from Indians and outlaws, but more died during epidemics in those days than ever died of arrow or bullet. Being isolated, far out in the country, was sometimes an asset. We probably missed more hazards than we realized.

One day a boy came out from town with a message from Laura Hines. The fever had struck her father suddenly, and in his weakened and spiritless condition he had died the second night.

Thomas struggled with his conscience. Not since his brother's death had he set foot in Stonehill. But the funeral of an old friend, and the bereavement of Laura, overcame his reluctance. He gave the two children into the care of Mrs. Fernandez, then four of us went to town in the wagon. Thomas hardly looked to right or left as we moved down the main street; his jaw was set in contempt for the place. Forgetting at first that Laura and her father had moved, he pulled the wagon up to the front of the large house that had long been their home. I had to tell him how to find the smaller one where they had lived since the war.

Laura was better reconciled to her loss than I expected. Maria hurried to embrace her. Laura accepted our condolences but said death had come to her father as a friend; life had lost its flavor to him.

The fever had people fearful about congregating indoors. The funeral was conducted entirely at the cemetery, a dry south wind blowing a skim of fresh earth into the open, waiting grave while the minister gave the eulogy. Maria stood on one side of Laura, Mrs. Canfield on the other, but she was strong enough; she did not need bracing up.

Branch Isom came to the funeral alone; his family was still in the comparative safety of San Antonio. He and Thomas did not speak, but their eyes met. Thomas' hatred flashed with the crackling reality of St. Elmo's fire. Isom quickly looked away. The uneasy truce of recent times had not overcome the open hostility of other years.

When the service was over Isom made his obligatory comments to Laura about the loss of a good man, the father of the town. Thomas watched him resentfully as he walked away.

"By rights he should not have come here," he said. "He robbed Mr. Hines of all he owned, even the will to live."

Laura shook her head, her voice quiet but firm. "Branch Isom did not cause our trouble. That came because Papa gave everything he had to the cause he believed in. Isom just picked up the pieces."

"He could afford to. He hadn't given anything away."

Thomas seemed to realize the subject was painful to

Laura, so he fell silent. But he watched Isom while the man's buggy was in sight.

Maria tried to persuade Laura to go to the ranch a few days, to get away from the unhappy town and the sorrow it had caused her. Laura shook her head. "I've fallen behind on the books. What I need most right now is work to keep my mind busy."

We followed her home but found a goodly number of sympathetic women there. She would not lack for company. Thomas made excuses, and we left. He was relieved to put the town behind him. On the way home, nobody talked much. Mrs. Canfield finally began to comment upon the fever, and how fortunate we were to live in the open country where God kept the air clean.

Her words were ironic, for Thomas' mother was struck down a few days later. No one knew much about the fever or its causes. We could only guess that she had caught it somehow at the funeral. Thomas immediately asked me to take the children to Maria's people in New Silesia. So far the fever had not struck that town. Little Katy did not mind; I had already seen how much she loved her grandparents. But the boy Kirby was silent during the wagon trip to the Polish town. His eyes were resentful when I turned him over to the old couple. He understood what they said to him in their language, but he stubbornly refused to answer them except in English. I sensed that I had been introduced to a shameful secret. Even as the Brozeks fawned over the children, it was easy to see they were covering up their hurt. Kirby came to the door of the stone house and watched me as I left for the ranch. He said not a word, but I felt his eyes following me.

Unlike Linden Hines, Mrs. Canfield had a strong wish to live. She put up a battle that she seemed for a time to be winning. But it was not enough. The doctor managed to see her only once, for he had more than enough suffering patients in Stonehill. Maria stayed beside the old lady constantly during the three days and nights she struggled. She was still on her feet, but barely, when the fever carried Mrs. Canfield away. Thomas just sat in his mother's rocking chair at the foot of the bed and stared. He did not talk; he did not weep. He just sat there, rocking.

Maria cried a little, then put that behind her and tried to comfort her husband. She seemed unable to reach him, and her silent eyes pleaded to me for help.

I said to Thomas, "I'll go to the preacher. Your mother was a believing woman. She'd want the words read over her."

A quick nod was the only sign that he had heard.

I knew without asking that he would want to bury her up on the slope, alongside his father and brother. Backing away, I said, "I'd better fetch the children home. They ought to see her laid to rest."

He stopped rocking. "No, there's fever here." That was all he said. He started rocking again.

Maria followed me to the porch, tears shining in her eyes. "He does not let me help him," she said.

I told her, "He's not a man who leans on people. He stands by himself." It struck me how thin and haggard she looked. She had slept little the last several days. "You'd better help yourself," I said. "You'd better get some rest."

She nodded, but she would not do it, not so long as she thought Thomas might need her.

The minister was almost as busy as the doctor. There had been other deaths since that of Linden Hines. He promised to come out to the ranch as soon as he could, but all preparations had to be made ahead, for he could not stay long. I tried to think of any people in town who should be notified. The only friend Mrs. Canfield had there, so far as I knew, was Laura Hines. Laura put a few clothes together and rode back to the ranch with me in the wagon.

Scarcely a dozen people stood at the graveside to hear the brief services. Thomas said little. He stood alone. When Maria reached once for his hand, he pulled it away and folded his arms.

I glanced at Laura. She frowned.

Laura did not like the tired, drawn look on Maria's face, and she offered to stay a day or two. Maria insisted she was all right; a good night's sleep was all she needed. Thomas took no part in the conversation. He seemed not even to hear it, though he was only an arm's length away. He responded to nothing until Laura said, "If you will then, Reed, please take me back to Stonehill."

The word "Stonehill" seemed to bring Thomas around. "You should get away from that place, Laura. It brings nothing but misfortune and death."

She gave him a look of surprise, as if not quite believing he cared that much for her welfare. "I have nowhere else to go."

It was in my mind—I had not given up—that someday *I* might provide her a place to go, when I was able to build my land holdings and my cattle herd some more, and after I put up a house of my own. But the thought passed when we sat in the wagon together. She glanced back, and what I saw in her eyes for Thomas, I feared I would never see there for me.

Maria started to climb the steps as we pulled away. She never made it to the top. I saw her sway, then fall. Laura cried at me to stop. She was down from the wagon and running before I could bring the team to a halt. I saw fear strike Thomas. He called Maria's name as he knelt and tried to lift her to her feet.

By the time I got the team still and the reins wrapped around a spoke, Thomas had Maria in his arms and was rushing into the house with her. Laura was directly behind him. I followed them into the bedroom, where Thomas gently placed Maria on their big hand-carved wooden bed.

"She's just tired out," he said desperately, more to himself than to the rest of us. He was trying to believe it, but it was obvious he did not.

Laura felt of Maria's hand and then her forehead. "It's more than that." Fear came into her face. She immediately took over, for Thomas seemed helpless, as he had been helpless when his mother was burning with fever. This was an enemy he did not know how to fight.

"Reed," she commanded, "run down and fetch Mrs. Fernandez. Then hurry to town and drag that doctor out here; bring him with a gun if you have to. Thomas, you help me get these clothes off of Maria."

Thomas had braced his feet, and he stood like an ox struck behind the horns with the flat side of an ax. Laura saw he was stunned. She gripped his shoulders and shook him savagely. "Thomas!" I waited in the door until he began to respond, then I ran down to the little Fernandez house.

What Laura said about bringing the doctor with a gun if necessary was not much of an exaggeration. He still had about all he could do without leaving town. I thought I would have to wrestle his hefty wife, who protested that *he* would be the next to die if he didn't get some rest. I sympathized with both of them, but I had to sympathize with Maria more. I took him to the ranch.

Nobody had to tell me the situation was grave. The hard-set look in Thomas' eyes said that, and the quiet desperation of Laura. Maria was talking irrationally, crying out in words I could not understand about things that had happened long before, or perhaps never happened at all.

I looked to Thomas to see if I could do anything for him. He seemed unaware of me, even when I spoke to him. Laura touched my arm and beckoned me into the parlor. Quietly, her voice trembling, she said, "You'd better hurry to New Silesia and bring her parents here. You'd best not lose any time."

"They have the children. I shouldn't bring the children to this fever."

"There's other family to leave the children with. But bring her parents, and hurry."

I never had been able to converse with the Brozeks very well because of the language problem. I went directly to the church and found the priest hunched over a giant Bible. I explained the situation. He went with me to the Brozeks'. Katy was playing in the front yard of the rock house with some other children, chattering happily in Polish. Kirby was off to himself, chunking rocks at some chickens. The girl recognized me and came running, shouting my name. Kirby walked only partway to meet me, then stopped, saying nothing. I could tell he hoped I had come to take him home, but he was too proud to ask, or to seem eager. He had much of Thomas in him.

Anguish came into the old couple's faces as the priest told them of my message. Kirby listened in silence. I could tell he understood it all. Katy cried and begged to be taken to her mother. The old grandmother picked her up and smothered her in her arms and hurried outside to call to a neighbor. In a few minutes she had the children placed with others of the family. The priest had a buggy, more comfortable than the ranch wagon, so he took the old folks in it while I followed close behind, one of Maria's brothers riding with me. The long miles I had made, first to Stonehill and then to New Silesia, began to tell on me, and the brother took over the reins. I tried to nap sitting up, but the wagon was too rough. I sat with my eyes shut and kept seeing all those anguished faces.

We arrived almost too late. Maria opened her eyes at the sound of voices. She recognized her parents and called their names and cried out for her children. Laura tried to explain that they had stayed behind to protect them from the fever, but I don't think Maria understood. She sank back into the fever. When the priest leaned over her with his beads and began to give her absolution, I knew the ordeal was nearly done. She cried out once and was gone.

The old couple crossed themselves and leaned into each other's arms. Mrs. Fernandez made the same sign and turned her face into a corner. I looked into Laura's tired, stricken face, then to Thomas, frozen, unseeing. His mind had carried him far away, denying reality, rejecting recognition of death. For several minutes he did not move. Then he gripped Maria's shoulders and tried to shake her awake.

"Maria! Maria!" he cried.

Laura gently touched his arm. "She can't hear you, Thomas," she whispered.

He shook Maria harder and kept calling to her. When realization finally reached him he pushed to his feet and stared down at that silent face now without pain. A terrible look came into his eyes, the look that had always frightened me a little. Instinctively I glanced at his hip, though I realized he was not carrying a gun. The dark thought came to me that if he had, he might use it on himself.

He spoke to no one, looked at no one, but turned and strode out of the room. The fear still pressed on me, so I followed him, keeping my distance. I thought it unnatural that a man could go through so much and never cry. I had not seen him cry when he buried his brother Kirby, or his mother. I saw not one tear in his eyes now. He walked carefully down the steps and toward the barn. Quietly I followed fifteen or twenty steps behind him, not sure what he might do or what I *could* do. He stopped at the horse corral.

His bay mustang Stepper was in there, pulling hay from a rack. He turned his head to watch Thomas, and he made a nervous, rolling noise in that long, ugly nose. Thomas walked in, shutting the gate behind him. I kept my distance, moving up quietly and looking between the poles. Thomas walked slowly toward the horse, his hand extended. The bay watched him suspiciously, little ears flicking in nervousness. Once he started to turn and run away, but something in Thomas' manner seemed to hold him. The bay flinched as Thomas reached out and touched his neck. Thomas slipped his left arm under the neck and up the off side. He patted the horse a while. If he said anything, it was in a whisper I could not hear. Then he had both arms around the horse's strong neck, his face buried in the dark mane, and Thomas did something I had never seen him do. He cried.

The horse, normally nervous as a cat, stood quiet and still, as if it understood, and let Thomas spill out all his grief.

I walked back to the house. The best help I could give Thomas was simply to leave him alone.

Thomas Canfield had long seemed a man the world could not touch, a man too strong to bend before the wind. Now, for a while, the fight was gone out of him. He held his ground on just one thing. Maria's parents wanted to take her to New Silesia for burial in consecrated ground. Thomas insisted she would be buried in the family cemetery up on the slope. That, too, he said, was consecrated ground, hallowed by so many he had loved. The priest blessed the place, and it was all right.

Beyond that one issue, he had no strength left. If the denizens of Stonehill had come then to drive off every head of cattle and to post a confiscation notice on his land, I do not believe he would have resisted. He drew into a shell where nothing from outside could reach him.

The girl Katy was too young to realize fully the meaning of death. Kirby knew. I never saw him cry, but I could see the pain and the helpless anger in his eyes. He did not know who to blame, so he blamed everyone. Some of the anger was directed toward his father for sending him away and some toward me for taking him. During the services I saw him resist attempts of Maria's parents to hold his hand. He stood alone, as his father stood alone.

The worst part of all was in returning to that big house, which must have seemed empty to the children. Thomas brought Mrs. Fernandez up from her own little place to live in the house and be a guardian of sorts. Her own sons were doing man's work if not drawing a man's pay. They slept in the little house where they had grown up, though they went to the big house to take their meals, cooked by their mother for them and for what was left of the Canfields. Much of the time they were not at headquarters anyway; they were often camped on one part of the ranch or another, looking after the cattle, batching. So, for that matter, was I. My hip had healed to the point that riding horseback no longer hurt me much, unless I let the work carry me too far into the night. I still had a limit.

I saw more of Kirby than of his sister because Thomas made it a point to keep the boy with him as much as he could. Where he went, Kirby usually rode by his side, on horseback or in the wagon. They talked little to each other. At least, Kirby talked little. His father volunteered points to him about the cattle or the horses, about the wild animals they encountered, about the land itself. Kirby absorbed this teaching without much comment. The long months went by, but he remained as distant as the day his mother was buried.

Despite our isolation, we heard things. Business began picking itself up from the floor where the lost war had left it. Union dollars, though still scarce, began to sift into the channels of commerce. Thomas had stubbornly held onto his ailing little store in New Silesia, not so much for its own sake as for the irritating competition it could give to Stonehill and to Branch Isom. Somehow he managed to pay off some loans and get himself back into reasonably good graces with the bankers in San Antonio, themselves hard put to find much real U.S. specie in circulation. An awful lot of scrip and plain old-fashioned barter were used in those days.

I had a horse in my string called Stomper, a name well given. He had a way of walking and trotting that jarred a rider's innards. Every time I rode him my hip would ache, but I could ill afford *not* to ride him, for a horse unused tends to forget his teaching and backslide into outlawry. I could have turned him over to one of the Fernandez boys, but they had not done anything to me that justified so sorry a treatment. I kept the horse as penance for whatever short-comings I might have in the sight of the Lord.

One afternoon the pain was so sharp that I quit early and rode back toward the house while the sun was still an hour or so high. I cut into the Stonehill road and heard somebody hail me. I stopped Stomper and turned him around, welcoming a chance to shift my weight in the saddle and perhaps ease the aching hip.

The rider who trotted to catch up to me was one I would recognize from a mile away. Branch Isom.

Thinking back, I could not remember ever seeing him on the Canfield ranch. I saw no pistol on his hip, though he carried a rifle in a scabbard beneath his leg. Everybody did; that was no sign of war.

He reined up and offered a few pleasantries. His manner was cordial enough that my initial suspicions were suspended, if not dismissed. He seemed no longer the unrepentant sinner that he had appeared years before, when we had first made our acquaintance. Perhaps it was the graying with the red in his hair, or the deeper lines in a ruddy face growing heavy with the weight of years and relative prosperity. He seemed to have mellowed. Or perhaps I had seen so much brutality in the war that he paled by contrast.

He spoke of regret for the sorrows that had befallen the Canfields. He said, "I'll admit I never felt any love for Thomas, and it's certain he's had none for me. But I've had only the kindest thoughts for his womenfolks, even that Polander girl he married."

That surprised me a little. I felt honor-bound to ask about his own family. He said they were fine; his wife and son had waited in San Antonio for the fever to run its course. "Boy's getting to be a goer. I'd like to have brought him, but I didn't know what kind of reception I might get from Canfield. Some things a boy shouldn't see or hear."

It wasn't any of my business, but I felt compelled to ask anyway. "What have you come to see Thomas for?"

"Business. A mutual profit for both him and me, I hope."

My suspicions revived, though not so strong as before. It had been a long time since much good had come to this place from Stonehill, Laura Hines being the exception. She had visited occasionally on Sundays to look in on the children, or so she said.

I rode into headquarters with him. He told me much I had not heard about the Union occupation army and Indian troubles farther west, and of business trends and hopes and fears. As we approached the barn I saw Thomas' wagon in front of the salt house. He was shoveling salt to carry to the watering places. Kirby stood in the wagon bed, evening out the load with a shovel whose handle was longer than he was tall.

"Thomas," I called, "you have company."

His jaw dropped and his face darkened as he recognized Branch Isom. He cut his eyes reproachfully to me as if Isom's visit had been my doing. *"Isom,"* he said. Not *welcome* or anything like that. Just "Isom." Recognition, but not approval.

Isom studied him a long moment before he said a word. Then he laid most of it right out on the table. "Thomas Canfield, you've never liked me, and I've never liked you. Men have been killed over differences smaller than we've had. But that's all in the past."

Thomas said nothing.

Isom said, "I have a business proposition. It could be profitable to both of us."

Thomas let his suspicions come bitterly to the surface. "More profitable for you than for me, I would warrant."

"Quite possibly," Isom admitted. "But I would carry considerable risk. Your profit would be guaranteed."

Thomas noticed his son watching Isom with unusual interest. Curtly he said, "Kirby, you go to the house."

Kirby was hesitant, and Thomas told him again, his voice brooking no question. "Go!" Kirby went reluctantly.

Thomas never invited Isom to step down from the saddle, so Isom sat there. He said, "Thomas, they're building a railroad west into Kansas."

Thomas pondered that fact a moment and failed to see significance in it. "You should not have to worry about that. They can't hurt you until they build one west from Indianola to San Antonio. Then you may be selling your freight wagons cheap."

Isom passed over the sarcasm and explained that the new railroad was opening up a market for beef in the East. "Cattle can be sold at the railheads to be shipped back there."

"We're a long way from Kansas. What good does that do us?"

"Cattle have legs. They can be walked to Kansas. I have started putting together a herd to take north. I'll buy cattle from you here and take all the responsibility and all the gamble. I'll pay you two-and-a-half a head for whatever cattle I can use. You won't have to go anywhere or take any risk. It's cash money, Union silver, placed into your hands right here at your corrals."

Thomas looked down, hiding his eyes. "What will you get for them, up in Kansas?"

"I won't lie to you. There is every indication they could bring fifteen dollars, perhaps more. But it's a long way and a risky trip. I'll lose some on the way. I *could* lose them all. If I make it, I'll earn a good profit. If I don't, I'll stand a loss. In either case, you'll have your money before the cattle ever leave this place."

Thomas said, "You've never handled cattle."

"I've handled horses and mules for years." He paused. "It's cash money. I'll bet you haven't seen two hundred dollars in Union specie since the war."

Thomas stared off into the distance, toward the slope where he had buried so many Canfields. When he turned I could tell from his expression pretty much what he was going to say. He would have dealt with Lucifer before he would deal with Branch Isom.

Coldly he said, "Isom, you were right when you rode up here. You never liked me, and I never liked you. What's between us is not forgotten. It never will be. I would not do business with you for a hundred thousand in Yankee gold."

Isom's face flashed to anger. I saw at least a little of the hostile Isom I remembered. "That's your final say?"

Thomas nodded grimly.

Isom had as much pride, in his way, as Thomas. He would not argue or plead. He said only, "I had hoped we could bury the past."

Thomas grunted. "Not until they bury *me*."

Isom's shoulders were stiff as he rode away. Thomas watched him as if half expecting him to turn and come back shooting. There had been a time, once, when that might have happened.

I could contain myself no longer. "If he offered you two-and-a-half outright, you could probably have carried him up to three. Maybe even three-and-a-half."

Thomas turned his back on me.

Next morning, without any word to me of what he planned, he left for San Antonio. Late the second evening he returned with two men following him in a buggy. One was a San Antonio businessman wearing a light duster over a good suit. The other was obviously a cowman by his clothes, his boots, his Mexican-style hat. He had the look of a man who had spent his life in the sun. Thomas introduced them as Mr. Jensen and Mr. Hayes.

"I have agreed to sell these gentlemen two hundred cattle at two dollars a head," he said.

I shook their hands and tried to look pleasant, though I quickly calculated that this represented a clear loss of one hundred dollars from Isom's offer.

Hatred could be expensive.

Branch Isom was by no means the only person putting cattle together for the trail to Kansas. These men had the same notion, Jensen putting up the money and Hayes the ability. Before the war Hayes had trailed cattle all the way to Missouri, and during the war he had taken some over into Louisiana to feed the Confederate soldiers. He had the look of a man who knew what the cow was about to think before she had time to think it. Those old cowmen bore a mark hard to explain but easy to recognize.

Thomas had us round up cattle from the end of the ranch nearest to Stonehill. Many people in town had become accustomed to helping themselves to Canfield beef. Thomas had done nothing about it because the cattle had been worth little anyway. Now times appeared to be changing. Thinning the cattle nearest to town might not stop the beef killing, but it made the thieves work harder. Hayes and Jensen were not interested in cows. A cow-calf herd was slow and difficult to trail. Anyway, the Yankees wanted beef, not breeding animals. The range was overstocked with long-aged steers and unbranded bulls born during the war years. They belonged to whoever caught them, if they bore no brand. As we gathered cattle, the two buyers were joined at headquarters by a crew of hungry-looking cowboys excited about the chance for a paying job that would put real silver in their pockets for the first time since the war.

Thomas had never been one to talk much, and he had said less in the time since Maria's death. He had shown little real interest in anything other than those two children. Now he spent a lot of time with Hayes, listening to all the old cowman volunteered to tell him about driving cattle. When the counting was over and the cowboys left with the herd, Thomas had a canvas sack that clanked with the heavy sound of silver.

"Sounds like more than it is," I remarked, remembering that he could have gotten better payment from Branch Isom.

"The devil always outbids the righteous," he replied, looking oddly satisfied as he watched the dust stirred by the departing cattle. "Reed, I want you to get an early start in the morning. Ride over west and see if the Ramirez boys want three or four months of work." They were among the men who used to go with us mustang hunting. "Get Abe Johnson and Farley Good and the Martinez brothers. We'll need a good crew who know cattle and horses."

"To do what?"

I could see something kindling in his eyes, a fire I hadn't seen there in a long time, a touch of excitement I had feared had died forever. "To put our own trail herd together and drive them to Kansas." He hefted the bag of silver. "This will be enough to outfit us."

I stood there with my mouth hanging open, thinking of a dozen good objections but undecided which to voice first. I didn't want to dim that light growing in his eyes.

Thomas said, "If their cattle can walk that far, so can ours. If they can get fifteen dollars at the railroad, so can we."

I said, "Branch Isom will throw a fit."

That, I realized, was one of the factors which put that new spirit in Thomas' face; that thought had come to him days ago.

"Yes," he said with satisfaction. "He will."

6

My circle took me two days. I brought some of the men with me. Others were to follow when they could put personal business in order. Seeing some of those faces again made me remember old mustang-running days, and I felt a chill as the dark face of Bustamante came into my mind. It was said he had gone down into Mexico and had been killed fighting on the side of the *Juaristas*. Yet, there were among the Mexicans some who swore they had come across him in the brush country, in one secret camp or another. Somehow, people never wanted to let any of the old outlaws die; they kept seeing them whether they were dead or not.

I took the Fernandez boys and the crew that had come with me and started putting cattle together. Following Hayes's advice and example, we sorted out steers and bulls and hazed them toward headquarters, pushing cows and calves back out of the way. We had no fenced pastures, so we kept a couple of riders circling the outside, preventing the gathered cattle from drifting far.

Thomas arrived with a couple of extra *gringo* cowboys and a Mexican cook he had come across in San Antonio. They brought two well-used wagons, one with high sides built for hauling freight, the other an old canvas-covered army ambulance, wrecked and partially rebuilt. The words "U.S. Army" had been painted over but still showed. The heavy wagon was full of food and supplies. The ambulance was empty.

I watched little Katy rush out of the house and down the steps to throw her arms around her father's neck. Kirby kept his reserve.

Thomas took for granted what had been done in his absence; he had expected no less. I watched the youngsters go reluctantly back up the steps as Mrs. Fernandez called them to supper. Thomas lagged behind.

I said, "It's going to be tough on them, you being gone three or four months."

"They'll go with us," he replied. "We'll fix bunks in the old ambulance for them and Mrs. Fernandez."

I had never been inclined to give Thomas advice, but I could not accept this without argument. "We can't take those kids."

He didn't even look at me. "I wasn't much older than Kirby when we left Tennessee."

"That was another time. They'd be better off here at home with Mrs. Fernandez. Or with Maria's folks over in New Silesia."

"They're *my* children. I won't leave them with anybody." His eyes cut at me, telling me the argument was finished.

Laura Hines came out the next Sunday to see the children. Her reaction was the same as mine. Thomas' decision remained as stern. "I know of no one I'd leave them with."

She thought on it a little. "Leave them with me."

He wavered, for a moment. That idea had not occurred to him. "You couldn't stay with them and work too."

"I can keep books anywhere. I can do it at home."

"At home in Stonehill?" He spoke the name with bitterness. The moment of wavering was past. "That town has brought grief to this family ever since it began."

"This trip could bring a lot more." She looked accusingly at me. "Why haven't you talked him out of this?"

"I tried." Nothing more needed to be said.

Laura spent longer than usual with her Sunday afternoon good-byes. She held to the girl, her eyes begging Thomas. "Katy, at least."

"They're my children," he said, ungiving. "They're my responsibility."

Thomas avoided a similar argument with Maria's parents by simply not letting them know of his plan until too late. The first day's drive carried us to New Silesia and a little beyond. Thomas departed the drive long enough to take the ambulance and Mrs. Fernandez and the children into the little Polish town. He left me in charge of the herd, so I did not see or hear whatever challenge they gave him. But when we camped on water at dark, Thomas rode up with the ambulance. The look on his face spoke of victory hard won.

Those were the earliest days of trail driving north. Trailing was still an instinct, not a science. The first drives had no clear pattern to follow, so each outfit felt its way along. Later, old drovers would look back and laugh at the mistakes we made and the time we occasionally wasted. What most of us did, at first, was simply to use what we knew of handling cattle on the open range. We knew little of lead steers, of proper pace, of avoiding stray cattle, of always being sure where the water was, of crossing strange and unfriendly rivers. We did not even have a proper chuck wagon. That was a refinement yet to come, credited to cowman Charles Goodnight and copied and altered to fit the fancy of every trail boss and herd owner who pointed their cattle north. We simply carried grub and cooking utensils in the bed of the old freight wagon Thomas had brought from San Antonio. A certain amount of it had to be unpacked and then repacked at every meal, which soon had us wishing for a better way. The invention of the chuck-box was inevitable, with its drop-down lid that became a work table for the cook. But we didn't have it on that trip. We did the best we could with what we had, hoping for better the next time. If there was to be a next time.

We pushed the cattle hard the first few days to keep them tired, less likely to spook and run, or to try to turn back south toward home. The cattle were half wild, many of the bulls dragged out of the brush and handled by men and horses for the first time in their lives. They were always looking for something to booger at, and they often found it. Those first three or four days they must have run at least twice a day. Usually it was in the wrong direction, so the distance they made was wasted. I never could understand why cattle had such an adverse way of stampeding every direction except north.

The wildest of the early runs was on the third day, not long after we had strung them out in the morning. A black cloud had been hanging low in the north since long before daylight. We had watched a distant flashing and knew the cloud was coming at us. After sunrise, thunder rolled from west to east like the sound of cattle running. A sharp clap put the herd into a panic, running past the swing men on the east. We spurred as hard as we could push our horses, for the ambulance with the kids and Mrs. Fernandez was in the path of those cattle.

Mrs. Fernandez was not one to lose her head in a crisis; she had seen a fair number in her time. She swung the team to put the vehicle into an easterly direction, same as the cattle were running. This would keep it from being struck broadside. The cattle broke and went around either side of the ambulance. A few bumped it going by, but no real damage was done. The worst that happened was that one of the mules got its forelegs over the wagon tongue and hung up in the harness. Kirby was hanging out over the front, watching, and the jolt bounced him off of the wagon. He jumped to his feet, waving his hat and shouting. The last of the cattle swung away from him.

Thomas had been on the far side of the herd, so he was one of the last to reach the ambulance. I saw that everything was all right with Mrs. Fernandez and the kids, so I waved the rest of the riders after the cattle. Thomas spurred up, slid his horse to a stop and hit the ground running. His face almost white, he grabbed Kirby into his arms and hugged him. I thought the boy was in more danger of being crushed by his father than he had been from those running cattle.

Mrs. Fernandez's face was pinched. Katy tried hard not to burst into tears. I turned to Thomas. "I can keep the herd moving. Why don't you take the kids back to New Silesia? You can catch up to us in a couple or three days."

He just gave me that look. "You never give up, do you?" he asked.

I saw in his eyes that he would not change his mind. "I do when I can see there's no use fighting it anymore."

If Thomas did not change, little Kirby began to. Looking back on it afterward, I suspected it might have begun when he managed to wave the last running cattle around and escaped unhurt from a bad situation. He began to develop an attitude that nothing could hurt him if he stood his ground, an attitude to which he had been amply exposed at home. Thomas could not watch him all the time. When his father was not nearby, Kirby would saddle a horse and leave the ambulance to ride with the herd. Thomas soon gave up forbidding him. He ordered Kirby to stay with the drags at the rear of the herd where nothing was likely to happen to him. In no time Kirby would move up to the swing position and often to the lead, where one of the older, more responsible men was riding point. He accepted no authority except his father's, and that only when Thomas was nearby. No one else could send the boy back where he belonged. If one of the hands became insistent, Kirby would tell him in either English or Spanish to mind his own business.

He took to sleeping on the ground at night with the rest of the crew. A wagon, he declared, was for women and girls. Only on rainy nights would he compromise his pride and go into the covered ambulance. As the days wore into weeks he settled into a position with or near the Fernandez boys

during days, and he rolled his blankets near theirs at night.
The other men had started the drive mostly as strangers to
him, and grown men at that. He never warmed to them
much.

Kirby seemed to avoid Thomas as much as he could,
pulling away on his horse when Thomas approached. I
took it as a natural thing, a youngster's desire to escape his
father's critical eye and reprimands for his shortcomings.
But Thomas took it for something more. Nights, sometimes, I would see him staring at his son across the campfire, his eyes troubled.

One day we came to a small creek that under normal
circumstances would be no challenge. Rain had fallen during the night. It must have been heavier upstream, because
the creek was rushing along at a goodly clip. Thomas motioned me up to the point, where we sat with Farley Good
and studied the brownish water, colored by the soil the rain
had carried into it. We quickly decided it didn't present
much danger to the herd. I could have thrown a rock
across it with a sore arm.

"Put them into the water at a run," Thomas said, "and
they'll be over before they know they're wet." He looked
back, seeking out the Fernandez boys. Wherever they were,
there Kirby would be also. "I'm putting Kirby in the ambulance."

I became too busy rushing cattle across to pay attention
to what was happening behind me. By and by I heard a
boyish whoop and saw Kirby spur his pony into the stream.
I yelled at him to come back, but the order was lost in the
noise of the cattle splashing into the swollen creek. Halfway across, the pony lost its footing and turned under. Juan
Fernandez hit the water before I had time even to move. I
went in behind him.

Kirby came up threshing. Almost as he surfaced, Juan
grabbed him, pinning him against his leg as he carried him
out of the creek and onto the far bank. I was beside him the

last few feet, ready to grab if Juan showed sign of losing his hold.

I was too scared to talk, and Juan looked as if all the blood had drained from his face. But Kirby was laughing.

I struggled to say something. Juan gave Kirby a strong shaking. "Your papa say you don't come on your pony. He say you ride the ambulance."

"I didn't get hurt," Kirby said defensively. "And neither did my pony. Looky yonder, he's coming out of the water. Go get him for me, Juanito."

"I get a *belt* for you," Juan said angrily.

Thomas rode up, his eyes afire. "Go catch his pony, Juan. I've got the belt for him." He stepped from his saddle and caught Kirby as Juan let him slide to the ground. Thomas unbuckled his belt and pulled it from his trousers, then held it at half swing. Kirby drew himself up to take the blow, jutting his jaw but not quite closing his eyes. He stared defiantly at his father. I sat on my horse, watching the conflict play itself out in Thomas' face. Slowly he lowered the belt without using it on his son.

In later years he *would* strike him. By then it was too late.

Sharply he said, "Next time I tell you something, you listen."

Kirby did not reply. He stood braced, still half expecting the belt to strike, but he yielded nothing.

"Damn it, boy . . ." Thomas said slowly, not finishing what was on his mind. Juan brought up the dripping pony. "Get on him," Thomas commanded Kirby, "and then you stay on this side of the creek. Don't you go back into that water for anything."

It was an empty order. There was no reason for Kirby or anybody else to cross that creek twice. But Thomas had to assert his authority, even if he had lost it.

Most trail drives were a long, slow stretch of boredom, with a few minutes of excitement now and again to take the place of the sleep there never was enough time for. Crossing rivers was one of the few times we had any reason to let our blood pump fast, once the herd wore the "run" out of its system. A few cattle naturally took the leadership, rising up off of the bedgrounds at daylight and setting out to graze. About all we did was point their direction, north. Most of the other cattle would gradually get up and fall into the positions their natures best suited them to. Like people, cattle developed a standing in the social order. The ones highest up protected their places with all the jealousy of a San Antonio matron. The ones which took the lead in the first days of the drive held it the rest of the way. The one which fell back early stayed back. After a time you would get to know the individual cattle and just where they belonged on the drive. Unless one went lame or sick, he would not vary his position much.

After the first days, when the cattle were used to walking and Thomas was sure Branch Isom hadn't started his drive yet, we let the Longhorns graze along and set a pace that suited them. Thomas occasionally dropped back a few miles to be sure nobody was catching up to us with another herd. He became touchy about our front position; he would not stand for pressure from behind. One day we saw dust way to the rear, and I went with Thomas to see about it. Another herd was pushing along at a pace faster than ours. I thought for a while it might come to a fight. Thomas held on to that lead like it was a gift from the Almighty, and anybody who challenged us was on the devil's string. Hot words passed, but the trail boss of that other outfit shrank back from the look in Thomas' eyes. He decided his herd needed a day of rest to make up for the hard pace it had traveled.

The nearest we came to a genuine scare was with the Indians. They had been in the back of my mind from the beginning because there was no way to get to Kansas from South Texas without crossing Indian land. I had always felt we were overdue for trouble in the old days when we ran mustangs in the wild country far to the west of Stonehill, but somehow we had never run into them. Now we were pushing through country the government had granted to them, and a herd of cattle was a hard thing to hide. The people who had been north ahead of us said the Indians wouldn't usually bother an outfit that let them have a few cattle, but this was never a sure thing. A lot of them hadn't settled yet and hadn't agreed to any reservation. You couldn't tell by looking whether they were treaty Indians or the wild bunch. If they took a disliking to you it didn't make much difference anyway, people said.

I was riding point the afternoon they came on us, out of the sun. In the first excited moment I thought there must be fifty, but later I recounted and found only seventeen. I guess it was always that way with Indians; there were seldom as many as there seemed to be. They made no warlike signs against us, but they all carried armament—bows, lances, a few old muskets worn out before they traded for or stole them. They stopped in a ragged line. One who made it clear he was the leader came toward me; walking his horse. He held up one hand to show he was peaceful, but I watched the other hand more; it held a rifle with a barrel four feet long. He started talking and making signs with his hands. I decided he had rather talk to us than fight us, though he might fight if the talk ran thin.

Thomas loped up to me, some of the other men just behind him. The ambulance had stopped. The two Fernandez boys had moved beside it, ready to protect their mother and the kids.

My first thought was that Thomas' sign language would be no better than mine, but I didn't consider the fact that he had been married to a Polander woman and had talked to both her and her family with his hands. It didn't take him and the Indian but a minute or two to find enough common ground that they could parley.

Thomas' face was cold serious. He told me, "He says he's got a lot of hungry people. He wants a beef for every man he brought with him."

By this time I had made the count and told Thomas how many that was, in case he had not counted for himself. He agreed with me that this was a San Antonio fancy-house price. He bargained awhile and cut the number to ten. The Indian looked satisfied; I suspected he had been willing to settle for less.

We had been so taken up with the Indians that the sound of the wagon chains right behind us came as a shock. I turned in the saddle and saw that Mrs. Fernandez had brought up the ambulance. I suppose she didn't consider her boys protection enough; people instinctively looked to Thomas for that. Kirby had his horse up real close to the ambulance, and real close to Marco and Juan. Little Katy stood behind the wagon seat, beneath the tarp cover, but she looked out around Mrs. Fernandez, her eyes as big as brown saucers.

The Indian stared at her, and a smile spread across his face. That took me completely off balance; I had never featured Indians smiling at all. He edged his pony up closer to the ambulance. It shied at the wind-flapping canvas, but he held it with a tight rein. Katy faded back under the cover, where we could see little more than her eyes.

The Indian motioned for her to come back out. I suppose he was trying to tell her he intended her no harm, but Katy was not interested in getting better acquainted. The chief laughed and turned to Thomas. Thomas was trying not to show his uneasiness, but the effort strained him. His hand was on his gun butt. The Indian made some more sign talk. Thomas gradually eased, but he contrived to work his horse around between the Indian and the ambulance.

"Katy," he said, "he wants to trade for you. He says he'll give us six ponies."

In later years Katy would laugh over it, but at that moment she did not laugh. Her fear gave way to a flash of anger.

"You're not going to do it, are you, Papa?"

He said, "Six ponies is a lot."

She leaned out from under the canvas, a long steel pothook gripped in both of her little hands. "I'll hit him on the head!"

The Indian broke into laughter. He turned back to the men behind him, pointed and said something about the girl. I knew he was approving of the fight he saw in her. Several of the Indians laughed, which only deepened Katy's anger. Thomas held out his hand to calm her.

"It's all right, girl. He didn't mean it. Nobody meant it."

The chief turned away from the jesting and back to business. He signaled a few of his men forward. They rode into the herd with him and started picking some of the fleshier cattle. The deal had been ten. I decided Indians didn't count very well, because they took an even dozen. But Thomas didn't count, either. As soon as the Indians were on their way he climbed down from his horse and into the ambulance to hold the girl in his arms.

When it was over, Thomas was shaken more than Katy. Kirby didn't have much to say that night, but he had stood his ground too.

Backing down had been bred out of the Canfield line.

We saw Indians only a couple of times after that, and just once that they actually approached us. Mrs. Fernandez kept the ambulance way back—Thomas had a long parley with her about that. Katy crouched down behind the canvas with the pothook in her hand, out of sight until the Indians had taken a few steers and were gone beyond the hill. I kept watch on Kirby out of the corner of my eye. He stayed by the Fernandez boys, who stuck to the ambulance like burrs. That night Kirby had more to say. He was bolder, now that he had experienced Indians close up for a second time without coming to harm. He talked about what he would have done if the Indians had made any threat. The Fernandez boys pestered and hoorawed him about his bragging until he started hitting Marco. They were friends again, after a while, but Kirby could flare like a match.

We made all the river crossings with a certain nervousness, mostly because of the kids and Mrs. Fernandez.

Rainstorms, hail, wind—all these things visited our drive and left us miserable, though they did not strike anywhere near the heart. We reached the railroad tired and thinner than when we had started in Texas, but we had lost no men and relatively few cattle.

The railroad was something new to most of the Texans, though I had seen a few in the war. That first train clanging and banging and smoking up a black cloud awed some of our crew. It came near stampeding the cattle. Both of Mrs. Fernandez's boys had to hold tight to the reins to keep the ambulance team from running away. The wagon team ran a little and bounced off some of the bedrolls.

Ours was one of the early herds. We were considerably ahead of the season's rush, when several herds might hit the shipping pens the same day. Most of our crew was primed to ride into town and paint it a bold shade of red, but Thomas stood tough. Nobody was to leave the herd until it was sold and delivered. I heard some grumbling, but Thomas did not.

Selling the cattle would have been easy except for Thomas. Three or four prospective buyers rode out to the herd where we held it on a flat above town. Each new one raised the bid a little. Thomas waited until he had a bid from every buyer, then told the high bidder he wanted payment in gold. That gentleman turned three shades of crimson and declared that his check was as solid as the U.S. mint. Thomas calmly told him he knew nothing about the mint, but he was familiar with the value of gold. Mr. High Bidder denounced him as an unreconstructed rebel and rode off talking to himself.

Thomas sold the cattle to a man who had bid him a dollar a head less, but he said it was better to lose a dollar than to risk it all to fraud. The buyer was friendly enough, a former Yankee major named Thome, who had his beard cut in the style of Ulysses S. Grant and wore a black coat even though it was summertime. He chewed a foul black cigar that refused to stay lit. Unlike some other people we ran into in Kansas, he knew the war was over, and he didn't throw it in our faces that we had been on the losing side.

"I'll have to send to Chicago for the gold," he said.

Thomas told him, "We spent three months getting here. We can wait."

The buyer smiled. "I can't blame you for wanting gold. They've thrown out the honest men in Washington and turned the treasury over to blackguards. It would surprise me none at all one day to be able to buy their paper money at ten cents on the dollar."

Some of the men itched for a frolic, but Thomas was as ungiving as an army sergeant. We loose-herded the cattle, watering them a bunch at a time in a natural lake that held water from the spring rains. Not a man in the crew got to drink anything stronger than Mrs. Fernandez's coffee, which she boiled with sugar in it. The enforced sobriety didn't bother me; I had been in the army long enough to work that foolishness out of my system. But some of these younger fellows had never been out of Texas, so even the lamp-lit windows of a little Kansas prairie town looked like Chicago. They thought they had seen the elephant.

They never got a chance to test it. The gold arrived with the same engine that fetched a string of empty cattle cars to haul away the herd. We eased the cattle up to the stock-pens and counted off a carload at a time. The engine chuffed and smoked, pulling the cars forward a notch each time we finished loading one and sealing its sliding doors.

I caught the distrust in Thomas' face as the train finally left, smoking slowly eastward up those shining tracks. But the Yankee major was an honest man. I accompanied Thomas inside the bank while the crew waited restlessly outside. Thomas and the major each counted out the gold coins on a table in a small side office while I stood at the door with a nervous deputy marshal who was sweating over his responsibility.

Thomas closed and strapped a pair of new saddlebags he had bought to carry the money. The major said, "I would suggest you lock it in the bank's safe until you are ready to leave town."

The deputy's jaw dropped. But Thomas relieved him of worry. He said, "We guarded the cattle. We'll guard the money." His fingers closed so tightly over the bags that his big knuckles showed dots of white. I saw something in his eyes not unlike the look men sometimes get from drinking too much. It was not the money itself which intoxicated him; it was the thought of the land he could buy with that Union gold. Money was a tool, like a pick or a shovel. *Land* was what counted.

The men still waited outside. Thomas told the major, "I promised the crew a drink when the business was all done. I would be pleased if you would join us."

"It would be my pleasure, if you will allow me to buy a round."

Thomas frowned at the men. "Just one. I need them sober."

The bartender pulled a pair of bottles up from beneath the plain bar as we walked in. He saw the major and put those bottles back, taking better ones from in front of the big mirror behind the bar. He started pouring the glasses full. Thomas stared dubiously at the two Fernandez boys, then held up a finger. "Just one," he told them. The first round was Thomas'. We were sipping the major's round and looking at our trail-beaten images in the long mirror when we heard several horses. In a minute boots were stamping off dust on the little porch. Three dusty, bearded Texans walked through the door. One of them took two steps and stopped.

Thomas pushed away from the bar and dropped the leather saddlebags to the floor, freeing his hands. He made no move toward his pistol, but he was ready.

I stared a moment before I recognized Branch Isom, but Thomas had known him at a glance. Isom had the wearied look of a long, hard trail, his red-and-gray beard untended, his clothes hanging in ribbons, his boots crusted in dried mud. Resentment rose in his eyes, then he shoved it away.

"Congratulations, Thomas," he said evenly. "You got here ahead of me."

"That was my intention."

"I never regarded it as a contest."

"It has always been a contest between us, Isom."

"It seems so, but I can't remember anymore why it ever started."

"I remember."

The men with Isom were strangers. They appeared as bewildered as the major. Isom told them, "I believe we will be more comfortable elsewhere."

Everybody stood in silence until Isom and his men were gone. The major seemed disconcerted, being drawn into a situation he knew nothing about. In all likelihood he would be called upon to bid on Isom's herd after being made to appear in league with Isom's enemy.

Thomas said, "We have things to do. We'll take leave of this town in a little while."

The major shook Thomas' hand. It was clear he thought leaving was a good idea. The men in the crew, by and large, would not have agreed, but they had not been asked.

As we rode toward camp I moved close to Thomas. I said, "You owe these men a night free in town."

Thomas shook his head. "I owe them wages, nothing else."

He had an effective way of shutting off argument simply by not listening anymore. We brought the wagon up to a mercantile store and loaded it with supplies for the trip home. Thomas had sold the extra horses, leaving us just the ones we rode and a few to meet any happenstance. Thomas would not brook much in the way of happenstance.

We were able to travel only a couple of hours before evening. It seemed to me we could just as well have waited until morning, but we put that many miles between ourselves and the temptations of the town and camped with a crew dissatisfied but sober. I had thought Thomas would ease a little as we headed south, toward home. But he was just as tense carrying the money as he had been driving the cattle.

I said, "If it'll make you feel better, we can set a guard over the camp." The men had been used to night guard on the way up. Thomas shook his head. "I won't sleep much anyway."

I hadn't been asleep long when I was jarred out of it by somebody hollering, out in the night.

"Hello the camp," he called. "I'm coming in."

I threw back my blanket and grabbed first for my pistol, then for my boots, which was all I had taken off.

Thomas shouted, "Who's out there?"

"Major Thorne," came the answer. "Is that you, Canfield?"

"It's me. Come on in." Thomas held a rifle.

The major was alone. The fire had burned down so that it did not throw much light on him, but he was easily recognized by the military set of his shoulders. His voice was urgent. "You had better rouse your camp, Canfield. I am not the only company you are going to have tonight."

There was no handshaking or attempt at pleasantries.

Thomas demanded, "What is the trouble?"

"Word has reached me that a gang of toughs is going to raid you for your gold."

Thomas spat. "Branch Isom!"

"No, not Isom. Some of the riffraff that have been hanging around town to see what they can steal from better men's labor. The whole town knows I paid you in gold."

Thomas was silent a minute, staring at the old ambulance. "This is as good a place as any to defend ourselves. But we have to get those children out of here, and Mrs. Fernandez."

We had crossed a dry wash just before we stopped for the night. We had ridden up onto higher ground to make camp, a standard precaution in country where a quick rain somewhere else could bring a rush of water down on a place that hadn't seen a drop. I suggested we hide the woman and children somewhere in that wash, where no stray bullets would find them.

Thomas agonized over it. "I don't want to be separated from Kirby and Katy."

"They could be killed if they stay here," I told him.

He called the Fernandez boys to him. "I want you-all to take your mother and Kirby and Katy and hide out in the wash yonder. Go far enough to be out of the way."

Katy did not want to leave. Kirby kept his silence. Thomas hugged the girl and handed her to Mrs. Fernandez, saying, "Take her and go, quick." The Mexican woman carried Katy while Kirby walked behind her, looking back at us with regret. The Fernandez boys each carried a rifle.

Thomas turned to the major. "I thank you, sir, for coming to tell us. Now I believe it is time you leave this place."

"I would stay and help."

"You've helped already. You have no stake in this, and there is no need for you to risk your life. I have good men here, all sober."

The major was an honest man with a good heart, but he was not rash. Extending his hand, he said, "Good luck," and rode off, making a wide swing away from the trail to avoid an unpleasant midnight meeting.

I had had military experience, but Thomas did not ask me for advice. He ordered that the horses be moved into a little grove that was like a black patch in the moonlight, a couple of hundred yards away. We tied them there, hoping they would be far enough from gunfire not to hurt themselves surging against the ropes. That done, we pulled back a little way from camp, from the ambulance and the wagon, leaving our bedrolls. Thomas carried the saddlebags over his shoulder. He spread us in a semicircle, covering the camp from the southeast so that no fire would be directed toward the kids.

We were prepared for a long and nervous wait, but they did not give us that much time. Almost as soon as we were positioned, we heard the soft plodding of hoofs to the north. The riders were walking their mounts, trying to make no noise, but a horse is not by his nature the most silent of animals. He rolls his nose, his stomach sloshes of water, and the more contentious will squeal and bite if a strange horse gets too near. For a while we could only hear them, then we began to see them, a vague dark mass moving slowly toward us in the thin moonlight. They drew close together as they spotted the two vehicles, or perhaps the dying light of the campfire. Some of the horses stamped nervously, but the men were evidently talking in whispers.

Suddenly they came spurring, fanning out to hit the camp broadside. Gunfire flashed in the darkness, roaring and ringing in our ears as the riders fired into our blankets, into the wagon. When one of them put three quick shots into the ambulance, Thomas came up from the ground with a curse and began firing his rifle. In a second or two we were all shooting. The surprised raiders shouted and screamed and fired back, but all they had to shoot at was the flashing of our guns. That, in the night, was half blinding, working against our marksmanship as well as theirs. The black powder burned our noses and put us to choking, the way I remembered it from the war. It brought up all the old feelings I had known of fear and hate and exultation, mixed up together and confusing.

Amid the fire and smoke and milling of frightened horses, we could not see much, but neither could they. Two or three men rode over and past us. One of them fell, crying out to God for mercy. The thought struck me that God hadn't sent him on this errand.

As suddenly as they had come, they were gone, the ones still on horseback. As best I could tell, half a dozen rode away. A couple more escaped afoot, limping and carrying themselves hunched over in pain.

None of us left our places at first, each waiting for somebody else to move. The smoke still clung thick and heavy, catching in our throats, burning our eyes. I saw men on the ground where our camp had been. Some moved, some didn't. Three horses were down, kicking and fighting and squealing.

Thomas was the first to move in. He walked warily, hunched over to present less of a target. He stopped to shoot one of the wounded horses, and I thought for a bad moment he was going to shoot a wounded man who lay nearby. The raider pleaded for his life. Thomas picked up a pistol, then poked his way among the other fallen men, kicking weapons from their reach. A couple of the men were beyond using them. Thomas shot the other two horses, putting them out of their pain.

We counted two men dead, another far into his dying. Three more were wounded but not in immediate danger unless Thomas lost his head and shot them. I could see the temptation rising in him.

"You," he seethed to a man sitting on the ground, gripping a bleeding leg, "you fired into the ambulance. If my kids had been in there you'd have killed them!"

"I didn't," the man pleaded, feeling death's cold breath. "I didn't shoot in there. God as my witness."

Thomas couldn't really have told one man from another, dark as it was, the gunflashes blinding us. He just fastened onto that man because he was available and seemed a little less shot up than the others.

Thomas demanded, "Where's Branch Isom?"

The man sobbed, "I don't know no Branch Isom."

"You're a liar!" Thomas shoved the muzzle of his pistol against the bridge of the man's nose. "Branch Isom led you out here."

The man was crying so that he could not answer. Thomas took that for answer enough, but I didn't. I said, "We've got no solid reason to think Branch Isom was behind this. The major told you himself it was a bunch of the town trash."

"It has the smell of Branch Isom," Thomas insisted. "He would have killed my kids!"

I was convinced he was wrong, but it was a waste of

time and breath to argue with him. He wanted so badly for it to be Isom that he would ignore any contrary evidence. If I had ever doubted how deeply his hatred had gripped him, I knew it that night.

A voice called from the darkness. "Hello the camp."

Thomas replied, "Come on in, Major."

Major Thorne dismounted. The smell of smoke and blood had his horse dancing in nervousness. The major made no idle comments and asked no empty questions. He could see the wounded and dead for himself. "How many hurt in your party?"

"None seriously," Thomas told him. "We have you to thank for that."

The major said, "I couldn't bring myself to ride far. I saw what was left of them tearing off for town. I knew you'd bloodied them."

Thomas stood beside the ambulance, poking his finger at the bullet holes in the canvas. His anger had not lessened. "If my children had been in there . . ." It seemed to strike him for the first time that the two youngsters and the Fernandez family were still in the wash, probably frantic to know what had happened.

"Reed," he said, "you and the men get up the horses and hitch the teams. We'll leave as soon as I fetch the kids." He started for the wash, trotting hard.

Thomas never had actually asked if any of us were hurt. He had seen everybody, and nobody was down. I did some quick checking and found one of the cowboys had taken a shallow bullet-burn along his hip. It did more damage to his clothes than to his body. We had the teams harnessed and the horses saddled by the time Thomas came back, carrying Katy. Kirby followed. Thomas turned the girl so she would not see the wounded and the dead. He quickly lifted her into the ambulance. Kirby stared at the carnage.

Thomas roared at him, "Boy, you get yourself into that ambulance." Kirby did not move fast enough to suit him, so Thomas grabbed him by one arm and the seat of his britches, hoisting him up.

The major said, "You're going back to town, aren't you? The law will want to know all about this."

Thomas' voice was bitter. "Where was the law tonight? If they want to talk to us they can come to Texas."

"What about these wounded men?" the major asked. "They could die if you just leave them here."

"Then let them die. Good-bye to you, Major." Thomas swung into his saddle and waved his arm. We pulled away from that unlucky camp, leaving three wounded men crying for us to help them. Thomas acted as if he never heard, but I did. I kept hearing them for years.

7

We traveled fast and hard the first two or three days, pushing until the teams were plainly giving out. Thomas looked back often. I thought at first he was apprehensive over possible pursuit, but that was not it. Toward the end of the first day he told me, "I didn't want to leave that place, Reed. If we hadn't had the children with us I would have ridden back into that town and faced up to Branch Isom and had it out with him for once and for all."

I tried to tell him again that I did not believe Isom had anything to do with the raid on us. He just rode off and left me. He never wasted time on things he did not want to hear.

He was not given much to talk, and he talked even less than usual as we picked our way south the way we had come. We met many trail herds pushing north, but we stayed on the upwind side and visited little. I would catch him rough-counting the cattle and mumbling to himself as he figured up how much money they might bring at the railroad. It was unlikely many would receive as much per head as ours; the market would go down as the season went on and the numbers increased. The fact that we reached the market ahead of him probably cost Branch Isom a dollar or two per head.

We were bone-weary as we moved into the familiar rolling country that meant home was just ahead of us. The sight of those South Texas prairies and occasional tangles of thorny chaparral was as welcome as a mother's face. We skirted around New Silesia. Thomas did not offer to explain, but I supposed he did not want Maria's folks to see the kids so trail-gritty and tired. He would clean them up and feed them up, *then* show them to their grandparents.

We came in sight of the homeplace, the houses, the barns, the corrals and fields. I sighed in relief. "I don't think I will ever leave again. This is one trip I never want to repeat."

"You will," Thomas said matter-of-factly. "There is money to be made taking cattle to the railroad, money to be invested in land. You'll make the trip again, and so will I."

I could think of a dozen arguments. The best one was in the ambulance, tailing up the outfit. "But the kids . . ."

"I made a mistake, taking them. I realized it the day Kirby nearly drowned. It was too late then. I'll rectify that mistake now."

He did not explain himself, and I did not ask him.

I never could understand how news could carry so fast. The morning after we reached home, Laura Hines arrived in a buggy, pulling right up to the big house. Katy shouted and ran down the steps. The woman and the little girl embraced one another and cried. Thomas and I watched from the barn, then walked up to the house. Kirby stood on the porch, looking at Laura but not running to her as his sister had done. Laura had to go up the steps to him. She tried to hold him, but he struggled away.

Thomas stopped at the gate and studied the woman with his children. I could not be so calm. I still thought Laura Hines was the finest-looking woman I had ever seen. I wanted to take hold of her but could not bring myself to do it. I shoved my hand forward. She hugged me. I melted to a mixture of delight and despair.

"It's good to have you back, Reed." She looked past me toward Thomas. "All of you. I haven't had a night's sleep the whole time, worrying about these children." She stepped back from me and put her hands lovingly on Katy's shoulders. "I'll bet you have a lot of stories to tell me."

Katy said, "An Indian wanted to buy me, but Papa wanted too many ponies."

Laura looked reproachfully at me. "You took these children where there were Indians?"

Kirby could not let Katy's story go unchallenged.

"Aw, it was just a big joke. Those Indians were scared of us."

Laura turned toward Thomas, watching him as he slowly came up onto the porch. The reproach drained swiftly from her eyes.

"Welcome home, Thomas."

"Hello, Laura. I'm glad you came out. I was going to send for you."

They did not hug; they did not even shake hands. They just looked at one another. Thomas reached for the screen door and held it open. "Come in, Laura. We have things to talk about."

He closed the door behind them, leaving me with the two youngsters on the porch. Katy went inside, but I heard Thomas say something to her, and she came out again, disappointed.

I said, "You-all haven't seen the colts. You'll be surprised how much they've grown while we were away." They followed me to the barn, and I kept them busy.

After a long time Laura came out looking for us. Her face was flushed. She was trying to hold down excitement. "Children, your father wants you at the house."

Kirby was brushing one of the colts and did not want to leave. He paid no attention to Laura. I told him sternly, "You go up yonder and see what your daddy wants." Katy had not waited; she had gone on ahead.

Laura stayed, trembling a little. I could not tell whether she wanted to laugh or cry, but she was holding back one or the other. She blurted, "He asked me to marry him."

I felt as if I had been kicked in the stomach. I knew upon reflection that this should not have come as any surprise.

Badly as I wanted her myself, she had never had eyes for any man except Thomas Canfield.

I asked a foolish question. "What did you tell him?"

"I told him I would."

It took me a while to work up the nerve to ask the next question. "Do you think he loves you?"

Tears edged into her eyes. "He was honest with me, Reed. He likes me. He respects me. But the only woman he ever loved lies on that hill yonder." She pointed her chin toward the family cemetery.

"Then why . . ." I started.

She cut me off. "He needs a mother for those children. The trail drive was a nightmare because of them. He wants to know they'll always be here safe, with somebody who cares for them."

"Katy cares for you, too. But I don't know about Kirby."

"I'll have to manage with Kirby. He'll learn. We'll both learn."

I was suddenly angry at Thomas, angry because it seemed to me he was buying Laura much the way he would buy cattle or horses or a block of land. "So Thomas gets a mother for his children. What do you get out of this?"

"A home. *His* home. I'll be near him from now on."

"Near him, but not really *with* him. Will that be enough for you?"

"It's more than I've had."

I slapped the palm of my hand against a post so hard that it hurt. "You can't be happy with half a marriage."

"Happier than I've been with none at all."

Over the years I had learned to tell from Thomas' eyes when an argument was over. I saw that look in Laura's. I took her hand and said, "I've never said anything to you, but I think you know how I've always felt."

"I know. Sometimes I've wished it could be otherwise for me, but it never will."

"Then, be happy, Laura."

"I will," she said. She kissed me and returned to the house.

The wedding was quiet, almost as if Thomas did not care to have it noticed. As usual he did not explain himself. Laura told me he felt that a show was inappropriate because it had not been so long since Maria had died. She did not have to tell me the rest, the fact that this was a marriage of convenience on his part, almost a business arrangement, done for the children rather than for himself. One did not throw a public celebration over the buying of property.

A handful of us, close friends all, watched the ceremony in the parlor of the house Thomas had built for Maria. He was solemn, almost regretful. Laura glowed. Kirby, young though he was, saw through it about as well as any of us. After the vows had been spoken he walked onto the porch by himself and stared darkly up the hill toward the cemetery. Katy went out after a minute. I followed them because I felt like a hypocrite, joining the other people in telling Thomas and Laura how fine a match they were, how everybody knew they would both be very happy.

Katy was puzzled by her brother's coldness. "Aren't you glad we've got a new mother?"

He turned on her in a flash of anger. "We don't have a new mother. She's just going to watch after us, is all. Mrs. Fernandez could have done that."

He walked out to the barn and proceeded to soil his new suit chunking rocks at the milkpen calves.

Looking back, it is hard to pinpoint just when Kirby started going wrong. At times I remember the river crossing on the drive to Kansas, but the seed may have been planted earlier. It might even have been there from birth, an inheritance of the wild anger which sometimes cropped out in Thomas. I was gone a lot of the time and did not fully realize the extent of Kirby's rebellion until later.

After the wedding I made up my mind I did not want to

live at the headquarters anymore, so near Laura. Of course I could not give Thomas my real reason, so I told him I had decided it was time to put up a house on my own land and see after my own interests. If he saw through me he gave no indication of it. He said, "I have been making some plans, Reed, and I was counting on you to help me with them. We can make money supplying cattle to the railroad market."

"I don't want to go back up that trail, not this soon."

"You won't have to. I can hire other people to do that. I want you to travel around the country buying cattle for me and shaping up herds for the trail. You have a knack for that kind of thing. You have an easy way of dealing with people, something I never learned."

I couldn't deny that. Thomas had just one way of dealing with people, on his own terms. If they didn't like those terms, there was no compromise, no deal.

When I still hesitated, he said, "You'll be my full partner in the operation. Whatever we make, half of it is yours. You can buy a lot of land."

I found that I enjoyed traveling. Over the next several weeks I saw a great deal of South Texas, visited a lot of ranches and became acquainted with a large number of people. It was my observation then, and still is, that as a class the people who make their living directly off of the land are among the most honest there are, probably because the land itself does not compromise or accept excuses. A person can lie to his fellow man and even to himself, but he cannot lie to or cheat the land. If he does not irrigate her with the proper amount of sweat, she will not produce for him. She will not be short-changed.

We put together three more herds in time to go up the trail that season, using the money received for the first herd at the railroad. Not many people in South Texas had any clear idea what cattle were worth up north, so prices hadn't increased much. They were glad to get rid of some surplus and lay their hands on real Yankee gold. Most trades in the outlying parts of the state were still by barter, and these people had little to barter other than cattle. They would gladly trade several steers for a barrel of flour or a sack of coffee beans. Poverty lay like a curse across the land in those first years after the war. Nobody had much, and a lot of people had nothing.

Once I unexpectedly met head-on with Branch Isom at a salt-grass ranch not far from the steamy Gulf of Mexico. Usually I was ahead of him, offering better prices and getting the better cattle. He wound up having to take a lot of the aged steers and the staggy kinds castrated too late in their lives. These too would fetch a price at the railroad, but not like the three- and four-year-old steers that could gain weight on a slow drive and arrive at the railroad in flesh enough for slaughter.

Isom and I sort of circled each other, wary as town dogs encountering a stranger. We shook hands and then stood apart, awkward and both wishing we were somewhere else. He said, "You've been busy, Reed Sawyer. Most places I go, you've been there and left."

"I don't plan it that way," I said.

He half smiled. "It would please Thomas Canfield if you did."

I didn't try to deny that. Isom frowned. "I heard he was blaming me for that robbery attempt up in Kansas. I want you to know, Reed, I had nothing to do with that."

"I never thought you did."

"But *he's* convinced I did, so the hell with him. He's a little bit crazy, I think."

I had never considered Thomas in quite so extreme a light. I changed the subject. "How's your family?"

"Fine, just fine. Got my boy with me out in the buckboard. Bet you haven't seen him in a long time. Come on out and let him say howdy to you."

I really wasn't wanting all that much familiarity, but I couldn't with any kind of courtesy turn him down. I followed Isom to his buckboard in the shade of a big moss-hung liveoak tree. "James," he said to the boy, "I want you to shake hands with Mr. Sawyer."

The boy was about Kirby's age, probably already taking some schooling. He had a bright, eager look about him, like a boy who would learn well because he wanted to. He looked me in the eye when he shook my hand; most youngsters won't do that without coaching. Kirby wouldn't; he never had. I glanced at Branch Isom and saw the strong pride in his round, reddish face. Whatever he might have been once, he was a father now. He did not have to tell me he was wrapped up in that boy; it showed all over him.

Isom said to his son, "Mr. Sawyer has beaten us here, James. I expect we'll have to go somewhere else."

I could see partisanship rise in the boy's eyes. I could not help thinking of Kirby, if he and Thomas had been in the same situation. Kirby probably wouldn't have given a damn.

I found myself asking, "Son, you really want these cattle here?"

The boy said firmly, "My daddy does."

I said, "Then your daddy will get the chance to make the first bid on them." Later, when Isom made that bid, I didn't raise it. I rode away from there wondering what Thomas would say if he ever heard what I had done. I wasn't going to tell him. It would have been worth going through the storm, though, just for the pleased look I saw on that boy's face when his father got the cattle he wanted.

Thomas was always a man to keep his promises, but occasionally things worked out so that he could not. He was unable to find anybody he thought was suitable to boss that third and last set of cattle up the trail. I had to do it myself. The snow was starting to fly a little by the time I sold the cattle at the tail end of the season's market and turned south, carrying Thomas' saddlebags heavy with gold coin. The raw north wind helped hasten my trip home, that and the memory of the robbery attempt the spring before.

I never told Thomas that Branch Isom and I pooled our trail outfits and rode back to South Texas together for mutual protection. Because some of the Canfield crew as well as his came from Stonehill, I remained with him until I watched his arrival at home, his little boy James running out onto the porch, then down the tall steps and into the yard to throw his arms around his father. Isom carried the boy up onto the porch where his wife waited, and Isom hugged both of them.

He had not made nearly so much money out of the trail season as Thomas and I had, but it seemed to me he was rich in one respect that neither Thomas nor I would ever be.

I turned loose the last of the crew and rode to the ranch alone, reining up in front of the big house a while before dark. I tied my horse to the fence, unstrapped the heavy saddlebags and walked wearily up the steps, thinking surely someone must have seen me.

Katy had. She flung open the door and shouted, "Uncle Reed." I received, in a distant-relative sort of way, the kind of greeting Branch Isom had gotten in town. Laura came into the hallway at the sound of Katy's shout. To a tired and lonely man she looked beautiful. I wanted to crush her, but I reached out my hand and took off my dusty old hat.

She shook my hand. "It's good to have you back, Reed."

Kirby appeared at the end of the hall. He stared at me with no more emotion than if I had been some stranger come to sell his father a load of hay.

"Where's Thomas?" I asked her.

Sadness showed in her eyes before she covered it. "Mr. Canfield is off looking at some land west of here. He had no clear idea when you'd be back."

Mr. Canfield. "He's gone a lot, I suppose."

"He works awfully hard."

I slid the saddlebags from my shoulder. "I'd best put this in the safe." Thomas had bought one in San Antonio after the first trip. It was in the parlor, where some people would have placed a piano.

Laura watched me close the safe and give the knob a turn. "You must be starved."

I told her I would eat at the bunkhouse. We had a full-time Mexican cook there now for the growing number of cowhands. Mrs. Fernandez had been relieved of all responsibilities other than the care and feeding of her sons Marco and Juan. But Laura would not hear of my going. She insisted I needed and deserved a good woman-cooked meal, served on a table with real dishes instead of tinware. After all that time on the trail I could put up no good argument.

By this time I had the use of the old double log cabin where Thomas' mother had lived so long. I cleaned up and put on some fresh clothes and made my way back to the big house with mixed feelings. Being that close to Laura was both pleasure and pain.

Katy was helping Laura in the kitchen, happily fetching and carrying. There had always been this free and happy and loving relationship between them. I did not see the boy. In a bit the table was set and ready. Laura stepped into the hall and called for Kirby. He did not come. Katy kept her head down when Laura asked her if she knew where her brother was. Reluctantly the girl said, "He went to the barn."

"I told him not to. He knew supper was almost ready."

Katy flushed a little, clearly wanting to defend her brother but knowing he was in the wrong. I said, "I'll fetch him."

I found him sitting on a mesquite-rail fence, studying a mare and a newly born colt. I said, "Your supper's ready."

He ignored me. I said, "Come on, son, before you get yourself in trouble. Your mother wants you."

He turned on me angrily. "She's not my mother. I don't have to do what she says."

Never having raised any kids of my own I didn't know how to answer that. I had a strong inclination to exercise my hand about six inches below the back of his belt. I just reached up and plucked him from the fence, took his hand and led him to the house. He pulled back on me all the way. He ate his supper in grim silence, pushed his chair away from the table and stomped off to his room. I tried not to look at Laura.

Katy said, "I'll tell Papa. He'll spank him."

Laura shook her head. "Don't tattle. We'll have to find a way to handle Kirby ourselves, you and I."

I asked her as gently as I could, "This happen much?"

She only nodded. I asked, "Does Thomas know?"

She nodded again. "He's done all he knows to do."

I thought I knew something but tried to keep the idea from showing. I guess she read my mind. She smiled uneasily. "He's tried that. He's tried love too. I guess the only thing that will work is time."

She was wrong about that. Time made him worse. He soon hit that period when he was growing rapidly, and all of it away from Laura and Thomas. By then Thomas had twenty-five or thirty cowhands scattered over the place, ranging from devout Christians to devout hellions. Kirby seemed, when he had the choice, to tag after the hellions.

When he was eight I caught him smoking tobacco swiped from somebody in the bunkhouse. When he was ten I found him slumped against a corral post in a stupor, an empty whisky bottle on the ground. I never told Laura or Thomas; they had enough worries.

I didn't enter the big house oftener than was necessary anymore. Remembering the warmth and happiness there in Maria's time, I found the place cool. From the beginning, Thomas had formed the habit of addressing Laura as Mrs. Canfield, and he was Mr. Canfield to her. The relationship was one of formality and respect on his part. On hers there was always a holding back, a love suppressed out of fear that it would be rebuffed. Only with Katy did Laura let herself go. She lavished on the girl all the affection she wanted to give her husband and stepson. Had she lived, Maria could hardly have been much closer to that flashing-eyed child.

That seemed only to widen the distance between Kirby and the rest of the family.

Katy was always eager to visit her grandparents in New Silesia, and Laura seemed happy to take her. Whatever reservations the old folks might have had about seeing their daughter's place in the house taken by someone else, they accepted Laura as a friend. The difference in language was always a problem, but Katy acted as interpreter; she spent enough time in New Silesia that she spoke Polish as well as she did English.

Kirby was another matter. He seemed always to have something he had rather do than visit his grandparents. At first I thought it might be simply that he did not want to ride in the buggy with his sister and stepmother, that he thought it unmanly. I offered to take him there myself. I had just as well suggest that he shovel out the corrals.

"They're just dumb old potato-eaters," he declared. "I don't want to see them."

If he had been mine I would have struck him across the mouth. Kirby glared, daring me. I might have done it had I not heard Thomas behind me, cold as December. He had been in the barn. He had a look in his eyes that usually meant blood to somebody. "Reed," he said very quietly, "I want to have some words with my son."

Badly as Kirby needed correction, I dreaded what that look bespoke.

"Thomas," I argued, "he doesn't know what he's saying. He's been listening to foolish talk from men who ought to be fired off of this place."

There had been more and more of those lately, men who laughed at the Polanders and condemned the Mexicans.

Thomas' voice took on an extra barb. "Go somewhere, Reed."

I went somewhere, but not so far that I didn't hear the crackle of heavy leather striking against cotton britches. Kirby did not cry.

His feeling against his grandparents seemed only to deepen; it was as if he blamed them for his punishment.

When he was about fourteen Kirby started running with the Hallcomb boys. Their father was a muleskinner by trade and had been fired by just about every freighting outfit from San Antonio to the Gulf. During one of his periods between jobs he was in the Alamo city helping create a boom in the saloon business when a prominent merchant was pistol-whipped one dark evening and the receipts of a busy Saturday removed from his safe. The crime was never solved. Some people thought it strange that old Goodson Hallcomb showed up back in Stonehill soon afterward with enough money to buy a little stock farm. In those days you didn't throw accusations around unless you had the facts. Nowadays they'll sue you for slander. Back then they were more likely to come looking for you with a pistol.

Hallcomb was good at raising and training draft stock for the same freight outfits that had fired him, and the San Antonio merchant soon made back all he had lost in the robbery, so most people abided by the old adage and let a sleeping dog lie. They wished he did as well at raising his boys as at raising and training mules, though. They were a salty pair, Bo about a year older than Kirby and Speck two years older. They were freckle-faced, tobacco-chewing, knot-fisted and knot-headed. Besides mules, old Goodson raised a crop of corn every year, part to feed and part to drink. Growing up, those boys of his put away more of the old man's corn whisky than of milk.

Thomas warned Kirby to stay away from that unholy clan, which made him turn to them all the more. At first it was mostly harmless things like riding the old man's wild mules. That led to drunken sprees in which they turned over farm outhouses and let pigs out of their pens into people's gardens and bobbed off the tails of some choice buggy teams.

Thomas was inclined to severe lectures and now and then a strong application of razor strop while Kirby leaned over the washstand by the back porch of the big house. It was always a case of punishment but never of correction. In no time Kirby would be back with the Hallcomb boys, dreaming up some new form of devilment for the community.

One Sunday Kirby and the Hallcombs, well supplied with the old man's corn, rode into New Silesia and fired at the church bell while mass was in progress. Then they tried to ride their horses into the church itself, to the shame of Kirby's old grandparents. Katy happened to be with the Brozeks. She pulled her brother out of the saddle, no hard chore in view of his condition. She then pounded him over the head with her grandmother's old-country Bible, which weighed almost too much for Mrs. Brozek to carry.

Kirby was shamed more by his sister's publicly administered retribution than by the words of the priest, who led him outside and reviewed the sacraments to him, placing particular stress on those sections that had to do with sin, punishment and hellfire. The Hallcomb boys, who had never received instruction in any of these subjects, stayed on the other side of the dusty street, grinning.

Thomas was outraged when the news came home to him. He nailed Kirby against the wall with his eyes. "Those are your mother's people," he said. "She would be mortified to know what you've done."

Kirby defiantly shook his head, denying any contrition. "They're not *my* people. I wouldn't claim them if she was *here*."

Thomas slapped him across the mouth, drawing blood. But he was too late. Much too late.

Afterward Thomas sat with me on the front steps, staring sadly toward the family cemetery. "I gave him a bad name, Reed."

"No, Thomas," I said. "Kirby's a good name."

"He's wild, like the other Kirby was."

Wild yes, but there the similarity ended, I thought. The first Kirby had never hurt anyone except himself. The second Kirby hurt everybody around him. I didn't see that my saying so would do anybody any good, so I kept the feeling to myself.

Thomas made up his mind to put Kirby's excess energies to use. He sent him to Kansas with two thousand head of cattle and a tough-minded trail boss who had the disposition of an old wildcat with one foot in a trap. The boss brooked no foolishness. He made no distinction between the owner's son and the poorest Mexican cowhand in the crowd. When Kirby came home three months later he was lean, tanned and sober. He bore a small scar high on his cheek to remind him of the folly of challenging authority that was a head taller and forty pounds heavier.

For a while he applied himself to business and the school Thomas helped finance for youngsters in that part of the county. Any sign of backsliding could be stopped by reference to the possibility of another trip with that hard-driving trail boss.

Katy had been a little chubby as a small girl, but around twelve or thirteen she started growing up instead of out, taking on some of the look of her mother. She had those same wide brown eyes, a shy, sideways smile that often made me remember early trips I had made with Thomas to New Silesia. She must have made Thomas remember, too, for sometimes I caught him watching her with a sadness that put a chill on me. He had never completely buried Maria. Her ghost walked his house and lay with him in that big wooden bed.

From things Laura occasionally told me, and more she did not, I knew she did not share Thomas' bed. I knew they seldom talked to each other anymore, not about the things that really mattered. They spoke of the weather and the crops and the cattle, and of news in the San Antonio paper. That was enough to carry them through the meals. Afterward, each had a place in the house apart from the other, a retreat from the responsibility of conversation.

As Katy grew older, Thomas became increasingly uncomfortable around her. He appeared confused, uncertain, and he kept a relationship almost as formal as his with Laura. When Katy was fourteen Thomas sent her to San Antonio to boarding school, over Laura's protests. Laura went with her to see her settled and secure and was a month in coming home. That seemed to suit Thomas all right; in seeing after Katy she was performing the duties he had married her for.

Thomas seldom felt obliged to explain anything, but one night as we ate supper in the bunkhouse—Laura was still gone—he said to me, "Katy's by way of growing up. She'll be a woman before we know it. We have too many young men around this place who have no attachments and no responsibility. She needs to be gotten to a better climate."

I could not argue with him about that. Even at fourteen she had begun to distract some of the young hands from their work. I never did tell Thomas about the boy who kissed her and then tried to take her behind the barn. I would have thrashed him, but that seemed unnecessary after Katy had blacked both of his eyes and split his lip. I just fired him and told him to leave before Thomas somehow found out.

By the time she was sixteen, there was no telling what the situation might be.

Somehow, neither of us considered that there were boys in San Antonio too. Not that Katy was one to let her head be turned, but you don't solve a problem just by moving it out of your sight. When she came home to spend that first summer she seemed to get an awful lot of mail and spend much time with a pen in her hand, answering it.

She was near sixteen when she came home for the second summer. Thomas was away on a land trip, for which I became thankful at the time. Laura had planned to take the buggy to San Antonio and fetch her, but all of a sudden and unannounced Katy showed up in front of the house in a buggy driven by a boy, or rather, a young man. He climbed down quickly and raised his hands to help her to the ground. Laura appeared on the porch, recognized Katy and hurried to the front gate with a smile I could see all the way from the corrals. The smile left her as she looked at the young man.

It was good to have the girl back on the place. I walked up from the corrals and hugged her like the uncle I was supposed to be. Katy pulled back and nodded toward the boy.

"Uncle Reed, I have somebody here I want you to meet."

The young man said, "We've met, Mr. Sawyer, a long time ago. I'm James Isom."

I've knocked down many a slaughter steer with the back side of an ax, and I felt as if somebody had just done that to me. An Isom here, on *this* place . . . It hadn't happened since the time Branch Isom had come out to try to buy some cattle from Thomas.

I shook the boy's hand and tried to remember how he had looked long ago when I had let his father have the cattle I had intended to buy. Now that I knew who he was, I could see he still had the same general features, the same big eyes that didn't look as if they ever had anything to hide. "It's good to see you again, son," I lied, thinking how fortunate it was that Thomas had gone somewhere.

Katy said, "James is going to school in San Antonio too, Uncle Reed. His mother and father went up to get him, and they offered to bring me home."

I could hardly believe what I heard. "You've been to Stonehill?" Her father had not set foot in that town since before she was born, except for a funeral. He had forbidden his children ever to go there. Kirby had violated that order for years, but I had never featured Katy doing it. I glanced at Laura but saw no surprise. I suspected she had known the Isoms were sending their boy to school in San Antonio. I also knew that if she had ever told Thomas, he would have moved Katy to Galveston, or maybe as far away as St. Louis or Kansas City.

Good manners meant I had to say something. All I could do was ask him how his folks were. "Fine," he said. "Just fine." I already knew that. Branch Isom had given up the cattle trade, mainly because of competition from Thomas and me, and had concentrated on business in Stonehill and on his freighting trade, which still thrived. So long as the freight line stayed busy he would prosper, and he didn't have to do anything illegal. So would Stonehill, for it lived from the commerce that passed through it going to and from the Gulf and the interior of Texas.

Katy said, "James, I hope you'll stay for supper."

Laura became very flustered. I pointed out how far it was back to town. Even if he left now, James would have to make part of the trip in the dark. I guess he understood the situation better than Katy, because he agreed that he could not stay.

"I'll see you when school starts again," he told Katy.

She looked disappointed. "That's a long time."

"Not when you stay busy. I'll be helping my dad with the business all summer. We'll see each other again before you know it."

Katy watched him ride away on the old town road we didn't use much. "He's a nice boy," she told Laura.

Laura put her arm around the girl's shoulder. "Come on into the house. We have a lot to talk about before your father comes home."

I was at the barn when Thomas rode in just at good dark, looking weary. I could have unsaddled his horse for him, but that was something a man did for himself. Worriedly he asked, "Have you seen Kirby?"

"Yes, I sent him down to the south camp to help brand out those calves."

"Good. I was afraid he might be off someplace with those Hallcomb boys, hunting for trouble."

I told him, "Katy came in a while ago."

Some of the weariness seemed to slide off of him. He smiled. "It sure is nice to have *one* child I don't have to worry about."

8

The railroad rumors had risen periodically ever since the war, about as regularly as the big crops of grasshoppers that plagued us now and again. They always seemed reasonable enough. Somebody, someday, was bound to decide there was a profit to be made hauling goods from the coast by rail instead of by trail. I figured this fear must sometimes have awakened Branch Isom in the middle of a long night. Now the rumors started again, but this time there was a difference. A surveying party moved through the country. They made no secret of the fact that the newly organized Gulf Coast and San Antonio Railroad planned to build along the general route of the old cart and wagon trails.

I expected Thomas to be pleased, but as usual he was looking farther ahead than I did. That was why I was still a little landowner and he was a big one. He said, "Sure, it'll be the end of Isom's mainline freight outfit, but they'll still need smaller lines to serve towns away from the rails. And a railroad will mean more prosperity for Stonehill than the freight trails did. Isom can throw the freight line away and still be richer than he ever was. He owns half of that wretched, damnable town." His face clouded over, and I was sorry I had brought up the subject.

There was a lot I didn't know about railroads. I guess I was like the fellow who buys crackers out of a barrel and figures they just grew that way. I had assumed somebody with a lot of money just came along and built the line. The people in Stonehill must have thought as I did. It came as a shock to them when the builder of the road arrived one day and asked for a sixty-thousand-dollar bonus to put his tracks through town. Their first inclination was to treat him to tar and feathers. As I heard it later, Branch Isom had a better grip on reality and advised that they study the proposition. Lamps burned far into the night at the big Isom house. Sixty thousand dollars was not a sum you snapped your fingers and called up easily, not in those days.

Our interest in the matter was only one of curiosity, because the route the surveyors had marked lay a couple of miles south of Thomas' land at the nearest point and a good dozen from mine. Thomas paid no attention to it. He predicted that the deal would blow apart anyway, and the railroad would never be built. Some sharp Yankee lawyer would get away with a lot of money and never be heard of again; it had happened before.

But one day while Thomas and I were at the corrals watching one of the Fernandez boys—men now, really—sack out a new bronc, a nice black carriage drew up to the big house. It had a Negro driver. A portly gentleman climbed down from the back seat and dusted himself. He looked up at the many front steps with dread.

Thomas called to him and saved him the climb. I followed along with Thomas. I had no real business there, but I gave in to curiosity, my biggest vice. We seldom saw such a rig at the ranch. It, and the gentleman who had arrived in it, reeked of money and importance.

I am sure the gray-bearded man sensed who Thomas was but he went through the polite motions. "I have come to see Mr. Thomas Canfield?" He put it like a question.

Thomas introduced himself. The gentleman wasted no time with me; he could probably tell at a glance that I had about as much authority over major business decisions as one of Laura's white chickens scratching about the yard. "I am Jefferson P. Ashcroft, sir, vice-president of the GC and SA Railroad."

I had known right off that he had not come to sell hay and that he was no horse trader. Well, maybe he was, but of a higher order than those of my previous acquaintance.

"I have come on a matter of urgent business, Mr. Canfield," he said, fanning himself with his felt hat. Thomas led him to a bench Laura had placed beneath a big tree in the front yard. The man looked too tired to climb those front steps right now. He said, "You have perhaps heard of the impasse we have reached in our negotiations with the businessmen of Stonehill? We have asked what we feel is a reasonable bonus for placing a terminal in their city. They have not seen fit to meet our offer."

Thomas shrugged. "Stonehill's affairs are of no interest to me, Mr. Ashcroft. I have no interest in whether that town gets a railroad or not. For that matter, I do not care whether your railroad is ever built or not."

Ashcroft frowned. "I am given to understand that you are the largest landholder in this region. You ship thousands upon thousands of cattle each year."

"Drive, not ship. I have them driven."

"But sooner or later they are put upon a train. How much more beneficial would it be to you, sir, if you were able to ship them from right here on your property?"

"To where? Your railroad will go nowhere except to San Antonio and to the coast. My cattle go to Chicago and points east."

"Our railroad will someday connect with others."

"Someday! Someday I will be dead."

Ashcroft was a horse trader, all right. He recognized when he had a lame horse on his hands. "I shall lay my cards on the table, sir. As our route is surveyed it will cost us several miles of extra track to pass through Stonehill. We could cut our cost by building across your land."

There was not a trace of "give" in Thomas' eyes. "I am sure you could. And I suppose you would want me to pay you for the privilege."

Ashcroft seemed surprised at the thought. "No sir. We would buy your right-of-way at a fair price."

Thomas did not study the proposition long. "I buy land. I do not sell it. I would be happy to have you stay for supper, Mr. Ashcroft, but our business talk has come to an end."

Ashcroft was inclined to argue the point, but that look came into Thomas' eyes, the one that always turned away argument.

Laura came onto the porch as Ashcroft's carriage rounded the barn. "Mr. Canfield, wasn't your company staying for supper?"

Thomas shook his head. "No, Mrs. Canfield. His digestion seems poorly."

I have always sort of blamed the Hallcomb boys for what happened to Kirby, though I know the fault was not theirs alone. Kirby rode right into it himself. And I know you could blame Thomas, for not knowing how to give him a more righteous upbringing. I even blame myself, remembering the times I should have put him over my knee instead of leaving that for Thomas when I knew he would not do it either, unless sorely provoked. A strong rod can sometimes help a tree grow straight and tall. Kirby bent with the wind.

It started, in a way, when the sheriff threw Speck Hallcomb in jail for beating up a San Antonio teamster he outweighed by thirty pounds. This put Speck in a mood for retaliation, a task for which he would need help. Kirby had not been running with the Hallcomb boys for a while; they had gotten along well enough without him. But Speck could not get out of jail, and Bo became tired of hunting up deviltry by himself, so he came out to the ranch and fetched Kirby when he know Thomas was away from home. When Thomas returned, Kirby had been on a double-rectified drunk with Bo Hallcomb in Stonehill for three days. He was nineteen then, going on twenty, and tall for his age. Buying whisky was easy for him so long as he had the money. Thomas would not go to Stonehill himself to bring Kirby home; he sent the Fernandez brothers.

They brought Kirby home grimly, all three looking somewhat the worse for wear. The brothers would not talk about it, but I found out later that Kirby had fought them, saying some sorry things about their being nothing but a couple of dirty Mexicans who could not tell him what to do. Those were things they would not have heard from him had he been sober, for Marco and Juan had taught him most of what he knew about horse and cow work and most of the decent things he knew about life in general. But the things a man says when drunk are often those which have been on his mind when he was sober. The brothers did not have much to do with Kirby after that.

Thomas put Kirby to the dirtiest, meanest work he could find around the ranch. As usual, the reformation was shallow and short. Speck Hallcomb got out of jail in due time, nursing his grudges. He and Bo sneaked out to the south camp and took Kirby away with them. He did not need persuasion, just an opportunity.

The first any of us knew about it, the priest came hurrying down from the church in New Silesia, the buggy team lathered, his face furrowed with trouble. Thomas was gone, as usual. Laura sent for me. I knew when I looked at her and at the priest that something was badly wrong. Kirby and the Hallcomb boys had ridden into New Silesia roaring drunk and had shot up the place, running all the "potato-eaters" off of the street.

It was a merciful thing that both of the old Brozeks had gone to their reward and did not have to suffer through another humiliation at their grandson's hands, the priest lamented.

Laura cried softly. She looked older than she really was; part of it was Thomas, but a lot of it, I knew, was Kirby.

"Reed, maybe you can talk to him. Please, bring him home," she said.

It had been a long time since Kirby had talked much to me, and longer since he had listened to me. I had to call on all the persuasive powers I had to convince Marco and Juan that they should go with me. They had not forgotten the last time, and probably they never would. I managed to convey to them my concern that Kirby might require stronger persuasion than I was physically able to give.

We arrived in New Silesia too late. Kirby and the Hallcombs had moved on to richer game, to Stonehill, where Speck still had a score he wanted to mark off. New Silesia normally was a quiet little place where you still heard more Polish spoken on the streets than English. The only local law was a little constable whose most strenuous normal duty was chasing schoolboys home at dark to study their books. Kirby and the Hallcombs had buffaloed him the first ten minutes they were in town; he had not come back outside again until they left.

He spent a minute or two telling me what he would do if they ever came back, then said darkly, "Stonehill is not New Silesia. They will kill somebody there, or be killed."

I did not want to take him all that seriously, but I got a cold feeling in my stomach. I glanced at Marco and Juan. Their eyes told me they had it too. We set our horses into a long trot for Stonehill. For the animals' sake I tried to hold the pace to that, but in a while I was loping, and the brothers were close beside me.

The New Silesia–Stonehill road led by the Goodson Hallcomb farm. As we passed it, Speck and Bo Hallcomb came riding out. I hailed them. They glanced at us but kept riding. I had to spur a tired horse to catch up to them. I rode past and turned around to face them before they would stop. They were cold sober, both of them, and scared.

"Where's Kirby?" I demanded. Neither would look at me. I asked them again. The Fernandez brothers pushed in behind them, adding to the pressure.

Speck still would not look at me, but he said, "It was Kirby done it, not us. We didn't figure on anything going that far."

I grabbed the front of his shirt and shook him. "Did what?"

"He shot and killed the sheriff. We tried to stop him, but he went and done it anyway. Now you got to let us go, Mr. Sawyer. Them people'll be coming after us."

"What people?"

"The whole town, I expect. We turned and lit out when we seen the sheriff go down. Seemed like the whole town was shooting at Kirby, and at us too."

"You went off and left him there by himself?"

"Them was awful mad people."

I put spurs to my horse, cursing and praying at the same time. I could hear the Fernandez brothers pushing to stay close behind me. We were still in a lope as we hit the edge of town. I reined up to look for a minute. The chill came back, for the place was quiet, much too quiet. Not a wagon was rolling. I saw a few horsemen milling around, and people standing in clusters. Whatever had happened was over and done. I could not bring myself to look at the brothers, but I knew they must share the cold dread that came over me like a winter fog. We walked out hard-breathing horses down the street. The people turned to stare, and I felt anger and hostility rising against us. Everybody knew who we were.

A familiar figure walked out into the street and stood waiting. Branch Isom had put on weight the last few years. He was not exactly portly, but prosperity had made him comfortable and soft, a far cry from the muscular, driving man I remembered from my first acquaintance with him in old Indianola town. I noted that he was not armed, though nearly everyone else on the street was.

We stopped our horses a few feet from him. He seemed to be looking beyond us. "Is Thomas Canfield on his way?" he asked.

I sensed right off that the town was braced for invasion. They took us for the vanguard. I hoped they could see we were not carrying guns. "We haven't seen him," I said. "Where's Kirby?"

Isom did not answer me directly. "You know what he did? He killed the sheriff. Wounded a couple of other people, too."

"We just heard about the sheriff from the Hallcomb boys. We didn't know about anybody else. Where's Kirby?" I was afraid I knew better, but I added, "You have him in jail?"

Isom shook his head and turned, beckoning. The people had moved out into the street as if to block us, but they stepped back and made room as Isom led us fifty yards to the open livery barn. Beneath a brush arbor, on a pile of hay, lay an old gray blanket. I knew what was under it and did not want to look as Isom pulled it back, but I forced myself.

Kirby must have been shot twenty times.

Isom said, "I wouldn't have had it happen for the world. But the way things were, people didn't have a choice. He had to be stopped."

I supposed he was right, but the grief and the anger and the cold nausea all came up on me just the same. They did not have to shoot him to pieces.

"Who-all did it, Branch?" I asked.

He let the blanket down gently. "All I can tell you is that I was not among them. Don't ask me to tell you more."

"Thomas will ask you."

"I hoped you would head him off, Sawyer. If he comes in here boiling for trouble, he'll find it. This town is in a black mood. I'll have a wagon fetched around so you can take Kirby home. Try and keep Thomas away from here. Please!"

It was hard to realize this was the same Branch Isom I had known so long ago. There had been a time he would have stood in the middle of the street and dared Thomas to come. Now he was begging me for peace.

"I have worked hard to get this town a respectable name, to live down what it used to be," he continued. "Now we have a railroad coming in. We don't want any more trouble here."

I said, "Bring the wagon."

The hostility of the people was silent but as real as a pit of rattlesnakes. Juan and Marco and I lifted Kirby into the wagon and covered him with the blanket. Nobody offered to help. Juan climbed onto the wagon seat. Isom handed him the lines and looked back at me. "For God's sake, Sawyer, keep Thomas away from here!"

A shout lifted from the far end of the street. My heart came to my throat as I saw a group of riders coming, fanned out in a wedge. Townspeople pulled back to the porches and wooden sidewalks, making room.

"It's too late," I said. "He's here."

Thomas' face was gray as he rode up the street. He stopped before the wagon, his jaw set like a block of stone. He stared at the covered form. The voice did not sound like his.

"Pull back the blanket."

Juan started to obey. I reined my horse in close and caught the corner of the blanket. "No, Thomas. You don't want to, not here."

Thomas' eyes cut me like a knife. He bumped his horse's shoulder against mine and pushed me aside. He lifted the blanket for himself. His cheekbones seemed to bulge. His eyes glassed over. When he turned, he was in a wild rage. He fixed his gaze on Branch Isom.

"Who did it?"

Branch Isom had lost color, but he did not back away. "Your boy killed the sheriff, Thomas. He was shooting up the town."

"I want to know who-all did this to him!"

"Nobody wanted this. I know how you feel, Thomas; I've got a boy of my own. If there'd been any other way . . ."

"Damn you, Isom! I don't want to take on this whole

town, but I'll do it if I don't see the men who did this to my boy. You call them out here!"

Thomas' hand was on the butt of his pistol. My throat went dry as I looked at the cowboys he had brought with him . . . gringos, Mexicans . . . he had never made much distinction so long as they did their work. They were scared, most of them, looking into the guns of half that town. But they also appeared determined. If Thomas said the word, war would explode then and there. Seeing those wild and ungiving eyes, I was sure Thomas was about to give that word. We were badly outnumbered, but not one man of Thomas' crew pulled back or showed any sign of the feather. No less was tolerated of a man in those days; he was expected to be loyal to the brand he worked for and die for it, if circumstances carried him to that. Marco and Juan and I were unarmed, but I knew we would be shot down with the rest.

I said, "Thomas, Kirby was in the wrong."

Thomas did not respond.

Cold sweat glistened on Branch Isom's round, reddish face. "For the love of God, Thomas, look around you. There's two men dead already. You pull that gun and there may be twenty."

"You'll be the first one."

Isom's shoulders slumped. I thought he had given up. Then he said something I would never have expected. "Shoot me, then, if it'll satisfy you. Shoot me and let my town alone."

Thomas seethed. "I should have shot you twenty years ago. I had the chance, once. I've always been sorry I didn't do it."

Fear was plain in Isom's eyes, but he did not back away.

Thomas said, "You're not armed."

"I haven't carried a gun in years."

"Get one."

Isom brought himself to look in Thomas' terrible eyes. "No. You'll have to shoot me as I am."

Thomas drew the pistol halfway out of the holster, and thirty men brought up their guns. Isom stood watching him, his face frozen. He did not plead. He did not move his feet.

Thomas seemed oblivious to the guns raised against him. He never took his eyes from Isom's face. "One last time, Isom, tell me who killed him."

Isom said nothing. He held his eyes to Thomas', and after a long moment it was Thomas who looked away.

"Whoever you are," he shouted to the town, "whoever shot my boy, come out here and face me!"

Nobody answered. Nobody came.

Thomas let the pistol slip back into the holster. His gaze ran the length of the street, touching on every man. His voice rose so that everybody on the street could hear. "Then you *all* killed him. This whole town killed him, the way it's killed almost everybody I ever cared about in my life. This town killed my father. It killed my brother, and my mother, and my wife. Now it's killed my son!"

He paused. I could not hear a sound except the nervous movement of horses, the squeak of saddle leather.

Thomas stood in his stirrups and raised his fist over his head. In a voice that must have carried out onto the prairie he shouted. "This town had killed the last of mine. I swear by Almighty God, I am going to kill this town!"

He reined his horse around and moved back down the street. The crowd melted aside as the Red Sea must have parted for Moses. The cowboys, much relieved, turned their horses and followed him. I felt weak enough to fall out of my saddle. I nodded at Juan, still on the wagon. "Let's go."

I tried not to look at the townspeople, though I had to give one more glance to Branch Isom. He looked drained and limp and incredibly sad. But he never moved.

We buried Kirby in the family plot on the slope, beside the uncle whose unlucky name he bore. Staring at the weathered stone with the first Kirby's name on it, I thought of the many ways in which the two young men had been alike, impetuous, even wild. But the first Kirby had sought nothing more than fun; there had never been anything little about him, or mean.

Mostly I watched Thomas during the ceremony. Laura held his arm at first, trying to give him comfort. But Thomas seemed to draw away, shutting her out. He stood alone. Laura put her arms around Katy, and the two women wept quietly together.

As the minister finished his final prayer, the little crowd dutifully came by in an informal line and expressed their condolences, the custom of the country, a burden the bereaved were expected to endure stoically. Thomas received them with a stony face and a mechanical manner. The last two men to come up were strangers, each wearing a circular badge with a star in its center. One of them asked, "Could we talk with you a minute, Mr. Canfield? Somewhere in private?"

Thomas blinked, taken by surprise. His stony look returned. "This is private enough."

The Rangers were ill at ease. The spokesman said, "We've been sent from San Antonio to keep the peace."

"It's a little late, don't you think?"

"We were sent to be sure nothing more happens. Our orders are to do anything necessary to see that it doesn't. Anything."

Thomas' eyes narrowed. His gaze dropped to the pistols both men wore prominently on their hips. "If I were going to shoot up Stonehill, I would have done it yesterday."

"You made a threat about killing the town."

"I intend to," he said coldly. "And there won't be one thing you or anybody can do about it."

He turned from the Rangers as if they were not there. He drew me away from the crowd and asked, "Do you have any idea where that railroad man is, that Ashcroft?"

I thought he might be in Stonehill, but there was no way to know except by going and seeing for myself. I did not want to go to Stonehill.

Thomas said, "Please, Reed, go for *me*. Go for Kirby. Find him if you have to ride all the way to San Antonio. Fetch him here."

I began to sense some of what was in his mind. It made me feel sad. "Thomas, you don't really want to do this."

He looked me in the eyes, and I could not hold against his stare. "If you don't go, I will," he said.

It was ticklish, riding into Stonehill. My skin prickled at the sight of the town. Its streets seemed deserted. Most of the people were at the cemetery, showing the sheriff's family their support at the funeral. The Canfield ranch had few friends left in that place, but I sought out one of those few who might know something of the railroad man. He told me Ashcroft had departed Stonehill in anger the day before the shooting, bound for San Antonio.

I spent the night on the road, stopping for a few hours' sleep on the ground. I found Ashcroft in the Menger Hotel bar, where he had been paying homage to the state of Kentucky for most of three days. He was in little mood to talk to anyone from Stonehill or its environs. "Robbers and thieves, all of them," he grumbled, "hoping to enrich themselves at the expense of the railroad."

I explained that I had nothing to do with Stonehill but represented Thomas Canfield instead. His resentment survived intact.

"I suppose Mr. Canfield has decided to sell us a right-of-way and enrich himself at our expense also."

He had no intention of coming with me. I thought of force but rejected that because I knew San Antonio had a high ratio of policemen to citizens and would not tolerate that kind of behavior. I sat with him in the bar and plied him with Bourbon until he went to sleep in his chair. Had he died then and there, the undertaker would have had nothing to do but place him in a box. I rented a carriage from a wagonyard, loaded him into it and started for the ranch. We had put many miles behind us before he rallied enough to realize he was on the road. He cursed me for twelve kinds of blackguard and threatened me with a lifetime in Huntsville penitentiary, but he had no wish to walk back to San Antonio. It was far past midnight when we reached the ranch, and he was cold sober.

Thomas dressed and met Ashcroft in the front parlor. He got right to the point.

"Mr. Ashcroft, are you still interested in a right-of-way across my ranch?"

Ashcroft blustered. "Kidnapping me and dragging me out here is a poor way of doing business. If you think we are going to pay you some exorbitant price . . ."

Thomas did not let him finish. He leaned forward, into the man's face. His eyes had the look of a hawk at the kill. "I'll *give* you the land!"

He had Ashcroft's total attention, and mine. "Give it?"

"With conditions. I want you to route your rails as far from Stonehill as you can."

Ashcroft blinked a few times. "We need Stonehill."

"No you don't. If you need a town, build one. I'll give you the land for that too."

Ashcroft was momentarily shocked beyond speech. He stared at me as if he did not quite believe, as if he feared he might still be drunk and dreaming all this.

"I don't understand."

"You don't have to understand. All you have to do is agree."

Ashcroft mumbled, benumbed. "I am not certain I can speak for the board of directors . . ."

"To hell with the directors. Just say *yes*."

Ashcroft was still looking for a catch but could not see one.

"Well, yes," he sputtered. "Of course, yes."

Not until that moment had I realized the full depth of Thomas' hatred, the sacrifice he was willing to make for revenge. I could not remember that he had ever sold a square foot of land; once he had gotten hold of it, he had held it fiercely. Now he was giving it away.

I stared at the fire in Thomas' eyes, and at the bewilderment in Ashcroft's.

I said, "There's a passage in the Bible, Thomas. Vengeance is mine, saith the Lord."

He shook his head.

"No. This time, it's *mine*."

9

The surveyors had been working their way across the ranch for several days before the people of Stonehill got their first inkling. Quickly Branch Isom consulted other community leaders and offered the railroad the bonus Ashcroft had originally asked. When he refused it, they raised thirty thousand more. It was too late. The railroad had signed the contracts with Thomas and saved itself thousands of dollars in right-of-way investment. This was at Thomas' expense, of course, but if he ever gave the cost a moment's notice he betrayed no sign.

Stonehill should have had a long, slow period of grace before its decline; railroads are not built overnight. But dry rot set in with the realization that the wheels were in motion and that there would be no reversal of plans for going around. Though freight lines still passed through the town, and would until the trains were running—and though wagon service would still be needed to the border and to towns that lay south and north of the railroad—the heart quickly was gone from Stonehill. One by one, businesses began to be boarded up or moved away.

Branch Isom tried desperately to hold the place together. He argued that branch lines serving the railroad would still bring commerce to Stonehill streets, that many ranchers and farmers would still choose Stonehill as their place to trade. He pointed out that it was the county seat and still had the courthouse. He even made rash guarantees of financial support in a desperate effort to keep his town alive.

The railroad platted a new town on its right-of-way. A few buildings were up even before the rails reached it, an evidence of more faith than I could have mustered. There was some question about a proper name. The railroad people first suggested it be called Canfield, but Thomas rejected that notion as self-advertisement. He wanted to name it Brozekville, for Maria's family. The railroad people thought that sounded too foreign. When Washington approved the post office, the chosen name turned out to be Ashcroft City. Thomas fumed over that a few days, but the cause was lost. One area always foreign to him was politics.

He still carried weight with the railroad, however, and the power of veto over who could buy property in Ashcroft City. At first he would allow no one from Stonehill to own property in his town. But soon he realized that the way to drain Stonehill and leave Branch Isom presiding over a dead town was to give people there another place to go. Once he made up his mind to that, and swallowed the fact that he would have to tolerate at least some of the Stonehill citizens in the new town, he saw to it that the lots in Ashcroft City were sold cheaply enough for anybody to buy one. He screened the buyers, turning away some of Stonehill's more notorious denizens. He put it down as an iron-clad rule that no property would be sold to Branch Isom or any of his kin.

Once the tracks were laid through town and stretched westward toward San Antonio, the exodus from Stonehill turned into a stampede. Thomas financed several of his cowboys who had higher ambitions. They invested in teams and heavy timber-moving equipment, which they converted to the moving of frame buildings. It was no great engineering feat to jack up a small structure, put runners under it and move it the ten or twelve miles from Stonehill to Ashcroft City.

Thomas was getting what he wanted, but he never smiled. I sensed it was not enough.

One day while we were working cattle on the south part

of the ranch, not far from Stonehill, one of the chuck-wagon mules became entangled in the traces, and the wagon fetched up in a gully with a broken wheel. I took the wheel to Stonehill to have a wheelwright fix it. The sight of the place hit me like a fist between the eyes. It looked as if half the houses were gone, jacked up and hauled away, leaving nothing but the cedar-post foundations on which they had stood standing like broken ribs of a wolf-eaten carcass. Most of the businesses still operating belonged to Branch Isom; the other storekeepers and artisans for the most part had left, bound for Ashcroft City or San Antonio or points west. Traffic was so slow that chickens scratched in the middle of the street.

The only smithy and wheelwright still operating worked in a shop which serviced the Isom freight wagons. He assured me he could get to my wheel right away; he had nothing else to do.

I walked down the street past empty stores, past empty lots where stores had stood. I stepped into a bar and had a drink. The bartender seemed glad to see me, though he knew full well who I was and who I represented. He and I were the only people in the place.

The drink seemed sour, and I did not tarry long. I walked on down to Isom's big mercantile store, where a lone farm wagon stood out front. I was tempted to go in but didn't know what, if anything, I could say to Branch Isom. Suddenly he was standing in the door, staring at me in surprise. I could not pretend I had not seen him. I said howdy, not knowing anything that seemed appropriate.

"You'd just as well come on in, Reed Sawyer," he said. "No use standing out in the sun."

I walked into the store and stood awkwardly, making small talk about the weather and how we needed a rain. I don't think Isom paid much attention to what I said, any more than I paid to his make-talk efforts. Finally I blurted out what was really on my mind. "Goddammit, Branch, I'm sorry."

Isom went silent awhile, then said, "I guess it would've been better if Thomas and I had shot it out with each other a long time ago. Whichever way it went, it would've saved a lot of people a lot of grief."

"Why don't you just leave here, Branch, and start over someplace else? You could do good in San Antonio."

"This is my town. Everything I own is tied up here. I have no choice but to ride it to the end of the line."

I was about to say it might be a short ride, but I kept that observation to myself. I said, "It's not much of a future for your boy."

"James will be all right. He has a good position in a bank in San Antonio. He's a smart boy, even if he is mine. You watch, he'll be a wealthy man someday. They'll put up a statue of him in a San Antonio park."

I caught that pride in his eyes, the kind of pride Thomas had never been able to have in Kirby. Strange, I thought, how the seed can sometimes produce a tree so much different than the one it came from.

I told Isom I had not seen his son in a long time. He said, "He's home for a visit." I heard a jingle of trace chains through the open back door. Isom turned an ear in that direction. "I'll bet that's him now."

In a moment a pair of shadows fell through the open door. A girl entered, followed by a slender young man. My mouth dropped open.

"Katy!"

Katy Canfield was so startled that she dropped her purse. James Isom stooped to pick it up and place it back in her hands. She stared at me with big, pretty brown eyes, disconcerted. "Uncle Reed, what're you doing here?"

"I'm a grown man; I can go where I want to. But you're not a grown woman yet, not quite. Your daddy have any idea where you are?"

She took a minute to answer. "Mother knows."

Somehow that did not surprise me. Kirby's raising, such as it was, had been mostly Thomas' doing. But the raising of Katy had been left mostly to Laura. Katy and Laura had always drawn together, two women combining their strength against a man's world of land and cattle and commerce.

Katy had much of the look of the mother she barely remembered. But I could not recall that I had ever seen so much trouble in Maria's eyes.

I said, "This is the last place in the world your daddy would want to see you."

"He's wrong; you know that."

"But he is your daddy."

James Isom touched Katy's arm, and she leaned to him for support. I had known they both went to school in San Antonio, and I remembered the time James had brought her home. But *this* . . . The idea had never entered my mind.

There was no pretending I had not seen. "How serious is it between you two?"

James said evenly, "It's serious, Mr. Sawyer.

I could see Katy's answer in her eyes. She said, "Uncle Reed, do you have to tell him?"

I studied the pair, clinging together. James was a clean-looking young man, his face appearing honest and without guile. He said, "I love her, Mr. Sawyer."

Branch Isom told me, "It's been none of my doing. I've tried to talk them out of it. But if you've ever been in love, Reed, I guess you know how little good it does to talk."

My stomach drew into a knot. I could remember.

Katy touched my arm. "Uncle Reed, if you think he has to know, let me be the one to tell him. Please, give me a little time. I'll have to find a way of my own."

I said, "You kids know he'll find out sooner or later . . . someday, some way. But it won't come from me."

They drew against one another, and Katy thanked me.

Though much of Stonehill's population wound up in Ashcroft City, it would be a mistake to think of that place simply as Stonehill transplanted. The building of the rail-road, a round-house and service facilities brought in a lot of new people, enough to give Ashcroft City a different politi-cal complexion. Even while Stonehill was still the county seat, Ashcroft City began electing most of the county offi-cers. And it was not meant that Stonehill keep the county courthouse forever. In the Ashcroft City plat was a block in the center of town, reserved for a new county courthouse. When Ashcroft City had the political power firmly in its grip, an election was called to decide whether to move the county seat. Branch Isom and his hangers-on tried hard, electioneering diligently among the country folk. But the issue was lost long before election day. Ashcroft City car-ried five to three. A bond issue was passed for a new stone courthouse, bigger and better than the old frame structure in Stonehill. In due course the building was completed. The only task remaining was the transfer of the county records.

This process, though it had the full backing of law, had caused bloodshed in several old Texas counties as they out-grew their original county seats and attempted a move. The ballot was one thing; possession was another.

The sheriff and one of his deputies, Ashcroft City men both, were met at the courthouse one day by a group of armed Stonehill men who blocked their entrance and served notice they did not intend to allow movement of the county records. They denied the lawmen access to their own office. The sheriff went directly to Thomas, who called in all his cowboys. I could see a grim satisfaction in Thomas' eyes as he stood on the steps of his house with the sheriff, the rest of us spread out on the ground. The sheriff swore all of us in as deputies. We rode together to Ashcroft City, where he swore in enough townsmen to give him a posse of sixty or seventy.

It was my bad luck to have been at the headquarters at all that day. I had begun trying to take care of my own business, my own cattle, and had even built a small frame house on my place. Personally I didn't much give a damn which town had the courthouse. I tried to tell Thomas so, but as always when he had his mind set on something he did not listen. He just nodded, taking it for granted that I was agreeing with him on everything.

I should simply have ridden away, but Thomas still had that power to pull people to him, and I was not immune from it.

We trooped down the wagon road to Stonehill like a ragged cavalry unit, guns bristling. A lot of the younger men were bragging about what they would do if it came to a fight, hoping it would. Pleasure showed in Thomas' face, too, which fed the uneasiness growing in me. Having been in that other war, I had already enjoyed about all this type of conflict that I ever wanted.

Behind us rumbled half a dozen empty freight wagons, enough to haul not only the county records but most of the courthouse furniture. Thomas and I rode up front, with the sheriff. Thomas said, "This is about what I expected from Branch Isom. If he puts up a fight, I want everybody to remember: he's mine."

I should have been angry at Stonehill for its resistance to the law, but I found myself angering at Thomas instead. I said, "The Texas Rangers could handle this, and nobody would get hurt."

Thomas declared solemnly, "We don't need the Rangers, or anybody else from outside. This is our business."

I let my exasperation rise into my voice. "You'll never rest easy till you've killed him!"

Thomas flashed me a look of surprise, which turned into doubt. His anger arose to meet mine. He said, "Reed, something has been gnawing at you lately. You've been partners with me for a long time, but if you're wanting to leave . . ."

I had not fully realized it, but suddenly I knew that I did. It was time to make a full break, as I had intended to years earlier when he married Laura.

I said, "I know Branch Isom a lot better than you do. At least let me go talk to him first. Maybe there won't be a need for anybody to get hurt."

His anger built. "You *don't* know Branch Isom. You never did."

"You just know him as he used to be. People change. He doesn't want to be your enemy; he hasn't wanted to in a long time. He's just old, and he's tired. Like us."

"I'm not tired." Thomas gave me a long, hard study. "If that's the way you feel, maybe you'd better ride on ahead and stand up with him."

"If the time comes that I feel like I should, I will."

I half expected him to explode, but instead he cooled. The look in his eyes was of hurt, of puzzlement.

After a time he said, "You don't mean that, Reed. We've been together too long."

"Like I said, people change. *You've* changed, and most of it hasn't been any improvement."

I watched him as we moved into Stonehill. I do not think he had seen the place since the day Kirby was killed. I do not believe he was fully prepared for the shell that Stonehill had become. It was as if a tornado had skipped through and had taken half the buildings away, damaging many of the rest.

"Good God!" he exclaimed.

I told him, "You *said* you'd kill this town. You've done it."

"I haven't killed *all* of it. *He's* still here."

We rode straight for the old courthouse. Its two stories had been built originally of green lumber so that the siding was beginning to twist and curl in places. The long comb along the roof had a gentle sag in the middle, like an old horse needing retirement to green pasture. But lined in front of it were fifteen or twenty men with pistols, rifles and shotguns in their hands. They were a pitiful remnant compared to the force Stonehill might once have offered; we had them badly outnumbered.

· The sheriff made a wide motion with his hand, signaling his posse to spread out. He rode in front, his hands high against his chest and far from his weapons, reins in the left hand, a sheaf of papers in the right. He tried to pick out the leader of the Stonehill defense. Branch Isom was not among them.

I glanced at Thomas. His eyes betrayed disappointment. Then they lifted. I swung around to see what he had seen. Branch Isom was coming out onto the porch of his big house on the hill.

The sheriff was saying, "Gentlemen, you all know who I am. You know the authority I represent. I have here the official canvass of the vote, making Ashcroft City the county seat. I also have here an order from the district court that all county records be duly removed to Ashcroft City. I ask that you step aside and let the law peacefully take its course."

Half the men talked at once, or tried to. This group had no leader. That could be good, or it could be bad. A leaderless group of angry men was unpredictable.

The sheriff, still in his saddle, made a move toward the courthouse. Three men jumped forward and grabbed the reins and bit. He shouted, "In the name of the law . . ."

Thomas drew his pistol. Branch Isom was running down the hill toward us, waving his hands. The commotion around the sheriff was so loud I could not hear what Isom was shouting. I put my hand firmly over Thomas', pressing down against his pistol.

"Wait," I said. He struggled angrily to free his hand, but I held tight.

Isom's face was flushed. He breathed heavily from the exertion of the run. Age and soft living had sapped the strength and endurance of his youth. "Sheriff," he said urgently, "please hold off a minute. Let me talk to these men."

Through gritted teeth Thomas said, "We don't care to listen to you, Isom."

The sheriff turned in a fury that surprised me. "Mr. Canfield," he said, "*I* am in charge here."

Thomas said, "The hell you are." He tried again to raise the pistol, but I pressed it hard against the horn of his saddle. He cursed me.

Isom turned his back on us and addressed the men who had chosen to defend Stonehill.

"Friends, I asked you before. I *plead* with you now. The law is with them. They have you outnumbered. Even if you beat them today they'll be back tomorrow with more. They'll bring the Rangers, or even the army. Give it up now, and let's not have anybody die. Too many have died already for lost causes."

Most of them seemed to be listening to him. Perhaps they were looking for an excuse to back away from a fight they could readily see they would lose. But it seemed to me they were listening to him with respect, the way men in this town once listened to old Linden Hines.

It came to me with a sudden jolt that Branch Isom, even in his wild younger days, had respected Linden Hines. He had respected him so much that—perhaps unconsciously—he had taken the old man's place.

Isom saw the men's hesitation, their doubt. He pounced on it.

"Tobe Haney, you have two good kids. You want to take a chance on dying now, when they need you the most? Bill, who's going to take care of your old mother? This courthouse means very little to her, but you mean all there is."

Thomas stared at Isom in disbelief and deep disappointment. He had wanted Isom to be the ringleader here, not the peacemaker. I let go of the pistol. Thomas burned me with a look of resentment.

He had watched Branch Isom so intently that he had not noticed James following his father down from the big house. Now James stood beside Branch, saying nothing but lending his silent support. Thomas studied him. I saw the sudden stiffness when recognition came. Thomas' jaw hardened.

He knew, I realized. Somehow, he knew.

The fuse still sputtered, but Branch Isom had pulled it from the powder. The Stonehill men began to draw aside, muttering grudgingly but without violence. The sheriff climbed the short steps and threw open the courthouse doors. He signaled for the wagons to be brought up. He was suddenly in a hurry, wanting to be done with this before someone fired the fuse again. The Ashcroft City men marched into the courthouse without fanfare, without cheering. A few were probably disappointed about the avoidance of a fight, but I think the majority were relieved whether they would ever admit it or not; the sight of the other side with guns in their hands had taken a lot of the romance out of the showdown.

Branch Isom moved closer to Thomas. "All right, you've won." Bitterness edged his voice, but resignation was there, too. "What little is left of my town, you'll be hauling away in those wagons."

Thomas seemed not to hear. His eyes were on young Isom. They were the hawk eyes I dreaded so much. He said, "You'd be Branch Isom, Jr., wouldn't you?"

"James Isom," the young man quietly corrected him.

"Well, Branch Isom, Jr., my quarrel with your father is an old one. My quarrel with you is new. You know what I'm talking about?"

James' eyes did not waver. "I guess I do."

"I intend it to stop, now! I'll send her to Europe, if I have to. And I'll send you to hell!"

Thomas cut his gaze back to Branch. "I had a son. You remember how I lost him. If you don't want to lose yours, you'd better talk to him!"

He pulled hard on the reins, turning his horse half around. He stopped and looked at me. "You have something to say?"

I did. "You'd have killed half the men here, just to settle your own private feud."

"Yes," he said flatly, "I would have. You coming?"

My stomach was cold. I said, "No."

"Stay here, then. Stay with Branch Isom."

I found myself giving voice to a notion that had been rising in me. *"He's* not Branch Isom, not anymore. *You* are!"

What I said never reached him, not to the point that he understood. He shrugged. "Suit yourself," he said, and left there in a long trot, his cowboys following him. I watched them until they were on the trail, then I turned and headed for the saloon.

I never had much luck solving my problems in a whisky glass. When the glass was empty the problems were still there, as big as ever. I nursed a couple of slow drinks, however, trying to decide what to do next. I did not lack for a place to go. My ranch was nowhere nearly so large as Thomas', but it was mine. I had gone there often to see after my cattle, sometimes staying several days. But always I had gone "home" afterward. "Home" had always been Thomas' place.

I knew it never would be again.

I heard horses on the street occasionally but paid little attention, mulling over my own problems. I became aware of a man standing in the open doorway, blocking much of the light. "Reed?" he called. "Reed Sawyer?"

I was startled to see Branch Isom there, a rifle in his hand. My heart bumped with the thought that the rifle was for me, because I had ridden into town with Thomas' invading army.

Urgently Isom said, "Reed Sawyer, I need your help."

The whisky had gone to my head a little. Whisky always had a tendency to make me sullen, one reason I drank so little of it. At that moment I was mad at everybody. "The hell you say."

"Reed," he said, "you've got little cause to look on me as a friend, but at least I hope you don't see me as your enemy."

The whisky's glow began to fade. "What's your trouble?"

He stepped closer. For the first time I saw a cut at the corner of his mouth, a bruise starting to purple. "It's James. That fool boy has gone to the Canfield ranch to get that girl. I tried to stop him."

I was cold sober. "Thomas'll kill him!"

"Not if I can get there first. You have any influence over Thomas?"

I shook my head. "*Nobody* has any influence over Thomas."

"I wish you'd come along and try. I don't want to kill him, but I'll do it to keep that crazy bastard from killing my boy."

In my haste to get up from the table I turned over the bottle. It fell to the floor and went rolling, spilling whisky. In a few long strides I was out of the place and into the saddle, riding out of town in a hard lope. I had to spur to keep Isom from pulling far out in front of me.

At times we could glimpse James at some distance ahead. He had seen us and knew we would try to stop him, so he held his lead. When we speeded up, he speeded up. We could not run the horses long at a time, or they would not endure to take us to the ranch headquarters. We would lope awhile, then slow to a trot to let them catch their wind. I told Isom there was a chance Thomas would not be at home. But the tracks along the trail told me Thomas and the cowboys had come this way ahead of us.

James arrived at the Canfield house a few minutes before we did. That was more than time enough. As we rode through the open gate of the outer corral, I saw someone fighting on the broad porch.

Isom's face twisted in fear. He shouted vainly against the wind. "Wait! Wait!"

Someone fell backward off of the high steps. It had to be

James, for Thomas stood on the porch, pistol in his hand. Katy struggled with him. As we spurred up I could hear her screaming, pleading with him. Laura was there too, trying to hold Thomas' arm. He gave her a rough push. Laura stumbled and fell backward over a chair. Thomas pulled free of his daughter and shoved her violently. She fell over Laura. Thomas started down the steps toward James, the pistol pointed.

"Canfield!" Branch Isom shouted. He jumped from his horse and sprinted defensively toward his son. James was on one knee. I knew at a glance that he was not armed. He had not come here to kill; he had probably realized that if he brought a gun he might be forced to use it.

Thomas swung the pistol toward Branch Isom. I was off my horse and running toward him. "Thomas, don't!"

Thomas fired. Branch Isom stumbled, his hat spinning from his head. He pitched to the ground. The rifle clattered from his hands. He had not had time to pull the trigger.

Thomas' face was a roaring fire. The pistol had leaped in recoil, and he lowered it to fire again. I managed to grab his arm.

"For God's sake, Thomas, come to your senses!"

I had never realized how powerful he was, especially with the fury pounding hot. He flung me backward, off balance. I saw the pistol swinging at me and tried vainly to throw myself out of its path. If my hat had not cushioned it, the heavy gun barrel would probably have broken my skull. I felt my face slam against the ground, and dirt was in my eyes. I raised up, trying to clear my throbbing head.

Now instead of Branch trying to protect his son, James rushed to his father.

"No, Mr. Canfield! Please don't shoot him again!"

Red and white flashes went off like fireworks before my eyes, and my head pounded. In spite of that, I saw Katy run down the steps and across the yard. She picked up the fallen rifle as her father raised the muzzle of his pistol against James.

Cold dread crawled up my back. Katy was about to kill her father. I said something akin to prayer, rolled onto my side and drew my six-shooter. As Thomas half turned, steadying his pistol, I squeezed the trigger. The recoil wrenched it from my weak hand. Through the gray smoke I saw Thomas stagger, drop to his knees, then sink awkwardly onto one shoulder.

Katy stared at him in horror, the rifle unfired but pointed at him.

Laura cried out and ran down the steps, taking them two at a time. Katy lowered the rifle, her eyes wide in shock. I believe that for a moment she thought she had shot her father.

Legs shaky, James hurried to her and took her in his arms. The rifle slipped into the dust.

Laura dropped to her knees and threw her arms around Thomas, pulling him against her. "Thomas! Thomas!"

He groaned, so I knew he was not dead. I glanced at Branch Isom. He was trying to push himself to a sitting position. Blood ran down the side of his face from the crease Thomas' bullet had given him. James pulled away from Katy and went to his father's side, crying out in relief that Branch was not dead.

Katy stood alone, staring in disbelief at her fallen father.

Laura hugged Thomas and begged him not to die. I managed to get my feet under me and stagger to Thomas' side. I slumped to my knees and tore his shirt open. I had put a bullet into his shoulder.

"Branch Isom," Thomas mumbled. "Seems like I'll never kill him. He got me after all."

I did not want to tell him, but I knew I had to.

"It wasn't Isom. *I* shot you."

He seemed to have trouble seeing me clearly. He could not reconcile himself to what I had said. "You're lying. It was Isom."

"It was me. I had to, Thomas. You went crazy."

He shook his head weakly, not accepting.

I said, "If I hadn't, Katy would have. I couldn't let her do that."

Thomas turned his face from me, searching for his daughter. She had not moved. He blinked, trying to bring her to focus.

"Katy . . . you'd have shot me?"

Firmly she said, "I was about to, Papa."

Thomas closed his eyes. He made no sound, but he was weeping.

By this time a dozen cowboys had come running. It took some strong talking on my part and Katy's to keep them from killing the two Isoms on the spot. They listened to Katy more than they listened to me. They had to, for they saw her eyes, the fierce eyes of Thomas Canfield.

The Fernandez brothers fetched a team and wagon. We managed to clot the blood with flour and bind Thomas up enough to hold him. I was lying when I assured Laura that he was going to live. At the time, I did not really believe it. But after Marco and Juan lifted him onto the blankets in the wagon bed and we started for town with him, I began to hope. Laura knelt beside him, oblivious to the bouncing of the vehicle on the rough road. "Hold on, Thomas," she pleaded. "Please don't leave me."

I had not heard her call him anything but "Mr. Canfield" in years.

Katy remained with James and his father. Branch was having trouble standing without support. The last thing I heard him say as we left was to his son and Katy: "You crazy kids. The whole world to choose from, and you had to pick one another."

The doctor said later that if it had taken us much longer to get Thomas to town, he would not have lived. Even as it was, he would suffer from a bad shoulder for however many more years the Lord saw fit to allow him.

I waited on the doctor's porch until Laura came out, weary and red-eyed, to tell me he was awake. She went in with me and sat in the cane-bottomed straight-chair where she had been from the first.

Thomas was pale and sick at his stomach from the chloroform, but his eyes locked on me with a challenge.

"I suppose you've come to apologize," he said.

"No," I told him.

He was disappointed. "You still think I was wrong."

"If I hadn't thought so, I wouldn't have shot you."

He chewed on that awhile, not liking it. "That wasn't a lie, about Katy fixing to shoot me?"

"She was about to. I couldn't let her do that, Thomas. I couldn't let her live the rest of her life knowing she had killed her own father."

"But *you* could live with it?"

"Yes. We used to be friends, Thomas. But I could have done it." I watched the hurt crowd into his eyes. I added, "Lucky for you I never was much of a shot."

He lay silent awhile. "Have you seen Katy?"

I hated to tell him. "She and James went over to New Silesia. They're talking to the priest about marrying them." I waited a minute before I told him the rest of it. "They asked me to stand up for them. I said I would."

Tears started in Thomas' eyes. "She didn't even come to see me."

"She was here. She stayed until she knew you were going to be all right. That's something, at least."

He closed his eyes. "The bitterest thing of all is to know she would have killed me for that boy . . . an *Isom*."

"He's a good boy, Thomas, better than you or me. You'll see that, someday."

"Isom." He spoke the name as if it were a curse. It *had* been, for much of his life. Acceptance would take time, a lot of time, for "give" was not in Thomas' nature. But ultimately he would have no choice. I suppose he realized that too, because somehow he seemed an old man, vulnerable, dependent.

He said with more despair than hope, "Katy'll come back to me, someday."

I told him, "She's got a Canfield stubbornness about her. You'll have to bend."

Dying would probably be easier. I could only hope he had it in him to bend.

I got up to go. He called for me to stay. I told him I had business of my own to look after.

He pleaded, "I wish you wouldn't, Reed. With Katy gone, and you gone, who have I got left?"

Laura sat staring at him, biting her lip to keep from speaking. A prayer was in her eyes. Up to that minute, I guess I had always hoped there might someday be a chance for me in her life.

I said, "Open your eyes, Thomas. God knows you don't deserve her—you never did—but you've always had somebody."

She reached out to him. He turned his head and looked at her a long time, then slowly raised his hand to hers.

I left them there together and walked out onto the porch, trying to blink away the blurring as the sun hit me in the eyes.